BERRINGTON

OR

TWO HUNDRED YEARS
AGO

BERRINGTON

or

TWO HUNDRED YEARS AGO

By

HIS HONOUR

SIR EDWARD ABBOTT PARRY

NEW YORK:
WILLIAM MORROW & COMPANY

Printed in Great Britain

CONTENTS

PREFACE i

BOOK I.—THE CHILD

CHAP.   PAGE
I. OXFORD ASSIZES 1
II. ENTER JONATHAN WILD . . . 10
III. A DISTURBANCE AT FRESTON . . 21
IV. A CASE OF WITCHCRAFT . . 31
V. THE CHILD GOES TO SCHOOL . . 45

BOOK II.—MASTER NIC

VI. EXIT JONATHAN WILD . . , 59
VII. MASTER NIC GOES ON HIS OWN . 71
VIII. OLD DOCTOR MORGAN . . . 83
IX. MASTER NIC GOES TO THE PLAYHOUSE. 97
X. A DINNER WITH MR. QUIN . . 108
XI. ENTER HETTY VERRALL . . . 119
XII. WESTMINSTER AND THE OLD BAILEY . 128
XIII. BARTHOLOMEW FAIR AND A FIRE . 138
XIV. THE PASSING OF BAGSHOT . . 149
XV. MASTER NIC GOES HOME . . 158
XVI. "IN THE SPRING A YOUNG MAN'S
FANCY…" 171

CONTENTS—*Continued*

BOOK III.—MR. BERRINGTON

CHAP.		PAGE
XVII.	Conferences at Cherry Croft	183
XVIII.	Counsel's Opinion	195
XIX.	Mr. Berrington Goes to Court	205
XX.	Exit Hetty	216
XXI.	Belinda	225
XXII.	The Comedy of Master Crowley	239
XXIII.	The Treaty of Hampton Court	251
XXIV.	The Enthusiasts	265
XXV.	Coursing at Blewberry Bottom	274
XXVI.	The Death of Turquet	285
XXVII.	Back to Hetty	298
XXVIII.	Mr. Berrington in the Fleet	309
XXIX.	The Diplomacy of Captain Johnson	323

PREFACE

BERRINGTON, or "The Child," as I think of him, was a figure of my own childhood. I narrated his history in my school days to open-mouthed comrades. He did a lot of splendid things in those days, other than what I have set down here, but these I have forgotten.

The cave of his adventures was, however, a real cave. Nearly sixty years ago I had an August leasehold, as it were, of Roger Johnson's cave. I led with my companions a double life. We were smugglers all day in our beloved cave, but returned home more or less punctually for meals and always late for bed-time. The cave was in the cliff to the left-hand side of Mr. Collins, R.A.'s pleasant picture of Seaford, in the South Kensington Museum. Alas, it has long since been scraped away by a steam navvy to make a parade.

I had forgotten all about Berrington and the cave when, nearly fifty years ago, I was cycling home from Wales on a 56-inch Timberlake, and somewhere between North Leach and Witney I read on a signpost, " To Stow-on-the-Wold." I remembered a nursery rhyme about this place, and concluded I would visit it. I turned left and coasted down into the valley, where there was a little hamlet with a church on the other side of one of those silver streams that are rushing down from the wolds to make for the Thames.

The open door beneath the sign of " The Golden Sun " suggested lunch, and whilst this was preparing, I thought I would visit the church. Here the door was not open, but an old woman from a neighbouring cottage, seeing me trying the lock, hobbled up the path to my help. I never grudge this English representative of St. Peter the modest tribute of sixpence. I stood outside, coin in hand, reading the inscription on the lintel, " This is the gate of Heaven." The old lady turned the key and, accepting my thank-offering with a curtsey, pushed the door open. Let us hope the gate of the hereafter will open as cheaply and pleasantly.

PREFACE

I find in the folds of an ancient oily and highly-coloured map the exact words of a memorial tablet that I found in the church of Steeple Berrington. It ran thus :

TO THE MEMORY OF

NIC BERRINGTON

Born at Steeple Berrington, 1708
Died at Coalville, Georgia, 1774

This tablet

is erected by his descendant

NICHOLAS VERRALL BERRINGTON

of Chicago, 1879

*" He will deliver his soul from going into the pit,
and his life shall see the light—"*

Job xxxiii. 28.

There were some monuments of Jacobean Berringtons lying coloured and cross-legged in marble state on either side of the altar. Outside there were more of the same beneath sunken box tombs. An artist was struggling with the elaborate perspective of these sculptured packing-cases and grumbling querulously at their inconsistent vanishing points and wrong lines of sight. He pointed out to me the strange mounds on the side of the hill across the glebe. These were the only remains of the great house of the family, which he said was burned down in the time of George II. After that I adopted this Berrington as my Berrington, and mentally made new and romantic ventures for him.

I had forgotten all about Berrington's existence, if you may call it by such a definite name, when many years afterwards he cropped up again in an even more interesting form. I was staying at the Lake Side Hotel at the south end of Windermere. It was a cold, wet night in June. The north-west wind was blowing half a gale down the lake. Darkness was setting in before its time. A few porters heavily draped in oil-skins sheltered in the sheds on the pier awaiting the arrival of the last steamer down Windermere. There was no one staying at the inn but myself, for a fortnight of "donking dozzling" rain, interspersed with what the natives call "girt pelts," which had made the place uninhabitable to strangers and trippers. I had a fire made up in my little sitting-room, and was, as I remember, dutifully plodding through "The Ring and the Book," a poem I still associate with interminable cloud and damp.

The boat was very late. Besides a few local people, there were only four travellers, and they were all Americans. There were three ladies, a mother and two daughters, and a grave, elderly man evidently not of their party. They came in cold, wet and hungry, and I heard them demanding supper and beds in tones of weariness and disgust.

Knowing what the temperature of the coffee-room must be like, I went in as they were finishing supper and suggested that there was an excellent fire in my little sitting-room if they would join me. The ladies, who were huddled and shivering in costly furs, said it was "real good of me," and the grave man smiled his thanks. When we were round the fire, I suggested some hot whisky, a drink the ladies had only read of in English books, but they found it to their taste, and I listened to their joyous accounts of how, since they landed at Queenstown five days ago, they had "done" Killarney, the Giant's Causeway, the Trossachs, Edinburgh, and a drive through the Lake District, and how they intended to do Chester on the morrow, thence to London, and be in Paris at the week-end. When the ladies retired, their silent companion would have gone, too, but I suggested to him another glass and a pipe. The glass he dismissed, but the pipe and the fire were accepted with gratitude.

It appeared that he was a very different character from his lively companions. He was, he said, interested in education, and had visited the Continent, taking and obtaining photographs of the houses of great men and the scenes of their boyhood for the purpose of making lantern slides to assist his lectures. Whilst he was in these parts, he had

iii

visited the haunts of Wordsworth, Arnold and Southey, and on the morrow was for making his way up Coniston Lake to see with his own eyes Brantwood, the home of John Ruskin.

Our candles were brought in, and we sat on smoking and talking of books and English customs and history. He was a widely-read man, and of the social memoirs of the seventeenth and eighteenth centuries he had evidently an intimate knowledge. Our talk flowed along, winding here and there, as talk does between two lovers of books seeking to learn each other's favourites, when he happened to ask me if I had read " Dorothy Osborne's Letters." I could not help smiling. "It is a book," I said, " that I hope to read in my old age." " Sir," he replied, with a touch of reproof and enthusiasm that roused my pride, " you must read it at once. I have not only read it more than once, but being chairman of our library committee, I have bought seven copies that each of our free libraries may have one."

" Then I am much your debtor," I said, " but I fear I cannot read the book as yet, since it is only a few years ago that I corrected its proof sheets. You cannot read a book whose proof sheets you have corrected."

" You are not Mr. Parry ? " he cried.

I nodded assent.

He rose and shook me vigorously by the hand. Nothing would please him but that I would write my autograph in his note-book, with my address and a favourite quotation from Dorothy Osborne which he dictated to me accurately. And when that was done, he sat smoking and looking at me curiously, chuckling the while to himself.

" Gosh ! " he said, " I had pictured you an old man with a white beard—yes, a white beard."

I laughed loud and made my apologies for his disappointment, and asked if he would let me know the name of my patron and fellow servant of Dorothy Osborne. He handed me his card across the hearth, and I read, Nicholas Verrall Berrington, Chicago.

" You are the last of the Berringtons, then," I said, " and set up that tablet in Steeple Berrington Church, and you must be the only man who can tell me who Nic Berrington

iv

was and why you chose the text you placed on the memorial."

At my knowledge of his family relationship with the old country, he was so surprised and delighted that his hand instinctively reached for the bottle and, pouring out half a tumbler, he asked me to join him in a toast to the memory of his kinsman, which I did with great content.

I sat listening with deep interest whilst this good man told me many of the deeds and adventures of Master Nic, or "The Child," as he often called him, which I have tried to remember and to set down in this volume. Some of the more historical deeds of his story belonged to the early history of Georgia and the times of the Governorship of Captain Oglethorpe, and the visits of the Wesleys to America. He said he thought of writing a record of these things when he got home, and he intended to see if he could find any manucripts relating to his family in the British Museum or elsewhere.

It was not until the early hours of the morning that we parted. I had taken a great liking to the old gentleman, and said I would accompany him and show him the path to Brantwood going by the steamer to the Ferry Hotel, and making our way over Hawkshead Moor. As he lighted his candle and rose to go, he took my hand and said very solemnly : "I am a Wesleyan and still believe with John Wesley and the early leaders of our communion that there is more than chance in such meetings as these. At least, I will say it has given me great joy."

I reciprocated his compliment, and told him I should like to know more of his ancestor's adventures, and why he chose the saying of that good young man Elihu the son of Barachel the Buzite, of the kindred of Ram, as a text for his memorial.

" If you knew the whole of that unhappy young man's story, you would know that those words are not mere poetry. They state a fact, a thing that may happen to any man through the love and care of the Father.

He pressed my hand, and with a kindly smile left me alone full of thought at the story he had told me and the strange chance of our meeting.

v

PREFACE

When I came down in the morning, I found only the three ladies snatching an early breakfast preparatory to rushing off to Chester. Mr. Berrington had risen early and taken a chaise to Coniston. The ladies had, it appeared, never met him before last evening, and did not even know his name. I felt vexed at his abrupt departure, though I had no claim upon his society. Very likely he had felt irritated with himself for having opened his heart to me over night, and no longer desired my company. For our morning thoughts are often less expansive than those of the evening.

I have never been able to discover that any history of Nic Berrington or of the Berrington family has ever been written, and therefore I feel I have a perfect right to set down as much of his English story as I am able to remember with such additions as seem " reasonable and probable," as the law would say. At the same time, it seems only fair to the deceased and his family representatives (if any) to acknowledge that I cannot claim for these pages a real historic basis, and that if I have done Nic Berrington any injustice in telling his story, I deeply regret it, for through all my life he has been a very real and pleasant companion of my dreams, and I am very fond of him.

BOOK I

THE CHILD

BERRINGTON

or Two Hundred Years Ago

CHAPTER I

OXFORD ASSIZES

THE Squire of Steeple Berrington had been summoned to attend the Lent Assizes at Oxford and serve upon the Grand Jury. Coming in the names of the High Sheriff of the County and Our Sovereign Lady Queen Anne of blessed memory, there was no gainsaying the invitation. Nicholas Berrington, Esquire—" Nic " to his friends and in his signature—grumbled lustily at being called from his horses and dogs and fields and pastures, not to mention his wife and child, but on the appointed morning, attended by his groom, he rode away cheerfully enough to do his duty to his Queen, his county and his country, as a good Englishman should.

The Manor House of Steeple Berrington stood on the brow of a hill on the southern side of the river valley. The length of the house, where were the best rooms of use and pleasure, had pleasant views of the opposite slopes and their fields and woods. Through the windows of the great parlour you stepped on to the terrace gravel walk, which was, they say, some three hundred paces long and broad in proportion.

The walk was fenced with heavy stone balusters, and on this morning little Nic Berrington—" The Child," as they called him, for he was an only son—had been lifted upon them that he might wave to his father when he should emerge from behind the mill and cross the ford. His mother, a tall, elegant woman, held him carefully, and both fixed their eyes on the well-known spot in the landscape to be ready with their farewell signal. Below them, reached by three descents of many stone steps, were the gardens. The flower parterres, my lady's own herb garden, and then the fruit gardens. On the right was a handsome cloister facing south and covered with vines, below which were the carp ponds. To the left was an orange house, then in the building, for the Squire was a busy architect and never happy unless he was planning and carrying out some new addition to his demesne. This you might see in the extensive mass of buildings to the east of the courtyard, where in the last few years he had erected from his own designs blacksmiths' and carpenters' shops, malting and brewhouses, wood-yards and a saw-pit, a dairy and a fine stable.

The Child, who cannot have been more than three or four years old, had in after years a dream-memory of the scene, and could recall to his mind's eye a beautiful lady in white lifting him on to the stone balusters, and the summer flowers and blossoms at his feet, and the tall figure of a stalwart man on a big black horse as he rode through the ford and waved to them from the top of the field before he disappeared in the wood to gain the Witney Road.

On his journey towards Oxford the Squire was joined by many of his friends and neighbours, magistrates like himself summoned on the jury, and the road became crowded as they neared the city with humbler persons who had duty at the Assizes. There were, it was said, nearly a hundred prisoners for trial, and what with witnesses, lawyers, constables and the friends of the unfortunate men and women in the gaol, together with the sheriff and his retinue, the judges and the gentlemen of the bar, there was a greater throng of folk in Oxford than had been seen there for many an assize.

In the days of good Queen Anne it appeared to our forefathers both seemly and reasonable that the warders and turnkeys of the gaol should make their livelihood out of the wretches committed to their charge. The State in its wisdom allowed the gaoler to purchase his place for cash and recoup himself out of such of his prisoners as could pay for privileges. The wholesale poor were crowded and herded in dens, where they were locked up all night, sleeping on the floor, sick and healthy, young and old, huddled together, in a condition of damp and filth and stench that made life unbearable, and disease, that ended swiftly in death, a blessing to be prayed for.

It never occurred to the country gentlemen and magistrates of this Augustan age that anything was wrong with the penal system. A few zealots like Captain Oglethorpe might disturb their complacency on occasion, a few kindly squires like Sir Roger de Coverley might be uneasy about the miseries of the poor, but the bulk of the ruling classes were as satisfied with existing conditions as we are to-day.

Had Nicholas Berrington given a thought to the matter, which he did not, he would have concluded that the prison arrangements for the poor were just as much a part of the divine order of things as squires, parsons, judges, grand juries, tithes and the gallows. That providence should make him a scapegoat in the business was fortunately beyond his imagination. He had heard of the dealings of Jehovah with the upper classes of Egypt at the time of the first industrial strike, but at the bottom of his heart he had never approved of Moses or his methods. That any such thing could happen to-day was, of course, absurd.

Now, as ill-luck would have it, the sun was hotter than was usual for the season of the year, and there was at the same time a piercing east wind to attack the sweating persons as they came out of the heated corridors of the Guildhall. The closeness and noisome stench in the crowded court were more overpowering than usual, and to a man like the Squire, whose life was spent in the open, it was extremely pestilent and offensive. The work of the Grand Jury lasted over two days, and their labours were concluded each day with much feasting and drinking. With a practical and commonsense desire to wash the foul flavour of the court-house out of his throat, the Squire poured down it several bottles of tavern Burgundy, which he shrewdly cursed as never having seen the province whose name it disgraced.

After three days of this purgatory it was little wonder, perhaps, that on his ride home he suffered the pangs of severe headache, which he endeavoured to relieve with ale and brandy at the various country inns on the road, so that

B

when he reached his beautiful home at Steeple Berrington
he tumbled off his horse in the courtyard and staggered up
the back stairs to his bed, leaving word for his lady that
he was far gone in drink and wished to be left to himself.

That a visit to Oxford to fulfil magisterial duty on a
Grand Jury should produce results like this created very
little surprise in the household, but when on the next day
the Squire was found to be shivering one moment and
burning the next, and yelling out that he was poisoned
and dying, it became time to send to Witney for such
medical aid as was available.

The next day the groom fell ill, and the doctor who came
over from Witney had heard rumours that the judge had
been taken ill, and that several of the counsellors were sick
of a fever, and many of the prisoners had died. Then old
people began to remember horrible stories of the Black
Assize, and others cried out that the plague had come
again, so that when the groom died in his cottage near the
stable and was hurriedly buried to avoid contagion, there
was a panic among the servants of the great house, and
many fled to their homes on the farms near by until Mrs.
Berrington was left alone to nurse her husband with the
assistance of an old woman who had no friends to fly to,
and The Child was left wandering about to care for himself
as best he might.

After this the poor child never saw his mother again.
She, poor soul, was stricken down, and husband and wife
passed away at the same hour. Then Master Luke Crowley,
the Witney lawyer, who managed the Squire's business and
found him ready money in exchange for parchments, arrived on the scene and took command. Two coffins were
hurriedly built, the house was draped with black by Mr.
Crowley's orders, and the family hatchment set over the
door of the hall in order, as he said, that all things should
be done decently and in order.

The old woman carried The Child to the far end of the
house beyond the kitchens, and there in a strange truckle
bed he cried himself to sleep and dreamed of his mother
and father, whose faces he had seen for the last time. Now
a suit of black was brought for him, and the fitting of this

annoyed him sadly. Then night came, and he was wakened out of his sleep and dressed in it, and Master Crowley took him by the hand, and he stood in the chancel of the church with many of his father's friends gathered round, all of them carrying links, the light of which made strange shadows in the oak beams of the roof. Two coffins were carried in, covered with black velvet palls and nodding plumes of feathers, and the curate (for the old vicar had fled to London) read a burial service. When the coffins were lowered into a hole in the middle of the chancel, Master Crowley and all the men round threw little boughs of rosemary into the grave. The old woman, who was by, gave The Child two little sprigs of rosemary, which he, with a child's glee, threw into the hole before him as the others had done, and this made him feel pleased and proud of himself.

Everyone seemed in a hurry to be away. One or two of the older men patted The Child on the head—all the neighbours called him The Child, and it was a nickname that followed him through life—and they sighed to think of his loneliness, but they had children of their own to consider, and could not offer to take him home from a house where two had died of the pestilence. It was enough for the sake of neighbourliness and good manners to attend the funeral. One by one they extinguished their torches by putting them head-down in the long, damp grass of the churchyard, and mounting their horses, rode homewards in the moonlight. Some of the younger men went down to the Vicarage, where Master Crowley had sent some bottles of Berrington's best wine, for a funeral without drink, even under these circumstances, was unthinkable.

The old woman carried the little, tired child across to the lonely house and put him back to bed, and again he cried himself to sleep, fretting that his mother did not come to kneel by his bedside and hear his prayers and tuck him safely in. In this way did Nic Berrington succeed to the estates of his forefathers, and with them to a tangle of misfortune which he had certainly done nothing to deserve. Luckily, he inherited from his mother a spirit of joy and cheerfulness that enabled him to bear the burdens of life more graciously than most.

There seems no evidence that at the moment of these tragic happenings Master Crowley acted with any intention of evil towards the luckless child. He was a man of business and respected in the county. The late Mr. Berrington had no near relations. Crowley held charges and mortgages over the Berrington estates, and these were valid enough, but before they could be enforced against the infant owner, a guardian must be appointed and legal formalities observed. The late Squire had made no will, and for the present the lawyer deemed that his wisest course was to wait and see. The ability to do nothing at a time of crisis is often more valuable than brilliant strategy.

With regard to the immediate disposal of the heir-at-law he was under no difficulty. When the curate, who was a brave and kindly fellow, had announced to poor Mrs. Berrington the death of her husband, she had dictated to him a letter which she had signed in his presence for him to give to Mr. Crowley, and he, having made a copy of it, had handed it to the lawyer on her death a few hours later. The letter was as follows :

" MASTER CROWLEY,—
" It hath pleased God, which works all things at His good will, to take from me my loving husband and to leave me lying at death's door here alone. If it please Him to take me from my dear child, I pray you that he be placed under the care of my dear nurse Mistress Johnson, the wife of Captain Johnson, of Cherry Croft, Freston, in the county of Sussex, where I was born.

" This, if by God's grace I am taken, is the last dying wish of

" ALICE BERRINGTON."

This letter was very welcome to Master Crowley. He determined for the present to pay off the servants, close up the great house and give formal notice to the tenants to pay him their rents, as they were used to do. Then he returned to Witney, carrying little Nic Berrington with him. At the lawyer's house The Child was handed over to Mr. Crowley's cook Rebecca, a large woman with a heart to match her stature, who nursed and fed and polished the light-haired, rosy-faced child with as much care as if he was one of her own well-loved brass candlesticks which were the pride of her kitchen.

When the day came for The Child to take the road, the good Rebecca packed up a hamper for him, with sufficient provisions to have fed a company of dragoons, and carried him out to her brother, Tom Sheard, the Witney carrier, who was waiting for him in the street with his three-horse waggon standing at the door-post. He had already received his instructions from Master Crowley, and watched his sister somewhat impatiently as she hugged the little orphan to her ample bosom, nearly crushing the breath out of The Child with her vigorous affection.

" Now then, Rebecca," cried Tom, " 'urry up, my girl, and remember the Queen's awaitin' for me in Lunnon."

Tom Sheard and his three brown Flemish horses and his great lumbering waggon, with the black tarpaulin cover, were the pride of the Witney road. From Witney to Uxbridge he was a known and respected character, and though his greatness lessened and dwindled to a minor glory as he neared the Kensington gravel pits, and threaded his way among the common traffic of the town to the " Saracen's Head " without Newgate, yet once reaching his native inn and stable, as it were, he was again a noted man in the circle of the exiles from Oxfordshire, who, living in the great city, came into the tap-room to bring and receive letters and news from the dear folk they had left at home.

Little do we think to-day how the hopes and fears of our forefathers rested on the waggons of the old carriers, that were the posts and railways of the seventeenth and eighteenth centuries. Out of the narrow streets of the City of London, each from his appointed inn, the well-known waggon, punctual to his hour and day, set forth, with goods and letters, for York or Lancaster, whence smaller fellows of less note would distribute them as far as Berwick, maybe, or to Kendal and across sands to Ulverston and Cockermouth. The Hereford carrier, who was to be found at the " King's Head " at Old Change, would pass on goods for far St. Davids ; on three days of the week the carrier for

Chester left the " Castle " in Wood Street, and you might send messages to Carnarvon and beyond the mountains to the ultimate fastnesses of the Lleyn ; whilst the Exeter men carried the western traffic for Plymouth and from there it found its way down to the Mount in Cornwall. In this manner was England served with safe and true carriage of letters and goods, and the villagers and county folk along the roads had even greater knowledge of what was going on in the capital than many of them have to-day.

Tom was a Burford man. He had known the Squire of Steeple Berrington, who often stopped him on the road to ask him the latest news from London. He was proud of his charge, and wrapping the little lad in a rug, for it was a cold morning, he set him by his side and gave him the slack end of the reins to hold, for he had children of his own and knew the ways of them. So The Child, shouting to the horses and full of the joy of the adventure, started off into the wide world with a laugh on his lips and no care in his heart, a state of mind which he continued to display throughout most of the strange happenings in the story of his life.

When The Child was tired of the burden of driving, old Tom found him some straw and made him a nest in the far corner of the waggon, where he slept contentedly. At the inns and farms where they stopped countrywomen had a peep at the soft, sleeping lad, and Tom shook his head mysteriously over the journey of the heir of the Berringtons, and gossips wondered whither he was going. Doubtless from this journey arose the many wild stories of his being spirited away and destroyed that were afterwards whispered round the countryside.

Little Nic Berrington had no memory of his two days' ride to London, nor could he remember being carried by Tom Sheard in a coach across the bridge to Southwark, where the Lewes waggon stabled at " The Tabard " in the Borough. Here they found Mistress Johnson, who had journeyed up to London at Master Crowley's orders, and was anxiously waiting for The Child. When she caught sight of his smiling, rosy face and light flaxen hair, and the laughing look in his blue eyes, she saw again her own little

Alice whom she had nursed in years gone by, and the good woman caught him to her heart and wept.

The Child in his trusting, loving way found the path to the hearts of women with less trouble than most, and accepted their homage easily and gracefully, but perhaps even he felt, though he could scarce understand it then, that the love of Mistress Johnson was near akin to that of the beautiful woman who used to play with him and worship his ways in the old garden at Steeple Berrington, and had now vanished from his life like a dream.

The journey to Lewes was made in much the same way as the journey to London, but, to The Child's disappointment, he was not allowed to drive the horses, and passed the hours either sleeping in the arms of Mrs. Johnson or sitting close to her side as if she feared someone would steal him. At Lewes old Jacob, with the farm cart, met the waggon at the " White Horse," and a ten-miles drive over the downs brought them to Freston and Cherry Croft.

In this way did Nic Berrington arrive at the Sussex farm, which in after life he always spoke of as his home.

CHAPTER II

At the time Jonathan Wild first met Master Nic, he was in the hey-day of his power. There was throughout the southern counties of England more law and sanction behind his name than attached to those of many real legal authorities, so ready is mankind to throw in its lot with any man who can do things and carry them through.

The history of Jonathan Wild is the common property of the world. Thief, receiver, smuggler and thief taker, the enormities of his villainy have earned him a prominent place in the gallery of criminal illustrations. But it is at least clear in all accounts of him that he was no journeyman botcher at his business. He was a master man with the mind and courage of a leader. In business or politics or state-craft he would have been a great figure, and dutiful party writers would have softened the edge of his wickedness and painted his enduring qualities in brighter colours.

It was no small feat, at a date when the rulers of the great city were utterly unable to police their streets and suburbs, that Jonathan Wild had organized the thieves and rascals of the country into a community of which he was the accepted chief. There were a few of these reckless outcasts who looked up to him as a beloved master, but all were his obedient servants and in the then uncivilised condition of local government many grave aldermen and citizens spoke of the rule of Jonathan Wild in the regions of crime as a welcome reform in the handling of municipal affairs.

In the early years of the eighteenth century there was no State provision for putting down robbery and restoring stolen goods, and Jonathan Wild, though his premiums were high and his business methods immoral, was what the able Victorian editor used to call a " felt want." In spite of the distrust and jealousy of an incompetent

magistracy and police, Jonathan Wild undoubtedly became
a well-to-do man, appeared in public in laced clothes,
wearing a sword and attended by his faithful body servant
Toby Billinge, in whose eyes he was as virtuous and worthy
of respect as the Lord Mayor of London himself. Nor
were thieves and ruffians his only prey. He might be met
with on occasion at the gaming house or the theatre with
that notorious gamester Count Turquet de Grillac, whose
friendship with his ruffianship was said to have begun when
the Earl of Romney employed Jonathan to rescue his son,
the Hon. Harry Camber, from the clutches of the Count.

The story of Jonathan Wild is, however, not to our
purpose except as it touches the life and history of The
Child. That the boy should have been sent into Sussex to
live with Captain Johnson, and that he should have found
himself face to face with a man who had once been the
accepted lover of his mother, are things which the thought-
less call coincidences and the more thoughtful regard as
the working out of the ways of providence. The happening
of them had a strange influence on his future.

For when Jonathan Wild lived in Freston long ago and
was a young sea prentice resting at his mother's cottage,
having sprained his ankle at sea, Alice Trustram, fair-
haired, blue-eyed, with her careless merry laugh, met him
in the fields and lanes as he began to hobble out again,
and with the proper sympathy due from the Vicar's
daughter to the lame and sick, she made inquiry from time
to time of his progress.

The old story ran its constant rapid course. He had his
adventures on the sea to tell with backward modesty that
enhanced their romance. She was ready with pity and
curiosity and tender questioning in her eyes to ask for more,
and at every parting he had the lover's wit to hint that
there were greater hazards to tell of, if there had been time.
The meetings became more regular, the walks lengthened
out into the fields and lanes and down into the river
meadows. Old shepherds and waggoners shook their
heads and grinned as they passed, but the lovers never saw
them, old gossips in the cottages peeped over their curtains
and chuckled with their neighbours over the comedy. A

young couple in the throes of first love are always a fresh delight to the old ones. The whole village took a merry human interest in the pretty romance of it all.

Only the Reverend Charles Trustram sitting at his study in the candlelight laboriously editing the Song of Solomon and drawing mystic parallels between the bride and the church had no inkling in his learned head that the young motherless girl, sitting demurely at his feet, was blossoming out into a rose of Sharon, and a lily of the valley, with a little panting heart listening for the voice of the beloved at the door of the garden.

There is an orchard at the bottom of the vicarage garden at Freston and a gate from out of it leads across the fields to the church. In the orchard was a little arbour where Alice used to sew and knit. How Jonathan found his way there love only knows. At first his visits were rare and cunningly disguised. At length they came to regard the arbour as love's bower and the orchard as their Garden of Eden, and were careless of discovery since the joy and happiness of these secret hours seemed so necessary and right. Nearly every evening Alice stole out of the library, crossed the garden and ran lightly toward the orchard. Jonathan was always there. At first she only stayed to give a hasty message about the morrow, but each succeeding evening brought more to say and a longer absence from the house.

It was a hot summer evening, the red glow of sunset had passed away, and a clear blue grey sky was darkening for the stars. The sea wind whispered through the trees with scarce a movement. An old woman from one of the cottages near the church crossed the fields and made through the orchard towards the vicarage. Her burden was to bring word of the funeral of a neighbour's daughter. The girl had died in child-birth. There was no husband to father the child and bury the mother.

The Vicar looked up from the pages of his manuscript, heard the story with some impatience and fixed a day and hour for the funeral. This done he would have returned to his literary work, but knowing the girl's story and remembering his duty as a shepherd of his flock he began a homily about the manifest judgment of God on the frail deceased.

The old woman listened for a while and her lips twitched.

" The girl was a poor kiddle creature but no bad," she murmured.

" I cannot hear such things said."

" You'm be hearing more said before long," muttered the woman.

" Such things are a disgrace to the parish and it is my duty as pastor to speak the truth about evil livers."

" There's a mort of human nature in evil livers."

" I have said my say, my good woman, you can go," said the Vicar, waving her away as one unworthy of his righteousness.

There is something peculiarly irritating in the phrase " good woman " to the feminine countrywoman.

" Good 'ooman, indeed," she repeated with a loud sniff. " Who's a good 'ooman oi'd like to knaw ? Oi aint a-going to be called out of my name for anyone, Oi can promise you. Oi'm born an' bred in the parish fifty-eight years come Michaelmas an' brought up sixteen children, all living 'cept them as died of small-pox an' a respectable married 'ooman as the register shows. 'Stead of preaching evil about the poor young girl as is taken," she cried, raising her voice in anger and contempt, " look after those as is living. You sit here in the candlelight, blinking like a mousehawk, where's your own girl ? All the village could tell you. Where is she this night an' every night ? She an' her lover young Jonathan. They're the laughingstock of the place and the soonder you get 'em wedded the better for all——"

Finishing on a top note of wrath the good woman flung herself out of the study slamming the door behind her.

The poor old man put down his pen. The whirlwind of feminine commonsense knocked the breath out of him. The Song of Solomon seemed to ring in his ears as a cold strain of lascivious delight. His brain spun round. The scholar and priest no longer existed. The coarse invective of the good woman had roused the human man in him. He was the father called to protect his child in danger. He did not fumble after the truth, he knew it by instinct. He did not stay to search the house. He knew she was not there. He went out to find her and save her. He passed through the garden out into the orchard as though his footsteps were guided to the arbour and when the guilty ones heard his voice in the orchard they were afraid. The dream of their love seemed to dissolve, they knew it was all ended and that their Garden of Eden was to be closed for ever.

She was weeping in her father's arms as he turned to denounce Jonathan. With righteous and godly wrath he challenged him with every evil deed that he had learned of his life, he enlarged with grave emphasis on the social wickedness of one of the lower orders daring to pay his addresses to the girl of good breeding, a sin that in those days struck more hopelessness into the hearts of the young couple than their moral wrong-doing, and he launched on the head of the abashed lovers a paternal curse of precedented dignity that struck terror into the soul of the shivering girl in his arms.

Jonathan was but a young fellow in those days and very young in crime and villainy. Through his love for this beautiful girl he had seen visions of a purer and better life. All these vanished in an instant. Alice made no effort to withstand her father's will. The old man stood with his protecting arm round the girl and his finger pointing to the village.

As Jonathan walked sullenly down the hill towards the church the figure of the old vicar seemed to tower in his mind as an implacable angel with a flaming sword in his hand barring the golden entrance to a lost Eden whilst he in his despair was a doomed soul hurrying along the high road of Hell.

It was two years afterwards that Nicholas Berrington, Squire of Steeple Berrington, married Alice and carried her away to Oxfordshire. On her death-bed her heart had travelled back to her Sussex home, and she could think of no one but her old nurse to mother The Child.

Cherry Croft, Freston, Captain Johnson's Sussex farm, was a square-built house of flint and brick with many

blocked windows to cheat the window tax. These gave it a
gloomy, forbidding, prison-like appearance. The farm-
house with its wide ample barns, its orchard and gardens
and the cottages for the farm-hands was nearly the whole
of Freston. There was the church, also built of flints picked
out of the chalk pit, with a tower capped by a wooden
spire, and higher up the road that led to the downs there
was the new Vicarage. A few outlying sheep farms were
within the curtilage of the parish.

This valley of Freston, sheltered from the east by solid
chalk downs and hidden from the wide river meadows and
the southerly gales that swept across them from the sea by
a rampart rookery of old elms, was Master Nic's new
world. Here he built up for himself memories of childhood
and boyhood, full of the joy of life. In this bold Sussex air,
living the sane life of a young animal, he learned to ride,
and swim, and fight with his village companions ; he fed
on good wheaten bread and farm milk, and later on English
beef and small ale, and increased worthily in stature, if not
in wisdom. The Child when he grew to a man's estate spoke
tenderly of the loving kindness and careful affection of
Granny Johnson, his mother's nurse, and never wholly
lost his hero worship for that man of wrath, old Roger,
who ruled his farm and his wife and all that was his with a
rough tongue of blasphemy and commonsense.

In a way this old sea captain was a noble figure of a man,
being as he was massive, tall and well set up. You did not
note at first that he had a kind face and his eyes twinkled
with fun. It was the aspect of his furrowed purple face,
white locks and brown bushy beard and whiskers, his
stern high forehead, his habit of shouting as if a gale were
trying to drown his voice and the strange mouth-filling
oaths that he hurled at you in his common talk that struck
fear into simple hearts.

Captain Johnson was still something more than a mere
farmer. He had been a sea-faring man in his younger days,
and it was generally known, across the downs and along
the coast, that he had more than a small share in *Kitty the
Devil*, as the revenue men called *The Lively Kate*, a
Hastings lugger whose nominal skipper was Master Ben

Cheal of Newhaven. This vessel did a lawful coasting trade between the Thames and the Cinque Ports, and if on occasion it sometimes strayed across Channel or to Rotterdam it had never as yet been found with contraband on board when visited by the Excise officers. These good fellows were very friendly with Captain Johnson who kept open house to all and sundry who visited Freston.

The Captain was a sufferer from asthma and later on The Child discovered with some interest that when the asthma seized him and he was forced to keep his room whilst Granny bewailed his illness to the village gossips over tea and brandy that were the glory of what was known as the Free Trade, his room was really empty and Old Roger had drifted down the river Cuxton and out into the English Channel to a trysting place with *The Lively Kate*.

It is not to be supposed that The Child learned these secrets on his first arrival. For many years he regarded the fat, furrowed purple face of Old Roger with as much awe as was in his composition. The oaths of the man and his drunken songs, however, gave a merry flavour to his company and in due course he and The Child became sworn friends and young Nic became jealous that his patron should have secrets from him. He was a mighty favourite with the Captain who swore by his liver and bones and much of his internal anatomy that the brat was a merry little devil and was not born to be hanged, a fate that he was wont to prophesy freely for all of his underlings and most of his friends and acquaintance. In such favour was the boy with the old ruffian that when Parson Oliver came down the hill, as he did many evenings a week, and the two sat in the kitchen drinking " Moonshine " which was smugglers' Sussex for Dutch gin, and smoking clay pipes, the " little devil " was allowed to sit up into the night against the protest of Granny Johnson and join his shrill treble to the rounds and catches they sang by the fireside.

For how long he had discovered the absence of Captain Johnson when that worthy was supposed to be lying ill upstairs one cannot say. It was no great mystery in the farm, but if a farmer from beyond or a stranger came across the downs and dropped into the valley, as happened on occasion, it seemed better to say that Master Johnson was laid up with asthma and kept to his bed than to excite interest in his movements by announcing that he had gone abroad. The Sussex world knew well enough about his ingoings and outgoings, but there was an etiquette about smuggling, as there is in every other trade and profession, and along the coast and for many miles inland the Captain's asthma was the accepted phrase for " not at home."

One summer evening when The Child was about nine years old he had noticed that Old Roger and one of his servants were loading the big farm boat that lay in the creek of the river beyond the elm trees, and was used legitimately for bringing hay off the river fields and rescuing cattle in the flood times. It occurred to The Child that the boat would disappear in the night as it had done before, and would return on the tide the next day with the shepherd, Jacob Napper, who would tell him that he had been down to the meadows looking for stray sheep. This stale falsehood and the mystery of the Captain's asthmatic absences were too much for the natural curiosity of The Child and he determined to discover the truth of the matter for himself.

With this in view he retired to his attic early in the evening and, as he had done before when the spirit of adventure seized him, dropped from his window on to the long barn roof, and creeping along the thatch gave himself a soft fall on to a heap of straw that lay in the yard. It was a moonlight night, though somewhat cloudy, but he had no difficulty in finding the boat. Lifting up one end of the tarpaulin he crept into an ample crevice between some casks and a large packing-case where he stowed away his slender frame on an old sail that was stuffed into the opening. Here he could await events in comfort.

He must have dozed off to sleep, for he was awakened by the clank of the chain being lifted from the staple and thrown into the boat, and two heavy men jumped into her and pushed off. Then to his great relief a well-known voice muttered under his breath : " Damn your fingers and shins, you lubber !—pull !— pull !—backwater !—pull ! " These orders were garnished with so many choice adjectives and pet particular expletives that The Child knew that Captain Roger and no other was in command.

Except for an occasional bump on to a mud-bank, which drew from the Captain new excursions and alarums of blasphemy, they drifted lazily down the river, The Child recognising from the short jerky strokes of the oars that old Jacob, the shepherd, was the motive power of the boat. He knew, too, when they passed out of the river fields into the wider estuary, and then the smell of the sea told him they were going down to the great shingle bank that ran out across the mouth of the river. He had wandered this way over the downs but why Jacob and Captain Johnson should row down here at midnight was beyond his ken.

The prow of the boat scrunched into the wet shingle and Nic knew the journey was ended. Then the chain was thrown on shore, carried up the slope and the anchor thrust into the loose pebbles.

" Blast your long legs and take yourself home over the downs," said the Captain pleasantly but with more circumstance of oaths.

" Ay, sir," replied old Jacob grinning amiably at his master's agreeable wit.

The gift of decorative blasphemy was better understood and appreciated then than it is with us.

The sound of the old man's tread died away across the shingle and now Captain Johnson was heard lighting a lantern, the conduct of the tinder and its refusal to take a spark being referred to the particular and immediate judgment of divine providence with forceful emphasis. His invocations were answered and, the lantern burning, he too moved away across the beach in the direction of the chalk cliffs and the sea.

The Child lifted up the end of the tarpaulin and peeped cautiously out. The boat was lying on the spit of shingle at the mouth of the Cuxton river. Captain Johnson was walking towards the undercliff. It was low tide. Once round the promontory of fallen chalk there was, as The Child knew, a small bay of shingle beach. Beyond that were stretches of cliffs and other bays, the sea in places lapping the cliffs day and night, and the cliff walls towering above. Except for a dangerous ascent from an open beach half a mile away known as Fox Gap, there was no way up the cliff when the tide came in, and then the Captain would be cut off. The Child chuckled to think of Captain Johnson trying to clamber up Fox Gap. He had done it, but the Captain? He nearly laughed aloud at the thought of it.

But the Captain, lantern in hand, stumped across the pebbles and disappeared round the edge of the cliff. The Child leaped quickly along and tip-toed over the cobble stones and fallen chalk boulders to look into the next bay. But when he could see round into it, there was no Captain, no lantern. The moon shone clearly. The brown shingle stretched along the edge of the sea, the little waves slapped the cobbles and sucked them down the slopes into the water with a regular constant sigh. Half a mile from the shore to the eastward, a three-masted lugger was hove to but there was not sight or sound of a human being on the shore.

A sense of loneliness and fear seized The Child and he began to wish he had left the adventure on the threshold. He started at the sound of a falling piece of chalk from the cliff above. Then other pieces fell, and then he heard strange voices, the sound of men clambering over the masses of fallen chalk right above his head. He hid behind a large boulder on the shore. Two sailor men climbed down on to the shingle and made their way towards the Captain's boat.

The Child at once concluded that where they came from the Captain must have gone to. He clambered up the broken chalk crags to a height of nearly thirty feet. He soon came upon a path where steps were cut in the chalk at the top of which the mass separated from the cliff itself and formed a sloping terrace, though this could not be seen from below. Peering down from the top of the fallen chalk he could clearly see in the moonlight a well-worn track leading into a cleft of the cliff which was propped in places with timber. The Child crept forward feeling his way with his hands on the side of the tunnel. In a few yards it

c

turned suddenly into a lighted chamber crowded with
casks and cases and ropes and spars and oars. On an up-
turned cask sat Captain Roger Johnson drinking a glass of
Hollands. Standing talking to him in short eager phrases
of command was a tall man in a dark surtout. His keen
hatchet face was shadowed on the chalk wall by the light
of a lantern. This, too, remained one of The Child's
memories throughout his life.

Nic must have uttered a cry of surprise at his discovery.
The tall man seized the lantern and caught him by the collar.

" Jesus God," he cried. " What have we found here ! "

He held the lantern full in the face of the boy and drew
a long breath. " It is Alice's boy—her very face."

" Damn my liver and lights," cried the astonished
Captain, " if it isn't The Child ! "

" Her child," said his companion softly. " I should have
known him anywhere. The child you told me of."

" He's nothing to you, Jonathan," said the Captain,
surlily, " but he's a lot to Granny and I like the little brat."

" He might have been all to me," said the stranger,
shrugging his shoulders, " but Jonathan Wild's luck wasn't
that way. Well, youngster, give us your hand. I'm glad to
meet you. I knew your mother in the old days. That's true
enough, Roger, isn't it ? "

" That's true enough, Master Wild."

The Child put out his hand and shook hands with his
new friend.

The man laughed, not a pleasant laugh, and the grim
sound of it struck a harsh echo against the chalk walls of
the cave.

" You never heard of Jonathan Wild, I suppose, eh, my
young gentleman ? "

Nic shook his head. Yet in after years he used to say
that a memory seemed to cross his mind of his father
and mother quarrelling, of his father hurling the name
" Jonathan Wild " at his mother as if in insult, and his
mother crying and sobbing as if her heart would break, at
which he had wept in sympathy with her. But he had not
really remembered such a thing. It was probably a dream
memory fashioned of things he had learned in after life.

CHAPTER III

A DISTURBANCE AT FRESTON

FROM the day of their first meeting Jonathan Wild became
the friend and patron of Master Nic. On his occasional
visits to Freston he brought him presents of clothes and
linen that rejoiced the heart of Granny Johnson, and when
the lad was twelve years old took him over to Lewes fair
and bought him a pony which The Child rode home in
triumph, and from that day was often to be seen cantering
across the downs or riding into Lewes with Captain Johnson when business took him into the town.

On one of his visits Jonathan took Master Nic with him
across to Rotterdam in *The Lively Kate,* an adventure
which the lad highly appreciated. With the Captain and
Mrs. Johnson Mr. Wild discussed Master Nic's treatment
by Mr. Crowley, the amount of his allowance, his rights to
his father's estates, and declared his intention of seeing that
he was fairly dealt with. But he warned them not to trouble
Master Nic's young mind with these matters. At this time
Mr. Wild was a man of power and property, feared if not
esteemed by the world he lived in, and Granny was overjoyed that her beloved child should have such a friend to
help and care for him. That Wild himself had a real affection
for The Child seems very probable. Few men are so utterly
degraded that they are immune from human love. Put it at
the lowest, Master Nic became a hobby of the great man,
he took the gracious little mortal to his heart, or what was
left of it, and The Child naturally responded to his advances.
Indeed even in later years, Nic Berrington could never
be brought to acknowledge the terrible crimes committed
by his extraordinary patron.

At the age of twelve Master Nic was the acknowledged

21

"cock" of the boys of the country-side. Nor was he altogether without some knowledge of the humanities. Old Granny Johnson with the aid of a horn-book had taught him some letters, and at Wild's suggestion the Vicar, at the cost of an occasional keg of rum, had been induced to teach him the Scriptures and to impart to The Child such memories of the Latin tongue as drink and the practice of farming had not wholly destroyed.

One memory of The Child we must not pass over as it is pat upon his story. In many of the lazy, mud-banked rivers that wind along the Sussex valleys there were in Master Nic's boyhood, and, indeed, in my own, an abundance of eels. Now the eel, as Master Izaak tells us, " seldom stirs in the day but then hides himself," and the best way to lure him from his hole in the river bank is by the art of snigling. The Child, who was an artist in all contests that required cunning, knew every hole in the banks and the best hiding places for eels. When he had raised the wrath of Granny Johnson by some extravagant piece of mischief, or had by his false quantities and errors in grammar roused the easy-going Vicar to threats of discipline,his habit was to wander off alone along the banks of the Cuxton river or up one of its little tributary streams in search of a basket of eels as a peace-offering to offended elders.

The way of snigling was, and still is, I trust, after this fashion. You tie a short line to a stout stick and then, baiting your hook with some choice guts or offal, you approach with knowledge the spot where your prey lies hid. You lower your bait gently in his neighbourhood and if he is at home and hungry he gorges the lure. This, however, is but half the battle, for though hooked he has yet to be landed and by the grip of his tail will weary out the patience of many who seek in too great haste to pull him to the shore.

There was a sluice with a penstock, which held back a dike from the river at low tide, across which ran a narrow wooden bridge. This was a favourite fishing-ground with Master Nic. One evening when he was following his sport with much success, he became aware that he was an object of interest to a young maiden of eight or nine, whose dark brown eyes were watching his proceedings with grave admiration.

She stood on the footpath some yards away and seemed to need an invitation to proceed across the bridge.

" Come along if you like," whispered The Child, " but keep quiet."

The girl walked towards him on tip-toe.

" He's under that plank in the floush-hole," explained Nic pointing to the tightened string which disappeared into thick muddy water under the flood-gate.

The patient struggle continued, The Child hanging from the bridge or the sluice gates at different angles to overcome the reluctant eel. He was evidently a strong fellow. The little dark-haired girl clasped her hands in excitement and gazed wonderingly at Master Nic's activities. It became a point of honour with him to succeed, for from the earliest the eyes of woman had always a great sway with Master Nic.

There is a saying that long warfare has often a sudden ending. Whether The Child attained the exact angle of extraction, or the tail of the eel became weary of well-doing, it is enough to say that he came away from his hole so unexpectedly that The Child fell over on the grass and the eel, which was more than a yard long, wound himself fiercely up in the string and frightened the little girl out of her seven wits.

She ran screaming wildly across the bridge, to the amusement of The Child who picked himself up just in time to see her catch her foot in the planks, stumble and roll with a splash into the dike.

Master Nic was after her in a second. He did not lose his head and checked his instinctive desire to plunge into the water after her. Swinging himself down by the piles and cross-staves of the bridge to the level of the water, he got a firm stance to grip her clothes as she came to the surface, and caught her firmly and held her with her head out of water, as she struggled and kicked and choked and he shouted for help. He was puzzling how he could drag her heavy body up the side of the dike when a man came running across the fields and helped them both on to the bank.

The first thing The Child did was to seek for the eel, but this in his absence had wriggled off into his native element, tackle and all.

"Damn my liver," cried The Child in pious imitation of Captain Johnson, "the little devil's got away."

"Silence, child," said the stranger sternly, "are the mouths of babes and sucklings for nothing better than blasphemy?"

The stranger flung himself on his knees and stretching out his hands to heaven, closed his eyes and cried out in a long-drawn rhythm: "Oh Lord who hast made this child Thy instrument in saving my little one from being overwhelmed in the waters of death, pour down Thy grace upon him that Thy Holy Spirit may sanctify him and his soul, which is doomed to eternal damnation, may be saved, and teach him to seek the Lord." He rose and lifted up his little one, who continued to sob bitterly in his arms, and strode away across the fields towards Foxhole, leaving Master Nic, who could make no sense of the fellow's talk, gazing after him in amazement. The lad was sufficient of a churchman to feel that it was bad taste in a common man to talk about sacred things, but the ardent language of Simon Verrall's sermon fell on indifferent ears.

"Seek the Lord indeed," he repeated with a chuckle. "I've got to find that damned eel first."

When the matter was reported to Captain Johnson and Parson Oliver, the Vicar declared that the man's name was Simon Verrall, who was a Baptist, staying with his cousin at Foxhole Farm, which was a nest of vipers where plots were hatched against the Church and the Crown. Captain Johnson agreed that Baptists in general, and the Verralls of Foxhole in particular, were damned villains who refused to lend their horses to run the cargoes of *The Lively Kate* to inland safety, and were believed to give information to revenue officers and other land-sharks who threatened the peaceful existence of the Free Trade.

The Child could not help feeling that it was a sad pity such a pretty little girl should belong to such undesirable relations. For many days he caught himself dreaming of large brown eyes gazing at him admiringly. He went back to the sluice gates and sought in vain for the eel. That, too, was never seen again, and within a week the whole incident seemed to have occurred in the land of dreams.

There is no more troublesome person to the normal magisterial mind than the man in search of martyrdom. Until the visit of Simon Verrall to this neighbourhood Parson Oliver with his two services on Sunday and his official attendances at funerals, weddings and baptisms as and when required, had seemed to the simple folk of Freston as the alpha and omega of the Christian religion as by law established. It is true that the Parson drank and swore like any other man, but these human traits in his character rather endeared him to his parishioners. He was a friendly character and would play a man's part at a wedding feast or a christening. Moreover, in times of sickness and distress he never came empty-handed. And though he said few prayers at the bedside of the sick man he could crack a joke and tell him the latest news from Lewes market about the price of corn and wool and he was never known to go abroad to comfort a soul in distress without his brandy flask in his pocket.

That Simon Verrall should seek to disturb the pastoral peace of this happy village was but a manifest sign of his vanity, wickedness and conceit, and of the evil ways of Baptists. As the Captain said on the Sunday afterwards as he and Parson Oliver smoked their pipes in the kitchen at Cherry Croft, " Who the hell wants any new religion in Freston ? " To which the parson, taking the sentiment to imply a righteous loyalty to Church and State, removed the waxed clay from his lips and lifting the mug of ale to his mouth gurgled, " Amen ! "

The trouble began on the Sunday. The parish church was well filled. Captain Johnson, Granny and The Child were in the square curtained pew in the chancel that pertained to the freehold of Cherry Croft, and Matthew Henderson, the substantial miller from the South Dean Mill, sat with his five daughters in the front pew. Master Nic used to gaze on the stout buxom eldest girl, Emily, a young woman of twenty, and critically considered her as handsome a piece of Eve's flesh as any in Sussex. Beyond them the farmers and their wives, each in their station surrounded by their boys and girls, and behind them their waggoners and farm-servants with their children, whilst on the back benches the rougher lads sat under the super-intendence of David Diggs, beadle and constable of the Manor of Gale, in which the parish of Freston was situated.

Up in the gallery were the men of music. Jacob Napper, the shepherd, who wrestled with the bassoon, Stephen Bunce, thatcher, who produced strange wailing notes from the hautboy, and little Tom Spiggot, the joiner, whose fiddle was at every fair and wedding in East Sussex, but who gave his gift to the services of the Church on the Lord's day.

Parson Oliver read the service in a clear voice and preached sound doctrine for the necessary twelve minutes looking every inch the established State official in his bob wig, full black gown and clean broad bands. Below the pulpit at his desk sat his clerk, Master Robert Rigby, his silver-grey hair lighted by many strange colours from the sunlight that streamed through the painted window in the aisle. He, too, played his part in the State worship with grave, natural dignity. He had been a seafaring man in his time and had been for many years the boatswain of *The Lively Kate*. Now he lived on a small croft up the valley and made a little money out of cobbling boots and shoes for the country-side. This trade of his combined excellently with his office of parish clerk. For, every Sunday in the church porch you would see a row of dirty old boots brought in by the farmers from the downs and another row of boots neatly repaired and cleaned waiting to be taken away by their owners.

The parish was proud of Bob Rigby. It is true he had some scriptural readings peculiar to himself, as in the 104th Psalm, where he trolled out with a sailor's en-thusiasm, " There go the ships and there is that lieutenant whom thou hast made to take his pastime therein." But few parishes could boast a clerk whose reading was so clear and precise and who took such a genial pleasure in the family ceremonials of the church. The Rev. Mr. Trustram had gently chided him on the subject of some of his quainter interpretations of holy writ, but old Bob, strong in ignorance and faith only smiled and shook his head saying : " My feyther read so, and oi read so, and our Sussex folk understand oi." So there it ended.

The Child noted with curiosity that the Verrall family filled their pew, for in spite of the taint of rumoured heresy they had not deserted the church of their fathers. With them was Simon Verrall and his little girl. She stood on a hassock and her searching brown eyes peered with vague wonder across the crowded church, and met the blue eyes of the curious child peeping round his curtain, and flashed a greeting to him.

The behaviour of Simon Verrall caused no little stir in the church. The bulk of the congregation took small part in the service. Parson and Clerk were there to do the duties they understood so well, and unless it was on occasion to join in a simple hymn the words of which they had learned in childhood, the people had the natural good sense and decency not to meddle with matters that they did not comprehend. But Simon in a loud voice challenged the Clerk himself in the responses and the sound of his " Amen " re-echoed through the aisles.

After the service the congregation gathered together in the churchyard and on the green between Cherry Croft and the church gates to converse about the affairs of their families and farms. It was noticed by some that Verrall of Foxhole endeavoured to get his cousin Simon and the little girl away with him, but that Simon refused to go, and after a short, angry talk the elder Verrall and his family walked hurriedly away from the church, leaving Simon in the churchyard.

The man had a small Bible with him which he placed on a flat tombstone near the churchyard wall. He pointed to it with his finger and the little girl, who seemed to know the part she was expected to play, turned it open at random.

Simon bent down to look at it and the text that met his eye was : " For which cause we faint not ; but though our outward man perish, yet the inward man is renewed day by day." To a visionary and fanatic like Simon this heathen method of casting lots, as it were, to encourage him in his own vanities, and pretend to himself that they were the will of God, was a common habit ; and whatever text he fell upon, generally gave him sufficient excuse to magnify his mission and disturb the public peace.

He threw himself on his knees for a moment and prayed in silence. Then rising slowly, he climbed upon the tomb-stone, faced the green upon which the villagers were standing and with his Bible outstretched in one hand, his eyes half-closed, in a loud sing-song voice, he called out : " The spirit of the Lord is upon me ; because he hath annointed me to preach the Gospel to the poor."

The puzzled crowd looked up at him in open-mouthed astonishment. A whirl of words that they scarcely heard or understood poured from the preacher. The familiar phrases of the Bible, jumbled up with abuse of their methods of life, threats of hell and promises of heaven, roused the sane Sussex folk to sudden anger.

The mob gathered underneath the wall shouting out angrily, " Knock his brains out." " Pull him down." Some began to throw clods at him, an amusement that the lads fell to very readily. One or two were for giving him a hearing. Old Bob the Clerk, speechless with indignation, kept warning him to descend whilst David Diggs, con-stable of the Manor of Gale, strolled leisurely across to Cherry Croft to debate with Captain Roger Johnson what were the duties and rights of a constable under such strange circumstances.

The mob got fiercer. Someone threw a stone which cut the preacher above the eye and blood flowed. A roar of joyous congratulation went up from their mouths. Some of the women shrieked and caught their men-folk by the arm to hinder them, so much mercy is there in the hearts of women even towards blasphemers. Then a cry of " Duck him ! " was raised, and with one heart and mind the stronger fellows of the crowd rushed for his pulpit, and were pulling him down when The Child, who had at the first trouble run across to summon the Captain, came rushing out of the gate shouting, " The Captain ! The Captain ! "

The sight of the wild preacher throwing out his arms and crying aloud, " The Spirit of the Lord is upon me," whilst

the mob pulled at his legs and pelted him with mud and
stones fairly staggered the good Captain.

" Damn my sockets and blind my eyes," he cried, " and
this in Christian England on a Sunday, too."

He beat his way through the mob with a thick oaken
cudgel until he reached the preacher. Diggs and one of his
own waggoners seized the fellow and threw him down and
the shepherd bringing up a rope they tied his arms and legs
securely.

There was, near the church gate, a small outhouse in
which Bob Rigby kept the shovels and boards and other
tools of the graveyard. This was the only public building
in the village and was dignified by the title of " The Lodge."
Here they used to place drowned stranger bodies from the
river on occasions, and the coffin of one who committed
suicide had rested there before it was carried to the cross
roads. This had caused The Lodge to be regarded by the
villagers as a place not wholly free from supernatural
terrors. Into this hovel Diggs threw his prisoner and locked
him in and Captain Johnson having dispersed the parishioners with a few well-directed and expressive oaths, the
peace of the Sabbath once more dwelt in Freston.

Whilst they were dealing with Simon and the mob were
clearing away to their homes, The Child remembered that
the little girl with the brown eyes had last been seen standing near her father when her cousins had left them and
gone home. He went back to the churchyard and hunted
about. At length he found her lying face down on a grass
grave sobbing as if her heart would break. As he could not
make her speak or listen to him he bethought him it was a
case for the healing kindness of Granny, and he went
across to the house and fetched her back with him.

The good woman soon soothed the little girl's terror
sufficiently to make her understand that Granny was a
friend and comforter. She raised her head from the ground
and saw Master Nic and Mistress Johnson bending over
her and knew that she had still friends in the world.
Granny, whose heart ached for the poor little lonely
wretch, picked her up and carried her into the farmhouse,
The Child running before to open the gates and doors.

Parson Oliver and Captain Johnson were in the kitchen
discussing the extraordinary affair; argument being the
business of men as merciful action is the province of
women.

"He shall be whipped at the cart's tail as a rogue and
vagabond," said the Parson fiercely.

At this moment Granny entered carrying the little girl
in her arms.

"Jesus God. What do you do bringing the fellow's
brat in here?" cries the Captain.

"I'd have her whipped out of the village, too," shouts
the Parson angrily. "It's a shame to let such devil's spawn
go without punishment."

"Poor litling," says Granny, holding her closer to her
breast, "how is she to blame?"

"Remember the commandment, Mistress Johnson,
which visits the sins of the fathers upon the children—
aye, unto the third and fourth generation."

"That's not my way," answers Granny in a huff.

"It is God's way, woman," says the Parson very sternly.

"Let it be how't wool, it's not my way."

And Granny, having scored the last word, turned her
back on the Parson and carried her burden quickly from
the room.

"Damn my liver and bones," chuckled the Captain,
"the old girl's in the right. What's the babe got to do with
it?"

"The words of the Scripture are clear," continued the
Parson in a tone of annoyance and rising as if to go. "The
woman is wrong——"

"Let the woman bide. It's the only way with them.
Clap a stopper on thy cable and bring thyself up. There's a
goose to dinner and she has the cooking of it. Do you stay
and help us to eat it, eh?"

"Well, well," said Parson Oliver as he sat down again.
"I suppose we must be charitable even to dissenters.
Mistress Johnson may not have opened her mouth in
wisdom but truly in her tongue is the law of kindness."

CHAPTER IV

A CASE OF WITCHCRAFT

THE lust of cruelty was the hall-mark of the eighteenth century. To an English mob the pelting of a wretch in the pillory or crowding the streets to see a petty thief, man or woman, flogged at the cart's tail from Newgate to Holborn was a holiday joy. Better-class people found their entertainment in visits to the Bridewell to see the women whipped by the men in blue. Bear-baiting, bull-baiting, cock fights, and prize fights, or even a fight between two market women, were sights that gladdened the hearts of all sport-loving Englishmen.

The good folk at Freston were no different from their fellow-men and women, and the delight of seeing Simon Verrall flogged at the cart's tail to the parish boundary, and then thrust out of the parish whose amenities he had so rudely disturbed, was looked forward to by all as a welcome amusement and a pleasant excuse for a holiday.

That evening after service a council was held in the kitchen at Cherry Croft. There were present Captain Johnson, Parson Oliver, Robert Rigby, and the constable of the Manor of Gale, David Diggs. A jug of ale, pipes and tobacco and glasses were set out on the table and Master Nic's function was to sit in the chimney-corner until such time as the Captain ordered him to descend to the cellar and refill the jug. Granny sat knitting in the window seat by the waning light.

To understand the trouble that they apprehended it must be remembered that at this time, a few years after the rebellion of 1715, political feeling ran very high. The Parson and his Clerk, though by no means Whigs, stood firm for Church and State and as much loyalty to the German King and Court as was necessary for safety. Captain

Johnson, like many other pillars of the Free Trade, was rumoured to be a friend of the King over the water and for reward was ready to carry across the Channel letters to and from that King's friends, or even the friends themselves. He therefore was very ready to show his loyalty in a matter of this sort. David Diggs, as a public officer, was longing to ply his whip, and looking forward like a good churchman to the pleasure of flogging a pestilent dissenter out of the parish ; but—and that was the trouble, he was a servant of the Manor of Gale, and held his office at the election of the Court Leet, and Mr. Gale, the Lord of the Manor, was a Whig. Not only was Mr. Gale a Whig, but he had been known to use his influence as a justice and Lord of the Manor to protect poor religious men and women whose churchmanship was unsound.

The Parson had brought with him a small leather-bound book which he laid on the table before him.

" What does the law say ? " asked Captain Johnson.

" The law is clear as I take it," said Parson Oliver, " and the punishment of rogues and vagabonds is after this way."

He read from the book before him : " ' The Constable Headburrough or Tythingman '——"

" That's oi, Sir," said David, beaming proudly. " That's oi. Oi was elected last Michaelmas and the Steward said——"

" Damn my ears," called out the Captain impatiently. " Let Parson read us the law."

" ' —The Tythingman,' " continued Parson Oliver, " ' assisted by the Minister, and one other of the Parish '—I think Bob Rigby the clerk should be that one—."

" Thank you, Sir. Thank you kindly," said the honest clerk, pulling the grey lock that rested on his forehead.

" ' —is to see (or to do it himself) '—"

" Oi'll do it myself, Maister," said David with a grin.

" ' —that such Rogues and Vagabonds etc. be Stript Naked from the middle upwards and openly Whipped till their body be bloody and then forthwith '—"

At that moment from across the green came the sound of a voice chanting in a tone of courage and challenge :

" The Lord trieth the righteous : but the wicked
and him that loveth violence his soul hateth.

Upon the wicked he shall rain snares, fire and
brimstone, and an horrible tempest : this shall be the
portion of their cup."

" Brimstone and fire and hell," cried the Captain.
" Close the window, Diggs, and let Parson get on with the
law."

Diggs obeyed and Parson Oliver continued :

" '—till their body be bloody and then forthwith to be
sent away from Constable to Constable the next straight
way to the place of their birth.' "

The Parson stopped, and picked up a clay pipe.

" Amen, Amen," said the clerk by mere force of habit
and buried his face in his mug.

" It all seems fair and square enough," said the Constable. "If the Captain will lend us a cart and the old mare,
the fitter thing will be to go round by the ferry road and
cast him off on Lewes highway. It's a bit longer than the
Seaford road but there's no hurry and it will save the
neighbours at the Ferry walking over here."

" Belay ! David, belay ! don't veer out such a lot of
jaw," said the Captain, holding up his hand. " I've listened
to the law, but as I hear it, it doesn't say that Verrall is a
rogue and vagabond, and hasn't the fellow got a right to go
before the justices and plead for himself ? "

" It be a part of my oath to take up all rogues and vagabonds and deal with them," said Diggs stoutly.

" Ay," said the more cautious Clerk, " but how do you
know who is rightly a rogue and vagabond as you may
say ? "

" There are minstrels and players and gipsies and
jugglers, it's all in the book," replied the Constable,
appealing to Parson Oliver.

" Read it up then," said the Captain. " Prove to me he
comes within the law."

" The law is full of pitfalls and hard to understand,"
murmured the Parson wearily.

" You may say the same of the Scripture," said the

Captain, " but the Law is our sailing orders in this world as the Scriptures our chart for the next. It's a pity they aren't simpler written for simple folk, but there it is. This business of Verrall's is above us, and the best thing to be done is for me to ride in to Seaford to-morrow and see the Steward about it and, if necessary, push on to Bishops Court and see Mr. Gale himself."

" Amen to that," said the Clerk.

" Another jug of ale, boy," said the Captain, " and then hike off, for I must be up and away early to-morrow. And look here, Diggs, take the poor devil some bread and cheese and a mug of ale and lock him up again and give me the key. I'll have no playing the fool whilst I'm away and I'll keep the key of his gaol in my own pocket. You may tell the village there will be no fun to-morrow till we learn what the justices say. The Law must be respected."

" That's right," said Parson Oliver.

" Ay, ay ! " said the Constable, and fetching a lantern he walked across the green where, having pushed the supper into the hovel, given his prisoner a parting kick and admonished him to ' shut his mouth and stop his psalm-singing,' he locked him up and coming back to the kitchen returned the key to Captain Johnson.

When they had finished a parting mug of ale they went homeward full of the worthiness of citizenship and a comforting sense of social duty well performed.

The Captain sat moodily at the table puffing rings of tobacco smoke at the chimney.

" Damn my liver and bones," he muttered sulkily. " We don't want stewards and justices and strange constables poking their noses round Cherry Croft."

" Why let 'em come, then ? " said Granny, looking up from her knitting.

The dear, good woman was perhaps the one soul in Freston who took no joy in the thought of a village festival with a rogue at the cart's tail and a howling, rejoicing mob of men, women and children running after him. Her heart was bleeding for the little brown-eyed child asleep upstairs.

"The Law is the Law, woman," said the Captain with a husband's superior wisdom.

" Seem's a pity he can't escape. It would save a lot of pother."

The Captain grunted at her foolishness.

" 'Taint likely with key in my pocket, is it ? "

" I reckon, Roger, mind I only say I reckon, that if he were gone in morning you wouldn't have any call to put yourself in a pucker about it."

" I'd not be snuffy about it, but I can't take no hand in it. It's too dangerous."

He whistled thoughtfully. There were a lot of kegs of spirits, bales of silk and dallops of tea under the hay in the big barn, and at the end of the week when all the hay was in and the horses free they were to be run inland. Granny knew all about that. It was not the moment to entertain justices, strange constables and other land-sharks whose hearts were hardened against Free Trade.

" You be off to bed, dear," said Granny with a comforting smile. " Put your clothes on the chair and I'll dust 'em ready for morning."

The Captain chuckled and felt in his pocket for the key.

" Nay," he said laughing. " I'm not letting you do what I don't dare myself."

" I ain't going to meddle with the Law. You be off and hang your breeches on the chair. If yon Child's up to mischief we ain't to blame. And if when you ride back tomorrow the man's gone, well, as Parson says, it will be God's way."

The Captain looked at The Child, who was sleeping in the chimney corner.

" He's downright sorry for the little girl and so am I," added Granny.

The Captain winked at his wife and, slowly rising from his chair, kissed her tenderly and then stood chuckling and gazing at her in admiration.

" Damn my thick old skull, but you'm the brains, my dear. I don't part with no key ! I can swear it never leaves my pocket ! You don't go near the lodge, and yet the man's up anchor and away and we get shut on him."

D

He laughed aloud at the scheme. " The little devil will do it all right. Leave it to him." He stopped again to roar with laughter. " Don't forget to dust them clothes, mistress. I must be smart to-morrow."

The Child awoke with a start. He saw old Roger kiss his wife and go tumbling upstairs to bed chuckling to himself. " Lord Almighty, but you'm the brains, my dear, you'm the brains. Jonathan himself couldn't have thought it out better."

The quick wits of The Child scented the unusual. Captain Johnson was in the main proud of and kind to the old lady but not demonstrative of these facts by outward endearments. There was something in the wind. Sleep left his eyes and he shook himself joyfully like a young dog who sees his owner with a hat and stick in his hand.

In a few minutes Granny went upstairs and returned with the Captain's coat and breeches, which she proceeded to beat with a bundle of twigs on the kitchen table. As she flung the breeches on the board there was a clanking sound as the key struck the table. She put her hand in the pocket and pulled it out.

" It's well for us there are no friends of Verrall's to get hold of this, but I'm sorry for the little girl."

" Are you, Granny ? " asked The Child. " I'm sorry for her, too. Give me the key."

" Nay, child. It would never do for me or the Captain to take his part. Lord knows what would happen if the Law got to hear of it."

" What's the Law, Granny ? "

" That's what they none of them seem to know, but it's agin Verrall and it's agin anyone who meddles with him, now he's in their hands, and to-morrow the Captain rides over to Seaford to see Mr. Gale and his Steward."

" Are they the Law, Granny ? "

" About these parts they be all the Law as far as I can make it."

For the idea of the Law as anything other than the divine will of county justices has never been very clear to this day in the minds of rural England.

Granny laid the key on the table and went off in search

of her work-basket for there was a button to make firm
on the Captain's coat.

The brown eyes and the tear-stained face of his little
friend were staring into the soul of The Child. To think
with him was generally to act. Sorrow at failure he had
often experienced and chastisement at discovery, but he
knew nothing as yet of repentance. He seized the key and
crept out into the darkness.

The sound of Verrall's chantings, now dismal and
hopeless in tone, helped to guide him.

" O my God, I cry in the daytime, but thou hearest not ;
and in the night season, and am not silent."

He kept repeating the same verse in a continuous moan.

The Child felt his way to the padlock. The key turned
in it and he moved it from the staple.

" It is the Angel of the Lord," whispered Verrall. " The
Lord is my Shepherd."

" Whist ! man," said Master Nic, catching the last word.
" You may thank your stars it is not the shepherd, and if
he's anywhere about there will be trouble."

Verrall recognised his voice. The Child went to him and
with some difficulty helped him to crawl out of the door
tied and bound as he was. Then he propped him up against
the wall, replaced and locked the padlock, and bidding Verrall keep still and shut his mouth, he ran across the green.

Granny was in the kitchen when he returned and appeared deeply intent on the sewing of buttons. She made no
movement as he slid the key back on the table, but he well
knew it was all play-acting and understood that it was done
in deference to the Law, of which Granny and the Captain
appeared to stand in great awe. Granny picked up the
clothes and putting the key in the breeches pocket carried
the things upstairs.

The Child's way to his room was up another stair, but
he made no pretence of going to his bed, for he quite
understood that this escapade of his met with Granny's
approval though not with that of the Law, but as he loved
Granny and had no glimmering of knowledge as to the
power or extent of the Law, he left the house again quietly
and returned to Verrall,

The untying of the shepherd's knots in the darkness gave The Child considerable trouble and every time he broke his nails he used language culled from the Captain's lips that made Verrall shudder.

" Cut it, boy, cut it. There's a knife in my side pocket."

" Cut it be hanged," said Master Nic angrily, " and have the shepherd after me if he found out who had done it. Besides, we can't afford to waste a good rope in these parts, and don't you think you are going to carry it off with you. This rope belongs to Captain Johnson."

Verrall had no desire to keep the rope which at length was untied and unwound, and The Child coiled it round his body the more easily to carry it until he had determined what to do with it.

Taking Verrall by the hand, for the night was very dark, he led him down to the boat-house and they sat on the ground for a while to consider the next step to be taken.

" The question is," said The Child, " where are you to go to now you are free ? "

" My first duty is to find my daughter that the ruffians carried away. Where is my poor babe, my little Hetty ? "

It was the first time Master Nic had heard the little girl's name. He said it over to himself several times and liked the sound and feel of it. " Hetty Verrall, Hetty Verrall." What a terrible thing it would be if he awoke in the morning and could not remember it. Granny was always saying she could not remember names. But " Hetty Verrall ! "—one must always have a name like that snug in one's heart and pat on the lips.

" The little girl is safe with Mistress Johnson and to-morrow she will carry her up to your cousin at South Dean."

" The Lord preserveth the strangers ; He relieveth the fatherless ; but the way of the wicked He turneth upside down. Mistress Johnson shall always be remembered in my prayers."

" That's very good of you, Master Verrall," replied Nic, " but it doesn't help. Here you are out of prison sure enough, but in another three hours or so Martin and the girls will come along this way with their milking pails."

" If you can put me across the river I can find my way up to South Dean."

" And how are you to hide there when the Law comes looking for you ?

" If I can get into Lewes I shall be safe."

" Then why not have said so long ago ? " cried Master Nic, jumping to his feet. " You can get to Lewes across the downs and never meet a soul. We'll go up the river half a mile and then we will make for Hindover."

They rowed up the sluggish stream to a little landing-place where the boat was made fast, and they were soon winding up a chalk pack-horse track along the side of the steep down until they reached a big barn with a large yard and sheep-shelter.

" This is Hindover and you can lie snug in the straw until sunrise. It's lightening already. You can't miss your way. There's a good track right across the downs to the Beacon, that's the highest point away there." He pointed into the gloom. " From the Beacon you will see Lewes below you. Now I must be off or someone will be wanting to know who took the boat out."

" The blessing of the Lord be yours, Child," said Verrall fervently. " First you are sent to save my little one from drowning in the waters——"

" It was the eel's fault, that. The beast frightened her."

" Then again you are sent to save my body from the scourging of the ungodly."

" I think Granny left the key my way on purpose. You ought to thank her," interrupted Master Nic, who felt that too much fuss was being made of an adventure that had really given him a deal of pleasure.

" Verily the hand of God is in these things and He has brought you to us for a purpose."

" Parson Oliver says the hand of God is in all things," answered The Child lightly, and he sprang away down Hindover Hill rather pleased to be rid of his strange companion.

Soon after sunrise Captain Johnson was up and about. His brown mare was saddled and at the door. Granny came down to the gate to see him away. As the man brought the mare round Martin and the girls came up from the fields with their milking pails.

"Where's The Child this morn?" asked the Captain.

"Asleep upstairs for aught I know," replied Granny.

"Nay, Mistress," interrupted Martin. "He's down on the river in the boat snigling for eels."

"Damn the little varmint," said the Captain chuckling, "then we'll have some eels for supper; do you hear, Granny?" and he waved her farewell.

Higher up the village he met the waggoner and the shepherd talking to David Diggs. The subject was, of course, the postponed discipline of Simon Verrall, and the two were grumbling to the Constable as Englishmen will about the Law's delays and the difficulty of coming by their well-known rights.

"If you can't punish him, Master Diggs, why are you the Constable?" enquired the waggoner.

Captain Johnson reined up and spoke to them.

"Now look here, you two. The man's in the custody of the Law and here's the key of his gaol," he continued, pulling it out of his pocket, "and if anyone interferes with him whilst I'm away, Parson says that it's pound-breach and that's felony and means transportation, or hanging may be for aught I know, but damn my liver and bones if I move a finger to save any of you."

Very early that morning Granny carried little Hetty up to South Dean and handed her over to her cousin, who was much relieved to learn that no vengeance was to be wreaked upon the wretched preacher until the Law in the shape of Mr. Gale and the Steward had been duly consulted.

That evening Parson Oliver had been up on the downs to look at a field of his turnips, and after gazing at them for some time in his slow country way had come to the conclusion that they wanted water. He then sat down to ruminate on the inconvenience of a world where the hay harvest required sun at the same time that his turnips required water. It was the more difficult to reconcile with a devout belief in the all-wisdom of Providence in so much as his own hay was already gathered and stacked, being down in the river meadows and earlier ripe.

Whilst he was musing on these bucolic matters he noticed a horseman on the Beacon Down, now but a small speck on the landscape, but he made no doubt it was the Captain returning and he moved along the upper valley to cross his track and meet him above the village.

" What news from Seaford ? " he cried as the Captain rode up to him.

" A day's journey for nothing," grumbled the Captain. " Mr. Gale attends the Parliament in London and the Steward has gone over to Pevensey and will not return until to-morrow."

" What's to be done then ? "

Captain Johnson shook his head doubtfully.

" You be Minister and Davy be Constable, so I doubt it's your business to deal with the fellow if so be as it is decided not to wait for the Steward."

They walked down to Cherry Croft, picking up David Diggs and Rigby on their way, and the Captain, taking the key out of his pocket, suggested that they should give the poor wretch some bread and cheese and a mug of ale as he had had no bait since supper-time.

Granny bustled about to get victuals for her man after his ride, and a fair portion for the prisoner, which Diggs and the Clerk, accompanied by the Parson, carried across the village green to the Lodge.

When they were gone, Captain Johnson enquired after Master Nic.

" Came in this morning with a creel of eels, and that's the last I see of him. He seemed mortal sleepy."

" He was up early, you know," and the Captain chuckled.

Granny said nothing, but set before her husband a large pasty, a loaf and some cheese, and a big jug of home-brewed ale.

He was lifting his first mug to his lips when shouts came from outside and David Diggs burst into the room, his eyes starting out of his head and wild with excitement.

" He's gone ! He's gone ! " he cried.

" Who's gone ? " asked the Captain impatiently.

" The man Verrall, sir," chimed in Rigby, who now came up with the Parson.

" True as I stand here," said Parson Oliver, who was pale with amazement, " the man is gone, rope and all, not a sign of him."

" Impossible ! " cried the Captain. " Damn my liver and bones, I can't believe it."

He jumped up from the table, and they all hurried across the green. There was no doubt the hovel was empty. The padlock was in perfect order. Diggs was clear that he left it fastened last night, and the Parson and Clerk, who were present when he opened the door, agreed that they found it untouched. They entered the hovel. There was a small shutter, but that was closed and barred outside. They flung it open. It was scarce a big enough opening for a man to get through, and there were no signs of any attempt to get out that way. Several villagers joined them, and many theories were advanced as to how the prisoner had escaped, but none of them seemed to fit in with the facts. Whilst they were chattering and raking about in the hovel, they disturbed an old white owl hidden away in the rafters. The bird fluttered about, hitting Mr. Rigby in the face.

" A witch, a witch ! " he cried in terror.

There was a rush to the door, the little mob tumbling over each other and shouting, " A witch, a witch ! "

The owl escaped through the little window and fluttered across to the elm-trees unnoticed by the villagers.

Parson Oliver, whose hat was knocked off in the rush, admonished them for their folly and walked away to the Vicarage. He suspected Captain Johnson, and was angry about the matter, but there were many reasons why he should not quarrel with his most important parishioner.

As for the villagers, the cry of witchcraft once started, they hugged it to their bosoms, and it almost made amends for the loss of their holiday and the whipping of Simon Verrall. Down at the Ferry Inn Mr. Rigby was the centre of interest as he described to an admiring circle the huge size and strange shape of the winged thing that attacked him in the Lodge. Many wondered how, when it escaped outside, it became invisible to their eyes, and yet several

who were there could swear quite honestly that they had
not seen it. The waggoner now remembered that his wife
had awakened him in the night because she heard a strange
rushing noise as of bodies racing through the air, and this
hint of witch-riding brought forward many other fearful
evidences of noises heard and not heard and appearances
seen and not seen.

But all these tales paled before the experience of the
shepherd, and when that became known there were few so
foolhardy as to disbelieve that Verrall's escape had been
planned and carried out by the Evil One and his servants.
Going in the evening to the barn to lock up for the night,
the shepherd had found the rope with which he had tied
and bound the prisoner coiled up and hanging tidily on its
wooden peg in its accustomed corner.

He carried it into the farm and laid it before the Captain
and Mrs. Johnson.

" Split my binnacle ! " cried the Captain, " that's a bit
of luck. That's the rope right enough. Where did you find
it ? "

" Take it ! Burn it ! The witch must have brought it into
the barn. Take it ! Burn it ! " called out the shepherd in
real distress.

" Leave it there, then, you swab, and go your way ; the
witch won't harm you as long as you get to your work in
good time of a morning."

" And keep away from the beerhouse when you are sent
into Lewes," added Granny.

The shepherd made mental resolutions to do his duty to
his master more fairly in future, but when he left the farm
he felt a social call upon him to go to the Ferry Inn and
carry his news there. This last piece of evidence was over-
whelming and solved the doubts of the few rationalists
who sought to maintain that Verrall's escape was not of
demoniac management.

" Put the rope away," said the Captain to Nic the next
morning, " and I'll take it down to the boat some day.
The rope is right enough."

The Child picked up the rope, but as he touched it something seemed to tickle his mind, and he burst out into peals

of laughter. The more he tried to stop, the more he laughed, until he stood limp and exhausted with Granny shaking him and the Captain threatening him with the end of the rope if he didn't cease his clacking.

"Damn the boy, is he bewitched, too?" asked the Captain.

"Bless us all, what's the matter with you? Are you pothery or what?" asked Granny, when she had shaken some self-control into him.

"Folk are so funny," sobbed The Child. "Folk are so funny."

"May the Lord bless all means to you, my child. You'd be in a poor way if folk weren't funny. Supposing folk had sense? What would become of the likes of you?"

CHAPTER V

THE CHILD GOES TO SCHOOL

THE pendulum ticks off the hours of our lives, and Master Nic's age of innocence was drawing to a close and Jonathan Wild's era of power and prosperity was nearing its climax. At No. 68 of the Old Bailey, the second door south of Ship's Court, the great man sat at the receipt of custom, interviewing owners of lost property, attorneys and molested travellers and, like the sound individualist that he was, doing competently those services for his fellow-men for reward, that are now done more cumbrously but perhaps more suitably by the State.

When Jonathan appeared in the streets he wore a laced coat and carried a silver mace as one in authority, and he was always attended by his servant, Toby Billinge, dressed in a sober but handsome grey livery. Toby was a simple fellow, but had been an expert cracksman in his day. He adhered to his master as a dog attaches himself to a shepherd. Of a florid complexion and round belly, in all appearance of a phlegmatic disposition and chary of speech, he was ready to take whatsoever orders he received and to obey them, asking no questions for conscience sake. An ideal servant for the man he served and faithful to the end.

The two made many journeys into Sussex, and Toby, finding that his master's interests were strangely wrapped up in the welfare of Master Nic, became honestly enough captivated by the gracious ways of the youngster and was always at his beck and call when his own master was not in need of his service.

Master Nic was now about fourteen, and Jonathan had long ago collected from Granny all the details of his first coming to Cherry Croft and the amounts of Mr. Crowley's quarterly payments, and had for some time been considering in his mind what Crowley's plans were for the boy's future and how far it would be worth his while to interfere

45

in the matter. Jonathan assured himself he had no weak sentiment in his composition. Alice Trustram had deserted him. Within two years of his leaving Freston she had made a good marriage for herself. This was her husband's child. What was Master Nic to him?

It was Granny Johnson who caught his eyes intent on The Child, who was teaching Billinge the art of making rabbit snares and jeering at his clumsy fingers and general lack of technical skill.

" I know what you be thinking, Master Wild," she said, " and you be right. Yon child is the very bly of his mother."

Jonathan, who understood her country phrase, nodded.

It was at this time that a letter was received by Captain Johnson from Mr. Crowley ordering him to convey Master Nicholas Berrington to London, where he would be met, as it was intended that he should be placed at a school in Yorkshire. Granny, and even the Captain, were in great distress. The Child was as their own child, and they loved him as such.

Granny, in tears, broke the news to him that he was to be taken away to school, but he only laughed the idea to scorn, saying : " As long as you want me, Granny, I'll stay here, and when you don't I'll run away to sea."

With that he gave the matter no further thought.

When Mr. Wild arrived on a visit a few days afterwards, he was shown a second and more peremptory letter from Mr. Crowley to the Captain, asking him to deliver Master Nic at Mr. Lee's, hatter and hosier, opposite the Mews Gate, Clerkenwell, on a date a fortnight later, with a threat that all money allowances would be stopped if this were not done. Parson Oliver and Mr. Wild both agreed that there was no question but that Mr. Crowley's orders should be obeyed, and as *The Lively Kate* was sailing in a few days from Newhaven to Gravesend, it was agreed that the Captain should take Master Nic thence to London in accordance with Crowley's instructions.

Jonathan Wild had intended making a voyage across to France and had, indeed, come to Freston for that purpose, but he now abandoned his intention and rode back to

London. It was clear to his mind that if he was going to take a hand in Master Nic's affairs he must cut into the game now or not at all.

The first step was to find out what Crowley proposed to do and whether he should come in as a partner or play his own hand. The position at Steeple Berrington, as far as Wild's information went, was that Crowley continued in possession and the world accepted him as agent for the heir, who was reported to be living with friends of the family in the south of England. That these friends should have appointed Mr. Crowley as their attorney seemed a very reasonable proposition. He was a respected citizen of Oxfordshire, and his neighbours would never have suspected him of any form of dishonesty or chicanery not sanctioned by law. He was a sound Protestant and a pillar of the church. Even his hobby savoured of learning and piety, for he took a keen delight in antiquarian studies, and Master Thomas Hearne, of Edmund Hall, Oxford, had written to him for information on the customs of Manors, on which he was a recognised authority.

It is quite an error to suppose that learning and culture are in any way inconsistent with moral obliquity. Otherwise two rogues like Crowley and the Rev. Daniel Adamson would not have met in London and fraternised over a discourse concerning the genuineness of the inscription on the grave of Robin Hood at Kirkleys Abbey.

The reverend antiquarian was a Yorkshire schoolmaster of Thirsk who kept one of those cheap schools which even at this date were notorious for their ill-treatment of unfortunate children. Crowley had made him small loans, and to assist him to work these off had proposed to him that Master Nic should be sent down to his school, intimating to him that he was a friendless youngster about whom no enquiries would be made. The Reverend Daniel Adamson quite understood that if an opportunity occurred to apprentice him to sea, or in some way to place him out of sight, a premium would be paid and no questions would be asked. In this way it was no uncommon thing for illegitimate and other unwanted children to disappear and be heard of no more.

Such was the position of Master Nic's affairs when Jonathan Wild, accompanied by Billinge, rode into Witney to visit Luke Crowley.

Master Crowley not only knew of Jonathan Wild by repute, but, like many other good citizens, he looked upon him as a man who had done good public work in mitigating the horrors and dangers of travel along the King's highway and restoring stolen goods. He was both honoured and surprised by his visit. Rebecca was ordered not to keep the great man waiting, but to show the visitor into the office, where, without wig and attired in an old green gown, Crowley was entering accounts in his ledgers.

Jonathan was dressed in a handsome brown riding-suit and wore his hanger by his side as any gentleman of position might do. He threw his hat carelessly on the table and flung himself into a chair opposite the old man, looking at him under his bushy eyebrows with half-concealed contempt.

" So you are Master Luke Crowley, the Witney lawyer."

" The same, Master Wild, at your service," and the old man finished his writing, slowly closed his ledger, and laid down his pen.

" I am in no want of your services, Master Crowley. I am here to do myself service," said Jonathan curtly.

" Surely, surely," said Crowley with a thin smile. " Everyone who visits me comes to do himself service, but in the end, yes, in the end, the service is often mutual."

" I am here on no borrowing errand. I want to know all about the boy they call ' The Child,' Master Nic Berrington, of Steeple Berrington, now living at Freston with Captain Roger Johnson."

The old man shrank at his bullying tone and drew back his chair, murmuring half to himself, " The Child ! "

" Yes, I hear you are for sending him into Yorkshire to a drunken parson named Adamson. I want to know about it."

" You want to know about it ? " repeated Crowley in a tone of polite curiosity. " You want to know about it ? Why should you want to know about it ? "

" That's my business," retorted Wild in his rough, bullying way.

" And mine also, my dear sir ! If it were my own business, it would be a pleasure to me that so eminent a gentleman as yourself, sir, should be pleased to be interested in
it. But you know, Mr. Wild, I am a mere agent, a lawyer.
A man of your learning understands the position. The
privilegium of the attorney forbids."

Mr. Crowley rubbed his bony hands and shook his head
pleasantly at his visitor.

" You damned old weasel ! " shouted Jonathan coarsely.
" I didn't come down here to chaffer and talk law jargon.
I came on business. You must make your terms. Either I
come in with you and share your gains, or I put the boy's
rights in other hands and see him through."

" Of course, Mr. Wild—business ! That is what always
appeals to me. But what can be done ? The estates must be
administered, and The Child will come of age some day,
and then——"

" Suppose the lad should not come of age ? There are
safer ways of ridding yourself of him than placing him out
at a Yorkshire school. Suppose we were to transport him
to the Colonies, say, or rid ourselves of him altogether ?
There are ways. Will you pay the price ? "

The old man's teeth chattered, and he trembled with
excitement. To be rid of The Child altogether seemed to his
avaricious soul like a gift of bags of gold.

" Two thousand pounds down," said Wild coldly, " and
Master Nic troubles you no more."

" It is too much. I cannot pay it. I have not so much
money in the world," he cried out.

" Liar ! " cried Jonathan with a grim laugh, drawing his
hanger and pointing it across the table. " If I slit your
throat now, I could take more than that from your money-
bags and no one the wiser."

This outrageous threat seemed to calm the lawyer. These
strange temptations had been a nightmare to him. Now he
awoke.

" You are quite in error, sir. I keep but little money here.
Parchments I have sleeping like infants in those chests and
thriving, yes, waxing day by day. They say I am a miser,
but I am no fool. I do not hoard gold. Your threats are

childish and ill-mannered. You would not cut my throat for a very sound reason. It would not pay you to do it."

Jonathan Wild put back his hanger with a curse. He saw that the bullying methods that overawed the thieves and scoundrels he ruled amongst had no effect on the clever, mean country lawyer.

" Pah ! my good man, I only jested. I like the lad myself. But let us finish the business. What do you say ? If I agree to take no steps to interfere between you and Master Nic, is not that worth two thousand pounds ? "

" May be it is worth more. To be as candid and open as you have been with me, Mr. Wild, I will admit that probably it is a fair price."

" That is very open, I agree," said Wild pleasantly, " and how will it be paid ? "

" It will not be paid," said the old man firmly. " The tempter hath not tempted me. I will leave things as they are. It is not for me to interfere with the decrees of Providence."

" You have changed your tune, sir," said Wild with a sneer.

" The best of us may fall into temptation. I am not a man of sentiment, but a lawyer. I do not pretend to be a well-wisher to Master Nic, but I bear him no ill-will. His father was my client. His mother I knew well. A very beautiful woman. I have not seen him since his parents' death, but as a babe he was very like his mother. The resemblance was much remarked."

" Other folk have noted that," said Jonathan absently.

" It was an extraordinary likeness," continued Crowley. "The same blue eyes ; the same fair hair. My lady was painted by Sir James Thornhill. The picture being of value, I had it removed from the house. Oh, yes, I can account, sir. I have been careful of the young man's affairs. I had it brought down here."

He pointed with his skinny finger over Jonathan Wild's head. Jonathan turned round in his chair and fell back.

" Her picture ! " he muttered, gazing at it intently.

The painting was a large drawing-room piece. My lady wore a ball dress of white muslin, with roses trailing over the hoop. Her hair was elaborately dressed. She stood out of doors on a terrace. In the background were the windows of a great house.

Jonathan Wild rose and walked to the wall, with his hands behind him. He smiled sadly and stood for several minutes looking at the face and figure of the woman who might have made such a difference in his life.

He turned on his heel to Crowley, who was still sitting at the table and wondering why the picture should charm the man so deeply. With a mocking laugh Jonathan threw up his head, saying : " God, sir, what wicked fools men are. You and I seem to be like two impenitent thieves plotting the destruction of the Son in the presence of the Holy Mother."

" You seem to forget, Mr. Wild, that I am a Protestant," was all Crowley's reply.

" A plague on all our religions," answered Jonathan Wild gaily. " I am glad, sir, you refused my offer. I tell you candidly, Master Crowley, you are a bigger hypocrite and rascal than I am, but we have fought a fair black-guard's game. I am going to ride down to Sussex and carry off your child and make him my child."

" You will ride on a fool's errand, then," retorted Crowley. " He left Sussex three days ago."

Jonathan Wild whistled.

Luke Crowley blushed slightly, for he could have bitten out his tongue for the blunder it had uttered. So they parted.

As Jonathan rode away from the house, he pointed out to Billinge the third window from the door, and Billinge, in his ignorant way, began asking questions about the chests and cupboards in the room.

" Whoever does the job," said Jonathan shortly, " is to remember that nothing is to be touched but the picture. Cut clean out of the frame, rolled up, and if anything else is disturbed I see to the hanging of the fellow. The picture I will pay for myself. It is a work of art."

" I don't understand art," said Billinge sulkily, and they rode up the street to the " Rose Tavern."

Master Nic received the news that he was really to go

E

to a Yorkshire school with his usual lighthearted philosophy. He disliked leaving Cherry Croft, and his pony and
all his friends, but there would be new adventures. The
parting with Granny would be a moist and miserable business, but the sail from Newhaven to Gravesend would be
jolly. As to school, he had no clear idea what that would
be like, but there would be a lot of boys of his own age to
fight and conquer. In any case, if he did not approve of the
change, he promised Granny he would run away and come
back to her. But he did not repeat his promise, as it made
Granny weep and hug him to her heart and chide him
and kiss him and call him her own dear child, and Master
Nic felt he was getting too old to sanction these exhibitions
of affection.

When they reached London and called at Jonathan
Wild's house, and found he was away from home, Master
Nic's confidence was a little dimmed, for he had intended
asking his patron's views about this new adventure and
taking his advice. When he arrived at Mr. Lee's and was
handed over with his portmanteau to the Reverend Daniel
Adamson, even Master Nic was rather dispirited, and when
Captain Johnson gulped down several incoherent oaths
and bade him farewell, he nearly broke into tears himself.

But there was no time for grief, for the Yorkshire waggon
was at the door, and he and seven or eight young gentlemen of a depressed and mournful disposition were being
promptly loaded into it with their belongings, whilst the
schoolmaster mounted his horse to ride alongside of it.

The reverend gentleman was a fat, roguish-looking
fellow, and told the lads that as long as they behaved well
they would find him good-natured enough, but any evil
courses would be sternly punished. With that he flourished
his riding-whip in the air catching his old horse a
dexterous smack as if to show his pupils what he could do
in this sort, and the cavalcade started away towards Islington
and the road to the north.

The lads were walking up Ridge Hill, near St. Albans,
to lighten the waggon's load, when one of them, more
adventurous than the rest, thinking that his reverend tutor,
who was conversing with the waggoner, was not observing

him, suddenly turned and darted down a green lane towards a small wood, where he hoped to find cover. Master Nic approved the lad's pluck, but doubted his intelligence. Indeed, it was a very futile and disastrous manœuvre. For the schoolmaster, cantering after the truant, caught him on the edge of the wood and seemed not displeased to have the opportunity of administering a severe discipline with the horse-whip, in which he paused from time to time to offer advice and monitions to his other pupils, which he did with the pleasantest of smiles and in most elegant diction, punctuated by skilful cuts with the whip and dismal howls from his victim.

This matter satisfactorily concluded, they continued their journey until they reached Dunstable. The Child had by this time fully made up his mind to part company with the Reverend Daniel Adamson as soon as it might be done with safety to his skin. They put up for the night at the " Wheatsheaf Inn," and The Child never doubted but that under cover of night an escape might be made. The pupils, however, were put in the stable loft for the night, and the schoolmaster personally supervised their undressing, and having offered up a short prayer with them and administered a further discipline to the runaway, with many merry quips about his failure and moral maxims on the virtue of obedience, all of which he supported by quotations from Proverbs and the wisdom of Solomon, he gathered up all their clothes and, taking them with him, bade them goodnight, locked the door upon them and went to supper in great good humour.

Jonathan Wild in his careful way had learned all about the plans of the Yorkshire schoolmaster. On leaving Crowley he had determined that he would adopt Master Nic and be responsible for his future.

He and Billinge passed the night at Oxford, but the next morning, to the latter's surprise, they did not take the London road, but, crossing the Charwell, passed through Headington for Thame, and after dining at Aylesbury, rode on to Tring and across the Beacon Hill down into Dunstable. Here they made enquiry for the Reverend Daniel Adamson, and Billinge found that he had not yet gone north, but was expected any day to arrive at the " Wheat-sheaf Inn."

It was one of the glories of the English law in the good old days that any person who would make an affidavit that another owed him twenty pounds could lock him up pending the trial, and unless the victim could find the money and pay it into court, he remained in a spunging-house until the trial came on. No one knew better than Jonathan Wild the procedure and methods of arrest by mesne process, and it was often used by the unscrupulous to put their enemies out of the way if only for a few days. Jonathan Wild himself prepared all the necessary legal documents for the discomfiture of the Reverend Daniel Adamson, since it was not worth his while to waste money in legal fees about so commonplace a matter.

Billinge was stationed at the " Wheatsheaf," and the next evening brought word that the schoolmaster had arrived, and was even now drinking rum in the parlour and eating a toasted cheese. Jonathan Wild, taking his papers with him and followed by Billinge, went straightway to the inn.

They both entered the parlour without ceremony. The Reverend Daniel Adamson looked up and wished them good-evening.

" Good or bad as may be," replied Wild rudely, " I am here to arrest you at the suit of Luke Crowley for thirty pounds. You will find the papers in order. I am to lodge you in gaol, and you are to hand over to me the custody of a young boy named Nic Berrington, who is with you."

The schoolmaster turned white. He did not even look at the proffered papers.

" There must be some mistake, Mr.——"

" Jonathan Wild," continued that worthy, picking up the phrase, " and let me tell you, sir, Jonathan Wild does not make mistakes, and Mr. Crowley is not the sort of man to employ him on a fool's errand."

The poor wretch buried his face in his hands. " I shall be ruined ! " he cried out in despair.

" Very likely," said Wild curtly. " Why not ? The writ is in order, and to-morrow you will be in Bedford gaol and can find security."

The man looked at the law papers in quiet despair. There seemed no help for him.

" Toby," called out Wild, handing him the writ, " here is your man. I will speak to the innkeeper. Lodge him here to-night and Bedford gaol first thing in the morning, and find this young lad Berrington and bring him here."

By this ingenious means was Master Nic rescued from the clutches of the Reverend Daniel Adamson and carried off by his powerful friend and patron, Jonathan Wild.

The next day they rode early to London and were joined at St. Albans, where they stopped to dine, by Billinge. Toby, in his simple way, told them a very merry story of how the schoolmaster had bribed him to set him free from the custody of the law into which he believed he had fallen. It was a jovial feast, and Master Nic rejoiced in his good fortune and gratefully worshipped his deliverer.

From this time until the end of his wicked career Jonathan Wild treated Master Nic as his own son, lavishing on him money and such affection as there was in his strange nature. Some weeks after the lad came to live with Jonathan there was hung in his own parlour a picture of a beautiful woman whose likeness to The Child everyone could see. There was an ugly scene between Jonathan and the woman Molly Straddle, who then ruled in his household, but Jonathan had his way after much violence and cursing. He kept his own counsel about Master Nic's origin. But the appearance of the picture and his affection and care of the lad caused many—and perhaps Mistress Straddle among the number—to believe that Master Nic was really a son of Jonathan Wild, a legend that was very detrimental to him in after life.

At first Master Nic attended the school of Mr. De La Place at Marylebone, where he was taught more of deportment and dancing than any more solid learning, but the restraints of school life were irksome to him, and he seemed to find his natural home among the thieves and wasters who formed the court of Jonathan Wild. Molly dressed up the pretty boy and took him in attendance with her to Ranelagh and Whitehall. Jonathan made no objection to his joining with Billinge and a lot of riotous youths in pocket-picking excursions at Bartholomew Fair and in other crowds. He frequented plays and cock-fights and the bull-ring with the wickedest, and became as clever with the cards as Count de Grillac himself, with whom he was a great favourite, and who never wearied in discoursing for his good on the maxims of polite morality.

And in judging of his future actions, though he himself in after life never sought to make excuses for his evil-doing, it is but fair to remember what a horrible upbringing this was for a youth of promise. All of his companions were men and women devoted to crime, wickedness, lust and profligacy, yet he seems to have remembered in them only those traits of wit, kindliness, honour and bravery which we cannot deny are at moments exhibited even by the worst of evil-doers. His smile never became false or bitter, his voice rang true, and his blue eyes looked on a world of crime and wickedness with the same merry sparkle of the joy of life with which they had shone on the pastoral delights of the valley of Freston.

But though he passed through this mire, less soiled than many would have been, yet when the end came and Jonathan Wild met his just doom on the gallows, it would have required a greater faith than that of Elihu to have spoken of the future of The Child those brave words with which Elihu encouraged his friend :

Lo, all these things worketh God oftentimes with man,
To bring back his soul from the pit, to be enlightened
   with the light of the living.

Yet in the end that was true also of Master Nic.

BOOK II

MASTER NIC

CHAPTER VI

EXIT JONATHAN WILD

THE sun shone brightly on Southwark on the twenty-fourth of May, seventeen hundred and twenty-five. Yesterday a great ruler of men had died a shameful death on the scaffold. Jonathan Wild had passed away and three of his lieutenants had fled across the river to Southwark sanctuary and were in hiding at the " Duke's Head " in Redcross Street.

For the Mint in Southwark was the last refuge of the outlaws of the great city. Westminster and St. Martin's no longer offered protection, Alsatia was a fond memory of an older generation of rogues, but the crooked, narrow lanes and low-browed roofs of the mean streets that surrounded St. George's, Southwark, were a district sacred from pollution by constable or bailiff.

Turquet, Count de Grillac and Master Toby Billinge sat at the table in the window of the inn parlour eating a paltry breakfast of salt beef and small ale, wondering in their minds whether they were to live their lives out in the filthy security of the Mint, to continue their career of crime without the protecting hand of the Master to uphold them, or to find some new outlet for their talents and energies.

Turquet de Grillac was a man of education and good manners. The story went that he was the illegitimate son of a noble house in France, and had been educated for the priesthood, and fallen into evil ways and worse company. Others said he had been a valet whom Jonathan Wild had saved from the gallows. No one could deny him good looks. His figure was of more than middle height. He wore his clothes with the air of a gentleman. His face had a melancholy expression which suited his olive complexion, and he had a furtive habit of half-closing the lids of his eyes and looking downwards along his well-modelled nose, as though he were surveying a hand at cards. Had you met him at a coffee-house and engaged in conversation, you might have taken him for an amateur in art and letters, for he had much to say not unworthy of attention on the topics that prevailed in polite circles.

But his business in life was cards, his play was suspect, and his reputation had only been maintained with difficulty through his skill with the sword and the patronage of Jonathan Wild. Here in this squalid sanctuary, at the age of five and thirty, sat this good-looking, well-educated cheat and scoundrel wondering how he was going to avoid starvation or the gallows.

Opposite him at the table sat little Toby Billinge, who for so many years had been groom, valet and confidential servant of the great man. There was no mystery in his story. The son of a publican who was hanged for robbery, he had been a house-boy with Jonathan Wild since he was ten years of age, and entrusted by him with the organizing of crimes. For him the normal life of man was stealing, smuggling, cheating and all chicanery, and to be the trusted servant of the greatest master of all these arts had been a stroke of fortune which made him hold his head high and cock his hat with a rakish slant. But now the master was dead, and to Toby Billinge the outlook on the future was dark and confusing. His cheery, round, rosy, apple face was soured and gloomy. His whistle was silent and he cast a squinting glance at the Count to see if there was hope there. But the Count was gazing out of the window moodily and did not seem to invite conversation, so Billinge continued to fill his mouth with beef and bread more by way of occupation than to satisfy hunger.

After a few minutes' silence the Count emptied his tankard and, setting it down with a sigh, said : " We have got to face it, Toby. The game is over and the gang is broken up for ever."

Billinge had his mouth so full of beef and bread that he could only assent to his companion's remark by a vigorous nod.

" The game is over and the only thing that remains to be done is to decide whether we stick together or whether we go on our own."

" We must stick together," said Billinge. "There is The Child."

" Drop that fool's name of ' The Child '."

" He was The Child when The Master found him. It was his name for him."

" He can't always be a child."

" I don't know that," replied Billinge obstinately.

" You will find that Master Nic will go to hell on his own, and do it very rapidly. "

" But we promised The Master that we would look after The Child," insisted Billinge.

" The courtesies of life, Toby, demand that you should promise to a man on his death-bed anything that may ease his mind."

" What will happen to him if we leave him to himself ? "

The Count made a clacking noise with his tongue and the roof of his mouth, and looped an imaginary noose round his neck with his forefinger.

" He will follow The Master. It is fate."

" It must not be his fate. We must see to it," said Billinge stoutly.

He rose and crossed to the fireside, where, on a settle, with his head on a cloth rolled up for a pillow, Master Nic was stretched at length in that sound sleep that comes to men and dogs in a state of youth and utter weariness. He had not altered much from the days of his boyhood, though he was now a youth of about twenty. His light flaxen hair was a shade browner, but he had still the same fresh complexion, the same delicately-moulded features and full, rosy lips, and had he been awake, the room would have been lighted with the sparkle of his blue eyes, and the hearts of his companions would have been cheered by his merry laugh. For in the den of thieves through which he had passed he had lost nothing of his bright outlook on the world and his careless delight in the joy of living.

He was dressed in a handsome suit of black of a superior cut even to the clothes of the Count, who was always a well-dressed man. Whether mere youth gave him the advantage over his fellows or he had sprung from a different stock, an onlooker would have wondered why so sweet a sprig of humanity should have found himself in such company.

"Well," said Billinge, coming back to the Count and looking him straight in the face, "as between pals, what are we going to do? Do you leave the job to me, or do you come in and work it? I shall not leave him; I promised."

"You are an old woman, Toby, and a sentimentalist like my countryman, Michel de Montaigne. It was he who said he had much rather break the walls of a prison and the laws themselves than his own word. In my day I have broken all three, and hope to do so again when it suits my purpose, but I will confess that I do not want to part company with Master Nic."

"You love The Child as well as I do."

"Love, you fool, is a word I have long forgotten the memory and meaning of, but a weary man of the world may well be refreshed by our young friend's merry ways. Were I a man of means, I would give him money if only for the pleasure of watching him ruin himself. But," continued the Count in a more serious mood, "would he ruin himself? I am by no means sure. Master Nic has the greatest gift the gods can bestow. He has luck!"

"Then you will keep your promise," cried Billinge eagerly.

"I am sorting my hand," said the Count, continuing his musings. "If it is for me to call, I'm hanged if I know what to call. A man does not want to go back on his word to one he carried to the grave twelve hours ago, and a man does not want to tilt at windmills like Don Quixote."

"Was he on the road, Count? I never heard of him," interrupted Billinge.

"He was very much on the road," replied the Count with the least shrug of contempt, "and looking after Master Nic in his wanderings in search of happiness would have been exactly the kind of madness that would have satisfied the Don's taste in adventure. Show me a plan, Billinge, and you and I will work together and do what may be done for the lad, but beggars cannot give largesse.

There is only one thing for it. Flight to foreign parts. *Sauve qui peut.* Our day is over. The impossible has happened. Jonathan Wild is dead."

" Yes," said Billinge, with tears in his voice, " The Master is gone."

" Snivelling will do no good," said the Count curtly.

" None whatever," agreed Billinge, gulping down his tears in a draught of small ale.

" The question is, have you a plan ? "

" I am not sure I have not," said Billinge humbly.

" Deal it out, then," said the Count.

Billinge leaned across the table and, looking at the door, beckoned the Count to draw near him. What he had to say was matter not for publication to the inhabitants of the " Duke's Head."

" You remember when I gave up active work in the housebreaking line some few years ago that I often went with the master as a tipstaff when he was out to arrest some fool who flouted his authority. In those days Jonathan Wild was hand-in-glove with the magistrates and officers at Bow Street. His word was law with them, and I had the run of the place and was well known to Sir James Hezlet and the other magistrates."

" That will stand you in no stead now, man."

" Peace a minute, Count. Peace. A few days after the master's arrest Sir James stopped me in Covent Garden and said in his jovial way : ' How now, Billinge, Othello's occupation's gone, eh?' I told him I had never heard of Master Othello, but that speaking for myself, I was out of a job, and that if the master did not pull through I should be in Queer Street. On that he took me aside into the ' Nag's Head ' and told me that from all he heard Master Wild was already in the cart, as the judges were determined to break him, but for his part he could not but admit that Wild kept the thieves in greater order than any magistrates or constables had ever done, and he thought the judges were acting a selfish game in destroying Wild and leaving them alone at Bow Street to tackle the scum that would be let loose on the city. It was then he asked me if I had ever thought of turning runner."

" The devil he did ? " said the Count, who was becoming interested.

" As he put it," continued Billinge, " he knew that I had been in at anything important the master did in the thief-taking business, and if The Master went, Bow Street would be in a bad way, and should I be in want of an honest job, I might do worse than turn runner."

" An honest job," said the Count contemptuously.

" It is something beyond an honest job, too," said Billinge, smiling. " There are pickings, you know, pickings."

" To think of a de Grillac in the red waistcoat of a Bow Street runner ! Turquet de Grillac, the Robin Redbreast! A filthy job for a gentleman."

" It is a safe job," continued Billinge, in a businesslike tone. " There is a salary, as I understand, and expenses, and beyond that there are pickings."

The word " pickings " seemed to attract the Count, and he repeated it in a thoughtful tone several times, and laughed to himself at the thought of such a strange career.

" Yet why not, Toby," he asked carelessly, " since the Devil only knows whether a thief or a constable is the greater rogue ? I will ask the Scriptures for guidance, as my old teacher used to say."

With that he dived into the pocket of his long coat and produced a dirty pack of cards and proceeded to shuffle them leisurely. It was characteristic of the Count to decide nothing of his own free will that could be as easily disposed of by the chance of the cards.

" So that is your Bible, Count," said Billinge, with a sneer, for he was a Protestant rogue and despised Papists.

" The good priest who taught me the philosophy of cards used to say there was no book in the world that brought him holier thoughts than a pack of cards. The ace reminded him that there is only one God, the deuce reminded him of the Father and the Son, the tray of the Holy Trinity, and when he dealt the four his thoughts turned to the Evangelists, Matthew, Mark, Luke and John, and in this way he spiritualized each of the cards. We will let the cards decide. If it comes the King of Hearts, I stick to the gaming table and the road; if it comes the Knave of Diamonds I turn Robin Redbreast."

The hazard was set, and he dealt the cards with leisurely grace. The future of three lives hung on the game, and Billinge clung to the table and watched the fall of each card with suppressed excitement. At the seventh turn of the wrist the Knave of Diamonds fell on the table.

" Good ! " shouted Billinge, jumping up with a shout of delight.

The Count packed up the cards slowly, accepting the result in a gambler's spirit.

" And what is the game ? " called out a pleasant voice from the settle by the fireplace.

" The game of fate, Master Nic, the end of which no player can either hasten or defer," said the Count wearily.

The Child was awake and sitting up looking on at the game with a child's smile of interest and pleasure. Billinge came across to the settle and sat down beside him.

" The game has decided it," he said, putting his hand on Nic's shoulder. " We are going into business and going to look after your future, as The Master ordered."

At the mention of The Master poor Nic, who was but just awake, remembered with a shudder the scene at Tyburn, the yelling mob and the meeting in the cold morning in the churchyard of St. Pancras. He buried his face in his hands and sobbed.

The Count walked to the window and looked down the narrow street at nothing in particular. No one knew better than he did that Jonathan Wild was a wicked scoundrel well hanged. But to The Child the master had always been a generous patron, and for a moment this soiled, worn-out man of the under-world felt that after death it would be well for you that someone should care enough about the event to shed tears over it. The idea was idle and absurd enough, but it filled his mind at the moment and brought a lump into his throat and a thought into his heart that he would be true to his trust and protect Master Nic to the best of his ability.

The lad's tears were soon brushed aside, and he was seated at the table munching bread and beef and drinking

small ale with the healthy appetite of youth whilst Billinge
explained to him their future plans. He waved them away
with an expression of disgust. The Count and Billinge
reasoned with him, but he turned their arguments to
ridicule.

" I can see you two Robin Redbreasts," he cried,
" rounding up your old pals and committing perjury at
Bow Street for the safety of your souls and bodies. Why
not turn Charley and call the hours of nights or sleep in the
watch-box till the boys knock you over in the morning ? "

" A philosopher once remarked," said the Count gravely,
" that in children silence and modesty are very advan-
tageous qualities, since it enables them to listen to the
wisdom of their elders. Toby and I have decided to follow
this course in your interests, and whether this arouses in
you amusement or gratitude is no matter."

Master Nic went across to the Count and seized his hand.
" Turquet, I was a beast," he said humbly. " I know you
and Toby are making this sacrifice for me, but don't you
see I am no longer a child. I cannot permit it. Either the
three of us will stand and fall together, or I will leave you
and go my own way. You seem to forget I am grown up."

" You will never grow up," replied the Count, with a
faint smile. " What could be more like a child than making
all this pother about a matter that is still on the lap of the
gods ? The first thing we have to see is whether Sir James
and his brother magistrates are ready to parley with us."

" And if they will not ? " asked Master Nic joyfully.

" Then it will be time to discuss other plans. Our first
step is to go to Bow Street."

" That is the game," said Billinge, " to Bow Street."

They called for another mug of ale apiece and drank
success and damnation to the plan, for Master Nic would
not toast the former. Then, having made a hasty toilet at
the pump in the inn-yard, Billinge and the Count left the
precincts of the Mint and made their way down to the
river at Cuper's Gardens Stairs, where they took a boat
to Strand Lane, and so to Bow Street.

Bow Street, as Master Nic knew it, was just passing out
of the ranks of wealth and fashion into the beginning of a

long career of good citizenship, in which its name should stand with London as a synonym for law and order and the suppression of vice and immorality. The wild oats of Bow Street were sown and its honourable connection with art and letters was already a tradition. The houses of the great ones, who added lustre to the name of Bow Street, were now owned by worthy citizens of smaller renown, and among these was Sir James Hezlet, magistrate and mercer, who had migrated west from the city.

Sir James was a magistrate of the City of London and the County of Middlesex. He had a pleasant estate near Hendon. He had recently been Lord Mayor, and was at the moment regarded with considerable favour by those in authority. He still affected the plain brown cloth of the citizen, but his buckles were of fine silver, his ruffles of the best cambric, and he carried a gold-headed cane. Not even at an assembly would he appear in the gorgeous silk coats and waistcoats that many citizens now wore on holidays.

Sir James was very ready to receive the Count and Billinge. They were brought at once to his parlour, where he sat behind a large table that reached nearly across the room. In front of him was a standish with ink and pens, and at his side were a few large volumes of statutes bound in well-worn law calf. Papers folded and docketed lay in correct order on the table, at one end of which a clerk continued his writing and paid no heed to the new-comers, who stood opposite Sir James.

Billinge had an uncomfortable feeling that he was not the first criminal that had stood in this place and shifted about uneasily, squinting from time to time at the engravings of learned judges that hung on the walls of the parlour. Turquet, with well-studied indifference, placed his hat and cane on the table and bowed to Sir James.

There was no beating about the bush. The magistrate came straight to the business in hand.

" Jonathan Wild is destroyed at last," said Sir James curtly, a gleam of satisfaction lighting up his grey eyes.

The Count bowed again slightly.

" I am going to break up his gang before they can find another leader."

F

Billinge put his head on one side and rubbed his ear thoughtfully. The Count smiled. It seemed wise to him at present to make no remark.

" I know it can be done," continued Sir James sharply. " I am going to take up each case as it comes along and run it to earth. I am well aware that in order to succeed I must have men under me who know the ways of criminals —so far Wild's methods of business were sound—I propose to give you two men the chance of taking service under me."

Turquet nodded approval. Sir James had now put forward a business proposal.

" We are ready to serve you, Sir James," he said, " but on conditions."

" Conditions," repeated the magistrate, and he stated in detail his proposals as to salary, service and allowances.

The Count listened critically.

" In the main these matters seem to us satisfactory," he said thoughtfully, " but there are other conditions that must be met."

" Name them, then."

" We must have a written indemnity against any proceedings for offences that may be charged against us prior to this date."

" That I agree to," said Sir James readily, and turning to his clerk, told him to draft the necessary documents.

" Further," continued the Count with much earnestness, " there is a young man who goes by the name of Nic Berrington——"

" He is reputed to be a son of Wild himself," interrupted Sir James.

" I know nothing of that," said the Count, " but it is not improbable that there may be charges against him, too, or warrants for aught I know."

" There are," said the magistrate, and he leaned across the table and picked up a bundle of papers, pulling over the ends that he might read the endorsements on them. " There are several charges against him."

" They must be dropped and not proceeded with," said Turquet firmly.

" Must be dropped ? " replied Sir James, opening his eyes and smiling at the Count. " Will Monsieur Turquet de Grillac give me a good reason for such a demand ? "

" It is one of our conditions," replied the Count quietly.

" These were some of the cases I wished to follow up," said Sir James testily, nursing the papers in his hand. " Why is this young criminal to escape ? "

" That is our business," said Turquet.

" There is no reason in such a request," said Sir James, annoyed at the Count's obstinacy.

" There is every reason," struck in Billinge. " It was The Master's last wish we should look after The Child."

" Jonathan Wild's ? "

" Toby here," said the Count smiling, " is a sentimental fool, but the fact remains that it is our whim or fancy, call it what you will, to see that this boy, who is indeed a child, and a fool of a child at that, should come to no harm. It is for that reason and no other that we consent to become runners."

" Then you think with me that this lad was Wild's son ? " said Sir James, looking at Billinge.

" I know nothing of The Master's secrets. He treated The Child as his own," replied Toby.

Sir James looked at the papers again and made a few memoranda on several of them which he picked out and made into a separate packet. This he carefully sealed and threw into a drawer in front of him, and this he closed and locked.

Billinge gave a sigh of relief.

" You may tell Mr. Berrington that bygones shall be bygones, but he must commence honesty from to-day. You two shall be sworn in at once. Is that agreed ? "

The Count bowed acquiescence.

" I will test you for a month. If you are honest and capable, I will extend your service. The first job I want you to take up is these Hertfordshire robberies. My men think they are the work of a man named Bagshot."

" The Captain," cried Billinge eagerly.

" Captain Bagshot, beyond doubt," said Turquet in a tone of quiet satisfaction.

"You know the fellow?" asked Sir James.

"The sooner we are about our business the better," said the Count.

"You seem eager to start."

"You could not have given us a task more to our minds," replied the Count joyously. "He was the Judas who sold Jonathan Wild."

CHAPTER VII

THE more consideration Master Nic gave to his friends' conduct the less he approved of it. Turquet and Billinge selling themselves to Sir James Hezlet was a sneaking, inglorious affair with which he could have no truck. If Sir James accepted their services, no doubt Turquet would return to his old lodgings with Mrs. Metyard at Wych Street, and he could hear of them there, but meanwhile the old life was good enough for him, and he would go on his own. He turned into the narrow Southwark streets feeling, despite his bravery, somewhat lonely at the thought of leaving his friends. But youth in search of adventure has no way of retreat, and he cocked his hat and swaggered along the streets whistling a merry air.

Turning out of Redcross Street towards Maiden Lane, he noticed on the second floor of a shabby lodging-house a girl leaning out of a window cursing a milkman, whose offence seemed to be the refusal to leave a can of milk on the door-step unless ready-money was received for it.

" What, Jenny, my girl," called out Master Nic in a tone of pleasant surprise. " Jenny ! They told me you were going to be sent across the water."

" Whist ! " she cried, putting her fingers to her lips. " Knock that devil over and bring his milk can upstairs, and I'll tell you all about it."

Master Nic, however, having some coin in his pocket, thought it better to acquire the milk by purchase, and taking a small can from the vendor, entered the house and carried it upstairs to Jenny.

The room he entered was little more than a garret. On a low bed in the corner lay an older woman in a drunken slumber.

71

"Molly!" said Jenny, with a jerk of her head. "She's been like that more or less ever since she left him at Newgate."

Molly Straddle, a fine woman of over thirty, had lived under Wild's protection for several years. A hundred and one clever shop robberies and gaming swindles were attributed to her skill in appearing as a lady of fashion not only in the west end of London, but at Bath and Tunbridge Wells, and even as far afield as Scarborough. The end of the Master had, indeed, brought her low.

Jenny Diver, a plump rogue of a girl of twenty, with big, dark eyes, pouting lips, a dainty carmine complexion, and two alluring dimples rather high on her cheeks, had followed her mistress into exile and was wondering, like The Child himself, whether the world of adventure which she had been brought up in was altogether played out and, if so, what was going to take its place. Her part had been the confidential waiting-maid to Molly, the fine lady, in her intrigues with elderly aldermen, or on occasion the simple-minded niece whose ample fortune had somehow got bruited about the Wells, and then Molly played the aunt and the dragon in the luring of young spendthrifts, who made fool plans to outwit the duenna and carry off the heiress.

The girl took the milk can from Master Nic's hand and blushed and smiled her thanks. She sat down on the only chair in the room to darn a hole in her skirt. The young man perched on the table beside her.

"The idea of finding you again; Billinge told me you were certainly booked for abroad."

"They say you can pick and choose a husband over there," said Jenny, lifting up her head and laughing in his face. "The old judge seemed to think there was no hurry for me to settle down as yet, and turned me on to the streets again with a lot of good advice about earning an honest living. Where is that to be done, Nykin?"

"God knows!" said The Child lightly. "I'm going to stick to the old game, anyhow."

"And what are your plans, then?" asked Jenny.

"Plans!" cried Nic contemptuously; "one does not

want plans in this world ; one just wants to enjoy things as they come along. To-morrow I shall very likely run through St. Paul's Churchyard and see what I can pick up."

" I can put you up to something better than that," said Jenny, nodding confidentially. " Come with me to-morrow ! "

The lad leaned down and put his arm round her waist, and she threw herself back and put her face up to his.

" Of course I'll come with you, Jenny. What are you after ? "

" I'll tell you in the morning. You come and fetch me about nine o'clock. None of this finery, of course. Just working clothes."

She patted him lightly on the cheek, and he stooped down to snatch a kiss. She was out of his arms in a moment and had slapped him on the face and stood laughing at his discomfiture. He seized her by the hand, and would have pulled her towards him, but she was too many for him, and pushed him out of the room, buffeting him with her fists in a friendly manner.

" It's a pity the lad is a pauper," she said with a sigh, as she mixed Mistress Straddle a cup of rum and milk.

" If Jonathan had lived to look after his affairs, some say he had big chances before him," said the older woman thoughtfully.

" What sort of chances ? " asked the girl sharply.

" God knows ! " muttered Molly, and then, after a pause, she added, " and possibly Turquet."

The next morning The Child laid aside his suit of black, put on the working clothes of a labouring man, and went down the street to call on Miss Jenny. She was attired in the fashionable dress of a young lady of the period, and Mrs. Straddle favoured the hood and cloak of the good mother or aunt who was to accompany Miss Innocence on her walks abroad. They both wore bunches of white roses on their bosoms.

The Child looked at Jenny with frank admiration as she dropped him a curtsey of ceremony.

" What part do I play in all this ? " he asked.

" Why, look ye, my dear," said Mrs. Straddle, " the

girl is a clever wench, and has bold notions. They say the
Bishop leaves the Tower this morning, and if that be so,
there will be a great mob of the White Rose people to cry
farewell to him. Now do you make your way to the Tower
and push through the mob towards the King's Stairs."

" When," continued Jenny laughing, " if you chance to
see a fair Jacobite maiden kneeling at the Bishop's feet to
take his last blessing, keep within touch, for his Lordship
has a ring of diamonds that we hope to save from exile."

The Bishop of Rochester's comedy was played out. His
correspondence with the King over the water had been
exposed, and he had been duly found guilty of treasonable
conspiracy and very leniently sentenced to exile, and was
now in the Tower waiting a summons to take ship for
France. The date of his Lordship's departure had been kept
a strict secret, but, like most official secrets, was common
talk among that section of the public from whom it was
particularly important to keep it. The White Rose party
knew all about it, and early on the summer morning the
whole neighbourhood of the Tower was densely crowded
by all sorts and conditions of people having a common
bond of union in a romantic love of the old dynasty and
a loyal affection for a worthless prince in exile.

There was a large number of women in the crowd, many
of them beautifully dressed, and carried to the scene in
their sedan chairs attended by footmen. The river was a
mass of boats. One of these, cleverly managed by two
young watermen, threaded its way towards the stairs, and
a young girl and her mother landed and, with some difficulty, made their way towards the passage which the guards
made from the Tower to the stairs.

At length the deputy-governor was seen approaching
with a large number of warders around him. A murmur of
disapproval ran through the crowd, but soon turned into
a cheer as the top of a sedan chair was seen behind them,
and it was observed that within it sat their beloved Bishop,
habited, alas, no longer in his episcopal robes, but in a
suit of plain grey cloth.

So great was the press of people towards the chair that
the guards were pushed forward, and it was with great

difficulty that the procession could make any progress. Women rushed forward to receive his last blessing, and others who could not get near shouted their blessing to him and cried aloud. The sedan chair stopped, and he extended his hand to such of the women as could get near. It was a scene of hysterical excitement. The beautiful young woman who had but just stepped out of the boat had pushed her way well to the front and, with tears and cries, had seized the Bishop's hand and pressed her face close against it, kissing it fervently and wildly calling upon him for a blessing. He spoke a few kindly words to the poor soul, and with difficulty drew his hand away from her lips. Two kind-hearted women helped the young creature in a fainting state to her mother's arms. A young labouring lad came forward to push a way through for her to her boat. Other women came to the Bishop's chair. Suddenly his Lordship called out, " My ring ! "

One of his purple footmen flung back the crowd and went to the door of the chair.

" That girl, the little one that wept so. She has stolen my ring ! "

A cry of " Stop the thief ! The Bishop's ring is gone," spread through the crowd, and the desire for a Bishop's blessing was forgotten by the mob in the greater pleasure and excitement of a woman hunt.

In vain did Jenny struggle to reach her boat. In vain did Molly Straddle tumble across her pursuers, whilst Master Nic, joining in the cries of the chase the better to effect his object, tripped up several of the crowd and pressed forward to protect her. Jenny made a fine effort to reach the boat, but finding this impossible, doubled and made for a side street.

But too many were after her, and by her flank movement she had got away from Master Nic, who was hemmed in by another wedge of the crowd. A dozen ruffians seized her. They tore some of her clothes off her back. They threw her down and dragged her skirts over her head, and pulled and hustled her towards the river. All that cursing, scratching, biting and kicking could do Jenny did, but the blackguards were too many for her. The tide was half ebb, and by the time they had got her to the beach the wretched creature had as little life left in her body as she had clothes to cover it. The deep mud prevented them from drowning her in the river, but they set her down in the shallow mud with intent to fling her in further, when an old fellow with a stout cudgel who had been laughing at the sight from a quay hard by rushed down on to the beach.

"Damn my liver and bones," he cried, "a jest is well enough and a romp with a girl is good fun, but this goes too far."

They stood aside, awed by Captain Johnson's words and manner, and allowed him to pull the girl out of the mud.

"By God, you've killed her," he said solemnly. "It will be the yard arm for some of you boys, thief or no thief."

The ruffian cowards began to slink away quietly, their lust of cruelty cooling rapidly at the thought of the gallows. The rest of the mob had already forgotten the incident as the warders had made use of the diversion to move along and carry the sedan chair down to the stairs and all were pressing after it to see his Lordship carried aboard the barge.

Master Nic now made his way down to the beach where Jenny was lying and found to his surprise that some men, under the direction of a stout old gentleman with a cudgel, were wrapping the girl's body in sacking and carrying it into a shed on the quay-side.

His first impulse was to run to their assistance, but remembering that in an inner secret pocket of his breeches there was reposing a diamond ring of considerable value after which there was certain to be a diligent and immediate search, he was for silently retreating when he heard a familiar voice call out, "Damn my liver and lights, but this looks like a case for the crowner. What's to be done with her?"

Nic ran up to him and tapped him lightly on the shoulder.

"I can tell you, Captain, and find her friends for you."

The old man wheeled round sharply.

"It's The Child, or the devil's picture of him."

Master Nic laughed merrily in his face. They had met on occasion at Jonathan Wild's house, but Nic had never forgotten what he called the treachery of his friends, and Jonathan had not encouraged renewed intimacy between them.

" We must get her away quickly. There will be hue and cry after her. It's Jenny Diver."

The Captain whistled. It had been one of his great principles in life never to be in at first-hand in any crime whatever. Smuggling was a trade or pursuit. The old man had often warned Jonathan against dabbling in these more direct ventures and had seen his wisdom justified by events. His first thought was to lock the naked, unconscious girl in the shed and send for a constable.

The Child ran along to the end of the short wooden quay and looked over the river. The great mass of boats were crowding round the barges, in which were the Bishop and his attendants and guards, and all were slowly making their way down the river. The wherry with Mistress Straddle and the two oars lay in the river a few yards from the shore. The Child waved to them impatiently. A few strokes brought them alongside of the quay. The Child ran into the shed.

" There is no need for you to be seen in it, Captain. Come Jenny, Jenny," he called, " pull yourself together. Here's Molly and the boat."

Jenny opened her eyes and feebly lifted up her arms to Master Nic. Her poor face was a mass of cuts and bruises, her hair was torn and dishevelled, she had scarce a rag of clothing on her body and her white limbs were smeared with the filthy mud of the river.

He caught her in his arms and carried her out to the boat. The rough fellows, Southwark watermen, to whom Jenny and Molly and her friends were not unknown, handled her body tenderly and kindly as Nic lowered her into the boat. Molly covered her with her shawl and one of the men threw his coat round her and they pushed away into the current.

The Captain was locking and closing the shed and giving directions to his men.

"There is no need for us to be seen together, young fellow," he said quietly to Master Nic. "You follow me down Thames Street and when I turn up towards the City keep close and we will find a place for some food and a talk."

Master Nic did as he was told. Somewhere beyond Billingsgate the Captain turned into a side street and entered the back door of a public-house. Master Nic was at his heels. The women in the kitchen knew the Captain and greeted him in a friendly way.

"Is there any one in the upper parlour? No? Well, send up a pasty and some cheese and a quart of ale and leave us alone until my skipper, Ben Cheal, calls for me. He should be here any time now."

They went upstairs and when the food was set the Captain took a long stare at Master Nic.

"Damn me if I think you ever will grow up. You'll always be The Child."

Nic's silvery laugh echoed round the room. "How is Granny?" he asked.

"Granny is well as old age and rheumatism will let a woman be. You must come and see her."

Master Nic shook his head and laughed again.

"Some day when I'm a rich man and my fortune is made, but not like this. But what brings you to London?"

"A fool's errand. Some of these damned Jacks seemed to think this Bishop of theirs might be rescued from the Tower and there have I been lying in the Long Reach this ten days waiting for the cargo. Now I find the Government are sending him across in the *Aldbourgh* man-of-war that is lying a few cables' length below *The Lively Kate*. Split my binnacle! their cause may be good enough, but their ideas of business would wreck any cause afloat. And what were you after this morning?"

"A fine prize, Captain, and we cut it out under the enemy's guns."

He drew forth the Bishop's diamond ring and held it aloft. The Captain put down his tankard and moved to the door which he locked quickly and silently. Then he took the ring in his hands almost reverently, and damned the whole of his anatomy in exhaustive praise of its beauty and priceless value.

Nic told him the story of its capture, and the Captain laughed at the trick until tears ran down his cheeks.

" Poor little devil," he said as he thought of Jenny. " She paid dear enough for her share of the prank. But you will never pass these stones now Jonathan is gone and if you are found with them——"

" Yes, yes, I know all about that," said Nic impatiently, " but I shall give it over to Molly and she can pass it with some of the Jews."

Roger Johnson shook his head doubtfully. " Put your trust in me, boy, and steer by the compass. Hand it over to me and I will get a reward for it across the Channel from the Bishop's friends."

Master Nic laughed and, taking the ring out of his hands, he placed it on his own finger and admired it critically.

"I shall want something on account of that reward, you know, Captain. Poor little Jenny would never hear of my parting with it for nothing."

" Ten guineas ! " said the Captain cautiously.

" Rubbish," replied The Child.

" Fifteen."

The Child shook his head contemptuously.

" Damn my liver and bones, you little Jew. Twenty," snapped out the Captain.

" And damn my finger if the ring leaves it under thirty," replied Nic, " and that's little enough, but we are old pals."

The Captain was no haggler. Whatever price he paid for it he could get a big reward and favour in the eyes of his masters across the water.   He counted out thirty guineas and The Child gave him the ring. A few minutes afterwards there was a knock at the door and the woman brought word that Master Cheal waited below. They had a parting glass of gin, which the Captain swallowed at a gulp.

" I must be off down the tide at once. You might do worse than come with me. What are you going to make of things here now Jonathan has gone ? "

Yesterday Master Nic might have listened to him, but he had thirty guineas in his pocket and they begat wild dreams in his young brain.

" I am going to enjoy life," he replied. " It seems to me that was what life was made for."

" There are worse things than sailing the sea and farming the land."

Nic waved his hand airily.

" To enjoy life you must live in London."

" To enjoy life you must breathe. Blast my lungs, you can't breathe in these hovels."

He took the lad by the hand and shook it firmly.

" You will be welcome Freston way any time," he said, " and if you want to hear of me in London this is the ' Magpie and Stump.' Come by the back door as I did."

He tumbled down the stairs and was gone. Master Nic finished his drink in a leisurely manner, and feeling that the day was yet young and that the possibilities of sport were not over he placed his guineas in various secure pockets of his garments and went down stairs. A merry compliment to the mistress of the house, a shilling and a romp with the girl in the kitchen, that they might remember him when he came next time, and then having surveyed the street and taken his bearings for a future visit he sauntered away towards the City.

St. Paul's was the great centre where business men were wont to meet, and The Child strolled along Cheapside wondering whether he should go to a clothier's and rig himself out anew or loaf about the Churchyard as he had often done before in search of spoil. He had made a complete circuit of the Church without any sign of sport when he noticed two gentlemen meeting on the other side of the road. The one appeared to be a gentleman from the country, the other a lawyer or man of business. They stood talking together very earnestly and The Child watched them as a poacher watches hares sporting on the landlord's demesne. The lawyer man pulled out a paper from the inner pocket of his coat and the country gentleman, taking it with a smile and a nod, placed it carefully in a leather case which he slipped into the left-hand pocket of his surtout. They continued talking for several minutes and parted with great show of affection, the younger man making his way East with Master Nic in stealthy pursuit of him. He stalked him warily round the Church, up Cheapside until near Milk Street where, to his delight, some waggons had met together and locked their wheels and a crowd had gathered to watch the waggoners punch each other's heads and encourage them to further blows by shouts and curses. Other conveyances and chairs drove up and there was soon a scene of wild confusion.

This was the craftsman's opportunity, and coming up against the gentleman, who was trying to make his way through the mob behind the posts at the side of the street, he fell heavily across him from the left-hand side and neatly knocked both himself and his prey into the gutter. He was up again just in time to escape a savage blow from the gentleman's cane and was away up Milk Street in and out of the alleys towards London Wall and beyond the fields of Finsbury with his precious booty.

There was no pursuit, and here in these rural surroundings he found a lonely spot where he could examine his treasure. It was a galley richly laden. There were papers, letters, bills of exchange and drafts, such as his dear master used to deal with so cunningly and profitably, restoring them to their owners for rich rewards. He must go in search of Turquet. There was Bow Street. Possible but dangerous. The Mint : not a place to enter with so much money on you. Old Mrs. Metyard at the lodgings in Wych Street. She might know something of Turquet's whereabouts. The idea no sooner occurred to him than it was acted upon and Master Nic turned his face south.

The old lady was overjoyed to see him. The Count and Billinge had ridden into Hertfordshire that morning and left their address for him, "The Black Lion," at Hoddesdon. Why they had gone she could not say, but gone they were. Nic determined to take up his abode in Turquet's lodgings, and throwing the old lady a couple of guineas bade her send for a roast fowl and some wine, and then go and tell Mr. Levy the tailor of Drury Lane, that Master Berrington had been robbed of his clothes in Finsbury fields and wanted a riding suit that he might shew himself in the world again. Master Nic had been a good customer of Mr. Levy in the old days. The man had a warehouse in Southwark at the back of the Church and Jonathan traded stolen clothing with him. In Drury Lane he was a fashionable tailor.

Dinner over, Master Nic made his way towards the " Cock Tavern," where he hoped he might see or hear something of his friends. As he passed Sir James Hezlet's house in Bow Street his eye was caught by a large board on which were placed notices by the Middlesex constables of articles lost or stolen, foundling children discovered, and rewards for the apprehenion of criminals. Some of these were merely written, others printed in the largest type.

A constable was pasting up a new notice, and a small crowd collected to read it. It was a hue and cry, and in the biggest letters a hundred pounds reward was offered for the capture of one, Bagshot, a highwayman, who had lately committed several robberies on the northern road. It was issued in the names of the County Magistrates of Hertfordshire.

As he read this the truth of matters sprang into his mind. He could see Turquet and Billinge in their new role of runners posting off with glee to Hertfordshire to run to earth the man who had betrayed Jonathan Wild. He clenched his fists and promised himself that within twenty-four hours he, too, would join the hunt and never drop it till he had caught his man and carried him to the gallows. Here was a real adventure worthy of his genius.

CHAPTER VIII

OLD DOCTOR MORGAN

IT was a fine summer evening when a gentleman plainly but handsomely dressed, followed by a servant in grey livery, rode up to the door of the "Black Lion," a snug little inn in the village of Hoddesdon.

Hoddesdon stands some seventeen miles from London on the Edinburgh road in the most beautiful part of Hertfordshire. Wealthy citizens and men of leisure found many pleasant country seats in the neighbourhood, so that mine host of the "Black Lion" expressed no surprise when the gentleman, who was no other than Turquet, informed him that he intended to ride round and look at any vacant houses there might be with a view to finding a country home.

Supper over, Turquet sat smoking at the window overlooking the street, envying his servant Billinge the more congenial company of the tap-room. It was part of the business for innkeepers and stablemen to be on terms of friendly neutrality towards the captain of the road. Had it been suspected that Turquet and Billinge travelled with a warrant in their pockets for the arrest of Bagshot, it is certain that in some way or other the Captain would have received warning of it.

Smoking at the window and wondering how they were to get at grips with Master Bagshot, Turquet was awakened from his reverie by the sound of hoofs clattering down the village street. A smart phaeton and pair driven by a stable lad dashed up to the inn. The only occupant was a very feeble old man wrapped in a thick dark cloak with a muffler up to his chin, a plaid shawl over his shoulders and his hands enveloped in thick gloves. He was wearing a pair of dark blue spectacles as if afraid of the soft summer evening light that was fast darkening into gloom. The landlord of the inn, seeming to know exactly what the visitor required, came out with a glass of brandy which he handed up to the old gentleman, whose hand shook as he pulled off his glove and lifted the glass to his lips. He swallowed the glassful at one drink with a masterly twist of the wrist that the Count greatly admired. A few words' conversation with mine host followed, during which he pulled out his watch, and then he motioned to the lad who drove the horses, and they sprang away to the north along the Ware Road.

"Curious," thought the Count to himself, "curious. I must make some enquiry into this gentleman." And he came downstairs, out at the inn-door and ran up against the landlord just as he was coming into the house with the empty glass.

"A fine pair of horses the old gentleman has," said the Count, looking up the road.

"A very fine pair!" assented the landlord.

"Smart steppers," said Turquet, looking to the landlord to continue the conversation with a new opening.

"Very smart, Sir," echoed the landlord who, unlike his kind, did not seem eager for gossip.

"Was the old gentleman going far?" asked the Count carelessly.

"Just a few miles round the county. It's his whim is driving. Nigh every evening he comes through the village and stops here for his draught. Yes, driving is his hobby. He says it does him good."

"Rather a dangerous hobby now the roads are so disturbed," suggested the Count.

"Exactly what I tell him," said the landlord, "but he only laughs at me and goes his way."

"An old character here?" asked the Count.

"No, Sir. He has only been with us a few months, if so long. Dr. Morgan, they call him, a retired physician I believe. He took the late Squire Byam's house for the summer—Jenning's Bury, it is called. The young Squire is at Oxford, Sir. You can see the chimneys from the main road. A quiet spot, Sir, very quiet."

Turquet strolled up the road. He went as far as the

lodge-gate of Jenning's Bury. The house was an old gabled house covered with ivy. He could only get a glimpse of it from the lodge-gate. He would have carried his investigations further, but a large bull-dog came out from the back of the Lodge and growled at him longingly. A woman's voice called the dog away and he went reluctantly towards the house, looking back over his shoulder every few yards and growling at Turquet. The Count returned to the inn.

Early next morning Billinge, according to orders, brought round the horses and they rode into Ware before breakfast. Here they heard news of a robbery at Wades-mill. The Dean of Lincoln, travelling to London, had been stopped and stripped of every penny he possessed, as well as two large portmanteaux, and had ridden on to London using anything but clerical language as to the magistrates of Hertfordshire and their methods of maintaining law and order.

That afternoon Turquet and Billinge held a council of war. Billinge had been making enquiries. It appeared that old Doctor Morgan drove out daily and every evening took a different route. Everyone knew the old Doctor and seemed to speak in a kindly tone of him. He drove out about seven or eight o'clock and often returned quite late at night. Sometimes he drove up to London. That was the sum total of Billinge's information about the old gentleman.

" What do you think of him ? " asked Turquet.

" I haven't seen him yet."

" He certainly drove through Ware last night."

" So did many others," replied Billinge.

" If it is the Captain, it is a wonderful disguise," said Turquet half to himself.

" For my part I think the Captain is in hiding in Ware," said Billinge.

" Then how does he get to the scene of action without being recognised ? Every story is the same. He appears, takes away a large booty and disappears. Now my idea is that this old gentleman is either Bagshot or a confederate and that his part in the game is to carry off the swag. To-night we will follow him. Have the horses ready at seven o'clock. We, too, will try an evening ride."

Billinge saddled the horses in good time and went in to tell his master they were ready.

" Is your master riding out this evening ? " asked the innkeeper as he met Billinge coming out of the yard.

" He said he might ride into Ware to see a friend," answered Billinge.

" Better carry his pistols, then. You heard of the affair at Wadesmill, I suppose," said the landlord.

" I'll tell him what you say," replied Billinge as he went up the stairs.

He was still with his master when the old gentleman's phaeton came clattering down the road. The landlord met him at the door with the brandy as before and had a few minutes' chat with his customer, who drove away towards Ware exactly as he had done the previous night.

" What do you make of him ? " asked Turquet, turning round to Billinge.

" What the rest of the world makes of him," returned Billinge. " He is an imbecile with a hobby."

" I can't make him out," said Turquet. " We'll follow him and see where he goes."

" Utter waste of time," grumbled Billinge as he went downstairs to bring the horses round.

The riders soon caught up the phaeton but they did not choose to pass it. At Ware the old Doctor had a glass of brandy. The two riders drew up at the inn as he left. Turquet had a glass of brandy and his servant a mug of ale.

" Nice horses in the phaeton that stopped here," said the Count to the tapster.

" Very fine pair, Sir. Old Doctor Morgan's of Jenning's Bury, Sir."

" Ah," said Turquet, " quite an old gentleman, eh ? "

" Very old man, Sir, feeble, very. Always stops for a glass, Sir, but never gets down, never."

The tapster collected the money and glasses and went in and the two pursuers trotted down the street. The phaeton took the Royston road and Turquet and Billinge kept it well in view, showing themselves as little as might be. It was getting dusk now and the old Doctor was evidently making for Wadesmill. As he must have heard of the robbery there on the previous night it was rather an extraordinary road for an invalid to take merely for the pleasure of an evening drive. Even Billinge seemed to think that the old Doctor might be in some way connected with the robberies.

There is a wood by the side of the road on the hill and the road dips down to the stream and then rises again. Turquet's belief was that the heavy portmanteaux that the Dean had lost had been hidden here by the thief, and that this expedition of the Doctor's was to bring them back to Jenning's Bury. They saw the phaeton disappear down the hill and waited by the side of the wood. Turquet was certain that they would not see it climb the opposite hill for some time. The Dean had been stopped on the bridge by one man, his portmanteaux taken out of his chaise and his postboy told to drive on with the promise of a bullet in his head if he turned to look back.

The two " runners " were full of excitement. If the old Doctor was after hidden booty it would be put in the phaeton and he would be taken red-handed with the booty on him. Whoever he was, they would have caught one or the gang and have justified their mission. What was their chagrin, then, to see in a few minutes the phaeton steadily climbing the hill, having evidently made no stay whatever in the little valley below.

" I told you so," said Billinge with a chuckle. " Utter waste of time."

" Well," replied Turquet in a gloomy tone of disappointment, " we will see the game to an end ; there may be something in it yet."

It was past midnight when the phaeton drew up at Jenning's Bury. Turquet was determined to see the end of the chase and, leaving his horse with Billinge, he braved the bull-dog and crept inside the gate along the shrubbery. There he saw a woman come to the door with a lantern. The stable boy with some difficulty helped the old gentleman down from the phaeton. Then the two of them between them helped him up the steps into the house.

Events moved slowly in Hoddesdon after this night's adventure and the new " runners " could make nothing of the business. Old Dr. Morgan went his nightly rides, news reached them of a postchaise held up near Waltham Abbey, and Sir James Hezlet began to write impatiently asking for tidings they could not supply. They had been at work for a week already but had nothing to show for it except a considerable tavern bill at the " Black Lion."

One evening they had ridden over to Waltham and were returning along the highway gloomily discussing their prospects and wondering if it were not better to ride back to London and tell Sir James they had failed.

Near Wormley there is a small wood, little more than a copse with barely enough cover for a horse and man and the last spot in the world that a sane highwayman would choose for a hiding-place. Billinge and the Count were very hopeful that on some of their evening rides they themselves might be tackled by Bagshot and in likely places were ever on the alert for a surprise. But here it seemed there was no need for vigilance and here, of course, the unexpected happened. A horse and man leaped out of the copse. Turquet's horse shied and threw him, and the thief put a pistol at Billinge's head before he could draw his pistol to defend himself.

" Stand and deliver," cried the thief. " Hands up, you on the floor."

" Not I. I shoot," cried Turquet, rolling round to get at his pistol.

" For Heaven's sake don't," shouted Billinge in an agony of fright. " It's The Child ! "

The hand with the pistol dropped, the mask was removed from the face, and a trill of joyous laughter confirmed Billinge's words.

" And what fool's game is this ? " cried Turquet.

" If it is anyone's fool game it is not mine," said Master Nic rather nettled. " Egad, if I had been Bagshot I should have finished the two of you."

Master Nic went off into a merry peal of laughter. There was just that touch of truth about his words that made silence the discreet answer

At supper Turquet made enquiry into Master Nic's movements in town. Receiving in reply obvious fairy tales concerning a lucky evening at the " Cocoa Tree " and a phenomenal run with the dice whereby Master Nic put himself in funds, Turquet nodded affable assent and gave the youth a truthful account of their own adventures.

Nic learned the failure of their quest and also heard that Sir James Hezlet desired their speedy return to London to take up the robbery of the Bishop's ring and the theft of a pocket-book belonging to Mr. Ambrose of Lancashire. He complimented himself on his restraint in not boasting of these triumphs and laughed heartily at his companions' adventure of their night-ride after the old Doctor.

" Of course it was a ' bite,' " he declared confidently. " I told you both from the very first that you are no more fit to be ' runners ' than I am. Turquet was intended by Providence to teach card games to gulls. Dear old Toby here hasn't enough brains for cards, but give him a crib to crack and he'll be in it and out of it again with the best of them. You should stick to the old game."

" But it isn't safe any longer. Don't you understand that ? " said Billinge.

" By the bye," said Master Nic, " didn't you say the old Doctor wore a diamond ring ? "

" On his right hand," said Billinge.

" Has he a watch and chain ? "

" A gold one," said Turquet. " I saw it at Ware."

" And do you mean to tell me he has never been stopped on the road ? " cried Nic, his eyes glistening at the thought of it.

" Never that I have heard of," said Billinge.

Master Nic whistled. He made up his mind that the diamond ring and the gold watch and chain should be the first fruits of his new career.

The next morning Turquet and Billinge rode over to Hertford where a prisoner who was thought to be connected with the robberies awaited identification. Nic rode part of the way with them, and on his return found the landlord and Dr. Morgan's stable-boy chaffering over the price of oats and must needs give his opinion upon inspection of a sample that the landlord's price was a fair one.

This led to the conclusion of the sale, and the landlord produced a flagon of strong ale to bind the bargain. Master Nic soon understood that his companions were pumping him, and took occasion to make it clear that his friend was gone to Ware and that after the mail came in he was riding over there himself in the cool of the evening. The stable-boy said he expected that he would be driving his master there that evening and the landlord remarked that " the Doctor seemed very partial to the Ware Road."

As Master Nic thought this over after dinner he became satisfied in his mind that Dr. Morgan was certainly not going to Ware that night. There are three roads out of Hoddesdon. You can ride south to London or north to Ware and the third road strikes across the hill by Hailey Bury and Hertford Heath. During Master Nic's short life he had always treated his instinct as other men make use of careful scientific calculation. He was certain in his young mind that the Doctor would take the Hertford Road, and he remembered passing a deep wood at the edge of the road near Woollensbrook. Here he determined he would commence highwayman and attain the glories of a diamond ring and a gold watch and chain.

The mail drove through about five o'clock in the afternoon, but there was nothing for Turquet, so Master Nic saddled his horse and, innocently answering all the landlord's enquiries as to his destination, made it clear to that worthy that he and his friend would spend the evening at the " Saracen's Head " at Ware. Indeed, so careful did he think it necessary to be that he rode as far as Amwell along the Ware Road and entered a little beer-house there merely for the purpose of telling the owner that he was making for Ware, and having thus satisfied all the promptings of his natural duplicity, he doubled like a fox up the hillside and across the heath towards Woollensbrook until he reached the wood he had observed in his morning ride.

The road had fairly wide grass sides to it and these merged without any clear boundary into thickets of brambles and shrubs and a wood of fine oaks and beeches.

Master Nic surveyed several spots on the road-side and at last chose a place on the right hand looking towards Hertford, where the springy turf ran like a green estuary into a deep grove of well-shaded trees. Through the branches in one place on his left hand was a natural window, narrow, but sufficient to enable him to see anyone approaching from Hoddesdon. Here a man could sit his horse unobserved and with a touch of the spur leap on to the highway and take his quarry on the stoop. Master Nic knew by the place of the sun that he would not have long to wait now, but he chuckled to himself at the thought that on his next expedition he would have a watch of his own by which to tell the time.

At his usual hour the old Doctor was driven up to the door of the " Black Lion," nodding and smiling at some of the villagers, who saluted him, and at the usual hour out came the landlord with the glass of brandy. He stood on the step to hand it to the old Doctor.

" They are all three at Ware," he whispered.

" Certain ? " muttered the old gentleman.

" Certain," repeated the landlord in a whisper.

" Then I can get across to the Hitchin Road," muttered the old gentleman, and tossing off the brandy he gave the signal to the boy to drive on.

It is the sign of a great sportsman to wait patiently in a sure belief that at last the game will come or the fish will rise. Master Nic sat his horse in the leafy harbour watching the lengthening shadows. Flippant and fidgetty as he was at ordinary moments, over a business such as this he became a different mortal. Cool, clear, collected and ready for the moment which his instinct had promised him should arrive.

And it did arrive. First a distant intermittent sound of gravel crackling under moving wheels, then a continuous rumble, then the clatter of hoofs and, all at once, the joyous sight of the phaeton—the prey approaching destruction.

Master Nic tightened his left hand on his rein, placed his pistol in position and sat erect and ready. His horse pricked up his ears with impatience as if he too knew the part he had to play. And all the while the luckless phaeton was rolling nearer to its doom.

It had come within about a hundred yards of Nic's hiding-place when suddenly, without any warning, as though it were doing a very ordinary every-day thing, it turned to the left at right angles to the road straight into the wood itself and the last Master Nic saw of it was the hind wheels bumping over the rough grass at the side of the road.

His first thought was that the horses had bolted, but then he could see enough to know that the driver had deliberately driven them into the wood. Then he made up his mind to follow them and would have done so, but peeping out from his hiding-place he saw a market-cart jogging along from Hertford and cautiously retired until the cart had passed away towards Hoddesdon. Tying his horse to a tree, he crept out behind some furze bushes to reconnoitre. The cart was out of sight. From the point where the carriage had disappeared came the sound of a horse pushing his way through the bushes. A masked rider on a black horse, one of those that drew the phaeton, came cautiously into the road. He looked eagerly north and south. There was nothing to be seen. Wheeling his horse towards Hertford he cantered rapidly up the road, passing within a few feet of Master Nic's hiding-place. As he rode by, Nic's eager eyes sought the rider's left hand. There were three fingers missing. Nic shuddered with hate as he gazed after him. It was the man who had sold Jonathan Wild to the law.

What had become of old Doctor Morgan? It seemed certain that Bagshot had met him and mastered him— unless—Master Nic whistled softly to himself—he began to think he had unravelled the mystery of the old Doctor. He would follow his trail and see. Either Bagshot had robbed him or—there was a greater alternative.

He left his horse where it was and, taking one pistol in his hand, skirted the edge of the wood until he came to the spot where the phaeton had turned off the road. Here he found there was a green track but little used running into the heart of the wood. In several places it seemed to have been mended with gravel and the wheel-marks of the phaeton were easy to follow. He stepped lightly along the turf for two or three hundred yards, then the track turned sharp to the right and dipped down at a steep angle. At this point a faint odour of wood-smoke passed across his face. He took stock of his surroundings. If he made a few paces to the right he could see where the downward road finished.

Master Nic's instinct was against descending into the unknown. He left the path. He stood on a hillock. He could not see enough for his purpose. He pulled himself on to the lower branch of a beech-tree and from there to a higher one and now he could see. He had a clear view of the dip in the road and the way it wound round and returned until just beneath him it ended in an old disused gravel pit. And in the the pit was the stable-boy and the phaeton, but only one horse. And the stable-boy had lighted a fire and was folding up a lot of wraps and cloaks and packing them into the phaeton. Master Nic's quick eyes noted a few sacks in the phaeton and a small coil of rope. The mystery of old Doctor Morgan and his high-stepping horses and his hobby of evening drives was solved and made manifest. Nic chuckled to think of the laugh he should have over Turquet and Billinge, but he chuckled silently, for he had to consider the fate of the stable-boy who was just underneath him whistling an irresponsible human tune from a comic opera, ignorant that his life and death hung on the judgment of Master Nic.

And at first he was all for shooting the boy. For one thing, the pistol was a new toy. Then again, he had never shot a man, and there was the excitement of it and the fun of recounting it with advantage to his friends, and the certainty that the law would excuse him for the manslaughter or even reward him. And these things, as Toby would have understood, were sore temptations to The Child, but the good sense of Master Nic prevailed. For he knew that he was an unpractised pistol-shot and even at that distance might miss the boy, and that would be a poor ending to the adventure since if it came to a fair struggle the boy might better The Child. So he mentally acquitted the boy with a sigh and waited and watched.

He was glad, as it turned out, that he had done so, for

when all was stowed away the stable-boy rolled himself up in a rug and threw himself on the ground near the fire. Master Nic watched him with the eye of a cat and listened to his breathing until at last he satisfied himself that his victim slept. Then he climbed cautiously down from the tree and descended noiselessly into the gravel pit below. He stepped on tip-toe towards the phaeton and secured the coil of rope. In drawing this away from under the sacks some noise was made and the boy rolled over uneasily. But he had no time to awake. Master Nic was upon him with his hand on his throat, and when he opened his eyes it was to see his excited captor gazing fiercely into his face and whispering to him that if he made any struggle he would be shot.

The boy was too bewildered to cause much trouble and was soon clumsily but satisfactorily tied up and, to make matters secure, Master Nic drew a sack over his arms and head and tied that firmly from the outside. Then he breathed freely and chuckled over the pleasant ending of the first act.

But the rest of the drama was to be played out and the next thing to be done was to regain his own horse. Satisfying himself that all was well in the gravel pit, he went back on to the highway and found his steed tied up where he had left him. His intention then was to carry the boy in the phaeton into Hertford and to come back with Turquet and Billinge to await Bagshot's return. But just as he entered the highway two horsemen came trotting dismally along from Hertford and he met his two friends returning from another blank day.

To tell them his adventure was the work of a few moments and the three turned off the road to the gravel pit where Turquet took command of the situation and proceeded to hold an examination of the unhappy stable-boy. Encouraged by a threat of Billinge to cut his liver out and stimulated by a very honest promise made by Turquet to tie him up to a tree and thrash the life out of him, the stable-boy gave a very clear and truthful account of his master's doings. The old Doctor was no other than Bagshot. His way was to drive into a similar hiding-place to this, of which he knew several in the district, and from such haunts to ride across country to his work and return about two in the morning and drive home. If the booty was heavy it was hidden and fetched some other evening. There were still two portmanteaux in a wood at Wadesmill and these would have been taken on the night when Turquet and Billinge followed the phaeton but for a friendly warning from the landlord of the " Black Lion."

All this being satisfactorily recounted, the stable-boy was replaced in the sack, the fire made up, a lantern, which they found in the phaeton, lighted and hung on the shafts, their horses made fast, and Turquet explained his plan of campaign for the proper welcome of Bagshot.

They knew they must wait for some hours. Turquet and Nic played a partie of piquet beneath the lantern, placing a cushion out of the phaeton on the body in the sack as a convenient table for the play of the hand. Billinge at the top of the gravel pit kept watch.

It was long past two in the morning. A chill breeze, giving warning of approaching dawn, swept the tops of the trees, waking the birds to song. The game was long over. Suddenly Billinge called from above :

" A horseman cantering along the road."

" Pull the sack off his head, Nic," called out Turquet.

It was done. Nic sat the boy up against the wheel of the phaeton and placed a pistol close to his ear and reminded him that what was required of him was instant obedience and that he, Master Nic, was sole judge and arbitrator of all matters of behaviour.

They could hear Bagshot's horse trampling through the soft ground and the rider pushing aside overhead branches. Then the horse stopped and the rider gave a long, low whistle.

" Repeat it," whispered Nic.

The boy repeated it without a tremble and Master Nic smiled satisfaction at his performance and let him live.

The horseman came merrily down the hill calling out joyously, " Hello ! Hello ! " Bagshot was in high spirits. He had shot a young gentleman near Stevenage that night and found a big purse of gold on him ; and the poor lad

wore a couple of rings which the brute could not pull off
his fingers. Billinge found the fingers with the rings still
upon them when he searched his prisoner's pockets
afterwards.

When Bagshot turned into the gravel pit he caught
sight of Master Nic standing behind the phaeton covering
him with his pistol.

" What the devil is this ? " he cried.

Three pistol-shots were his answer. His horse reared
and he fell back on the ground badly wounded in his arm
and chest. His captors were upon him and had him tied and
bound before he had realised what had happened.

This was the way of the capture of Bagshot and Sir
James Hezlet and his new runners got great credit for the
affair. For Master Nic would scarcely own that he had any
part in the business. Like the deputy of Achaia, he was
shamed to be mixed up with minions of the law and their
warrants and arrests and he openly declared that he cared
for none of these things.

CHAPTER IX

MASTER NIC GOES TO THE PLAYHOUSE

THEY carried their prisoners towards London guarded by a posse of Hertfordshire constables. There were capital charges against Bagshot in Middlesex and Sir James Hezlet determined that he should be lodged in Newgate.

Sir James met them at Edmonton and, having heard their story over a friendly bottle at the " Bell," complimented Mr. Berrington upon his pluck and resource. Master Nic received his commendations very graciously, explaining that it was quite by accident he had met with his friend de Grillac and that it was a mere chance that he had been able to assist him. Pleading urgent business in London, he said farewell to his friends, promising to dine with them next day at an ordinary near Temple Bar.

" I must do something for that young fellow," said Sir James as he left the room. " I like him. He has a very charming manner. What a sad pity he fell into the hands of Wild."

" You go the way of all of us, Sir James," said Turquet smiling. " The rascal has given us medicines to make us love him."

That night after Bagshot was securely loaded with irons in Newgate, Turquet had the honour of taking supper with Sir James, who wanted him to take up an urgent case concerning the loss of a pocket-book.

" It appears," said Sir James, " that a Mr. Ambrose of Preston was talking to his banker in Paul's Churchyard the very day you left London and had occasion to take out his pocket-book to place in it a bill which the banker handed to him. He is certain that he replaced the book in his pocket. He walked up Cheapside and somewhere near Milk Street a lad fell up against him and shortly afterwards he found that the pocket-book was gone."

" An old street trick," said Turquet.

"He went at once to the City Magistrates and has offered a reward of a hundred pounds, and he remains in London, being very desirous of finding the book and having it handed to him without examination, as it contains family papers, so he says, of a very private nature."

"I should say that before long the thieves will carry the book direct to Mr. Ambrose."

"That is what I fear," said Sir James, "and I want you to get in touch with him and, if possible, prevent his handling the book until we have seen it. I have had special instructions from Sir Robert Walpole himself to see that Mr. Ambrose does not get his pocket-book back until it has passed through his hands."

"Mr. Ambrose is suspected, then?"

"His brother was out in '15 and is now in France," replied Sir James, "and Mr. Ambrose is a friend of Captain Oglethorpe."

The young Captain was then Member for Haslemere and his Jacobite sympathies were openly avowed.

"Where am I likely to come across him?" asked the Count.

"He is often at White's or the 'Cocoa Tree,' for he is fond of the dice."

"Then I shall find him easily enough."

"He frequents the theatres, too, especially the Jacobite House at Lincoln's Inn Fields."

"I understand," replied Turquet as he rose to depart, "and I will bring you news of Mr. Ambrose before many hours are passed."

But his enquiries after Mr. Ambrose had not made much progress when the three friends next met and dined with each other as Master Nic had arranged. After dinner they adjourned to the "Cock" for a quiet smoke and a bottle of wine. It was, as Master Nic acknowledged, a pleasant change from Redcross Street. Instead of skulking in the purlieus of The Mint, here they sat at ease in good clothes with money in their pockets, free from the necessity of thieving and cheating and in good odour with the magistrates and the law.

Turquet, to his friend's delight, informed him of his

intention to visit the theatre in search of Mr. Ambrose, and the two agreed to set out forthwith for the playhouse in the Fields where Mr. Quin was billed to play Falstaff in the " Merry Wives." Billinge went off to make a tour of the mug-houses for news of the thief.

There was a crowded house when the two elbowed their way into the boxes. The great chandelier was already lighted and the snuffers were lighting the candles at the side of the boxes. The pit, from the spiked barrier that enclosed the musicians to the very back of the house, was a sea of grizzled heads. The orange girls drove a brisk trade with the laced and jewelled gallants of the boxes, beautiful ladies made smiling advances to fashionable youths who sat in their neighbourhood, and from the gallery came the noisy chaffing of the footmen who entered that part of the theatre as if of right and exercised their privilege to praise or damn as fancy moved them.

The play began. The Count scanned the boxes and the pit for any who should answer to the description of Mr. Ambrose. Meanwhile Nic, who always loved the play, sat with his eyes riveted on the scene drinking in the rollicking folly of the old knight and his gay companions.

As the curtain fell at the end of one of the acts the Count brought him back to earth by tapping him on the shoulder and asking him if he would come along with him to the " Cocoa Tree."

" And leave this ? " asked Master Nic in amazement. " What for ? "

" I can see no one here like Mr. Ambrose, and I am not wasting more time in this place. I shall try the ' Cocoa Tree ' and perhaps White's."

" Try the cellars if you like," replied Nic scornfully. " I see the end of this play."

The Count shrugged his shoulders and turned away.

" And, Turquet," asked Master Nic as his friend was leaving him, " do you know Mr. Quin ? "

" I have not that honour," said Turquet gravely.

" I must know Mr. Quin."

" By all means."

" But how am I to get an introduction to him ? "

H

" A bottle of wine and a supper at the nearest tavern is an introduction to any actor," replied Turquet lightly.

At this moment the curtain rose and Turquet walked out of the playhouse, leaving his young friend intent on the scene. Nic's awe and respect for the great James Quin convinced him that he was not to be approached in the vulgar manner Turquet had suggested. Would such a genius demean himself to sit at a table with common men ? In all ages we find the actor poised between the heaven of faithful adoration and the earth of careless contempt.

The play ended and the next piece was to be a farce in which Mr. Quin had no part. Master Nic having refused to buy an orange for an over-dressed and highly-painted young lady who had squeezed herself into Turquet's vacant seat, and by this neglect having moved the damsel to a volley of the strangest blasphemy, sat looking down at the throng below him and marvelling at the buzz of the critics' tongues.

For some time his eyes rested on the face of a handsome gentleman of middle age, rather taller than his fellows who stood at the side of the pit just beneath him. Nic recognised him at once. He was plainly but handsomely dressed in a brown suit and wore a scarlet waistcoat. In the button-hole of his coat he carried a very small white rose. Nic watched him curiously. Twice had he seen gentlemen approach him, hold the lapel of his coat as if admiring the rose and offer him a word of greeting. To this the tall man replied with some query and each of his friends had replied with the same word " Passionately." After this they had entered into conversation.

" Turquet has too much youthful enthusiasm," said Master Nic chuckling to himself. " If he had waited patiently here I might have introduced him to Mr. Ambrose."

The curtain rang up. The owners of the grey wigs settled down in their seats. Master Nic was again The Child, and gave himself up whole-heartedly to the coarse humours of the farce. Mr. Ambrose and Turquet were soon forgotten. The comic man was knocked backwards and sat on his hat. A roar of honest English laughter filled the house, led by the joyous shouts of the delighted Child.

Outside the Playhouse in Lincoln's Inn Fields linkboys were shouting, chair-men wrangling, the gallants were assisting ladies to their coaches, as the gaily chattering crowd poured into the street. The play was over, and for a moment the Fields were awakened to a sudden activity.

Master Nic, coming out at the centre door, found himself squeezed by the crowd against a pillar, and in his immediate neighbourhood was Mr. Ambrose. It seemed to him that this gentleman was staring at him as though he had met him before, as indeed to his cost he had, and it further seemed to Master Nic, in accordance with the matchless impudence of his nature, that it would be amusing to discover if his theory of the white rose were correct.

The movement of the crowd brought him nearer Mr. Ambrose, and going up to him he said, " Good evening, that is a pretty rose you wear," and he touched the lapel of his coat.

Mr. Ambrose started.

" Good evening, Sir," he replied courteously. " I have not the pleasure of your name."

" I have no name for the moment. You are Mr. Ambrose of The Clough, Preston."

That gentleman bowed saying, with marked emphasis, " I gather that you are fond of roses ? "

" Passionately ! " replied Master Nic, slowly and distinctly.

Mr. Ambrose glanced at him and then held out his hand, which Master Nic caught in a friendly grasp. They were by this time just outside the theatre and pushing their way through the crowd. Mr. Ambrose requested his companion to follow him and turning out of the Fields they made their way towards Drury Lane. Here Mr. Ambrose entered the " Rose Tavern " and telling the landlord to send up a bottle of Hermitage and not to allow him to be disturbed, walked upstairs to a little upper room followed by Master Nic, who was wondering how his adventure would end.

" And now that we are alone, Sir," said Mr. Ambrose, setting down his sword and hat upon the table and motion-

ing his visitor to a chair, " will you tell me your name and
credentials, from whom you received the signal and what
is your message ? "

" Very willing," replied Master Nic, throwing off his
hat and stretching himself at ease in a chair. " For the
moment my name is my own affair, for the rest I will be
frank with you. I have no credentials and no message. As
for your signal, that was so clumsily acted by your friends
in the pit that by way of jest I thought I would mimic it for
my own amusement. Faith, if all the friends of the King
across the water have no more skill at affairs than you and
your friends there will be more deaths on Tower Hill
before the end of it."

" Young man," cried out Mr. Ambrose angrily, springing out of his chair and putting his hand on his sword,
" are you a spy ? "

" Whist ! " said Master Nic, putting his finger to his
lips and smiling pleasantly at his friend. " The wine ! "

A drawer entered with the Hermitage, and when Mr.
Ambrose had paid for it and poured out a couple of glasses,
his anger was gone, and he could not but look at the slight
figure of his strange guest with an air of curiosity and
amazement and wonder what my Lord Impudence would
say next.

Master Nic raised his glass and nodded to his host in
his friendly and engaging way.

" The Royal Exchange ! "

Mr. Ambrose's eyes lighted up with pleasure. " ' The
Royal Exchange,' " he repeated solemnly.

For by such subterfuges did convivial Jacobites express
to each other their desire that the hated George should
be exchanged for the beloved James.

" You must not take my political views very seriously,"
said Master Nic, pouring out another glass of wine.
" Politics is not one of my vices, and you will, I am sure,
pardon the freedom I have taken of making your acquaintance in this way, but I heard accidentally that you
had lost a pocket-book. I have information of it."

Mr. Ambrose grew serious. Master Nic was no longer a
jesting youth, but rather the figure of Fate standing with

a sword in his hand menacing the destinies of kings and kingdoms.

" How may I be sure that you really have information of the book ? "

" I have copied the words of His Majesty's letter in which he tells you what the Queen says of Lord Inverness and thinks of all Protestants : ' S'il est infidel a Dieu sera t'il fidel a son Maitre.' " He handed him the slip of paper.

" Peace," called out Mr. Ambrose, " you have indeed seen the book."

" I have it in my custody," replied Master Nic calmly, pouring himself out another glass of wine.

Mr. Ambrose looked at his sword and the slight figure of the smiling youth, but his sense of honour forbade the attempt.

" Besides," added Master Nic, who was watching his eyes and instinctively guessed his thought, " it would spoil all. The pocket-book is in my possession but not upon my person. I take better care of it than its former owner."

The young man laughed pleasantly at his jest. Mr. Ambrose was pale with excitement.

" I ask your pardon for any thought of harming you," he said with real regret, " but I must recover the book."

Master Nic accepted his apology with a generous wave of his hand.

" And now tell me," continued Mr. Ambrose beseechingly, " how you came possessed of the pocket-book and on what terms you will return it to me."

" The book " said Master Nic gravely, " was taken from you by a poor lad who was starving. He is a linkboy and is now in honest employment. He used to attend me on occasions, and noting his troubled look I wormed his story out of him, and he gave me up the book which had been hidden in his garret. He has spent the gold contained in it but all else is intact. The first term is that no effort shall be made to follow up the thief."

" Agreed ! " said Mr. Ambrose.

" The next term is that inasmuch as there is a public reward of a hundred pounds for the book you will give me that sum which I promise shall be carefully spent in the best interests of this young lad."

"Agreed," said Mr. Ambrose, very heartily, "and may I say I think it kind of you to interest yourself in his career."

"Not at all," replied Nic hurriedly, "not at all. And now that being settled we come to my reward."

"Name your own sum, Sir."

"I do not wish for money," replied Master Nic loftily, "but I understand you have friends among the players. Have you the honour to know Mr. Quin?"

"Mr. Quin the actor?" said Mr. Ambrose in surprise. "Certainly I have what you justly term the honour to be well liked by him, Sir, for I take the friendship of a man of parts to be an honour."

"And I too, Sir," said his companion with genuine enthusiasm. "And the reward I ask of you is that you will introduce me to Mr. Quin as your friend."

"Really, Sir——"

"It is the price of the pocket-book," said Master Nic firmly.

"You take me up too readily. It is so small a thing to ask. I will do it with pleasure—the greatest pleasure. I have interest with Mr. Quin and he shall be here to dinner with me to-morrow. Here, Sir, to-morrow at two. I had asked Captain Oglethorpe to dine with me, but perhaps——"

"By all means," said Master Nic, bowing politely. "I shall be honoured to make his acquaintance. At two o'clock I shall bring you your pocket-book here."

"I rely on your good faith, Sir," said Mr. Ambrose with a tone of anxiety in his voice.

"And why not, Sir?" asked Master Nic simply as he bade him good-night, "Have I not relied on yours?"

They shook hands and parted.

Next day at noon Master Nic, who had taken a room for himself with Mrs. Metyard in Wych Street, began to apparel himself in his greatest glory to do honour to the banquet, his host and Mr. Quin.

Master Nic looked more fascinating than usual in his well-fitting, pearly-grey suit, his smart, flashing paste buckles, and the new auburn wig curling on his shoulders.

He was arranging his lace ruffles before a small square of cracked looking-glass when his two friends entered the room and he pirouetted round the floor laughing with delight at the thought of his own beauty.

" What is the meaning of this ? " asked the Count, crossing the room to a seat in the window.

Billinge stood at the door in stupid, squinting amazement. The glamour of dress has always had a mighty charm for the lower-class mind. To the Count The Child in rags, or The Child in purple and fine linen, would always be The Child, a problem to puzzle over, giving him that occasional tug at his heart strings which came as a pleasure rather than a pain to a man of the world long weary of it. To Billinge The Child was a sacred possession, an image to be worshipped, a Child to be protected.

" What is the meaning of it," repeated the Count as he pulled out a box of his favourite Brazil tobacco and loaded a pipe and puffed the smoke out of the window.

" I am invited to dine at the ' Rose Tavern ' in Covent Garden."

" The wine will be good enough at ' The Rose,' " said the Count, " but with whom do you dine ? "

" With Mr. Quin for one," replied Master Nic in an off-hand tone.

" Then the food will be as good as the wine or there will be language used," said Turquet laughing.

For the epicurean habits of Mr. Quin were the common talk of the town, as actors' failings often are, and Turquet told Nic how he had once met him at an inn in Plymouth, to which seaport the great actor made annual excursions for the joy of eating the John Dory and the pilchard fresh-caught from the sea.

" And who asks you into Mr. Quin's company and throws good wine and a good dinner over your uneducated palate into your utterly unappreciative gullet ? " asked Turquet with a laugh of good-natured contempt.

" Mr. Ambrose," replied Master Nic with a smile of triumph.

" Our Mr. Ambrose ? " shouted Billinge and Turquet together.

" My Mr. Ambrose," said Master Nic in a tone of patient rebuke. " My friend Mr. Ambrose of The Clough, near Preston in Lancashire, who has no wish, as far as I can make out, to become acquainted with either of you. But, being a gentleman who loves the company of men of parts, he has asked Mr. Quin, Captain Oglethorpe the Member for Haslemere, and myself to dine with him at ' The Rose.' And this reminds me," continued Master Nic, pulling out the late Doctor Morgan's gold watch and looking at it with affected carelessness, " it is time I was on the way. Billinge, do me the kindness to fetch me a chair."

Billinge turned round with the eagerness of a poor courtier who is graciously permitted to do a favour to his prince.

" Stop," said the Count.

He spoke in a tone of command and as one who was serious. Billinge stepped back into the room and even Nic's smile died away for a second.

" Stop," said the Count, " we must know where we are in this affair. The point I want made clear is this," continued Turquet gravely. " I have told you the history of Mr. Ambrose and the pocket-book. Are you going to make use of that information and play your game with him without partners, or are you going to tell your pals as much of your game as they have told you of theirs ? You must cease to be The Child with us, Berrington. It is for you to decide. Are we three going to stand together or is this the parting of the ways ? "

Master Nic was chagrined and penitent at his friend's tone. In his vain, child-like way he loved Turquet and Billinge. He knew, too, with his sure instinct for human good-will, that the two men loved him and had made sacrifices for his welfare. He was conquered. Indeed, but for the thought of his new suit he would have flung himself at the Count's feet on the dusty floor and asked his pardon.

" Turquet," he cried in a conscience-stricken voice, " Turquet, my friend, I am a pig and a brute. I will tell you the whole affair. I should have done so at once."

•

" Good," said Turquet, his eyes glistening with pleasure. " Let us hear your story. I knew you would not play us false."

Master Nic was himself again and called out to Billinge in a tone of sprightly command : " Pull the bedstead across here. Hurry, man, I must not keep Mr. Quin waiting."

Billinge wondering, did as he was bid.

" Toby," ordered The Child, feeling by now quite restored to his natural impudence, " pull up that loose board. I do not want to dirty my fingers."

He tapped the board lightly with his foot to indicate to Billinge the one he wished moved, and with some injury to his finger-nails and several oaths Billinge got it out from its fellows.

" You should have put your heel on this end," said Nic, laughing at him, " then it flies up a little."

" How the devil was I to know that ? " muttered Billinge. " What next ? "

" Put your hand under the next board—the other side— that's right—and give me Mr. Ambrose's pocket-book ! "

Toby the dumbfounded did as he was commanded, and Master Nic, taking the book from him, threw it lightly across to the Count.

" Turquet, I make you master of its contents, but when I took his book I never proposed to play this game with you, and I must keep my word to my friend Mr. Ambrose. I have promised to return him the book with all the papers intact."

" Monsieur Michel says that the only excuse for a broken promise is where one has promised something that is wicked or unlawful in itself. You shall take the papers back to Mr. Ambrose when I have looked at them. I will not steal them."

The word " steal " made no impression on the shallow waters of Nic's young mind. He was intent upon the coming joy of the afternoon.

" Turquet," he said, placing his hand lovingly on his shoulder, " you are a kind fellow and would never spoil my fun. I knew it. Toby, off with you and fetch me a chair. I must not be late."

CHAPTER X

A DINNER WITH MR. QUIN

THE Count took the papers from the pocket-book and replaced them one by one.

" How did you come by this book ? " he asked.

" Well, I took it at Paul's, and now I am going to take it back."

" And claim the reward ? "

" Better than that, Turquet. I am going to dine with Mr. Quin."

" Let me take the book to Sir Robert Walpole," said the Count. "No questions will be asked how you came by it."

" It is impossible," said Master Nic. " Mr. Ambrose has my word."

He held out his hand. Turquet handed him the book.

" As you will," he said. " But I must report the affair to Sir James Hezlet this evening. Mr. Ambrose is already under suspicion, and he will be wise to be out of London after eight o'clock to-night."

" He can please himself about that when I have dined with Mr. Quin," replied Nic with a merry laugh. " Think of it, Turquet. Don't you envy me ? "

The Count sat smoking silently and gazing at Master Nic with curiosity and affection. Perhaps he was remembering his own youth and the days when the actors of Paris were his heroes, and the world was a nursery of sport and adventure.

" A penny for your thoughts," cried Master Nic.

" It might have ended at Tyburn," continued Turquet.

" I suppose that is bound to happen some day," said the lad, as though Tyburn was the canonical portal through which men of adventure generally approached eternity.

" Possibly," said Turquet drily, " but to be hanged as a pickpocket is a poor ending for a lad of your figure." He

rose and put his hand on the boy's shoulder, speaking to
him very earnestly. " Nic, I want you to give it up. I want
you to run straight. You have chances in the world."

" Turquet, I can't," replied The Child with equal earnestness. " I love it ! "

" Do you remember a picture that hung over the mantelpiece in Wild's parlour—the portrait of a woman ? "

Master Nic nodded.

" Do you think if that beautiful woman could come to
life and asked you what I am asking now, you could have
refused her request ? "

" We are growing mightily romantic and mysterious,"
said Master Nic with a sneer. " I should tell the good
woman to——"

" It was your mother," said Turquet quietly.

Master Nic sprang up and seized his arm. He almost
shook him.

" How do you know that ? "

" Wild told me the last time I saw him, when he asked
me to befriend you."

" And my father ? "

" Wild never spoke of that. I believe the Johnsons know
more of you than any. But do you never think that all this
business is utterly unworthy of you, that you were born for
better things ? God knows, you may make your life a feast
of pleasure at the first, but the bread of it is sad eating in
the end. I have been down to the bottom of the pit and
crawled out on to the edge of the world again. I don't want
to see you sliding down into it and do nothing to help
you."

" Hillo ! Hillo ! " cried Billinge from below stairs. " My
lord's chair blocks the way ! "

" Turquet," said Master Nic, taking his hand, " you are
a good friend to me, but I can't promise what I don't
expect to perform. I'll promise you this, though ; I'll do
my best to keep away from picking pockets."

" After all," said Turquet, patting him on the shoulder,
" you promise as much as a friend and a man of sense
should do."

Billinge, holding open the door of the sedan chair, was

as proud as a hen with a duckling chick, as heads came out
of the windows and passers-by stopped to gaze at the fine
leg and handsome figure of Master Nic, who stood awhile
on the steps of the house to treat the rogues of the kennel
to a glimpse of the real St. James's.

The Count from above gazed after the chair as it went
swinging up the narrow street. He, too, looked after it with
love or pity of a kind in his heart. There were few, who came
within the radius of Master Nic's sunny carelessness, that
did not want to help and protect him.

Long before two o'clock Mr. Ambrose was waiting at
the Rose Tavern with some anxiety, and ran to the door
with a sigh of relief when he saw Master Nic stepping out
of his chair. Taking him by the arm, he led him to a handsome room now prepared for dinner. The Rose Tavern
was kept by a son of the late famous Pontac—Pontac, the
son of the President of the Parliament of Bordeaux, whose
portrait swung over the tavern in Abchurch Street, which
his son, by his acknowledged skill in cookery, vintnery and
philosophy had raised to a house of European reputation.
Even now at the " Rose," Pontac, Junior, boasted that he
served the vintages of Pontaq and Haut Briond, the wine
of his grandfather's estates which Evelyn had praised in
old days. Here, too, at the " Rose " you could have those
modish kickshaws, hams boiled in champagne or burgundy,
fatted snails, and chickens not two days from the shell,
which the elder Pontac had made famous, but to-day Mr.
Quin and other wise epicures had set the taste of the town
towards more honest English fare, for which also the
" Rose " was equally famous.

The room was handsomely furnished with mirrors and
rich curtains, and a large portrait of the late Monsieur
Pontac hung over a long sideboard which was heavily laden
with silver. The oval table in the centre was laid for four,
and on a smaller buffet stood several bottles, well-filled
decanters and many glasses, with a drawer in attendance
upon them.

Master Nic took Mr. Ambrose aside to the window and
handed him the pocket-book, asking him to look through
the papers.

Mr. Ambrose scanned them hurriedly and gave a sigh of satisfaction.

" Here is a draft for the hundred guineas for the young linkboy," he said, handing him a paper. " My bankers, Barclay and Tritton, of Lombard Street, will honour it. I wish I might offer you some reward."

" You give me that," replied Master Nic, " in the pleasure of your friendship and the introduction you afford me to Mr. Quin."

" At least, sir, let me know the name of the gentleman who has rendered me so great a service."

" My name is Berrington—Nicholas Berrington, at your service."

" Of the Berringtons of Oxfordshire ? " asked Mr. Ambrose. " My wife knew a Mr. Berrington of Steeple Berrington——"

Master Nic was wondering how he should reply when a bustle was heard downstairs, and Mr. Ambrose ran to the door. Captain Oglethorpe and Mr. Quin had arrived at the same time, and were received with honour by Pontac's lackeys. The Member of Parliament, however, was of little account in their eyes compared with the great actor. Waiters flew hither and thither to take Mr. Quin's hat and relieve him of his cane and escort him to the dining-room. The popular actor was a noted figure in the neighbourhood of Covent Garden, and everyone in the tavern was anxious to please him, well knowing that where Mr. Quin dined with satisfaction to-day many of his friends and patrons would dine to-morrow.

James Quin was an ample figure of a man. He had an expressive countenance, an inquisitive eye, a clear melodious voice, and a memory packed with the verse of Shakespeare. Moreover, he was an Irishman and the beloved of women, as the men of that gallant race always have been, and he had the Celtic accent on his tongue from which pearls of wit and epigram fell without effort, but the great glory of the man was that he was a master-craftsman in the art of dining.

He shook off the civilities of Monsieur Pontac and his satellites, threw his hat and cane to the servants and, taking

Captain Oglethorpe's arm, to the young soldier's great gratification, mounted the stairs to the dining-room, where he greeted Mr. Ambrose almost with an embrace.

"Harry Ambrose, my dear friend," said the great man, rolling the letter R with a pleasant Irish burr, "I am proud to be your guest. Go bid the servants spread the dinner. Introduce me to your young friend. The Captain and I are well acquainted—I am happy to meet you, Mr. Berrington. There was a Jack Berrington in Dublin, a navy captain."

Master Nic shook his head and blushed. This desire to link his name and identity with others was a new and irksome experience to him. He had wandered into a world the ways of which were strange to him. But the genial actor rambled on without noticing his confusion, or perhaps out of a kindly desire to cover his shyness.

"And now, my young friend," continued Quin, patting the delighted Master Nic on the shoulder, "sure 'tis no sin for a man to labour at his vocation; let us to work, and let me offer you in whispering humbleness a piece of sage advice: always begin your dinner with a 'whet.' But take none of your fancy 'whets,' as White and Wormwood or Ratafia or the like, but plain, wholesome sack, and that in moderation."

And to show what he meant by moderation, the great man went to the buffet and poured out four half tumblers of sherry, which he offered to his companions, and they tossed them off at a draught.

"And now," said Mr. Quin, "to business. What have we here? No funeral baked meats when I dine with you, Harry."

Indeed, the banquet was one for a king, or rather many kings. As the mode was, the servers loaded the table with soup and fish and roast ducks, a pigeon pie, fresh green peas from Marylebone, and a dish that Mr. Quin approved of in no small measure, which was called a bean tansy. And Master Nic, who had expected the great man to discourse of poetry and the theatre, was amazed at the fervour and learning of his soliloquies in praise of the minor art of cooking and the craft of the cook.

"The man who made that bean tansy," said Mr. Quin

with judicial emphasis, " deserves to be decorated by a grateful monarch. The king who has such a subject may be adjudged happy. We will drink the fellow's health."

And the cook, a burly, red-faced fellow, was introduced by Monsieur Pontac himself, and came up hot and perspiring from the kitchen in his clean white cap and apron. Whereupon Mr. Quin, taking the jug from the tapster, filled him a bumper of claret with his own hands, and they all drank his health. After which Mr. Ambrose and his guests listened with awe as cook and actor discussed with the companionable freedom of great artists the proper architecture and composition of a bean tansy.

" For you see, gentlemen," said Mr. Quin, as the cook departed, " your bean tansy as a general thing is but bruised beans and bacon, with cloves and mace and the yolk of eggs and butter, so that at a feast like this it is but a heavy addition to better fare. But this fellow mixes his beans with biscuits, sugar, sack and cream, and bakes the whole in a dish, which he serves with a garnish of candied orange-peel. And let me tell you that when the table is crowded with good food, the graceful appearance of a dish is a pleasant inducement to appetite."

With such discourse did Mr. Quin delight his hearers, and there was plenty more good talk and glasses were going round rapidly and merrily, when Monsieur Pontac entered, and whispered Mr. Quin, that his dresser had called to say it was time he was at the theatre.

" By heavens ! " he said, looking at his watch and jumping up, " I should be in the Green Room. Do you come to the play to-night. It's Mr. Addison's ' Cato.' "

" I am sorry it is impossible," replied Mr. Ambrose. " I have several things to do, and to-morrow I ride for the north."

" Then you have found what you sought ? " asked Mr. Quin in a lower voice.

" Thanks to Mr. Berrington here," said Mr. Ambrose gratefully.

" Ah, then," said Mr. Quin, seizing Master Nic's hand and pressing it warmly, " you shall be more my friend than ever. Perhaps it may be your pleasure to see the play to-night and I shall be proud if you will join me in the Green Room afterwards, and we will go to supper together."

Master Nic was in the seventh heaven of delight, and the great man hurried away with his dresser. Captain Oglethorpe was eager to get down to the House, and now took his leave, expressing a wish to meet Master Nic on some future occasion, for he had been pleasantly impressed by his frank, innocent bearing and courteous manners.

Mr. Ambrose suggested to Master Nic that they should have another bottle, but this he resolutely refused.

" You are anxious to get to the theatre, I see."

" I am sorry, sir, to have kept you here even these two hours. It was selfish of me. I have been wasting your time for my pleasure. The papers in your wallet have been seen by friends of Sir Robert Walpole, and he will hear of them to-night at eight. If I might advise, you will be away from London to-night."

" My dear Mr. Berrington, you overwhelm me with service."

" I am happy to have had the opportunity, sir. I am your humble servant."

He picked up his hat and cane to depart.

" At least give me some address where I can find you if I am in London again——"

" I have no address, sir," replied Master Nic frankly. " Indeed, I do not even know if the name I have given you is my own to give."

There were tears in the boy's eyes. Mr. Ambrose looked at him with compassion. The youth had found a way to his heart. He shook him warmly by the hand.

" You have been very kind to me, sir," said Master Nic, and he hurried from the room and ran downstairs out into the street, and so away towards the Fields.

To his great pride and delight he was received by his friend Mr. Quin in the Green Room, and in the glory of his surroundings soon forgot his troubles. The great actor introduced him to Lord Morden, Lord Bassett, the Honourable Herbert Wyndham, and several young aristocrats who honoured the stage and hampered the drama by sitting at the wings to watch the play.

Mr. Quin was supreme. Whether it was the port, or the claret, or the bean tansy, or some sudden inspiration in the actor himself, certain it is that all the grizzled heads in the pit nodded approbation of Mr. Quin's magnificent performance of Cato, and rose as one man to encore the well-known soliloquy, a compliment that Garrick himself never received.

And some think that this compliment so elated him that he was guilty of a singular breach of good manners, the consequences of which sat heavy on his kind heart for many a year beyond. There was a poor wretch of an actor named Williams—a Welshman—who was full of the fiery temper and conceit of his nation, and spoke the English tongue with that quaint accent that you meet with among the hills across Dee sands. The fellow was but a hanger-on in the theatre, being cast occasionally for small parts and at other times snuffing candles or doing such odd jobs as made him worth his few shillings a week. But for all his poverty he had the true heart of the actor, as many have who cannot fit the role, and being, as I have said, a Welshman, he had worthy ancestry, the soul of a gentleman, and was nobly sensitive of insult. Moreover, it must be remembered that he had not drunk claret or eaten bean tansies and sipped the good red wine of Portugal. His dinner had been his breakfast, and was but a mug of small ale at noon with a crust of bread and an onion. It was a cruel act that the great Quin in his triumph as the blazing star of the evening should have stooped to crush out of existence the little Welshman's rushlight.

Williams was cast for the part of Decius, Cæsar's ambassador. When he entered he spoke the words in his mincing voice, murdering the true line as thus :

" Cæsar sends health to Keeto."

Quin, looking at him with all the scorn and contempt he could muster, replied in solemn, tragic tones :

" Would he had sent it by a better messenger."

The critic pit, who for their credit should have resented the blackguardism of the gag, leapt at the wit—as they called it—of their favourite, cheering Mr. Quin and jeering at the wretched ambassador. The scene proceeded but

I

lamely, and at its conclusion, when Decius retired, he put real sorrow and passion into his last words :

"When I relate hereafter
The tale of this unhappy embassy,
All Rome will be in tears."

The audience caught the pathos of it, and a low murmur of sympathy for the man they had insulted ran through the house.

But the wrong was done and past repair. The angry Welshman left the boards with murder in his heart ; the blood of kings and heroes coursed through his veins and the fury of red dragons glowed in fire from his eyes as he swore by the glory of all his ancestors that he would never sleep until he had wreaked vengeance on his enemy.

At the end of the play, when Mr. Quin passed into the Green Room from his triumph, the little man was there pale and trembling to challenge the great actor to mortal combat. And though Mr. Quin good-naturedly sought to laugh the matter off as a jest, the fellow flew at him and would have struck him in the face had not Master Nic tripped him up, and so he measured his length on the ground. My Lord Bassett and Master Nic held him firmly down until the lackeys of the theatre, hearing the noise, ran in and seized him and shot him out of the stage door into the kennel.

"Well, well," says Mr. Quin, "the fellow has a right to be angry, and I would willingly have asked his pardon, and to-morrow, when he is more reasonable, I will make it right to him."

This sentiment Master Nic thought very noble, for he had not then learned that the morrow, when we hope to put right the wrong of to-day, is a day that seldom comes. It came not to Mr. Quin. For that night my Lord Bassett must entertain Master Nic and Mr. Quin and the rest to a bowl of punch at "The Cock," and so from one bowl to another, until chairs and coaches carried the young fellows off to their houses in the west of the town, and Quin and Master Nic went out to walk to their lodgings.

It was a mor night night, and as they rolled along arm

in arm by the Piazza at Covent Garden, near where Mr. Quin lodged, out sprang my little Welshman, right in their path, drew his sword, and demanded to fight Mr. Quin. The great man was but too ready for the nearest folly at hand, and cursing Welsh and Scot and Saxon with drunken Irish good nature, he flung Master Nic aside, drew his sword, and rushed at his adversary. The clash of steel echoed through the piazza. Master Nic strove to part them, but feared to injure one or the other in the attempt. Truly, when Celt meets Celt, it is like the fighting of frenzied dogs, and the safer course is to stand by till one is laid low.

But now a citizen in a grey suit, accompanied by his servant with a lantern, rushed to the scene and, raising his cudgel, would have thrown himself between them, crying out in loud tones, " Peace in the Lord's name. He that killeth his brother is in danger of hell fire. Fetch the watch, Ziba, the watch ! " The good man had undoubtedly run on their swords and been killed or grievously wounded had not Master Nic thrown his arms round him and pushed him back. A posse of the watch came hurrying up, and the sound of their approach seemed to drive the Welshman to fiercer efforts, and he flung himself at Mr. Quin. It was then that the scuffle ended. A random pass drove Mr. Quin's sword through the little fellow's proud heart, and he sank with a groan, his life's blood making a spreading puddle on the cobble-stones.

Mr. Quin stood aghast. His sword dropped from his sobered hand. The watchman ran up and seized him. He made no effort to resist. Master Nic was kneeling down and had placed the head of the fallen man on his breast and, lowering his ear to his lips in answer to the call of the poor creature's glassy eyes, caught his dying message.

" Thank Mr. Quin," he whispered. " Tell them I asked him for satisfaction. It is my own fault. They must not punish him."

His head fell limp across Master Nic's wrist, who lowered it gently to the ground. The man was dead.

When the watch, who were now in force, would have lifted up the body to carry it to the Watch House, the citizen in grey put up his hand and, kneeling on the ground, stretched out both his arms and called out in a loud voice :

" Oh, most gracious Father, Lord of Heaven, Who hast decreed that this Thy servant should go hence and be no more seen, without time for repentance and restitution, let the miracles of Thy compassion and Thy glorious mercy supply him the want of the usual measures of time, and the periods of repentance, and the trimming of the lamp. Forgive him his sins and redeem this our poor brother's soul from the dangers of an eternal death, and make him partaker of the gift of eternal life, through Jesus Christ our Lord. Amen ! "

Mr. Quin breathed a deep " Amen," and many of the watch and the curious crowd that had gathered from nowhere out of the darkness and pressed round to see what was forward, echoed the word in mumbling tones. Only Master Nic uttered no sound. He was watching the face of the praying man kneeling on the cobble-stones, lighted, as it was, by the moon streaming between the pillars, and wondering where it was that he had heard and seen him pray before. And when the man put on his hat and rose from the ground, Master Nic remembered that he had parted with him years ago on the Sussex downs, and that his name was Simon Verrall.

CHAPTER XI

ALL the parties to this affray were detained for the night at the Watch House at St. Paul's, Covent Garden. The next morning Mr. Quin was taken before Sir James Hezlet at Bow Street, who decided that he must stand his trial for the killing of Williams. When they had been bound over as witnesses, Simon Verrall begged Master Nic to accompany him home to the City and take dinner with his family.

"It seems to me," he said in his grave manner, "as if the hand of the Lord had brought about our meetings. Again I owe my life to you, and I should wish at least to assure you of my gratitude and my desire to serve you in any way that is possible."

Master Nic thanked him and accepted his invitation. As they walked away, Mr. Verrall told him that in the days of his wanderings in Sussex, he had but recently lost his wife, little Hetty's mother, and was married a second time. He still at times felt the call of the Lord to go forth and preach but he humbly hoped that what he was now doing was right, and that his wife and daughter were messengers of the Lord when they dissuaded him from further missionary efforts.

Master Nic thought they were undoubtedly right. He was beginning to find that the world he had lived in, the world of crime and roguery and adventure, was not the only world, and it began to dawn upon this young mind that it would be entertaining to step aside from it and explore new social continents. His meeting with Mr. Ambrose and Mr. Quin had been a strange adventure, and as this seemed the sequel to it, he made up his mind to follow it through.

They walked along the Strand and Fleet Street towards Fetter Lane, Mr. Verrall continuing his apologia. "It seems almost another life since I was in Sussex, and you saved me

119

from the constable," said Master Verrall, " and some of the brethren would say that I am a backslider and have sought the paths of Mammon and left the straight way of right-eousness. As the Reverend Silas Westerman says, ' There must be some to toil and gather in the harvest, and it is better that they should be men of God so that they are ready to spend their substance in his service.' "

With such discourse did the good man seek to excuse himself to The Child for the fact that he no longer lived a life of wandering enthusiasm, but was a substantial glover in the City of London. The truth of the matter was that on the death of his first wife he had married Miss Deborah Flood, a well-to-do spinster and a member of Mr. Wester-man's congregation. This good woman, though strict in the practices of her creed, was fond of money and capable in management, and had spurred on her husband until they now had a most flourishing business. She herself ruled with a rod of iron over the apprentices in the workshop, most of whom were girls taken from the poorhouse or brought up from the glove-making districts in Somerset and Here-ford to serve their time.

" And now Mr. Berrington, you shall see our hive of industry," said Verrall, as Ziba opened the door to them and they entered a spacious hall, from which a handsome staircase led to the upper chambers.

A cry of delight from the gallery above made them look up. Master Nic's eyes rested with satisfaction on the tall, graceful figure of a girl of sixteen or thereabouts, with dark hair and large brown eyes full of joy at the sight of her father. She came tripping rapidly down the stairs to greet him.

" Ha ! " cried Verrall in mock anger. " Why are you not at Westminster selling gloves ? We are all workers here, sir ! Why are you holiday-making, Hetty ?"

" We were so anxious when you did not return, father, that I could not leave home until I saw you safe back again."

She placed her two hands on his shoulders and he leaned down to kiss her.

" Thank the Lord in the first place, Hetty dear, and then His instrument, Mr. Berrington."

Young Mistress Verrall curtseyed low with practised grace, her long eyelashes modestly closing her eyes to The Child's appreciative gaze. He, too, put forward a handsome leg and bowed gallantly. The old man frowned slightly at the sight of these fripperies.

" The ways of the Lord are past understanding, Hetty," said her father. " Many years ago this gentleman saved me from danger, and though you will not remember it, pulled you out of a dike where, but for him, you might have drowned. Last night I was for trying to separate with my cudgel two men fighting with swords—a mad project truly for an old man—when he stepped in and pulled me back. So, under the Lord, we both owe him our lives."

Hetty had a vague child's memory of falling into a pond and being rescued by a merry boy, a hero who caught eels and rescued damsels in distress. Her father rarely spoke of those wandering days now and, indeed, she hardly remembered whether such an event had really happened. She turned her brown eyes smiling thankfulness on Master Nic, and the gentle glory of them entered into his soul. Would that he could plunge into cataracts or mountainous seas and save her life again and keep it for his own, was the thought that stabbed him to the heart. He had felt like that with Jenny and others, and yet he swore to himself that this was something new and wonderful and different from any experience he or any man had ever countered since the waking of Adam.

" Where is your mother ? " asked Verrall.

" She is with the apprentices, I think," said Hetty carelessly.

" See that we have dinner in good time. Come, Mr. Berrington, let me show you my workshops."

Master Nic seemed rooted to the sacred spot where he first met Hetty, but seeing that the young lady had danced away towards the kitchen regions without so much as a parting glance towards him, he aroused himself and followed his host down a long corridor to the workshops.

" I have knocked two houses into one, as you will see," said the glove-maker as they left the living apartments.

It was not extravagant to describe the place as a hive of

industry. Industry was another new note in the music of the world as far as Master Nic was concerned. That one should beg or borrow or steal a pair of gloves was natural enough, but that these should be made by human workers toiling skilfully for long hours and living laborious lives was to him, as it is to many of the idlers of to-day, difficult of realisation.

Here it was to his eyes. Down below were skins of dogs, goats, sheep, and of chamois, stored and kept by several workmen. Simon Verrall handled them with knowledge and called to his workman to bring out some choice specimens for Mr. Berrington's inspection. In another room men were damping the skins with horsehair brushes some six inches wide, the horsehair being nearly three inches long. These implements the men handled readily and quickly, dipping them into clean water, drawing them lightly over the skins and then piling the treated skins carefully upon one another.

In another room the skins were being planed. The men laid them on a slab of marble and scraped away any surplus flesh that remained with a flat knife set on a wooden handle. Then they were cut into tranks or glove shapes and given out to the sewers, after which, as Verrall explained, they went back to the workmen, who damped them again and stretched them. In this room Ziba Grime was the foreman. Master Nic recognised the thin features and lank hair of the servant who had been with Verrall at the Watch House.

Simon Verrall picked up some of the gloves from a pile on the table and showed his guest how well they were sewn. One, however, did not please him.

" This should not have been passed," he said in a vexed tone, showing a glove to Ziba.

" Mistress Verrall commands the sewing room," replied Ziba. " It is sent to us so. You cannot gather grapes from thistles. There are too many raw apprentices upstairs. What you save in wages you lose in craftsmanship."

Verrall picked up the glove, and they climbed upstairs into a huge attic that ran the length of the two houses. It was crowded with women and girls sewing at low tables. At a higher table, in a better light near the window, sat Mrs. Verrall. She was a tall, spare woman with hard, glittering eyes, thin lips and a beaky nose. They came up to her table. The sight of these girls bending painfully over their work and the stifling atmosphere depressed the joyous spirit of Master Nic.

Mr. Verrall introduced him to his wife, and mentioned that he had asked him to dinner, and Mrs. Verrall received him with a look of suspicion. Her mind was on the business of the day, and she rather resented the bringing of this elegant stranger into her kingdom.

" There are some new skins come, Simon."

" I have seen them, my dear," replied her husband.

" Ziba says you have been cheated over them," said his wife not without a malicious smile.

Verrall threw the glove on the table. His wife snatched it up and examined it.

" Collins," she said to the forewoman, " how came you to pass such work ? "

Miss Collins, who had also been looking at the glove, might have reminded Mrs. Verrall that she, too, had passed it, but she said nothing.

" Whose work is it ? " asked Mrs. Verrall angrily.

Miss Collins looked at a mark inside the gloves.

" Mary Martin's," she said.

Mrs. Verrall picked up a cane off the table, walked across the room to where Mary was sewing and, showing her the spoilt glove, struck her across the shoulders smartly several times, scolding her angrily and promising her a sound whipping if her work did not improve, with the added threat of sending for the beadle to take her back to the poorhouse. The poor girl promised amendment and burst into tears.

Master Nic's soft heart felt angered at her treatment. He hated Mrs. Verrall, and had difficulty in restraining himself from expressing his wrath. He was glad to leave this portion of the hive of industry. In his ignorant way he wondered if gloves could only be made by men discontented with their wages, and sewn by poor girls huddled in an upper chamber governed with the rod by a harsh, ugly woman. But seated at the hospitable table of Simon Verrall with Hetty of the brown eyes opposite to him, he soon forgot the sorrows of others in the hive of industry, in his own delight in the garden of love.

The grace was long and the fare was substantial. At the upper end of the table were the family. Mrs. Verrall carved the joint for the foremen and forewomen, who sat in the order of their status below the salt. Ziba, as a favoured servant, replied now and again to a remark from his master or mistress, but the others uttered no word, being intent on their food and ale. At the end of half an hour, a clanging bell rang in the workshop. All rose. Master Verrall pronounced another long and unctuous grace and the servants departed.

" Ziba," said Mrs. Verrall, as the fellow reached the door, " be you ready to accompany Mistress Hester to Westminster ? "

" I shall be in the workshop. She can call me."

" Really, ma'am," said Hester, pouting, " I think Aunt Nan might give me a holiday for once."

" What do you say, wife ? " asked Verrall doubtfully.

" You know best what your Aunt Chilcote is like, Simon. Hetty is not her only great-niece, and if she be treated lightly, she may find another lass to sell gloves in Westminster Hall and not our gloves at that."

" You had best go, child," said Verrall humbly.

" Might I have the honour of being her escort," said Master Nic, looking across at the girl to meet an invitation in her eyes. " I shall be walking that way."

Mistress Hester was pouting and gazing down at her fingers, which played idly on the tablecloth.

Ziba, who was still standing at the doorway, looked eagerly across the room at Mr. Berrington.

" By no means, Mr. Berrington," replied Mrs. Verrall. " It is Ziba's place to go."

" Ay, ma'am," said Ziba willingly, and he turned on his heel and went into the workshop.

Hester followed her stepmother from the room without so much as a glance at Master Nic.

Verrall went to the buffet and brought a decanter of wine and two glasses, which he set on the table before them, and the two were left alone in the parlour.

Nothing was said for a few moments. Master Nic was trying to invent excuses for his departure and wondering what the links might be between beautiful brown eyes, Westminster Hall and great aunt, Nan Chilcote. At length Master Verrall set down his glass and delivered his message.

" Mr. Berrington, since the Lord brought you into my life to save me from destruction I have had it on my mind that He must have some service for me to render to you, since all His ways are just. I have asked you here to show you that I have worldly means beyond my own wants. My good wife brought me money and helped me to make more. I have but one child, and I can provide well for her and my business increases. I do not know your present position in the world, sir, but I am your debtor, and if you can tell me how I can best pay my debt, I shall be under an obligation to you."

Master Nic did not know how to make reply. There was something in the fatherly mien, in the strange medley of piety, worldliness, honesty and gratitude, that was new in his experience of men. He felt he could trust the man. Moreover, he wanted an excuse for revisiting the house in Fetter Lane, which for him had become a holy shrine lighted by celestial brown eyes. He would seek Master Verrall's advice. He was shrewd enough to know that such a course is the most acceptable form of flattery to old men.

" You have very little reason, sir, to be grateful for anything I have done," he replied modestly enough. " These things are the incidents of life, but since you wish me to make use of your services, and you seem to be a man well acquainted with the business of the world, I would not ask money of you—of which at the moment I have no need, but I would ask your advice."

" By all means," replied Master Verrall.

" What I tell you is in confidence."

Master Verrall bowed.

" It will be necessary to tell you a long story, but I will make it as short as may be."

" My time is yours," said his host gravely.

The Child rehearsed, as nearly as he could remember it, the story of his life. There was a dim recollection of a large house in the country, of a funeral, of journeys in waggons, of his life on the Sussex farm. Then he said something of his dead patron, touching lightly on the industries in which he had been engaged. He spoke of the picture which he had been told was his mother's portrait, and passing over all the evil he knew of him, related only the affection and care that Jonathan had lavished upon him.

In the end he said simply : " I begin to find the world I have lived in is not all the world. I have a feeling sometimes that I was not born to it, that I do not belong to it. I want to know who I am."

The last phrase was almost a cry of despair, and Master Verrall replied in a gentle voice of sympathy, " What you tell me is very strange, and I wish I could help you on the moment. But this I do know. A year or two ago I visited my cousin in Freston, and saw Mrs. Johnson, with whom you used to live. We spoke of you, and she with tears in her eyes longed to hear news of you. I gathered that she had been a servant in your mother's household, and that in some way the man Wild had been a figure in your mother's life. There is no doubt that Mrs. Johnson could give you the information you require. From what my cousin said, the belief in the village was that you were of gentle birth and were brought into Sussex from Oxfordshire."

" The Berringtons of Oxfordshire," murmured Master Nic, remembering Mr. Ambrose's question.

" Is there such a family ? " asked his host.

" I know nothing of it," said Master Nic, wearily putting forth his hand, reaching for the decanter and pouring himself out another glass. " What do you advise, sir ? "

" It seems to me," said Verrall thoughtfully, " that Mrs. Johnson can tell you all about your parents and why you came to be in Sussex. Why not go down into Sussex and find out all she can tell you ? "

Master Nic emptied his glass at a gulp and smacked the table heartily with his open hand.

" Damn my liver and bones, sir, you are a regular Solomon ! I'll go home again like the prodigal son." He laughed merrily at the thought of beginning a new adventure.

" Not even from my guest and my preserver will I allow swearing in my house ! " cried Verrall, standing up hastily.

" I beg your pardon, sir," said poor Nic, greatly abashed at his incivility.

" It is not for me to pardon you, sir. Ah, how I wish you were of His fold. I shall pray for you that the Lord will open your eyes to the blessings of His service."

Master Nic could not help thinking of the blessings that had fallen on the apprentices in the attic upstairs, but he was silent on that score, for as he rose to go a thought flashed across his mind that if the beauty of brown eyes beckoned him within the fold, he would leap lightly over the hurdles of dogma and her faith should be his.

All he said was : " My upbringing has not led me in the same paths as yours."

" It is never too late. Nothing is impossible to the Lord," replied Verrall. " Remember if in the future I can be of any service to you in holy things or in matters of this world, I shall not forget my debt."

They shook hands and parted, and as Master Nic walked westward he felt he had found a friend in the world whose value was enhanced a thousandfold in his eyes by the fact that he was the father of the only woman in the world who at that moment was worth a man's winning.

CHAPTER XII

MASTER NIC during the next few days turned over in his mind many cleverly-invented excuses for a further visit to the Verrall household, but the thought of the harsh step-mother, the coldness of his beloved, and his distaste for Mr. Verrall's homilies, kept him from acting upon them. Whilst he was pondering these things over an early cup of chocolate, he suddenly remembered the talk at Verrall's table about Hetty and great-aunt Chilcote.

He cursed himself heartily for not having sought out Mrs. Chilcote at once, and springing out of bed, spent a considerable time in adorning his person for so delicate and important an expedition. Then, seeing that the sun was shining and the streets were dry, he took his best hat and cane and sauntered down to Arundel Stairs, where he hailed a skiff to take him on the flood to Westminster.

Master Nic had never before entered Westminster Hall. It had been a common saying amongst his late friends that where the lawyers were gathered together there was no harvest for smaller thieves. The sight that met his eyes as he pushed in among the throng was a very strange one. At one end of the Hall sat the judges of the Chancery and Queen's Bench, the lawyers crowding before them to listen to the arguments of the cases that were being heard. On the right, in a small, boarded enclosure, was another court in which a trial was pending. The vast floor was crowded with ser-jeants in full-bottomed wigs, barristers in smaller wigs, attorneys and clerks carrying blue sacks filled with books, papers and briefs, anxious clients catching at their lawyers' gowns and pouring their grievances into impatient ears, idle loafers, seedy bail-men, witnesses of both sexes, and a miscellaneous crowd of sightseers and customers pressing round the stalls, which lined either side of the Hall and drove a thriving trade in books, millinery and other wares.

The Child went up to one of the stalls and idly turned

over some prints. The assistant was at his call and rattled
off a string of trade phrases descriptive of their rarity and
beauty.

"By the bye," asked The Child casually, "do you know
if a Mrs. Chilcote has a stall in the Hall?"

"Widow Chilcote?" said the man, laughing. "They
say she has been here since the time of William Rufus." He
pointed to her shop on the other side of the Hall. The Child
threw down the prints and elbowed his way through the
throng, his heart beating impatiently at the thought of his
proximity to the beloved.

A number of counsellors and others were gathered round
Mrs. Chilcote's stall. Some of the bolder of these were
chaffing an old woman who sat in a corner of the small stall
like a witch in a cave, her long crutch stick clasped in her
skinny hands, her little, beady eyes watchful of her stock
of gloves, perfumes, toothpick-cases and such fandangles.

A tall gentleman, elegantly dressed, was leaning over the
counter, that the girl who was serving him might measure
the gloves to his hand. As he came nearer he observed with
annoyance that the customer was my Lord Bassett, and he
hated him with a great hatred. The gloves were bought and
paid for and my Lord still lingered at the stall, leaning over
the counter and whispering to the girl, who laughed and
blushed at his follies, shaking her head.

"But a masquerade, I protest and vow—Mistress Chilcote will bear me out. It is a most harmless pleasure. All the
best people go to these entertainments." My Lord turned
to the old lady with his pleasantest smile and added, "You
were at many in your day, madam, I can swear."

The old lady nodded her head and chuckled at his
flattery.

"Old Nan is wiser than young Nan. Let the girl be, my
Lord. She is a good child and not for such places."

"But a masquerade, Mrs. Chilcote—'tis pure, let me
perish." He caught sight of Master Nic. "What, Mr.
Berrington here. He is a man of fashion, my dear, a friend
of Mr. Quin. Berrington," he called out as Master Nic
came up to the stall, "I want your good word. Let me
ntroduce you to Hetty Verrall, the beauty of Westminster

Hall. She treats me cruelly, and I tell Mistress Chilcote she will lose her my custom. You must help me to persuade Mistress Verrall to make one of a party to a masquerade, and you will join us, eh ? "

" I will see you damned first, my Lord," cries Master Nic, with his cheery laugh, which took all offence out of the menacing words.

" Heroically spoken, faith ! " says my Lord with equal good humour, " but I must have good reason for your threats," and he turned round and looked Master Nic full in the face.

" Indeed you shall, my Lord. There is no offence in it. I have had the pleasure of knowing Mistress Hetty since she was a child. I am a friend of her father. When she goes to a masquerade I trust it will be with me, and three is no company, eh, my Lord ! "

Lord Bassett bowed and moved away.

" And now, Mistress Hetty," said Nic, with an air of an old friend of the family, " I want to buy some gloves."

He stepped boldly into my Lord's place and put his hand across the counter for the girl to measure. And as she lifted up his hand in hers to stretch the glove across it, he was thrilled by her touch and closed his eyes with a sigh of rapture. And when he dared to open them again, the great hall of Westminster, the judges, the counsellors, the throng on the pavement, and even the old woman at the back of the stall, swam out of his vision and vanished into space, and there were only two beings in the universe, Master Nic and his beloved of the brown eyes.

This was the beginning of Master Nic's suit at Westminster. Like many another suit in the old Hall, it ambled along its ancient paths, but slowly and with small profit to the suitor. For Nic found very little opportunity of becoming better acquainted with Mistress Hetty, since the Widow Chilcote kept a keen eye upon him and all the other young sparks who visited the stall to bask in Hetty's brown eyes and when the purchases were made she bade them give place to other customers who were waiting their turn. To speak with the girl on her way to and from her home was not possible unless she had encouraged such a meeting, and when he had made the attempt he found her so distressed at his advances and Ziba so surly and fierce in his demeanour, that he could only turn away, hiding his chagrin beneath a compliment and an elaborate salute.

Even the news that the date of Mr. Quin's trial was fixed did not interest him, and when Billinge told him that it was probable that Bagshot would be sentenced the same day, he only muttered, " Poor devil ! "

" Devil if you please ! " said Billinge hotly, " but why poor ? "

" Our young Lord and Master," said Turquet, smiling, " is full of humour. Nothing is well with him to-day. He sighs when he picks up four aces, and having won three parties at piquet, throws up the cards and curses his luck."

" Then it is a woman at last," said Billinge miserably, but under his breath.

Master Nic either did not hear him or did not heed him. " Billinge," he called out, turning round suddenly, " I want your help. You can remember coming down to Freston when I was a boy there, and you were with Jonathan Wild when he stole me away from the schoolmaster."

" What of that ? " said Billinge, rubbing his broad nose thoughtfully. " What is it you want to know ? "

" I want to know who I am. Why am I called Nic Berrington ? Who do I belong to ? Have I a right to the name, or am I an outcast and a mere adventurer ? "

For the first time in his life Master Nic feared to hear that he was a son of Jonathan Wild. It began to dawn upon him that to be the son of such a man barred him from all hope of winning the hand of Hetty Verrall.

" You remember what you told me, Turquet, of the picture of the beautiful lady that used to hang in Wild's room ? "

The Count nodded.

" What became of the picture, where has it gone, and where did it come from ? "

" I can answer both your questions," said Billinge. " The bailiffs seized all the Master's property, and there was a sale, so the Lord only knows where the picture went to, but I know well where it came from."

K

" Where ? " cried Master Nic eagerly.

" It was hanging in the house of Mr. Luke Crowley, a lawyer of Witney, and the Master taking a fancy to it, I went as instructed and slit it out of its frame and brought it away."

" And Witney, where is Witney ? " asked Nic excitedly. " Not in Oxfordshire ? "

" Where else should it be ? " said Turquet, who began to be interested. " I never heard this story before, let us know all about it."

Billinge told, in all the circumstance he could call to mind, the story of Wild's ride into Oxfordshire and his long interview with Crowley, and how on coming away from Witney they made straight for Dunstable and rescued The Child from the clutches of the Reverend Daniel Adamson. Master Nic listened intently, looking at the Count as if to see what he made of the story.

" Does it seem to you, Turquet, to solve any difficulties ? " he asked anxiously.

" At least it makes your task no harder. Clearly Mr. Luke Crowley, the lawyer of Witney, could give some information of your history if he will do so, but the person who must know about it is Granny Johnson, if what Verrall told you is true. There seem to be Berringtons in Oxfordshire, and it seems reasonable to believe you are connected with them."

" I must know all about it," said Master Nic earnestly.

" A philosopher said that the mind anxious about the future is unhappy," said Turquet, laughing at his eagerness.

" I must know the best or the worst of the past," replied Master Nic, " and to-morrow I ride into Sussex."

" The day after to-morrow," answered the Count, " to-morrow you give evidence for Mr. Quin."

Early on the morning of Mr. Quin's trial Master Nic arrayed himself in a suit of very sober apparel carefully designed for the occasion, with the assistance of Turquet, who also superintended the dressing of his wig, so that he might appear before the jury as a young man of good family and of a peaceable and studious disposition who honoured with his patronage and friendship the great actor.

They all went in a coach to the Old Bailey and found a

large congregation of well-known men of the world had
already secured places in the court.

The Grand Jury brought in a true bill against Mr. Quin.
A jury was now empanelled and sworn, after the Crown
had challenged two Irishmen, who left the jury with marked
regret. Counsel opened the case, and called Simon Verrall
to the witness-box. His fair-minded account of the matter
put heart into the prisoner's friends. Then Master Nic's
own evidence was given, and he was pleased to find that
he was allowed to bring out everything he wished in Mr.
Quin's favour.

At the end of the evidence it seemed very unfair to his
young mind that though two lawyers had had their say
against Mr. Quin, he was not allowed to hire a lawyer to
speak on his behalf. But this, as Master Verrall explained
to him, could never be permitted, since if it were, all
criminals would hire lawyers to plead for them, and there
might in that case be grave difficulty in obtaining con-
victions.

But when he heard the clear sonorous voice of Mr. Quin
openly admitting, in tones of well-restrained grief and
sorrow, his honest confession of the wrong he had done his
fellow-actor upon the stage, and his deep regret that he
could not have avoided the accident that caused his death,
Master Nic felt that no advocate, however eloquent and
ingenious, could have done so much for his friend's defence
as he was doing for himself. He was deeply overcome when
he depicted his poor friend Williams dying in the arms
of his friend Mr. Berrington, and twice repeated poor
Williams' generous dying message to the jury. " Tell them
I asked him for satisfaction. It is my own fault. They must
not punish him."

Reminding the jury that two Irishmen had been asked
by the Crown to leave the box, he said he was glad it was
so, and thus, placing one hand on his heart and opening the
other outstretched in appeal to the jury, he brought his
modest discourse to an end in a passionate burst of eloquence : " Confident, gentlemen, of my own innocence and
the English discernment to trace out the truth wheresoever
it may be hid, I would not have it said that I owed my life,

or what is dearer, my honour, to the undeserved favour of my own countrymen—I am proud to have been tried by a jury of Englishmen, for if my honour is not saved, I cannot much wish for the preservation of my life. Thus I wait, gentlemen, the determinations of yourselves and the court with that confidence, I hope, which innocence has a right to enjoy."

There was a deep murmur of applause as Mr. Quin concluded and the usher called out " Silence ! "

" A damned fine piece of play-acting," whispered my Lord Bassett.

He was standing near the dock by Master Nic, having been called as a witness to prove on his honour as a peer of the realm the high moral character of Mr. Quin.

Master Nic was wiping tears from his eyes, and My Lord's words grated on the fine edge of his feelings.

" How dare you ! " he sobbed, " it was beautiful ! "

My Lord smiled pleasantly at his young friend.

" Beautiful ! I should say it was beautiful. Johnny Gay wrote it for him, and he gave it us at the ' Rose ' last night after supper. But when Quin speaks it—ah, you are right, Mr. Berrington—such acting deserves tears."

The Recorder's summing-up was short and very favourable to Mr. Quin, and when it was ended it was seen that the jury made no movement to leave the box, but seemed ready to give their verdict without delay. Master Nic in his ignorance feared for a moment that they had already made up their minds against Mr. Quin, but in a few minutes the jurors stood up and, to his intense joy and relief, acquitted him of murder and manslaughter, and found a verdict of self-defence.

Mr. Quin bowed gravely to the court and the jurors and stepped gracefully from the dock, shaking Master Nic cordially by the hand as, with a few whispered words of thanks, he passed him and made his way through a crowd of sympathisers and friends out into the courtyard.

Master Nic, who, with his two friends, had to wait until Captain Bagshot was put in the dock, to his great regret could not join him. And now the Grand Jury carried in a sheaf of true bills and handed the indictments to the clerk, and the warders brought up from a room below a dozen or more wretched-looking men, thieves, murderers, and other villains, and among them Bagshot. And Master Nic had perforce to listen to several trials in which poor wretches were proved to have stolen small amounts of money or trifling articles of property, and in a few minutes they pleaded guilty or the necessary oaths were taken and they were swept away to the gallows or transportation. And just before the dinner-hour of the court, Bagshot was put up and pleaded guilty to one of several indictments for robbery that were read out against him. The counsel for the prosecution were satisfied with this course, but Master Nic and his friends were intensely disgusted at the turn things had taken, for they feared that some deal had been made between him and the authorities, as in those days not infrequently happened.

And although he was duly sentenced to death, Master Nic had no joy in it, for it was openly rumoured that he had offered in Newgate to betray further comrades to the law and had prayed in aid his betrayal of Wild, so that it was whispered round the court that his plea of guilty might even yet save his neck and his sentence be commuted to transportation.

But on Sunday Billinge came in with the pleasant news that Bagshot was among those unlucky ones who were seated in the condemned pew at Newgate, and this confirmed Turquet's advice from Sir James Hezlet that Bagshot would certainly be hanged on Wednesday, though he had made several offers of providing fresh food for the gallows from among his former comrades.

These tidings gave the three friends great pleasure, and Master Nic informed the others that on Monday he intended to make arrangements to go down to Sussex after the execution, and would be up early and go in search of Captain Johnson, for if he happened to be sailing down the river, he might give him a passage. This course Turquet strongly approved, and early on Monday morning Master Nic made his way across the Temple, through Blackfriars, and along Thames Street to Billingsgate, until he arrived at the back door of the " Magpie and Stump."

"Is Captain Roger Johnson in town, ma'am?" he asked when an old woman opened the door.

"Bless you now," she said, recognising him and pulling him inside, "the Captain only left yesterday morning."

"It matters little," said Nic cheerily. "I shall reach Sussex more quickly on horseback."

But the old woman, who was a seafaring man's widow, shook her head at this.

"You must never think of journeying by road if a ship is to be had. What with foot-pads and robbers, it marvels me how any can be found to travel in a post-chaise by road when they can have a snug berth in a tight boat for half the money. Now let me see, Annie!" she called to a serving wench, "run up to the parlour, my dear, and see if Captain Gregory is there and tell him I want a word with him."

Captain Gregory, master of the schooner *Medusa*, of a hundred and twenty tons burthen, came rolling down into the kitchen at the landlady's call. I say rolling, because he was a little round tub of a seafaring man with a pock-marked, pudding face framed in a fringe of scanty red tow. His bandy legs caused him to walk with a swinging see-saw gait which may have steadied his motions on board ship, but seemed to give the little kitchen the rolling motion of a ship's cabin.

Master Nic was not favourably impressed by the little man, but he was so courteous and civil in his rough way when he heard that the young gentleman was a friend of Captain Johnson, that Master Nic, who was himself without guile, shook him frankly by the hand and accepted his invitation to a morning draught of old ale in the friendly spirit in which it appeared to be offered.

He now opened out his business to him without delay. He explained that he had come to the inn to find Captain Johnson to sail with him to Newhaven, and if Captain Gregory was going down channel and could drop him at Newhaven, or better still at the mouth of the Cuxton river, which runs into the sea between that harbour and Beachy Head, Master Nic would willingly pay him for that service.

"I'm more than half a sailor," he added, "and have made

many a voyage with *The Lively Kate*, and a couple of days at sea will be a treat to me."

"The devil it will!" said the Captain. "Then I'm your man."

" Where are you bound for, Captain ? "

Captain Gregory closed one eye and looked at him thoughtfully.

" As a friend of Captain Johnson's, sir, and as one who has sailed with him and has the run of this house, I take it I may tell you in confidence that there is cargoes and cargoes, and that cockets and cargoes ain't always what they seem to be."

The Child nodded as one to whom these things were not information.

" I'm chartered this voyage, and it all depends on Gravesend. London customs house officials is men and brothers. I can deal with them. But these Gravesend fellows is a spiteful, mean, prying lot. They want to keep you there under the Tilbury guns and go poking about the hold making you lose the tides, and you haven't only to buy one of them, you have to buy half-a-dozen. I may have to run Gravesend. That's the truth."

This candid conduct of the Captain convinced Master Nic how wrong he had been in judging of the Captain by the mere look of the man. The plan of running Gravesend and outwitting the Custom-house fellows was so thoroughly suited to his outlook on life that he closed with the Captain then and there. He agreed to send his portmanteau down to the inn and meet the Captain on Wednesday afternoon. This would enable him to see Hetty before he left and go with his friends to the hanging at Tyburn on the Wednesday morning.

" A likely young fellow enough," said the Captain to his landlady when Master Nic was gone.

" There, don't you play him no tricks," said the old woman, " for he is well in with Roger Johnson."

Now Captain Gregory had had the misfortune to carry away a portion of *The Lively Kate's* taffrail as he was taking up moorings alongside of her at Havre some eight or nine months ago, and since then the two captains were only on cursing terms. But of this incident the good landlady was ignorant.

CHAPTER XIII

MASTER NIC was full of his good luck in having met with such a jolly fellow as Captain Gregory and a trifle nettled at himself for not discerning his good qualities on the first view of him. It was a glorious summer morning. He sat himself down on a seat in the Temple Gardens to watch the boats drifting up the river, for there was little breeze to fill their sails. The joy of future achievement filled his young mind, a joy which brings to youth more lasting pleasure than can ever be obtained from present industry.

This was his dream. He was the scion of a noble race, the Berringtons of Oxfordshire. Granny Johnson would reveal to him the mystery of his birth. He would then return to his ancestral home. The good lawyer, Mr. Crowley, would introduce him to his family. He would find relations ready to acknowledge him. He would acquaint Master Verrall of his new position. The glove-maker would favour his suit. Hetty would no longer treat him coldly, but would throw herself into his arms, and he would carry her off in a chaise and four to be met in his native village by a peal of church bells and the rejoicings of the inhabitants.

Master Nic sighed contentedly over his daydream, and was beginning to repeat it over again with added detail when the pleasant sound of a girl's voice brought him back to earth and the Temple Gardens again.

" Strike me dead if it isn't The Child ! "

Nic started to his feet and found himself face to face with Jenny, dear, delightful Jenny. She wore a large hoop of the latest fashion, and her hair was a small mountain crested by a large hat and feathers.

" Jenny," said Nic saucily, " those are better togs than what you wore when I last saw you."

He gazed at her in frank admiration. Jenny pouted.

" You might have come to see me and brought me those

138

guineas for the ring instead of sending Toby. But I will forgive you. You shall take me to Bartholomew Fair."

"I should have thought you had had enough of picking pockets," said Master Nic. "For my part I have left it alone."

"Picking pockets, indeed. I have apartments of my own in Bond Street nowadays, only my lord having gone with some friends out to Richmond, I came as far as the New Exchange to buy a tea-board and some other toys, and now I have found you we will go to the Fair together."

She looked so daintily pretty in her clever fal-lals, which seemed cunningly made to deck out her figure—all except the hoop, and that was provokingly tilted to show her elegant silk stockings—that Master Nic would have been less than a human youth if he had not stopped a moment to gaze at so much prettiness ere he told her that he must deny himself the pleasure of taking her to Bartholomew Fair.

And what we pause to deny ourselves the devil often insists on making us a gift of at the instant. For the girl, catching the youth's eye gazing at her, began laughing immoderately so that he was fain to ask her what amused her, and she, between her outbursts of mirth, conjured up a blush beneath the paint on her face and, striking Master Nic with her fan, declared he was thinking of the time he had last seen her, and had carried her into the boat, and that he was a nasty, low wretch to remember such shame of her. To which it became necessary for Master Nic to make many protestations of the innocence of his thoughts, and by the time he had convinced the fair Jenny of his respect and affection for herself, her arm was in his and she was leaning on his shoulder, and they were strolling together up the Middle Temple Lane. For The Child, as we may still call him, was like any other young fool, only too proud to convey so much beauty, glorified by such fine apparel, and to notice the nods and smiles of approbation of the passers-by in the street as he handed my lady into a hackney coach and, jumping in after her, ordered the driver to make for Bartholomew Fair.

Bartholomew Fair was a joy after Master Nic's own heart. There was noise and gaiety and shows and feasting, and man, woman and child were all intent on their coarse, human, senseless way of throwing off the cares of the world and revelling in the fun of life. Nor could you have a jollier companion for such a jaunt than pretty Jenny. There was no squeamish niceness about the girl that hindered her from seeing this sight, or joining in that romp, or listening to the players' gibes. Jenny was a London lass and, like all her sort, loved a show or a fair, and knew well the ins and outs of Bartholomew's and how to get the best and the merriest of it all.

" We will have the day of our lives," said the delighted girl, clapping her hands together as the coach rattled up Fleet Street.

" And this time you shall kiss me before we start," said Master Nic, slyly alluding to their last adventure and gallantly pulling her towards him.

" Curse you ! " cried Jenny, only half in anger. " You will ruin my hair. Be easy now ; be easy. You are crumpling my sash. Oh, do a-done ! "

Master Nic remembered a saying of Granny's that when a girl said, " Oh ! do a-done ! " it was an invitation to more caresses, so he plied her with kisses till she shouted, " A-done do ! " when he knew from the same authority that the girl considered the fun had gone far enough.

And whilst this merry comedy was forward in the coach, the driver had turned up Fetter Lane and on the doorstep stood Mrs. Verrall, her thin, grim face peering curiously at the romping boy and girl, maliciously pleased at the thought of telling her husband what she had seen of his friend, and full of pious gratitude to the Lord that she was not as other women are.

As they neared the Fair-ground they seemed to enter a procession of coaches and foot-passengers all making their way towards the same goal. At length, so thick were the people and carriages on the ground, that Jenny and her companion, impatient of their slow movement and tired of shouting and chaffering with the mob, jumped out and joined those on foot, and in that way, with a deal of elbow labour, pushed as far as Pye Corner.

The first thing to be done was to eat roast pork, and here

were all the cook-shops, the cooks standing at their doors bellowing out the excellencies of their pigs and pork. Master Nic and Jenny entered one of these and sat down in a suffocating kitchen to large platters of pork cut from a pig that a fat fellow was roasting at a spit in front of a large fire. The pig sauce at this establishment was a special brand of spice and apples, the secret of which was much vaunted by the proprietor, though others said their sauces were more wholesome and savoury.

After the cook-shops, with their pork and ale, they scrambled through the crowd towards the booths, stopping on the way for a tot of Geneva from one of the many gin stalls that were to be found in every part of the Fair. After that Jenny must eat some sweet cakes, and then Master Nic must buy her some fancy at one of the ribbon shops, and all this amid the wildest confusion of tongues and trumpets and drums and whistling cat-calls and bawling that ever was heard. For some shouted, " Nuts and damsons ! " " Buy my cucumbers to pickle ! " " Here's your rare Holland socks, four pairs for a shilling ! " " Knives to grind ! " all in different tones, but never ceasing to repeat their call ; whilst drolls and mountebanks rushed out of their booths crying out, " See Jephthah's Rash Vow ! " " See ' The Tiger ' ! " " See ' The Horse and No Horse, whose tail stands where his head should do ' ! " " See ' The Double Girl ' ! " " The Grimacing Spaniard," " The German woman without hands or feet," " See ' The greatest rope dancers in Europe ' ! "

Truly there was such a profusion of sights that one did not know where to make beginning, and it was not worth while to pay money to go inside the booths until one had made the round of the Fair to see what could be seen outside for nothing.

Jenny and her companion went from booth to booth, laughing and wondering at the racket and buffoonery with the rest of the crowd. And as evening came, the tents were lighted with lanterns without and candles within, and the throng became thicker, for in the dark of the night many who did not care to be seen in daylight made parties from the West End and came down to the Fair. You might often see Sir Robert Walpole and his friends, or even the Prince of Wales and some of the Leicester House circle, enjoying the fun of the fair with the best of them, and the people liked them the better that they did not despise the holiday of the mob.

The happy couple had more cakes and gin and joined a circle of other young fools like themselves, and ended on the roundabouts, mounted on their hobby-horses, blowing trumpets and shouting snatches of ballads, sitting in the great wheel which carried you up towards the stars in swinging carriages, so that you could look down on the crowd lighted up by smoking flares and the Fair appeared for all the world like a merry parody of hell.

" The largest elephant in the world except himself " had fired off his cannon and stood with his four feet on a tub, and nothing remained to be seen but the rope-dancers. They had kept that show for the last, and pushed their way into the tent with the crush. They sat close together among the stifling press of folk on the low benches, and stared their eyes out at the wonders of the dancers. Each out-did the other in their perilous activities. And now the German woman came of whom the whole town was talking. Her trick was to dance on the rope in the costume of a peasant woman, in clogs or sabots, and bit by bit throw away her foot-gear, and skirts and petticoat and bodice, until the final garments were reached, and the men roared and the women giggled and cried shame, but all enjoyed it mightily, and then in a blaze of fireworks, as she leaped in the air, everything disappeared, but the lady bounded on to the stage in the modest tights of the circus-dancer and, kissing her hands to the cheering audience, departed through the curtains at the back of the tent.

" That was a fine show," said Master Nic critically. " I could see it a dozen times."

" These foreign women will do anything," said Jenny scornfully. " Fancy undressing like that in a tent full of people ! "

They were outside pushing through the crowds.

" You must find me a coach, and I must be getting back west," said Jenny.

"I'll find you a coach sure enough, but you don't go home yet," said Master Nic, holding her arm tight in his. "We have supper at 'The Rose' to-night."

"If my lord only knew, he would kill me!" said Jenny, clinging the while more lovingly to her friend's arm. "He's very jealous."

"Damn my lord, whoever he is!" replied Master Nic valiantly. "You are mine to-night, and we have supper at 'The Rose,' and then I'll drive you home or anywhere you have a mind to go," and he pulled her to him and kissed her, which was a very proper and natural thing to do at that time of evening at Bartholomew Fair.

Outside, near Smithfield, they found a hackney-coach, and bargained with the man to drive to 'The Rose' in Covent Garden.

"How I wish you were rich like my lord," said Jenny with a sigh, as she put her head on Master Nic's shoulder, "and then I could live with you always."

"Who knows but I may be rich some of these days," said the young fool with appropriate mystery.

Jenny remembered what Molly Straddle had said.

"Have you come into your kingdom, my king?"

"When I do, will you be queen of it, Jenny?"

She threw her arms round young Nic affectionately, and all his fleeting thoughts of right and wrong dissolved beneath the warmth of her caresses.

It is an accursed thing that so sweet an idyll of love should be disturbed by the rough humours of a political mob, but the truth of history cannot be gainsaid, and as the coach rolled into Drury Lane it was encountered by a shouting mass of drunken Jacks with torches and picks and axes cursing the dissenters and praising the Church with fierce oaths and loyal execrations.

These outbursts occurred from time to time, and at long last culminated in the great riots that burned half this part of London. The cause of the trouble on this occasion was an indiscreet sermon of the Rev. Mr. Westerman, the pastor of a little chapel near Lincoln's Inn Fields.

The driver of the coach had carried them right into the mob before they knew where they were. Some men seized the horses, and a rough shock-headed fellow with a link in his hand pulled open the door and demanded to know whether they stood for the Church.

"The Church for ever!" shouted Master Nic tactfully.

"Hurrah!" shouted the man. "A friend, my boys. A friend. Come with us, sir."

He caught him by the wrist to pull him out. Master Nic whispered to Jenny: "Shout for the Church, girl!" as he jumped out among the rest.

"Hurrah for the Church!" he cried, throwing up his hat. "Drive on, fellow!" he called out to the coachman.

Jenny put her head out of the window and waved her kerchief, screaming her enthusiasm for the Church. The mob cheered her loudly, the horses were released, and she drove away in triumph. Master Nic was swept up in the crowd, and away they went towards Lincoln's Inn Fields crying, "To the meeting-houses! Burn them! Westerman's first!"

Master Nic remembered with a chill at his heart that Simon Verrall and his household worshipped at the meeting-house of the Reverend Silas Westerman. But it was Monday. The little chapel would probably be empty.

Unfortunately, the congregation on this very evening had met for one of their love feasts, which often lasted well into the night. The main business of the evening, which always excited great enthusiasm, came after the service, when members of the congregation came and poured forth their spiritual biographies.

Hetty, who had come with her stepmother, watched the service from a pew in the gallery. Her father was not present, having made a journey into Somerset on business affairs. Hetty had never been moved to share her spiritual history with the rest of the congregation, but she listened with awe to the horrible revelations of her saved sisters, and prayed for them fervently and added her sweet voice to their prayers of praise or despair.

It was about nine o'clock, and the service was at its height, when shouts and tumults were heard in the street, the noise increasing as the mob approached the Fields. Ziba Grime, who was seated near the doorway, had gone out

into the street to see what was the cause of it, and rushed
back to the meeting-house, calling out in the middle of a
hymn, " There is a huge Church mob mad with drink.
They will pull the meeting-house down."

The congregation, already excited and exalted, flew into
a mad panic. Many on the ground floor escaped at the centre
or side doors. Mrs. Verrall ran down the gallery stairs and
out at the back door, but Hetty, giving way to some older
women, was too late to escape. The Reverend Silas Westerman strove to get control of the excited congregation. He
ordered the doors to be closed, and this was done. Then, in
stentorian voice, he offered up a prayer for the sinners and
outcasts who were led astray by the idolatrous priests of
the Church and incited to destroy the meeting-houses of
the Lord's people.

Outside the mob approached with shouts of triumph. An
old watchman going his rounds turned his steps away from
the wrongdoers, an over-bold constable spoke to one of
the ringleaders, and was hustled along with the mob, held
by two or three stalwart fellows that he might not get away
and bring the soldiers on them. There were several footmen
in the crowd, and the leader of the mob was a tall fellow in
green livery, with red buttons and red stockings. He carried
in his hand a tall pole with a green curtain attached to it,
a trophy they had carried off from the Reverend John
Bradbury's meeting-house at Hatton Garden, which they
had already wrecked.

When they came to Westerman's meeting-house the
fellows who had hold of Master Nic let him go, for all were
now mad on burning it down or wrecking it.

The footman captain threw up his wig and hallooed for
the Church. Shouts went up in execration of the dissenters,
and the sound of the minister's prayer in the meeting-house
seemed to incense them to deeper rage.

" Burn the devils out like rats ! " cried some.

" Huzza ! Fire ! Damn the Dissenters ! Damn the guards !
Damn the Parliament ! Three cheers for the Church ! "

With these wild cries and hallooing like madmen, the
mob brought scraps of laths and timber from a new building
near by, and some got a couple of bavins from a wood-

store, and before any had time to think of the result, a tin of oil and a match had made a blaze which jumped to the upper windows of the meeting-house.

There arose from inside a shriek of women in terror and agony that went to the heart of the senseless mob, and they stood for a second of time silent and horror-struck at what they were doing.

Master Nic, who was near the door, jumped on the steps of the meeting-house and shouted, " Have done with this, boys. Let the women out."

" Are you an enemy to the Church ? " shouted the red footman with an oath.

" The Church doesn't want to burn women and children."

" That's right, master," said a couple of drunken sailors, and the footman, with great political wisdom, seeing that the mob were for deserting him, gave orders for the door to be broken open.

One seized a pick and tried to prise it open, others battered it with an axe, and several pulled the burning brands away to get at the job. But the fire kept its hold, and it was some little time before the door fell in with a crash, and through the smoke and dust burst a crowd of frenzied men and women, mad with terror, into the arms of the drunken mob. Some escaped down alleys or were dragged into neighbouring houses, but others were caught by the ruffians and the men knocked down and trampled upon, whilst the women had their clothes thrown over their heads or torn off their backs, and were slapped and cuffed through the mob amidst drunken cheers and coarse laughter. All of which was done with many " huzzas " and much hallooing and cursing of dissenters to the glory of God and the Church and to the unfeigned delight of these stalwart Churchmen.

Whilst this devil's chase of the wretched women continued, the minister came to the burning threshold of the meeting-house, his pale face glowing in the fire.

" For God's sake, if you be men and not fiends, help to put out the fire."

Ziba rushed out, his face blackened with smoke, shrieking : " The stair has fallen. The women in the gallery are doomed ! "

You could see the poor things at an upper window and hear their piercing cries. The mob, who had been all for maltreating them or even murdering them a moment ago, were now seized with a desire to save them, but no one had a notion how it could be done.

Master Nic and his drunken sailors were working hard to pull down the burning laths, some neighbours fearing an extension of the fire had brought pails of water and were throwing it on the flames with but small results. When Master Nic caught sight of Ziba, he rushed at him and seized the dazed man by his arms.

" Is Miss Hetty here ? " he cried. " Tell me, she is safe."

" The gallery ! The gallery ! " called out Ziba, choking. " The gallery ! "

Master Nic remembered seeing a ladder at the new building where the laths came from. He yelled his commands to the sailors, and several others ran to him ready to follow the word of a man who knew how to lead. The ladder was tied to the scaffolding. A sailor ran up it like a cat, a clasp knife in his mouth, and cut the ropes. Master Nic slashed the lower ropes away with his sword. The fickle mob cheered as they ran it across the street and reared it up against the window.

Master Nic climbed up with one of the sailors, and willing hands held it firm below. Several women were passed down it and saved. Poor Hetty was so dazed with terror, she could only cling to Master Nic and cry to him not to leave her.

" You must go now, Hetty," he whispered.

The sailor went down first to hold her. Master Nic loosed her arms.

" Be brave, dear. It is safe. Be quick. Now ! "

" I durst not. I can't do it," she cried.

" Then there is no hope. I am content."

She understood what he meant, and calmed herself for the effort.

" I will go," she whispered.

He lifted her on to the ladder. The sailor steadied her.

L

"I kiss you good-bye," he said, holding her by the arms and lowering her gently down. As he reached over the sill and leaned down, now holding her only by the wrists, the sailor called upon him to let go, and he kissed the dear hand that still clung to him, and heard the men below call out, "All's well!" and several cheered lustily. He pulled himself back, turned and threw his leg on to the ladder, and was following her as quick as might be, when the wall itself fell in with a crash and he disappeared into a mass of bricks and beams and dust and smoke.

The cheers died into a groan, and then all was silent. The mob listened intently. From the west came the roll of drums. The Guards were upon them from St. James's. The rabble sneaked away southward to the Strand or north towards Finsbury, and when the Guards rode in to the Fields they only found a few citizens helping to put out the smouldering fire. But there stood the ruins of the little meeting-house as a memorial of how Christians loved one another two hundred years ago.

CHAPTER XIV

THE PASSING OF BAGSHOT

WHEN Jenny had escaped from the mob, leaving Nic in the hands of the Philistines, she had made straight for Wych Street, but finding no one there, had left word with Mrs. Metyard of what had happened. Billinge, coming in later, had rushed to the spot and, with the help of the soldiers and other willing citizens, had rescued Master Nic and carried him home in a coach. A doctor had been sent for. There were no broken bones, and but for some bruises and a spoilt suit of clothes, Master Nic was little the worse for his adventure.

Toby nursed him tenderly all Tuesday and prevailed upon him to remain in bed that he might be fit to enjoy the outing to Tyburn on Wednesday. It would have been a sad disappointment to both of them if they could not have gone together to Tyburn to see Bagshot hanged.

Wednesday was London's hanging day. Men, women and children flocked to Tyburn to see the carts arrive and the criminals turned off by the hangman. Master Nic cursed Toby merrily when he wakened him from his slumbers on Wednesday morning, for he was roused from a beautiful dream of which he was the hero, in which, after a long string of adventures, he was at last carrying a lovely princess with brown eyes across the tops of raging waves, stepping lightly from crest to crest towards a golden island of eternal blessedness.

" Bagshot's to be hanged this morning," announced Billinge with grim pleasure.

Master Nic yawned. Billinge repeated the announcement. Master Nic stretched himself. He did not seem as eager about the treat as he should have been. Toby was puzzled, and again repeated the news.

" Well, well," said Nic, rubbing his eyes. " I'm all right

this morning, and I suppose I ought to go. Yes, I'll get up at once. I must go and see Hetty later, I suppose."

" Hetty ! " grumbled Toby. " Hetty ! What do we want with Hetty ? "

Turquet, who looked in at that moment, threw up his head and repeated mockingly, " What do we want with Hetty ? My good Toby, what did Adam want with Eve ? What did Anthony want with Cleopatra ? What did Romeo want with Juliet ? "

The Child sat up in bed and nodded pleasantly to the Count.

" You, sir," he said with a show of dignity, " can appreciate the happiness of a man who discovers that he is not unacceptable to the only woman he ever loved."

" Child," replied Turquet gravely, " it is an experience I have gone through half a hundred times, and hope I am not too old to recapture its joys once again ; but I, too, ask, why Hetty ? For when I had the honour to attend Sir Robert Walpole to Bartholomew's Fair on Monday afternoon, I could have laid odds the lady's name was Jenny."

" A fine strapping lass, too, and all you want for the present," cried Billinge enthusiastically. " None of those psalm-singing city madams."

" Stow that, Toby ! " cried Master Nic angrily, jumping out of bed and reaching for his clothes.

" Our friend," interrupted the Count, " is provokingly inarticulate, but his meaning is, I think, sound. What he means you to understand, Toby, is that just as a seafaring man learns his business in light vessels on short voyages, so a wise mariner in love may do worse than make short excursions with pleasure craft before he ventures on the unknown ocean of matrimony."

" That were treachery to the woman I love," said Nic, gravely shaking his head in sublime forgetfulness of Bartholomew Fair.

For since Monday afternoon he had gazed close into Hetty's brown eyes and pressed his lips to hers and carried her in his arms. The sun had gone down on his past and risen brightly on a glorious dawn.

Turquet, who had seen many such sunsets and sunrises,

laughingly replied : " Business first and pleasure afterwards. It is eight o'clock now, and if we are to get good places it is time we were away. When we have seen the end of Bagshot, you can fly to your mistress and tell her all about it."

The three friends took a hackney-coach and drove through Piccadilly and Berkeley Square to one of the side lanes running into Oxford Street, where they joined the merry throng that was swarming along the highway to Tyburn.

Arrived at the scene of execution, they found three good places reserved for them on a stand, which was a business speculation of a Charing Cross publican, an old friend of Billinge. From this eminence they could see all the fun going on in the crowd below them. At stands or barrows, gingerbread, nuts, apples and the favourite Geneva were doing a brisk trade at cheap rates. Ballad-mongers were selling the latest doggerel from Grub Street descriptive of the life and crimes of Captain Bagshot. Cripples were begging, low-class pickpockets were dodging in and out of the crowd, men and women, the scum and riff-raff of the City, were quarrelling and fighting among themselves, and the merry ones among them were hoarding dead cats and dogs and rotten fruit to hurl at the unfortunate fellows in the carts, as a last parting salute to their fellow human beings who were to be pushed off from the world's edge to that last voyage into eternity that each of us must make in his turn.

The waiting mob yelled with pleasure as the Sheriff's coach came into view. Master Nic craned his neck with the others to see the first glimpse of the procession. Yes, there was the hated Bagshot lying in the cart. He had spent his last night on earth drinking to drown his misery, and his yellow, sodden face and sunken, dull eyes might have brought pity to any heart. But the crowd hated him. Jolly, roystering highwaymen they loved and honoured, but this fellow was a cruel brute and cut off his victim's fingers, and tortured as well as stole, so out came the dogs and cats and rotten vegetables and refuse, and the soldiers had to force a way through the crowd to bring him to the gallows. Even

Nic was weak enough to feel a sneaking sense of pity for him.

In the next cart a girl was sitting on her coffin, a baby in her arms. She had been a shoplifter, and the law, in its supreme wisdom, demanded the life of the young mother. A groan of pity arose from the hoarse throats of the mob— strange music from such an organ—but the change seemed a relief even to themselves after so much cursing and exe- cration A curious, uneasy silence fell on the crowd as a man tore the child away from the fainting woman and handed it to the parish beadle, who stood near, and the poor wretch was carried on to the large cart that stood beneath the fatal tree. But all was merry again in a moment. A sailor lad, who had knifed another boy in Thames Street, was bowing and smiling to his pals as they crowded round the cart to shake him by the hand, and gave him a jovial send- off into the Everlasting. He was a popular figure with the crowd, and they greeted him with loud huzzas.

And now seven fellow-men and women are drawn under the triple tree in their carts, and caps are pulled down over their faces and the ropes properly arranged by the hangman, who goes about his business carefully, as a good craftsman should. Turquet's eyes are fixed on Bagshot with stern satisfaction. The game is over, his adversary has lost the rubber, and the Count is pleased. Toby stares at it all with open delight, his only sorrow is the natural human regret of a child at a show which he loves when it comes to the fall of the curtain. But that poor, weak child, Master Nic, dared not look up for fear he should see the frail figure of the little shoplifter dangling at the end of the rope. He closed his eyes and thought of Hetty, and then his mind passed to Granny and the days of his childhood, and he was seated again in the little church at Freston, and he seemed to hear Parson Oliver droning out the text: " For if ye forgive men their trespasses, your heavenly Father will also forgive you : but if ye forgive not men their trespasses, neither will your Father forgive your trespasses."

A few hours afterwards, Master Nic, having dined well with his friends at a cook-shop in the Strand, had recovered his natural spirits, and was seated with Turquet at the " Cock

Tavern " over a bottle of Mountain. Billinge had gone to Bow Street on business, and Nic was impatient to run off to Fetter Lane, but the Count had matters of importance to discuss with him and, somewhat against his will, had carried him off to " The Cock."

" I am going to ask you a straight question," said the Count, leaning across the table so that Nic might hear his words without their reaching others in the room. " Do you propose to marry this girl, Hester Verrall ? "

Master Nic looked in his face with a radiant smile, his eyes sparkling with youthful astonishment that such a question should be asked.

" Why, Turquet ! My dear Turquet, can you, can any man believe——"

Turquet interrupted his rhapsody ere it had got well under way.

" Enough," he replied. " I propose to help you to that desirable end."

Master Nic seized him by the hand and pressed it affectionately ; he filled their glasses and drank " To Hetty, the fairest of the fair." The Count repeated the toast solemnly.

" In the first place," he continued, " let me put forward my point of view. You must know that when I reported the matter of your Mr. Ambrose to Sir James, he carried me off to Sir Robert Walpole, who has been graciously pleased to wish to take me into his service. He is a man I can serve under. True, he has not the *tournure du monde* that our good friend Jonathan Wild possessed, but he has the same great qualities. Moreover, his trade and business, though similar in essentials to that of Master Jonathan, has a wider scope, and it is a safer service, since roguery on a large scale has always been safer from the pains of justice than crime of a petty character. Sir Robert has work of importance for me in France if I will undertake it."

" And what hinders you ? " asked Master Nic carelessly.

" I will put it this way. If you were married and settled in the world, I should go with a more equal mind."

Master Nic laughed.

" You are still under the absurd impression that you and Billinge are looking after me. I love you for it, Turquet, really I do—but if you think of it, is it not almost the other way about ? "

" Senility must bow to the wisdom of manhood. But as I may be called away to France for a short visit at any moment, I want to give you a few words of advice. In the first place, I should go down to Sussex and find out what is known of your birth and station."

" I have already made arrangements to go into Sussex. So far we are agreed."

" Assume, then," continued the Count, " you return with the certainty that you are a gentleman by birth. You go to this glove-making dissenter and demand his daughter. These mechanical traders have strange notions. He may refuse his consent or ask you to wait until you recover your position in the eyes of the world, and your estate, if there be one."

" And what then, Turquet ? "

" Then you marry your fair one. Once marry her and her father must use his wealth to support your claims and help his daughter to a greater position in the world."

" But Hetty—you don't know Hetty—she would not leave her father in that way——"

" Hetty ! " cried the Count, laughing derisively. " I don't know your Hetty, but things which are equal to the same thing are equal to one another, and I know any number of other Hetties and Lucies and Sophies and Maries and Clarettes. As Nicholas Berrington, a gentleman by birth, you will appeal to the vanity and love of your fair mistress. She falls into your arms first and marries you afterwards, or if your lordship pleases, you take a hackney coach to the Fleet and then enjoy the honeymoon. The great thing is to marry her, secure her father's money-bags, and with them restore your fortunes."

" You are talking nonsense," said Master Nic angrily, rising from the table—"offensive nonsense ; at least," he added in a pleasanter tone, " it would be offensive it if was not you who talked it, Turquet. I don't think you half mean it. Of course you don't understand. Hetty is so different——"

" Different from what ? " asked the Count.

"Different," said Nic, seeking words to express his meaning. "Yes, different—of course—different from any other woman that ever lived."

Master Nic felt like an orator who had hit on the finest, most expressive and original phrase in the world. Waving Turquet a kindly farewell, he walked out of the tavern with confidence and joy on his face and love and hope in his heart.

"My God!" groaned the Count, as he called to the drawer for a pipe of tobacco and another pint of wine. "What a beautiful thing it is to be as green as that!"

The drawer came to the table to take his order. "The young gentleman who just left says that your honour will pay the reckoning."

"The devil he did!" said Turquet, laughing, and not a little nettled.

It was one of his principles in life never to pay for drink until dice or coin had been thrown, and it was shown by the lot of providence that the call was on him; and he knew that young Nic was now walking along the Strand chuckling in his green soul that he had bettered his friend to the extent of a quart of Mountain.

Master Nic knocked at the door of the Verralls' house in Fetter Lane, with the pious timidity of an acolyte who approaches the door of the temple in which is enshrined the Holy of Holies. The door was opened by Mrs. Verrall herself, who stood with the handle in her hand barring the entrance like a priestess on the threshold of the shrine.

"Your servant, madam," said Master Nic, with his most winning bow and smile.

"What dost thou here?" asked Mrs. Verrall with no invitation in her voice.

"I came to see Mr. Verrall."

"If that be true, you waste your time; he has ridden into Somerset on business."

She was closing the door and her visitor added in haste—"and to ask after Mistress Hester."

"What is our daughter to you?" asked the woman, a touch of anger raising the pitch of her voice.

"I did her some service at the meeting-house," said Nic humbly.

" Ziba tells us you were one of the mob who started the fire," said Mrs. Verrall, beating her foot on the ground.

" Ziba is a liar, and I will beat him into a jelly ! " shouted Nic angrily.

" Ziba is a precious vessel in the sight of the Lord," said the woman, shouting back at Master Nic.

" Then the Lord will have the pleasure of seeing him broken into pieces and kicked into the kennel, for he is a damned liar."

This horrible blasphemy, which might have taken away the voice of many a less courageous woman, seemed to put strength and courage into the heart of this gaunt priestess of the Verrall household, and she burst forth into a torrent of abuse of Master Nic.

" It is you who are a liar, and blasphemer, and a corrupter of women, an unclean person and an idolater, who as the Apostle Paul truly says, has no inheritance in the Kingdom. Did I not with my own eyes at this very hour on Monday see you in a coach cuddling a light woman in the open day ? "

Master Nic started, not, let us hope, without guilt on his conscience.

" You are a man of sin, a railer, a drunkard, a wolf of the evening ! Go and assemble with your fellows in the homes of the harlots, and leave this dwelling alone. My husband's daughter is not for the like of you ! "

The angry woman slammed the door in his face as a practical full stop to her oration, and left Master Nic shamefully laughing in the street.

" Faith ! " he said to himself, " old Turquet is right. There is no dealing with such canaille. A gentleman must treat such muckworms as they are worth, but Hetty must be mine ! "

Arrived at the " Magpie and Stump," and finding Captain Gregory was out, he made up his mind that he would waste no more time in an endeavour to see his Hetty until he returned from Sussex. Calling for a standish, some paper and a glass of Geneva, he composed a letter to her with some natural difficulty, for his scholarship was not of the first order. After several unsuccessful efforts, the first letter to his lady love was at length satisfactorily penned in a bold round hand, and the author of it read it aloud not without a reasonable note of pride and gratification in his voice.

"My Dearest Mistrisse:
  "If the Ship did not wait to carry me downe into Sussex on grate affairs I wold have remained in London for your good Father's return who I hope is my good friend but at onct on my coming back I shall aske to kisse that deare and pleasant hand and till then I shall remane your most affectionatly faythfull servant unto death.
                                         " Nic Berrington.
  "To my most passionatly beloved Mistrisse Hester Verrall."

When this was sealed and directed to his lady at the "Sign of the Gauntlet" in Fetter Lane, Master Nic handed it to a ticket-porter to be specially delivered into her hands, feeling that it was too precious a document to be entrusted to the penny post.

CHAPTER XV

MASTER NIC GOES HOME

ALMOST as soon as Master Nic had despatched his letter Captain Gregory rolled into the tavern and declared that it was time for them to take oars to the Custom-house. Arrived there and entering the long room, the little Captain seemed to know everyone, and was on specially good terms with the grave clerks behind the counters, who made out his ship's papers for him without delay. Nic wondered at the dense crowd of sea captains, merchants, Turks, Chinese, orange women, and watermen all jabbering and hustling to get their business done.

"When does the *Medusa* sail?" asked a grave man, one of the senior clerks, who was walking through the room.

"Must catch the ebb tide to-morrow morning," replied the Captain.

"Must, eh?" replied the other with a smile.

"Now, my dear Mr. Blinkhorn, you will send the Custom House men on board to-night to clear the ship."

"I fear it is impossible," said the other. "Rules must be obeyed."

The little Captain drew him aside into a corner of the room, talking to him very earnestly and jingling some coins in his pocket as he spoke. This music seemed to charm the grave man, for presently the Captain came back to Master Nic smiling and said: "That's all right. We can be off now ; Mr. Blinkhorn says he will come on board himself and sign the papers, as they are short-handed and very busy. I call it good of him."

They went down to the quay and, with some little difficulty, for there was a throng of folk shouting for boats, they got a skiff to put them on board the *Medusa*, which was lying at anchor in the Upper Pool. She was a schooner of a hundred and twenty tons. The waterman swung the skiff round and brought them under the rope-ladder. Master Nic caught it and, running up it easily enough, sprang on to the deck. Captain Gregory, having paid off the man, followed more leisurely.

"This is not the first time that you have been on board ship, Mr. Berrington," said the Captain admiringly, as he took him into his cabin.

Master Nic laughed and began babbling stories of his exploits on *The Lively Kate*, and how from the days of his childhood he had been used to handle the sheets and take his turn with the watch.

Towards evening Mr. Blinkhorn arrived and came down into the cabin to clear the ship's papers and examine the cargo. Master Nic went on deck and left the Captain and the Custom-house official together. In about ten minutes or so he was sent for to join them and found Captain Gregory preparing to mix a bowl of punch whilst Mr. Blinkhorn was putting his official signature to the papers to the effect that he had made a careful examination of the ship's cargo and it tallied with the manifest.

Mr. Berrington and Mr. Blinkhorn were made known to each other, a lantern was lighted by the cook, who came to and fro from the galley with the kettle, more lemons and sugar were commanded, and the little Captain having brought out a fat Dutch flask of spirits, the three sat down to make a night of it.

The talk at first was nautical and official. The Captain wanted Mr. Blinkhorn to accompany them to Gravesend.

"No, no," said Mr. Blinkhorn. "I told you, Gregory, I could do nothing for you there. You'll take your own risk. I cannot interfere outside my own district."

"But a word from you, sir, to those Gravesend fellows. They're terrible sharks."

"It is not for me to judge other men, sir," said Blinkhorn, raising his glass. "God forbid! I know you, Captain, for an honest man and a generous, kindly soul. I'm sure if you tell me your cargo is straight, it is straight."

He drank the Captain's health. They drank Master Nic's health and then Mr. Blinkhorn's, and the Captain proposed "To hell with Gravesend!" but Mr. Blinkhorn objected and asked the Captain for a song. Whereupon the Captain, placing his hands on his knees, trolled out a long ditty which seemed more complimentary to Gravesend and began thus:

"As lately I travelled
Towards Gravesend,
I heard a fair damsel
A seaman commend,
And as in a tilt boat
We passed along,
In praise of brave seamen
She sang this new song:
Come tradesmen, or merchant,
Whoever he be,
There's none but a seaman
Shall marry with me."

How many verses there were and how many times Master Nic sang the last two lines he could never remember, but he caused considerable annoyance to the Custom-house official, who invited himself afterwards to sing "Drink to me only with thine eyes," by bursting in at the end of every verse:

"There's none but a seaman
Shall marry with me."

" Gad, sir!" cried Master Nic, inflamed with the punch and the high ideals of a seaman's life as expressed in the Captain's song, "why was I not a seaman?"

"Plenty of money in your pocket!" shouted the Captain.

"Drink and food galore, my boy! said Mr. Blinkhorn, filling his glass.

"Maids, wives and widows waiting for you in every port. Believe me!" said the Captain, chuckling.

"I'll sail with you, Captain, by heaven I will!" said Master Nic. "You're the best fellow and make the best punch in the world. I'll sail with you round the world. It's a bargain."

He caught hold of the little Captain's hand and wrung it fervently.

The little Captain was in tears, and put his hands on Nic's

shoulder and pressed him down on to the locker and filled
him another glass of punch. And then Mr. Blinkhorn said
he was a fine fellow and drank his health, and the Captain
said he should sail as mate, and he would put him on the
ship's books there and then, and Master Nic continued
between his sips of punch to assert in song that

> "None but a seaman
> Shall marry with me."

He seized the quill offered him by the Captain and nearly
fell into the ink in his eagerness to join this glorious profession. What he signed or whether his name was truly on
the books of the good ship *Medusa* he never knew, for
his next memory was that he was lying on the floor of the
Captain's cabin with an accursed headache and a tongue
three sizes too big for his mouth, and through the open
porthole came a cooling breeze and the pink flush of dawn.

"Where the devil am I?" he murmured miserably. Overhead he heard the regular tramp of men's feet on the deck
and the well-known chanty he had joined in many a time
with the crew of *The Lively Kate*.

> "In Amsterdam there dwelt a maid,
> Mark well what I do say,
> In Amsterdam there dwelt a maid,
> And she was mistress of her trade,
> And I'll go no more a-roving
> With you, fair maid,
> A-roving, a-roving
> Since roving's been my ru-in,
> I'll go no more a-roving
> With you, fair maid."

"Capstan work!" muttered poor Nic. "Then we'll be
drifting down with the ebb. Gad, what a head I've got!"

My young gentleman pulled himself up, stretched his
stiff, painful limbs and climbed into the Captain's bunk,
where he fell very heavily asleep.

The morning sun was high in the heavens before Master

Nic came on deck and found that the *Medusa* was slipping down Woolwich Reach before a pleasant westerly breeze. The boatswain, a lusty, tall fellow with a large nose and several warts on his face, was at the wheel, and Captain Gregory was pacing the deck near by. He seemed in a cheery humour. Nothing was said about the carouse of the night before, and he called out a jovial good-morning to Master Nic as he came up the ladder.

"A fine sight, sir, this," said the Captain, as he waved his hand towards Woolwich yards, where the men-of-war were building. "That's the old *Royal Sovereign* and that's the *Royal Prince*. No, it ain't. They call her the *Queen* now, don't they?"

They passed a guard-ship at the lower end of the reach, to which the *Medusa* dipped her flag. Nic was full of admiration for the way in which the Captain handled his vessel, as he ran round some ships at anchor and pulled in his sheets to head the *Medusa* down Gallions Reach towards Barking.

"I should have thought you were shorthanded with a vessel of this size, but I will say they are a smart lot," said Master Nic in a patronising tone.

The little man screwed up his eyes and grinned, and the big boatswain gulped down a big guffaw and then stared straight ahead.

"Keep her well off Maggot Ness!" shouted the Captain angrily, and then, turning to Master Nic, he continued: "You are perfectly right, Mr. Berrington. I had to sail shorthanded this morning, but I hope to pick some fellows up at Greenhithe when we anchor to-night."

Master Nic enjoyed the sail down the river in the merry spirit in which he accepted all new adventures in life, and gained the good opinion of Captain Gregory and his men by being always ready to handle a rope when the schooner made a new tack, and doing it w th a willingness and knowledge that showed he was no landlubber.

They had a fair voyage down the river through Erith Reach and Rand's Reach, steering by trees and wharfs and church towers, past Dartford Sands, until they got into the full waters of Long Reach, where all is clear, and you may

anchor at safety in any part of it with the solid foundation
to a seafaring man of six or seven fathoms of water beneath
your keel. Here they anchored for the night above the little
village of Greenhithe, and Captain Gregory went ashore,
returning after dark with two drunken sailors and a couple
of boats laden with barrels of gunpowder to add to his
clandestine cargo. These were stowed away in different
parts of the hold among more innocent merchandise.

After supper the boatswain was sent for and a council of
war was held. Captain Gregory explained that it was not his
intention to have any trouble, if it could be avoided, with
the Gravesend devils, and if they had a fair wind he would
endeavour to run past the town and not come to anchor to
pick up the searchers from the Customs who came on board
at that town to make a second clearing of the ship.

Master Nic expressed himself full of delight at the prospect of cheating the Custom-house fellows of their bribes,
and offered the Captain to take a part in the manœuvre, a
suggestion that was gratefully accepted. And when they had
found him some rough seafaring togs to take the place of
his town clothes, it was settled that he should be placed in
control of the jib sheets, at which work he had showed
himself to be quick and clever during the day's sail.

Early next morning they woke to find a good breeze
from the west, and were soon under way with all sail set
and tacked up Fuller's Reach to Old Man's Head. And when
they opened the reach, which is called Gravesend Reach,
coming down apace with the tide of ebb under foot, and a
fresh gale of wind astern, they should have handed some of
their sails, hauled up a foresail or mainsail or lowered the fore-
top sail, to signify to the Custom-house men that they
intended to bring to. But nothing of this was done, and
they ran free down the reach with all sail set.

On seeing this the sentinel on the block house on the
Gravesend side fired his musket to signal the Captain that
he must bring to. But the Captain kept his course, and as he
passed broadside with the block house, the sentinel fired
again.

It was the first shoot of the ebb, and as luck would have
it, there was a great fleet of colliers and lighters and other

M

ships under sail coming up from Hope Point trying to reach Gravesend before the tide became too strong that they might anchor in the channel. And this was the Captain's salvation. For when the sentinel at the block house saw clearly that the *Medusa* was making a run for it, he fired his musket a third time as a signal to the fortress over the river at Tilbury that a vessel was to be brought to. The gunners of the east bastion should have let fly at her, but the Captain kept his ship so skilfully hidden among the other vessels in the reach that for the life of them the gunners could not fire at the *Medusa* for fear of damaging some of the other craft, and when at last she did clear and they could fire, the shot fell wide.

The officer at Tilbury, seeing with disgust that the *Medusa* was slipping past his guns, manned out several boats with soldiers in hopes to overtake her or, at the worst, to make signals to some men-of-war that were lying out at the Nore to cut her off. But the gale freshened and went round to the south-west, and the ebb tide now running stronger, the *Medusa* showed them so clean a pair of heels that before the boats got down to Hole Haven she was beyond the Nore and making for the channel.

They set a course nearly due south, and the Captain called the crew aft and a special ration of grog was served out. All the men had taken part in handling the ship past Gravesend, and the Captain promised that each should receive his due reward according to his grade, when they were paid off, with which everyone was well pleased. The watches were now set, and when the names were called out by the boatswain, Master Nic was startled to hear that Berrington was allotted to the starboard watch.

" I don't mind doing my share until we reach Newhaven, Captain," he said pleasantly, " and I don't care which watch I serve on as you are short-handed. We will talk it over at dinner-time."

"The devil we will !" replied the Captain gruffly. "We don't want talk on board the *Medusa*, young fellow, and the men don't dine with the skipper."

The boatswain and one or two of the sailors standing by laughed pleasantly at the Captain's humour.

"What do you mean?" asked Master Nic angrily, garnishing his question with several quotations from the vocabulary of Captain Johnson.

"None of that, my lad, unless you are looking for trouble," said the little Captain, poking his head out at him provokingly. "The foc'sle is your place till we reach Virginia, and if I've any nonsense with you, there are plenty of planters there in want of likely young fellows such as you; so if you don't do your work briskly and pleasantly you won't be one of the crew on the voyage home."

"I'm a passenger on this ship," shouted Master Nic in a fury, "and you promised to put me on shore at Newhaven."

"You paid me no passage-money, and the owners object to the master taking friends on board," said the Captain pleasantly.

Master Nic clenched his fist and would have flown at the Captain, but the big boatswain strode up to his chief's side, and he had the sense to see the odds were too many for him. His heart sank within him, and he could have wept with vexation to think he was ass enough to have been tricked by a fool's plot such as this.

"You crimp!" he muttered under his breath, scowling at the Captain.

"I won't have that said on board the *Medusa*," replied the Captain loftily. "You signed on the ship's books the night you came aboard. It's all fair and square as far as I'm concerned. You are like all the rest of the young city fellows. You'll carol and chirp in your cups about a seaman's life for you and all that sort of thing, and you sign on and drink the skipper's grog, but when it's your turn to keep your part of the bargain you turn sulky."

Master Nic, as he went off to the foc'sle, remembered bitterly enough something of the scene in the cabin. He had played the fool and lost badly, and he had the sense to see that the game had gone against him. After all, there were worse things than a voyage to Virginia.

At least Master Nic could be thankful that he was on a well-found vessel whose captain knew his business. For when they had passed the Nore and got round the North Foreland, they ran into squally weather and beat out to sea, and there encountered one of those terrible gales that on occasion burst on our shores at the end of summer or in early autumn with a fierceness very terrifying to landsmen.

Topsails were taken in, storm-staysails set, and the good ship laboured and plunged in the seas which swept over her day and night, and the pumps were constantly going. Master Nic had known rough weather on *The Lively Kate* but he had never experienced such a gale as this, and was thankful enough when the storm abated and they found themselves off Folkestone. His hope now was that the Captain would have to put back, as the cargo had shifted and there was considerable damage to the rigging and tackle of the schooner, but the Captain preferred to run the risks of the seas rather than put in among land-sharks after his recent adventure at Gravesend, and busied his crew with storing the cargo afresh and making good his own repairs.

They were now off Dungeness and the wind being still from the west and but light, although they made the best use of the tides, it was four days before they rounded Beachy Head, and then, night coming on and the tide being against them and a mist falling over the sea, they took soundings and finding they were in shallow water, the Captain deemed it wise to cast anchor.

Master Nic came on duty with the morning watch at four o'clock. There was a thick pall of sea-fog hanging over the ship. The tide was running up-channel. The poor prisoner leaned over the gunwale and peered into the drifting mist. He knew they were somewhere in the neighbourhood of his beloved Sussex. They had been beating off Beachy Head for several hours the day before, and by the call of the man with the lead and the amount of cable that was paid out when they let go the anchor, he knew that they must have run well in shore, and that if the fog rose they might see the Seven Sisters or the high chalk cliff with the Roman camp on the summit that overlooks the little town of Seaford.

He had a mad impulse to plunge into the sea and swim for it, but he was too full of youth and the joy of life to put an end to it in that way. Within an hour or so he heard the gulls calling, and some flew down wind screaming at the ship as they came up to it through the mist. Over the stern

of the vessel the thick air seemed to get lighter for a moment, but he could see nothing, and again the mist darkened
everything.

Tears stood in his eyes as he thought of Granny Johnson,
perhaps within half-a-dozen miles of him at this moment,
sleeping peacefully in the farm at Cherry Croft. And Hetty!
Poor Hetty, with the brown eyes, which would never look
lovingly at him again. He pictured her at home thinking he
had run from her, and believing every lying tale of scandal
that her wretched lean stepmother poured into her ears—it
was maddening.

Poor heathen Master Nic had forgotten how to pray, but
that he had a fluency of commination in advance of his years
is beyond doubt. With all the fervour and piety of his
nature he cursed Captain Gregory, who had taken advantage of his trust and innocence, and called for divine vengeance on every hair of his head and each pit in his pox-
marked face, and outdid King David himself in his suppli-
cations that when the Captain was destroyed evil should fall
upon his mother, his widow and his fatherless children, if
any. Then he cursed the *Medusa* in ample detail, including
every bolt, bar, sheet, rope, spar, halliard, mast, sail and
plank that went to the making of her. And, in conclusion,
that justice might be done, with all the solemn righteousness of a self-convicted sinner, he particularly and specially
cursed Nic Berrington, rightly called The Child, as an infant,
milksop, calf, numskull, greenhorn, ass and fool, unfit for
the game of life and rightly punished for his sins.

Exhausted by grief and emotion, he sank on his knees and
covered his face with his hands. And at that moment there
came a gentle wind from the west along the grey waters and
lifted up the mist and fog in wreaths, so that when he took
his hands from his eyes he could clearly see the brown edge
of the shingle and the white curves of the low waves running along it. Then for a few moments the early yellow light
shone through the curtain gauze of the mist, and he could
see the whole beach and the footings of the white chalk
cliffs, though the upper heights were still hung with clouds.
And now he could see the river and hear its stream running
over the pebbles into the waves. He knew he was at home!

He threw off his heavy sea-boots and stripped off his clothes. There was no one near him at the fore part of the ship. Silently he climbed over the gunwale and handed himself down the cable, slipping quietly into the sea. Then he struck out boldly for the shore. From time to time the mist fell and lifted again, but he had faith that if he swam across the tideway he was making for the shore. At last he was in slack water, and then he felt the soft touch of weeds about his limbs, and knew the rocks were beneath him. A few more strokes and the friendly brown Sussex shingle welcomed him back to land.

He pulled his heavy body wearily out of the backwash of the little waves and sat down cold, benumbed and half-exhausted on the beach. Then, like a hunted hare that hears the music of the beagles she believes she has long outdistanced, Nic's heart almost ceased to beat, for there came through the mist, which was now rapidly clearing, the shrill note of the boatswain's whistle, the cry of "Man overboard," and the call to stations to lower a boat, and he knew that peril was upon him, for the Captain was not a man to let a sailor slip out of his hands and so fold them again and do nothing.

Naked as when he was born and stung to energy by the rattling of tackle and blocks and the shouts of the boatswain and the men, he ran up the shingle beach to the chalk cliffs, his eager mind full of a last hope. He knew if he could find the opening in the cliff without being seen from the schooner, he might lie snug in Captain Johnson's cave without any fear of capture. He looked back anxiously to seawards. The mist still hung between the shore and the vessel, and now he ran and jumped from one chalk boulder to another, looking wildly for the entrance to the cave he used to know so well. At length he found the fallen heap of chalk at the base of the cliff where the little path began that led to the cave.

Out on the water he could hear the splash of oars and the voice of Captain Gregory cursing and swearing and calling on the men to look this way and that to see if he was still swimming about in the sea. But he was safe. He had gained the entrance to the cave and stumbled into the dark sanctuary and fell among bales and casks like a little frightened child rushing from danger into a mother's arms.

Captain, boatswain and men spread themselves over the shore and hunted in and among every boulder and rock for half-a-mile or so east and west. Master Nic, wrapped in sacking at the back of the cave, could hear their voices now near, now far. At length they seemed to gather together on the edge of the shingle, and his pulse leaped to hear the men pulling the boat down the shingle again into the water.

" He's gone and drowned hisself," said the boatswain in a melancholy voice.

"That lad wasn't born to be drowned," said the Captain decisively.

" Well, what I think——" began the boatswain.

"Think! You were not made to think, you fool," shouted the Captain angrily, "you were made to keep your eyes open. I told you to keep your weather-eye on him, and you let him slip through your fingers like an eel."

"Well, I thought——"

"Damn you, stop thinking then, or you'll sink the ship. I've a good mind to cut the whole ship's company's grog for a week and yours for the whole voyage."

This threat threw a gloom on the party, and they entered the boat and pulled to the ship in silence.

Master Nic dozed and listened for several hours, and it must have been eight o'clock before he dared to crawl to the mouth of the cave and put his eyes above the entrance. There on the water rode the *Medusa*, her sails rapidly clothing the spars and masts. The anchor was catted and fished, the breeze filled the sails, and she got slowly under way and headed off to the open sea. Never had he seen a sight that gave him greater joy than that of the *Medusa*, with every rag set, making steadily away down channel with a fair wind.

Master Nic could now look about him in safety and, finding a crow-bar, broke open what looked like a case of brandy, and discovering what he sought and a bag of ship's biscuits, made a most glorious meal, and raising his bottle from time to time in a spirit of charity and forgiveness, he drank *bon voyage* to Captain Gregory and the *Medusa*.

Then he found more sacking and an old horse-rug and some straw, of which he made a bed. The fatigue he had endured lent a softness and comfort to his couch that was real luxury to his poor, tired body. Without taking any thought for the morrow, and with thankfulness in his heart for the mercies of the day, he drew the rug over him, laid his head on a lump of twine and fell fast asleep.

CHAPTER XVI

"IN THE SPRING A YOUNG MAN'S FANCY . . ."

MASTER NIC, more dead than alive from shock and fatigue, lay half asleep and half unconscious until late in the afternoon. What would have been the end of him had no one visited the cave, who could say, but that evening Captain Johnson had occasion to come down the river with Jacob to fetch some stores.

The Captain walked across the beach and made his way along the shore and climbed up the path to the entrance of the cave. Here he groped for a lantern, which he lighted, and was proceeding to enter the cave when he saw the broken case.

Instinctively he grasped his pistol and held the lantern down to see what had been done.

" Damn my liver and bones!" he muttered. "Has someone run us to earth at last?"

He gazed anxiously about, wondering almost in terror who could have penetrated the secret which meant so much to the success of his trade. As he held up his lantern, he saw the figure of Master Nic hidden under the rug. He put his pistol at his head and shouted: "Hands up, or I fire!"

Master Nic raised his face and, rubbing his eyes, stared sleepily at the lantern which the old man nearly dropped in his astonishment.

"Split my windpipe, it's The Child!" he shouted.

"Who on earth asked you to call me at this hour?" muttered Nic, wearily. "Can't you let a fellow sleep for a while without all this noise? The whole place might belong to you the way you go on. The brandy is on the floor. Have a drink. It's not bad stuff. And, for heaven's sake, don't make so much row!"

He wandered drowsily in his talk for a moment or two, and then put his head back on the lump of twine and fell fast asleep again.

"Split my windpipe!" said Captain Johnson in tones of supreme conviction, "it *is* The Child."

He soon saw that the poor wretch was in no condition to give any account of himself. His teeth were chattering when he spoke, and when the Captain felt his hand he had sense enough to see that the lad was in a high fever. He went to fetch Jacob, and the two carried him feebly protesting to the boat. He did not know them and wept copiously in his weakness, begging not to be taken back to the ship. They carried him home to Granny, who put him to bed whilst the Captain rode into Lewes for a doctor.

And in Granny's good hands we must leave him whilst we turn our attention to poor Hetty, slowly returning to consciousness and the memory of the terrible ordeal of the fire, and wakening to the narrow life around her. She lay tossing on her bed of sickness, listening with deaf ears to the pious jargon of her stepmother's prayers and her sly stories of the utter unworthiness of Master Nic as a spiritual complement of virtuous woman. Her heart was full of anger that Master Nic had ever been brought into her life. She recalled the days of her father's wanderings of enthusiasm, hard and uncomfortable as the life had been, with regret that they were over. She loved her father and rejoiced to see him contentedly following his trade and religion with that happy sanity that seems a special gift of heaven to prosperous dissenters. But it was this very prosperity that had been the cause of her misery.

She had never had occasion before to peer into the future. Her father and stepmother in their care for her may have shaped it in their minds, though the matter had never been openly spoken of, that in due course she would marry honest Ziba and carry on the family business in accordance with biblical precedents. Of late she had sometimes wondered herself if this was to be her fate and she had not shrunk from it. Ziba was a sounder man than the sprigs of humanity who leered at her across the counter in Westminster Hall.

But this possible future was now impossible. A burning kiss on her lips and the sheltering embrace of a man's arms had awakened in Hetty what to her was a sinful affection.

Happy Master Nic, proud and beautiful in his young man-hood, full of the joy and pleasure of life, reared among the bad surroundings of wicked men and women, was to Hetty a being to be shunned, a warm glowing vision to flee from, whilst she sought safety among the cold spectres of a melancholy faith.

Mrs. Verrall wrestled with the Evil One when the ticket-porter handed her Master Nic's letter. She longed to destroy it and indeed had gone so far as to hold it over the fire when she saw the words "Thou Shalt not Steal" blazing in the flames. Her native honesty triumphed. She took it to her stepdaughter, who laid it at the side of her bed.

When Hetty was alone she opened it and read it again and again and kissed it fervently and bedewed it with tears. She dared not keep it, lest someone might discover her unhappy secret. Every word of it was graven on her memory but the beloved paper must perish. Bravely she held it in the candle and clapped her hands on the black ashes to destroy them. No one should ever know her secret, which she would carry with her through life until she might sleep alone with it in the grave.

"Was your letter from Mr. Berrington, Hetty?" asked her stepmother when she returned to the room.

"He wished to know how I was. I have burned it."

Mrs. Verrall's quick eyes saw some fallen ashes on the floor and her mind was at rest.

"You did wisely, dear."

The girl turned on her pillow and closed her eyes.

When Mr. Verrall returned from Somerset he was deeply grieved at his daughter's condition. He consulted a worthy physician of the City who prescribed with as much effect as doctors always have and will for a mind in trouble, and bright, lively Hester sat weak and moping in the parlour, the light of her brown eyes dimmed until the sight of the man she loved should bring the sunshine back to them again.

About this time old Nan Chilcote came to see her assistant. Trade at Westminster had been suffering from the incompetence of a series of impudent wenches quickl cashiered by the irate old lady. She discussed Hetty's illness with Mrs. Verrall and the two ladies acidly disagreed in their diagnosis. When Mrs. Verrall sighed and said she feared the child was going into a decline, the tough old woman took snuff and scoffed at the notion, seeing the stock she sprang from. She related at much length how in her girlhood she had been deep in love with a young sailor who was drowned, and the sorrow of it had thrown her into a sad state which caused all her relatives to despair of her life.

"A fine lad he was, too, Hetty," she said as she related the story to her more attentive niece. "Not unlike that young Mr. Berrington who was always hanging about our stall down at the Hall, but a finer, broader built sort of man, worth a dozen of my good man Chilcote any day, as I used to tell him. But God willed it and so it was."

The old woman took a pinch of snuff and waved the incident away with her skinny fingers as though it was a matter of no great importance nowadays except as an interesting fact in her own interesting history. Hetty gazed at her, wondering whether it was really true that any man had ever looked into those dull eyes and pressed kisses on those thin, dry lips.

"You may well take stock of me, Miss Hetty, with your brown eyes," said the old dame, shrewdly guessing her thoughts. "Just as many a young man came dangling after me as ever you saw making sheep's eyes at you in Westminster Hall."

"Do not put those notions in the girl's mind, cousin," said Simon Verrall, reprovingly.

"Pah!" she cried, laughing at him, "they are there already, I expect. Instead of letting her sit moping there, Simon, why don't you take her away for a change somewhere? Here's all the beaux from the Court coming back in a week or two and no Hetty. You don't expect the young fools to buy their gloves and toothpicks from an old woman like me? I will say Hetty is worth her wage, though most girls nowadays ain't worth their keep."

A sentiment which seems to be uttered by all sensible matrons of each succeeding generation.

"I think, cousin, there's a lot of sense in what you say," replied Verrall, who had a great respect for Mrs. Chilcote and her business and wealth and liked to see her affection for Hetty, coarsely as it was expressed. "I have had a mind for some year or two to go down to Sussex to see our cousin there. Why not take Hetty down to stay with them for a while?"

"A real sensible idea," said the old lady. "Why, see the very thought of the fresh air from the sea brings the colour into her cheeks. Go with your father, girl, and come back as hale and pretty as ever you were."

She bent down and kissed Hetty on her brow.

"And give old Verrall my love. I remember him a boy in a smock. He is plagued with the ague now, I hear. God be thanked I shall see you all out yet."

And the old lady hobbled away on her crutch, having done Miss Hester more good than a hundred doctors and administered better spiritual consolation than a bench of bishops or a council of elders.

Chance, or the long arm, having drawn these young folk back to the village where they met as children, would that we might chronicle a happy marriage without more ado and give Granny Johnson the joyful toil of preparing the marriage feast and so sing an epithalamium and waken the happy couple next morning with the music of bones and cleavers and end the story.

But not in this way is veracious history to be written, and whilst Miss Hetty has been moping in stuffy London poor Master Nic is being tended through a long illness by his devoted Granny, whose chief idea of nursing was to shut every cranny in the room through which the pure air of Sussex might bring relief to her patient and dose him with nauseous drenches.

At last surly winter was gone, the birds were singing, the lambs frisking in the fields, the primroses peeping in the woods, and here and there a cowslip might be found in the marsh fields. The call of spring was answered by the echo of youth and Master Nic stole out into the orchard and once more picked up the threads of life. Granny acknowledged his convalescence on her knees with tears of gratitude and pride in her heart at the success of her cunning pharmacy.

Nor did she abdicate her position as high priestess of Hygeia, but left the mystic chapel of the still room for the altars of the kitchen, which were continually heaped with savoury delicacies. There was now a glorious regime of chickens and jellies, butter and eggs, milk and ale and, later on, good beef and mutton. Master Nic improved in weight and colour.

"Damn my innards," said the Captain with enthusiasm, "if belly timber don't beat drugs."

It was during his convalescence that Master Nic learned from Granny something of the story of his life. He listened with experienced sympathy to Granny's tale of his mother's love for Jonathan Wild, and how some years afterwards Mr. Trustram and his daughter left Freston and Granny heard that she had been married to Mr. Berrington. Then she told him of his mother's dying message that Granny should receive her child and care for him. According to Granny Jonathan Wild had from the first taken an interest in him, and she firmly believed that had he lived Jonathan intended in due course to see that Master Nic came into his kingdom.

Ever since he had begun to picture himself as Nicholas Berrington of Steeple Berrington his dream, as human dreams do, repeated itself with stimulating monotony. Every day he rehearsed the pleasant scenes of his drama. He would ride into Oxfordshire. He would announce himself to Luke Crowley as Nicholas Berrington, heir to the estates of Steeple Berrington. The good old lawyer would welcome the prodigal's return. The village bells would ring. He would take possession of his house and lands and in due course he would bring to the home of his fathers the most beautiful bride the world had ever seen, Hetty Verrall.

The spring breezes from the Channel, the sunshine, the good food and the dreams of future bliss had a splendid effect on Master Nic's health. He became tired of inaction and insisted to Granny that he was fit and ready to open the campaign.

The Captain had gone across the Channel for a few day

but the impatient young man could not await his return. Granny, who could resist him in nothing, provided money from her own stocking, and borrowing one of the Captain's horses he rode into Lewes to fit himself with apparel worthy of his station that he might make his way into Oxfordshire without further delay. In the matter of clothing the outer man, the young rascal had from the earliest been a student and a scholar; and when he returned to the farm arrayed in a handsome brown wig and fine ruffles and a purple riding suit, the "latest from London," as the Lewes tailor assured him, foolish, loving Granny gazed at him as a staid, shabby ewe will stand admiring with sheep's eyes her well-groomed white frisking lamb. Nor, indeed, was she satisfied until she had gone through the contents of his portmanteau and admired the cambric shirts and lace ruffles, silver buckles, and velvet coat and breeches and silk waistcoat, in which costume he told her he proposed to enter into his kingdom.

In vain she begged him to wait the return of Captain Johnson or to consult Parson Oliver before he went his way. To no purpose did she assure him that he was not strong enough to bear the fatigue of the journey. The headstrong youth laughed at her advice and her fears and the next morning he saddled the Captain's horse and rode away across the downs, leaving the old woman leaning over the gate watching his departing figure through her tears and murmuring prayers for his safety with trembling lips.

He took the upper road by Verrall's Farm. Beyond that you could gain the east downs and ride on the turf across to the London Road. Above the farm on the hillside was a chalkpit overgrown with bracken and bramble, and as the horse's hoofs clattered on the loose flints in the chalk a big blundering sheep dog tumbled out of the bracken and bounded at his horse. The sight of the farm had recalled to Master Nic's mind dreams of brown eyes, and when his horse shied he was holding the reins but loosely, so that his body swerved and the animal broke away for a moment until he recovered command by instinct and, to excuse his own carelessness, swore wicked words at the offending dog.

But these froze suddenly on his lips as he heard from

within the chalk-pit the sound of a voice re-calling the dog
to its owner. For the voice was the voice of a woman and in
it was the melody of love, though the mere spoken words
were only a repetition in a note of command of the word
"Bobbin," which we may assume was but a dog's name.
Nevertheless, for Master Nic the voice was a herald's
trumpet of unspeakable joy, it was not only the voice of a
woman, it was the voice of The Woman—he was in the
presence of Hetty, and the houses and lands of Steeple
Berrington had vanished from his vision, for he had come
into an even greater inheritance.

He leaped from his horse and left that sensible animal
cropping the grass, in no way interested in the great events
he was witness of, and ran down into the chalk-pit. The
sure instinct of his love was not at fault. It was Hetty. Her
pink hood had fallen on her shoulders, her hair was loose-
ned and waving in the sea breeze, her cheeks glowed, and
as she recognised the intruder she dropped her basket
with a cry of joy and held out her hands to him.

The boy and girl were in each other's arms, their lips had
met, and she was resting her head on his shoulder and
crying softly and happily. Bobbin, with a dog's instinct of
being in the human picture, jumped up with his rough,
dirty feet and scraped the nap off The Child's purple suit
by way of offering the happy ones his canine blessing. The
old horse munched the grass and sniffed contempt for
Bobbin and his utter equine indifference of human affairs.
A seagull wheeled up from the valley and shot a cry of joy
back to his mate when he saw the lovers, for the love-story
of the birds is the first of all the love-stories in the world,
as the nest is the model of a lover's home. But the boy and
the girl heeded none of these things. When he could find
his voice Nic murmured: "My beloved!"

The girl heard him repeat this beautiful phrase, and each
time it was uttered there came a song into her heart : " the
winter is past, the rain is over and gone; the time of the
singing of birds is come." And she knew that her time, too,
had come and she took her fate in both hands and she too
dared to murmur "Beloved!" and then hid her face and
her blushes somewhere beneath his chin.

"Hetty!" he cried proudly, as if he was naming a kingdom he had conquered by his own valour.

"Nic!" she whispered humbly as if she were uttering the title of a king of kings.

"I have found you at last!"

"I have been longing for you to come!"

It was nearly two hours afterwards when Jacob put his head into the kitchen at Cherry Croft and astonished Granny with the joyful news that Master Nic was riding down the hill on his way home again. She ran out to the garden gate and there was Mr. Berrington with a sad, but alas, hypocritical, look of weariness on his naughty face.

He let himself down from the saddle with an exaggerated pantomime of fatigue that went to Granny's heart.

"It's no use, Granny."

"I knew it wasn't," said the triumphant old lady.

"I'm not nearly strong enough," said the youth with a sigh.

"I told you so," she said, with a chuckle of delight.

"You will have to keep me here for a few more days yet."

"And more than that, lad. Ah!" she said, shaking her head, "if only you young folks knew what was right for you, and knew that you didn't know so much as you think you know, and would do what your elders told you, it would be a better world."

"It couldn't be a better world," said Master Nic with sudden enthusiasm.

"Bless me! You seem almost yourself again."

This gave the young rascal the cue to remember his part; and taking Granny's arm he hobbled as if dog-weary, drawing his feet along the brick paving to the farm porch.

Granny celebrated her triumph in the kitchen. She roasted fowls, baked apples, and while these were in the making, feasted her prisoner with cakes and ginger wine, and chuckled over his failure in taking the road, with sly allusions to her own superior wisdom in warning him from the attempt. All these things, and particularly the feasting, Mr. Berrington took in excellent part.

That evening as they sat by the candle light at each side

N

of the kitchen fire, Granny knitting and The Child seeing faces in the flames, he suddenly put a question to her.

"Granny, do you know the chalk-pit on the downs above the Verrall's Farm?"

"I should think I do," said Granny laughing. "Why, Roger and I used to meet there of a summer when we were courting."

At first in Master Nic's heart there was a sense of sacrilege at the thought that this hallowed spot should have been so used in the past, but his quick instinct guided him at once to the opening it made for his purpose.

"Granny dear," he said, as he slid from his chair and sat on the rug before the fire with his hands round his knees and his face turned from her, "I am going to tell you a secret, the most wonderful thing that ever happened in the world."

"My poor boy!" said Granny, for her shrewd wit told her what was coming.

And as he told the story of his love she put her hand on his shoulder and leaned her head towards his and, for ten minutes by the clock, was the happiest old woman in the world.

And when she had heard his tale out she placed her hands on his head and said in a low voice: "May the Lord bless all means to both of you my darlings."

BOOK III

Mr. BERRINGTON

CHAPTER XVII

CONFERENCES AT CHERRY CROFT

SIR ROBERT WALPOLE had conceived a great regard for the Count de Grillac's abilities, and had personally instructed him to undertake a secret and somewhat dishonourable mission abroad, which Turquet accepted as a compliment to his genius.

As Sir Robert dismissed his ambassador he warned him of the danger of his task, and hinted that to travel by the Dover route would be unwise.

"As you give me no safe conduct, the route I take is my own business," said Turquet with dignity.

The Secretary's secretary looked shocked.

Sir Robert laughed heartily: " Damned sensible, Monsieur! Damned sensible! Trust no one, least of all in this house, or in any government office, for that matter."

He waved him away good-humouredly and straightening his wig before the glass nodded to his secretary, saying: "That fellow will do the trick," and plunged into other business.

Turquet obtained leave of absence for Toby and took him with him, riding south to Lewes. His idea was to consult with Captain Johnson about the most secret route to France.

Meanwhile, as if to celebrate the lovers' happiness, the sun shone on Freston every day. The young couple were inditing in their memories a calendar of love from which in after years they could recall the scenes of each wonderful day. Sacred to their love was a stile on which they sat and watched the sunsets, the path through the woods, the great open lonely waste of rolling downs across which they wandered arm-in-arm, talking about little else than their marvellous love for each other, and preening themselves on the strange fact that such great happiness could never have been vouchsafed to others before and that perpetual and lasting bliss had been reserved for them alone.

Already there was a vague thought in Master Nic's mind that it would be only right that Hetty should know something of his past life and he lay awake rehearsing to himself how the matter were best introduced and dealt with. To Hetty also, when he was absent, an undefined fear came over her that her devoted Nic was not really a Child of God, and that it was her duty to carry him with her to the stool of repentance at the meeting-house. She had an uncomfortable feeling that her beloved would not look his best in a posture of penitence and this thought puzzled and pained her. But when they were together the shadows of past sin that lightly burdened poor Nic and the gloom of a narrow religion that shut out the light of the world from Hetty's soul were unreal phantoms and mockeries of life, the happiness and reality of which was the presence of love.

Hetty had written to her father and he had replied that he would come to Freston as soon as business matters would permit. His worldly knowledge taught him that this might be no bad match for his daughter, his religion forbade the banns, his human nature compelled him to like the youth, and his enthusiasm saw the hand of God in the bringing of the two together.

Captain Johnson was no great friend to the business. He disliked psalm-singing and psalm-singers as inimical to Church and State and the glories of Free Trade and smuggling.

Such was the state of things when Turquet, who had sent Billinge to Newhaven, arrived at Cherry Croft and Mr. Verrall came into Sussex to visit his cousin. Experience tells us that each generation, as it arrives at years of real discretion, looks with amused pity at the love-affairs of its children, without the least recollection that there was a time not so very long ago, when these wise elders themselves were wandering through the labyrinth of blessed dreams in which their youngsters are now entangled. Some good women and a few wise men have sympathy, sense and patience enough to help the dreamers to a happy awakening. If Granny had had her way the young people would have married and settled down in the farm, to cheer her old age with their presence, and the Berrington Estates might have remained for ever with Luke Crowley. But the common sense of wise women never did rule the world else it were less of a fool's paradise than it is.

A family conference was held at Cherry Croft after dinner in the farm-parlour. Hester and her father had dined with Captain Johnson and, overawed by her first public appearance with her beloved, she had kept her eyes on the table and spoken in monosyllables, gaining for herself the Vicar's verdict that she was a very "proper behaved young woman." When the pipes and Geneva were set on the table the Captain moved to his wife that she and the girl should retire, but Master Nic saw the glance and stopped them.

"Hetty and I are not going to waste the sunlight, are we?"

She looked at him gratefully. Simon Verrall felt he ought to say something, but the words were not to hand.

"Damn my liver and bones, my boy," said the Captain. "You must stay. It's your affairs we're going to discuss."

"Well, I'll leave Granny as my representative and I'll do anything in reason you decide, but I'm not going to waste this lovely day indoors."

Laughing lightly and taking Hetty by the arm he carried her boldly out of the house and left the elders to their conference.

"It is as well as it is," said Turquet. "We can speak more freely."

Granny picked up her knitting and retired to the chimney-corner. The four men sat round the table and filled their pipes from a large jar of tobacco whilst Captain Johnson poured out a stiff glass of Geneva for himself and passed the bottle. The Vicar who, by virtue of his office, was evidently expected to say the first word, looked at the substantial, well-dressed figure of Simon Verrall and could not but remember how they had met in this very room to discuss the whipping of him at the cart's tail and smile to think how absurd an affair that seemed to-day. This embarrassed him for the moment.

"It seems to me, Sir," he said after a pause, "that as you are the father of the girl we ought to hear your views first."

Simon Verrall bowed. "I will tell you in a few words how I view the matter. The girl is my only daughter. She tells me she is in love with this young man. I am, as you know" (he looked full at the Vicar), "not of the Church. I should have hoped to see her choose one of my own creed. Nevertheless, I will own I am drawn to him. Under Providence I owe him my life. I will not stand in the way of their happiness if indeed this is the way."

"That is all very well," said Captain Johnson impatiently, " but you say nothing about his inheritance. Of course you will be glad to make the match, if as we believe, he is heir to these Oxfordshire estates. The matter is, how is he to come by his rights?"

"Master Simon is in the right," said Granny from the chimney-corner. " Their happiness is all that matters."

"Hold your foolishness," called out the Captain.

"Mr. Verrall," said the Vicar holding up his hands for peace, "rightly places the happiness of his child first, but there are the young man's claims to consider."

"I may add," replied Mr. Verrall, "that some time back when I first met Mr. Berrington in London he sought my advice then, and I offered to help him either with money or in any way he wished. It was my counsel to him that he should come here and see what was known of his birth and parentage. He seems, when he left here as a child, to have fallen into strange and unhappy company."

"As one who knew him in early life," said Turquet quietly, "I can assure you, Mr. Verrall, that what you say is true."

"Curse me," cried the impatient Captain, "all this is to no purpose. Here's the lad come to life again and fine estates waiting in Oxfordshire for him to take possession of them. How does he go about it?"

"I fancy that what he will want to know is how does he go about getting married," said Granny.

"Surely, Madam," said Mr. Verrall, "Mr. Berrington will wish to make his position in the world clear before he thinks of marriage? They are both young and——"

"Therefore the less likely," interrupted Turquet, "to put money before matrimony."

The Parson chuckled.

"You are a student of the world, Sir," he said, raising his glass to the Count, who returned the compliment.

"I suppose," said Mr. Verrall thoughtfully, "the matter is one for the lawyers."

"Damn lawyers," ejaculated the Captain.

"Roger!" said his wife warningly.

"I say again, wife——"

"There is no necessity to condemn lawyers," said Turquet. "The Vicar will tell us that Providence has already ordained that matter. The difficulty of the position lies here. I understand that when Squire Berrington died, the estates were involved in debt. They have been managed since by a certain Luke Crowley, a lawyer of Witney. He may choose to dispute our young friend's claim. If I were not bound for France I would have suggested that I approached Mr. Crowley to see if we could make terms with him to admit Mr. Berrington's rights and leave him the stewardship during his minority."

"We had best consult our lawyers about that," said the cautious glove-maker, "and if I may make a business proposal it is this. I am returning to town to-morrow and if Mr. Berrington will go with me I will place the matter in the hands of my lawyers forthwith. I will be responsible for the cost of the matter and will use my best endeavours to speed it along."

"That is the right course," decided the Vicar.

"Well, have it your own way," grumbled Captain Johnson, "but I mistrust the devils."

"My advice has been given," said Turquet quietly.

"But not mine," interrupted Granny, rising from her chair. "Leave these young people with me. Let us have a wedding here and when the Vicar has joined them together let the young man go and battle for his estates and I will keep his wife safely here until his new home is ready."

The wise men smiled wisdom and shook their heads.

"Dear old woman," said the Captain in a kindly tone, "let the children be. If they are married in three years' time they will have enough of it and to spare. You talk foolishness."

But Granny could not let it end there. She had sat and listened to their folly and now she would speak hers as the spirit moved her.

"I don't say much, Roger, most days, but I see a lot of foolishness round me that I give the go-by to. I know it's not for me to try and put it right. The boy is the son of my dear girl who broke her heart when her father wouldn't let her marry Jonathan. What kind of a man she would have made of him God knows. You know what he made of himself. You bid these young things bide for years. Love won't wait."

"Jacob served twice seven years for Rachel," murmured the Parson.

"Aye, but Jacob waited on the farm and she was to be his wages. If they were farm-hands with hard work on six days of the week, and church and courting on Sunday I wouldn't say aught. But you men know what the great city is like. I only know what comes out of it. Whilst you and the lawyers are seeking the money and estates what are the young folk going to do till the day comes when they can enjoy them? You can't feed love on hope by the measure of years. The lad has no work or trade or business. He's a fine lad and I love him, but he's been brought up in a bad school. Give him a wife. Someone to love and live for and let the rest take care of itself. I've spoken too much perhaps. But I had to." With that Granny swept up her knitting and hurried out of the room to cry over the matter and pray for her loved ones.

The men sat and smoked in silence for two minutes of regular ticking of the old clock. Then the Captain spoke in a low tone of amazement.

"Damn my liver and bones, I never knew her like that afore!"

"She's right about the whole business," said Turquet.

"Only the world isn't made as we should wish it," added Verrall sententiously. "The wise course in matters of law is to seek the advice of lawyers."

"Maybe you're right," said the Captain doubtfully.

"Of a certainty," said the Vicar with conviction.

Turquet sat smoking in thoughtful silence.

The conference was at an end.

Out in the sunlight there is another conference of two going on, at least as earnest as that within doors, if less practical and contentious.

Hand-in-hand the lovers wander through the churchyard out at the south gate and across the footpath to the river meadows until they halt at the very bridge where they had first met in childhood. They lean over the railing, Hetty clinging close to her protector and glorying in the memory that here he had saved her life: Master Nic receiving her homage with complacent pride but peering with the practical eye of a fisherman into the muddy water below for signs of eels.

"Strange," she whispers, "that we have never been here since the day we first met."

"It was ages ago."

"A whole life-time."

"Then there is more than a whole life-time in front of us, dear one."

"I hope it may be so."

She places her hand in his shyly and he lifts it to his lip

"Tell me, Nic, when did you first know you loved me?"

"I have alway known I loved you."

Youth lives in the present. The Jenny of Bartholomew Fair is not even a memory with him to-day. She repeats his words to herself with a sigh of content.

"I wish we could live for ever and ever in this village. No place will be quite the same to me as this."

"You must not think that, beloved. If I had not a home to take you to I dared not have asked you to be my wife. It is no evil that we are to have riches and horses and servants and a noble house to live in. I wish it were a palace since you are to be the princess in it."

She shakes her head with a little sigh.

"I am no princess, I am not even a lady."

"Hush! You are my princess, my lady."

Lest the words should not be conclusive to her doubting, timid soul he takes her in his arms and seals the covenant with kisses.

"Will it take very long to settle all these great affairs?" she asks timidly.

"Impossible," replies young ignorance splendidly. "When it is made clear that I am the heir they must give me my estates and we can be married."

"It should be so."

"It is so. What can hinder it?"

"I do not know. I was never brave. I shrink from going back to London. I fear to lose you, to be dragged back into the old life at Westminster Hall, my stepmother, Ziba, it can never be the same again. Now you are mine I want to be with you always."

The Child tries to rouse her with pleasant mocking laughter.

"Ha ! I see what it is. You cannot trust me out of your sight."

"I can trust you always with or without me. But we have lived such different lives. Whilst I am working and praying and waiting I cannot even shut my eyes and dream what you are doing."

It flashes across The Child's mind that such a test of fidelity must lead to an uneasy life. He has soared to greater heights than he wots of and currents of strange thoughts tend to unbalance him.

"Do you want me in your dreams as well, Hetty?" he asks with a proud smile.

"I want you ever and always. I want to know you better and better every day so that I may do right by you. I know how good and clever you are. I shall always think you are perfect, but you must find something to tell me, to make me believe, I am not unworthy of such happiness."

High as he soars, she outsoars him in the ecstasy of her love and the wise Child seeks the safety of earth in a phrase.

"Let the past bury the past."

The words awaken the memories of the chapel. Mary vanishes in Martha. "You have the text wrong," she says with some accent of pride in superior knowledge. " Jesus said: 'Follow me; and let the dead bury their dead.'"

" I was thinking of a saying of Turquet," he replies lamely.

"I do not like the Count. He is always looking at me. Is he a good man?"

"He has been a good friend to me."

"Then I will try to like him," she says humbly.

The pat quotation of the text had chilled Master Nic's heart. He began to see that the religion which was part of Hetty's life, of which, in his wretched ignorance, he scarce understood the meaning, would thrust itself between them unless he could wean her away from it, or that worse might happen and he might be captured and be overwhelmed in its folds himself. He thought of Simon and Ziba and the meeting-house and compared them in a mental picture with Parson Oliver and the village church. A glow of orthodoxy warmed him with the thought of the wider comfort of life under the shadow of the Established Church. He spied the boathouse across the field and it offered a welcome escape from complicated thoughts.

"Let us go and see how the tide runs."

Hetty, too, felt they had strayed on to dangerous paths and was pleased to move away from the bridge of memories that had roused these topics. She, too, became deeply concerned in the flood and the ebb and listened to Nic's wisdom on the signs of the moving waters with reverent attention. At the boathouse he decided that it was but an hour off low tide and they would bale out the boat and float down to meet the incoming flood to return with it. Hetty had never stepped into a boat in her life. The men and women she had seen in the Thames wherries had always seemed to her of the heroic type. She watched all the arrangements that her beloved made with the deepest interest. A cushion for his princess was made out of a couple of sacks covered by his coat which he had taken off, and timidly clutching his hand she stepped into the boat and took her seat. When he shot out into the stream with a waterman's mastery of the craft all fear dissolved in pride. Once more he was her beloved, her lord, her king, and her governor. Brown eyes met blue in smiling content and the dear souls were the happier that they ceased to trouble each other with words and thoughts and accepted cheerfully the best happiness the gods have left to lovers, to be together and alone.

When they returned to the house and heard the decision

of the conference, Master Nic was full of active joy at the prospect of riding to London and getting the lawyers on the track of his inheritance. That evening he and Turquet sat up after the Captain and his wife had retired, the Count listening with half-closed eyes and an ever-filled pipe to his child's prattle of love and beauty and hope and glorious happiness.

"But what is the use of my talking, Turquet? You cannot understand it. No one can understand it."

"It is the incomprehensible," said Turquet with mock solemnity, " yet is it not an uncommon experience. In my youth I too have loved. Also I have eaten sweetmeats, but now I have lost my taste for them; also, at a still earlier period it is on record that I thirsted for milk, but I no longer drink it."

"Have your laugh at me, Turquet. All I know is that I am going to live in a new world."

"If your head is not too full of visions to find room for it, let me offer you some sense by way of furniture for your new world. I am going to France to-morrow."

"For how long?"

"The cards are not on the table. I cannot say. I have left Billinge at Newhaven. I want you to keep him by you until I return. He has leave of absence to go with me, but he would be a hindrance. If you are in want of money he can find you some."

"I have sufficient."

"I have never had sufficient, nor met anyone who has. Secondly, you must keep away from your old friends. If you intend to see this thing through they will not help you."

"Why, of course——"

"There is no 'of course.' Jenny will desire to help you when it becomes known you are heir to Steeple Berrington."

The Child blushed and frowned.

" Cultivate the Verralls and have patience with their ways. They are not our ways and you will not like them."

"How sourly you talk, Turquet."

"But they are her ways," he went on coldly, "and if

you want your princess you must make them your ways. Such is the way of women, especially religious women. A priest I knew used to be always saying, 'At least bear patiently if thou canst not joyfully.' It is the keynote to good manners which keep affection alive."

It was the truth of the dim revelation on the bridge bluntly expressed. Master Nic sat looking into the fire and yet felt cold.

"With the lawyers you will want more patience. For my part I should have gone to Crowley and made terms with him, but Verrall thinks otherwise. He is a man of business. Let him guide you."

"Is there anything else, Turquet?" said The Child sulkily.

"Yes. Keep away from the cards."

"Has Simon Verrall converted you or how do you come by so much wisdom and morality?"

"Experience," sighed the Count, wearily knocking out his pipe. "Experience; and like many another old fool I am flattering myself I can teach you how to acquire the same knowledge without burning your wings."

Master Nic's merry smile brightened his face again.

"You were always like that, dear friend, and I have never ceased laughing at your kind folly. Who could be happier than I am to-day and whose prospects could be brighter?"

"And as nothing one can say or do can alter fate, what foolishness all this talk has been. You are right, Nic, and I think you told me before that giving advice is the pet folly of old men."

He put his pipe on the mantelshelf and altered his tone.

"I must be back in time for the wedding, my boy."

"Of course, Turquet. It would be nothing without my best friend. When do you return?"

"I know nothing of it. A week or a month. Who knows? Sir James Hezlet may have news of me if you want to write to me."

"We shall have to wait at least a month, I suppose," said Master Nic, thoughtfully.

"I should say so," said the Count, smiling rather sadly,

"but if I do not return in time there is a phrase of the old woman that seems to fit the case. She's a good sensible old lady and she loves you, Nic. She had more sense than the rest of us this afternoon."

"And what would she say?"

"Her phrase has no sense to me, but it sounds well," said Turquet, taking the lad's hand in his. "She says, 'God bless all means to you,' but I stick to my creed and say Good-luck, and so good-night."

CHAPTER XVIII

COUNSEL'S OPINION

MR. BERRINGTON made a high endeavour to live up to the ideal of the faithful lover. He put away his finest clothes and assumed a sad-coloured coat of grey satin which he flattered himself, as he stood before the glass, combined an air of wisdom and discretion with the hint of riches.

The sacrifices he made to the gods of his beloved scarcely met with an adequate reward. For nearly a month he had dined almost daily at the austere table of the Verralls. He had accompanied his beloved to the meeting-house, and smiled at the antics and mouthing of the preachers, until nature and the stuffy heat of the crowded building overpowered his honest efforts and, to the shame of the family, his head nodded in obvious slumber.

Poor Hetty watched him struggling to make headway in these strange scenes and threw beacon glances of encouragement from loving eyes. But the lovers seemed to grow apart from each other rather than to be drawn nearer. They treasured silences of their own which each feared to share with the other. A condition of things always fatal to true comradeship.

For Hetty dared not speak seriously to her lover of her religious faith, and she on her part was waiting for her beloved to tell her in greater detail the story of his past life. But it had already dawned on Master Nic that his past and the glorious activities of his early days were not episodes in the career of Mr. Berrington that would be useful evidence for his lawyers or support his claim to his property; nor were they triumphs that he could lay at the feet of his mistress, to the end that he might bask in the sunshine of her praise and admiration. Therefore in his careless, merry way but with sound dramatic instinct, he determined to kill and bury his past. The past was dead and no one should dig up the corpse of it to disgust the living. And, after all, it was his own past, and if he chose to disinherit himself and adopt a quieter and less adventurous past to please others, was he not carrying out the text of Mr. Westerman's sermon of last Sunday: "old things are passed away; behold all things are become new?"

In what he deemed to be the spirit of this text, Mr. Berrington drew up a discreet narrative of his early life, for the use of his lawyers. This he read to Billinge, who expressed the candid opinion that it beat the truth hollow.

Mr. Oldcastle, Verrall's lawyer, carried this away to place it before the famous counsellor, Mr. Annesley, who had devilled in the old days for the great Jacobite counsellor Christopher Layer, and after his execution, had attained to a wide practice among the landowners of England. It was said that the cupboards of his chambers were filled with the skeletons of the families of the great.

Soon afterwards Mr. Oldcastle sent for Mr. Berrington, who took a coach to his attorney and found Mr. Verrall awaiting him there. Mr. Oldcastle informed them that Counsellor Annesley had read the papers and was kind enough to say that he would like an interview with Mr. Berrington before he advised or offered to appear in the case.

The three of them walked to Middle Temple Lane, where they climbed up a narrow winding wooden staircase and were received by the Counsellor's clerk and ushered with much solemnity into the presence.

Mr. Annesley, a tall, gaunt man of about fifty with bushy eyebrows, a long hatchet face and wide, firm mouth, sat at a table heaped up with papers and parchments, over the top of which his thin raw neck stretched out that his eyes might peer at the intruders.

Mr. Oldcastle introduced his clients and "The Vulture," as Master Nic named him on the view, fastened his eyes on the heir of the Berringtons as if he could discern the very nakedness of his thoughts and was ready to tear the truth out of his vitals. But his client was not abashed and smiled back a sunny smile as he bowed and took his seat by the window.

"The case seems clearly made out to the date when Mr. Berrington leaves the Yorkshire school, but after that?" asked the Counsellor.

"I have no instructions," said Mr. Oldcastle.

The Vulture gazed curiously but not unkindly at Mr. Berrington.

"Is it at all important?" asked Master Nic lightly.

"It is all important," replied the Counsellor.

"Mr. Oldcastle never told me so," said Mr. Berrington mischievously.

The Vulture shrugged his shoulders and lifted his eyebrows wearily. The ways of attorneys were beyond fathoming, but they brought grist to the mill and were therefore to be accepted without rebuke. Mr. Berrington's words were true and stung Mr. Oldcastle, who felt the silent contempt of the Counsellor. Like many another lawyer, he had sought the information from his client by every other method than that of direct inquiry, and, of course, Master Nic had gloried in the task of putting him off by skilful equivocation.

"If it is of importance to you, Sir, shall I tell you my history from the moment I left the Yorkshire school?" asked Mr. Berrington frankly.

"I shall be obliged if you will do so, Mr. Berrington."

"I will for the present omit all names. For the story is not wholly my own and there are reasons why I may not agree to bring others into my affairs unnecessarily."

At this The Vulture turned his eyes piercingly upon his client and listened intently to his statement. The main features of it were those he had rehearsed in the morning before Billinge, but occasionally new features seemed to come to his remembrance; the cruelty of the schoolmaster, the kindness of his patron, for he had woven Mr. Ambrose into his story, the excellence of the education he received at his London school, and some of the learning he had acquired there, here he was on sure ground or he was describing facts, and his last meeting with his patron at a dinner with Mr. Quin when he had urged him to follow up his claim and offered to supply him with money for the purpose.

Oldcastle listened to the story with satisfaction. Given the names of the patron and the schoolmaster, it could easily be proved. Verrall accepted the narrative simply and gladly. He had feared to hear worse things. The idea that it was anything but truth and fact never entered his honest mind. The Counsellor continued to sit listening intently with his eyes set on his client as his head swayed slowly circling from side to side, his habit when very deep in thought.

When the story was finished the Counsellor sat upright and after a moment's silence, said: "A good story: but for our purposes useless without the names of your patron and the schoolmaster."

"As to that, Counsellor Annesley, I will tell you if you wish it, but in confidence. You will then understand my reasons."

"I take it," said the Counsellor slowly, "that the school where you acquired so much learning and added correctness of deportment to your natural gifts—."

Mr. Berrington blushed and bowed to accept the compliment.

"Was the establishment of the excellent Mr. De La Place at Marylebone. There is no other that meets your description."

Master Nic sat erect, startled. Here was a different class of man from Verrall and the attorney. He was vexed that he had been betrayed by the pleasures of memory into so much useless description, but there was no going back upon the story.

"You knew my schoolmaster, then?" he asked.

"My only son was at the school."

"Cecil Egerton Annesley," said Nic, slowly as the vision of the boy leapt to his eyes. "Of course. He was one of the party when we raided the orchard at the farm at the end of Love Lane and the farmer peppered young Burton with small shot." Master Nic laughed at the memory of it. "Well, he will remember me there."

"He died of smallpox more than a year ago," said the Counsellor gravely, and then, eager to return to the case, he hurriedly continued. "But the evidence of De La Place will be of value to us, and he will have known your patron from Lancashire."

"I do not think he ever saw him. The business was arranged by an agent."

"Then we must know the names of the agent and of your patron and their evidence must be taken."

"It is not possible, Mr. Annesley," said Master Nic decisively.

"I cannot advise in a case where the whole facts are not put before me."

"The facts are not my facts. I have always heard that Christopher Layer might have kept his head and been sitting in these chambers to-day if those who knew his secrets had not betrayed them. You do not advise me to that course, Counsellor."

"It will be very difficult," interrupted Mr. Oldcastle, "if we are not to take the proofs of these witnesses to substantiate our case. I can, of course, see Mr. De La Place at once."

"You will do no such thing," said Mr. Berrington promptly, "until," he added, "Counsellor Annesley gives the word. It seems to me we are trespassing on the Counsellor's time. He has heard the whole story now and can give us his advice."

The Counsellor gathered up the papers in front of him and tied them firmly together and leaned back in his chair. He looked at the youth before him and the shadow of a kindly smile lighted his weary grey face. "I will tell you honestly, Mr. Berrington, what I have to say about your case. When Mr. Oldcastle first brought me these papers I was, I confess, inclined to believe that you were an impostor, excuse the word."

"It was a reasonable enough thought," said Master Nic laughing.

"I remember the death of your father very well and the terrible losses the Bar sustained at that Black Assize at Oxford. I have friends in the county. Your disappearance as a child was talked of at the time. Crowley was a man of good reputation and it was known that your father's estate was heavily encumbered. I am absolutely convinced to-day

that you are Mr. Nicholas Berrington and your father's heir."
Turning to Mr. Oldcastle he continued, "I will put my
advice on the case in writing. Meanwhile I think, Mr.
Oldcastle, that you should make a distinct and direct claim
against Mr. Crowley that he acknowledges your client's
rights, and put a time limit upon him for his accounts to
be delivered. These letters of his show a disposition to
dally and waste time. Either he must accept Mr. Berrington
as heir to the estates or we must fight. That is my advice
to Mr. Berrington."

"I wish we could start the fight straight away," said
Mr. Berrington with a sigh. He felt the danger of inaction
to himself and his beloved.

"Let us hope for everyone's sake there will be no fight
and that Mr. Crowley will take a wise course and make
peace. And now, Mr. Berrington," said the lawyer rising
from his chair, "may I invite you to walk across to Nando's
with me for a pipe and a cup of coffee? I should like to have
a talk with one who knew my poor boy. I ask this favour
as a father, Sir, and not as a lawyer."

Mr. Berrington was very willing to please the old man.
He had no qualms of conscience at the fictions he had imposed upon him, but he was puzzled in his own mind how
far the lawyer had really believed in them. Verrall and Mr.
Oldcastle went their way and the tall lawyer and his gay
young client, a strangely assorted couple, walked across to
Inner Temple Lane and entered the lawyers' Coffee House
where the Counsellor, who was a respected customer, led
the way to a quiet box at the end of the room.

Here over pipes and coffee Master Nic recalled as many
anecdotes as he could of his school-days at Marylebone and
the pranks and comedies and tragedies of school-life. And
in all his stories young Annesley was made to play a hero's
part, and the old man sat and listened with a soft smile of
content on his worn features as a happy child will welcome
old nursery tales.

When the stream ran dry and Mr. Berrington rose to go,
the old lawyer put his hand on the young man's arm and
said: "You have fairly conquered me. The story you told
me in my chambers is very far from the truth, and a lawyer

is a fool to touch a case where his client is deceiving him
but, God knows, my own boy might have been just such
another as you, and in the same trouble, so if you want a
friend as well as a lawyer you may trust me."

Nic's eyes sparkled with grateful thanks. He looked
across the room. There was no one within hearing. "I will
tell you anything you wish to know," he said simply.

"It were better so if I am to help you," said the lawyer,
his features stiffening again as if his mind stood at attention
once more.

"You do not believe in my patron, perhaps?"

The Vulture, for so he seemed again, shook his head.

"He is a Lancashire man. Christopher Layer knew him.
Mr. Ambrose of The Clough."

The Vulture raised his eyebrows. "Mr. Ambrose," he
said in a tone of surprise. "Has he been in London of
late?"

"Now you understand my difficulty," said Master
Nic.

"But did you live in the north with him?"

"Never," said his client simply. "Nor did I ever go to
school in Yorkshire with the Rev. Daniel Adamson. But if
need be, Mr. Ambrose will help me in any way I choose
to ask. I had the pleasure to do him a service. You have
asked me for the truth as a friend. Some day I will tell you
the whole story. Meanwhile, the story I have told in your
chambers seems to me to meet the occasion."

And before the lawyer could utter any protest or take up
the matter in argument, Mr. Berrington had seized his hat
and cane and pulled out his watch as if late for an engagement, and shaking the lawyer firmly by the hand had
thanked him with his bravest and most engaging of smiles
for his kindness and friendship and hurried out into Fleet
Street in a cloud of excuses and apologies and the necessity
of haste to fulfil other duties. And as the old man stood
looking after him with amazed curiosity, he felt that this
bright young being had found a place in his heart.

Mr. Berrington strolled west, keeping his place by the
wall against all comers. The fact that The Vulture had
accepted him as the heir of the Berringtons gave him new

heart. But when he pictured himself telling falsehoods to his beloved his bravery forsook him. He would walk in the Park and take counsel with himself by the banks of the canal.

As he was passing the Royal Mews at the bottom of Leicester Fields a noisy mob of weavers and their friends came up behind him. There had been trouble in Spittlefields over the importation of calicoes, and now some Irishmen had started working at a lower rate than the Londoners. And though the weavers were staunch Whigs, their grievances turned them mad and they came in gangs to the west end of the town, cursing the Germans and reviling the King and Queen. In such-wise in all ages is the fire of mob violence kindled by stray sparks and if it be not stamped out in the beginning may spread from the kennel to the palace.

Mr. Berrington stopped at the bottom of the incline watching a sedan chair ambling towards St. James's. The chairmen wore the livery of the Prince of Wales and Nic stood aside to let it pass. In it was the Princess Caroline going to the Palace, wholly unattended, as her custom was, for she and the Prince were beloved of the people and it was part of her wise policy to show her trust in them.

Master Nic swept his hat to the ground as he bowed gracefully to the first lady in the land. Caroline of the bright eyes nodded a laughing greeting to the handsome youth. Just at that moment some ruffians rushed out of an entry with coarse cries about "the King's Woman." Doubtless they thought the lady in the chair was the Duchess of Munster or some other of the King's mistresses. The weavers joined in the cry and mobbed the chair. The chairmen set down their burden and, drawing out their poles, drove the mob back. A hulking brute of a fellow, no weaver, let us remember, but a chairman who had joined the mob for fun, thrust his filthy head in at the window of the sedan chair and shouting, "The Princess by God," spat three times in her face.

Berrington, who saw his beastly action, flew at him like a terrier as he turned to fly down an entry, flung himself on the back of the ruffian, and throwing his arm round the

throat of the beast well-nigh choked the life out of him. By
this time the cries of the Princess's chairmen had brought
several citizens to her rescue. The mob of weavers now
made way for a mob of loyal subjects. They bound the
ruffian and would, indeed, have torn him to pieces had not
Mr. Berrington urged them to save him for the cart and the
hangman's whip. And now the friendly crowd so mobbed
the chair huzzaing and shouting for their dear Princess that
the chairmen could not get near the chair again. But her
Royal Highness, who to the end of her days never learned
what fear was, stepped out of the sedan chair and raised her
hand, beckoning Mr. Berrington to come forward.

Casting no look at the ruffian at her feet and as if she
were in her own drawing-room, she placed her hand on
Mr. Berrington's arm and bade him escort her back to
Leicester House. The crowd parted and made a lane for
their heroine to pass—she might have walked over their
bodies had she willed—cheers rent the air, the great heart
of the people, as the phrase goes, was filled to overflowing
at the spectacle of the great princess, gowned, bejewelled
and adorned for a royal drawing-room, walking in their
midst on the arm of a fellow-citizen. No wonder when His
Majesty heard of the little drama that he called poor
Caroline "cette diablesse Madame la Princesse." Indeed,
the good lady knew more about the sane management of
English democracy than any other German royalty that
ever reigned, and who can teach that knowledge but the
Devil himself?

By now news of the fracas had reached Leicester House.
The lackeys had rushed for orders to the Chamberlain, they
had penetrated to Lord Hervey and his lady, and Prince
Prettyman himself had been roused from his lethargy to
take the field.

Lord Bathurst was the first to run down the steps of the
house and meet the procession. He would have offered the
Princess his arm, but she smilingly refused and mounted
the stairs of the portico leaning on the arm of her young
squire until she saw the Prince, who by now had reached
the doorway.

Safe in her husband's arms she, as was her wont, whispered a few stage directions to the Prince. The little man came forward and the mob saw with delight that he said a few words of gratitude to Mr. Berrington and raised the royal fingers for him to kiss, which the hero of the occasion did with much grace and loyal fervour.

At this touching scene men yelled, women's eyes filled with tears, the mob shouted themselves hoarse, and English hearts beat with joyful patriotism and pride that Providence had brought such noble creatures to rule over the destinies of their land.

CHAPTER XIX

STRANGE it is, in a great city, how an obscure person, unknown to his neighbours, suddenly becomes a hero of gossip in coffee-house and tavern, the talk of the town, and a bone of fierce contention between contending parties who know nothing authentic of his rights and wrongs. Dame Gossip and her acolytes in Grub Street welcome their puppet hero. Fables and tales are invented by opposing journals and dished up as truth by clever writers to tickle the ears of their patrons cunningly garnished with romance for the gulls who swallow such garbage and call it news.

Upon this foundation the knowing ones build new edifices of rumour, add fictions only to be retailed in whispers, slander the dead—a safer task than libelling the living—until at last the city buzzes and booms with wild stories which fools repeat to each other with unholy joy until the game is stale, some new incident seizes the fancy of the mob, and merely to mention the old myth is to prove yourself out of the world and no man of fashion. As it was in the eighteenth century is now and we may readily suppose ever will be.

It must be remembered that at this time there were two courts: George I and his fat German women at St. James's, who were cordially hated by the citizens, and Prince George and Princess Caroline at Leicester House, who dutifully hated the old man who stood between them and the throne and stuck at nothing in the way of catchpenny public display to please the mob and annoy the King. And Berrington's London was a city of saunterers, men of leisure who cared for little else but either to tell or to hear some new thing.

It is not surprising, therefore, that this story of the attack upon the Princess and her rescue by a manly unknown, a youth of beauty and presence, who had been honoured by the Prince himself, was like a handful of meal thrown over the farmyard gate bringing the poultry clucking and fluttering to one place to scramble for their share of it.

For the next few days the journals and news-sheets had varied accounts of what had happened and strange stories were put about in the coffee-houses of the origin of the riot and the conduct and personality of the rescuer. The Whig politicians at St. James's Coffee-House or the Smyrna in Pall Mall were gravely exercised about the extent of the plot and discoursed nervously of their fears of a larger rising of the mob instigated by foreign gold, and there were loud demands for further arrests and stringent measures against Tory speakers and writers. The Tories at the "Cocoa Tree" or "Ozinda's" disclaimed all interest in the matter, shocked that the malice of their opponents should dare to blame them for the foul deed of a base mechanical ruffian who was like as as not set on to the battery by some Whig spies who went about promoting disorder for their own wicked purposes.

From Nando's and the Temple came rumours that the hero of the affair was the claimant to great estates and a youth of unbounded riches who had been stolen by gipsies in his youth and recently discovered by his relatives. Many of the wits and literary gentlemen at Button's or Will's had stories of their own making about the attack on the Princess and the mystery of the young fellow who had saved her, and it was said that Mr. Quin, the actor, knew the youth and his history and that he was a young Jacobite recently returned from France whose name was Berrington. When this story reached the "Cocoa Tree" there was great rejoicing, since the rescue of a woman in distress was the natural privilege of a gentleman of the old school.

The first principle of party politics is that what your party finds convenient to believe is true, and what the other fellows foolishly or dishonestly pretend to believe is false. The Tory world was ready to welcome Berrington as the rightful heir to the Oxfordshire estates whilst the Whigs, with the honourable exception of Toby Billinge, were inclined to rank him as an impostor.

Master Nic accepted his popularity with cheerful resignation. It seemed to him a natural flood-tide in his affairs, sent to carry him in to the haven for which he was making. When his acquaintance, Lord Bassett, who had been sent by Lord Hervey, the Princess's favourite, met him in Westminster Hall with a command that he should attend the Prince at Leicester House he betrayed no undue elation. Indeed, in his child-like way he regarded it more as an opportunity of visiting tailors, perruquiers and haberdashers than a great stroke of fortune and honour to himself. Master Verrall had insisted upon advancing him money to carry on his suit, and this was properly secured by deed. But now that he had money in his pocket the world of credit was open to him and he had too soft a heart to offend the willing tradesmen by offering them coin when all they pleaded for was custom.

The Vulture became more than ever interested in his client. Mr. Quin and his friends welcomed him to the playhouse. His social engagements became very numerous and he found less time for visits to Fetter Lane. When he did meet his beloved, his rosy pictures of his triumphs, his cackle of the coffee-houses and his new friends, and the business talk of the assured success of his claims roused little enthusiasm in poor Hetty.

Day by day she mourned over her own unworthiness to be helpmate of so brilliant a creature. The higher she appraised his wealth, his nobility, his easy carriage in the greatness of his new circumstances, the more clearly did she discern the narrow station of life to which she had been called and a nameless terror struck her soul at the thought of deserting the home she knew and the father who had protected her all her life, for a position she could never fill with honour to her beloved.

She had her own pride. At Cherry Croft, on the downs, and in the chalk-pit they were lovers and equals. Here in the great city she had awakened from the dreams of first love. She believed he would be true to his word. But that was not enough. She could not bear the thought of his stooping to lift her to a throne where she would always be an inferior in the eyes of all about them. Daily prayers and tears brought her nearer to a clear resolve. She must set her beloved free to fulfil a destiny she was not born to share. How often afterwards did she regret that she had never had the courage to speak the words of farewell when he held her in his arms.

The Princess Caroline had walked through the great drawing-room and the levee was over. She had spoken a few words of nothingness to those who had pleased the Prince's party, and thereby put them into the seventh heaven of delight, she had ignored those who had displeased the leaders of their faction by some act or speech of malice or neglect and left them wondering who had betrayed them, and she had flattered the powerful leaders of the King's government by assiduous and gracious attentions. A word of thanks to Mr. Berrington, who was brought forward by Lord Hervey, had raised him as if by magic to a pinnacle in new social altitudes. When Her Highness left the drawing-room many came round him to make themselves known to him and offer him those services and hospitality that are always at the disposal of new favourites. For, as the Princess turned away from him to welcome another courtier, she was overheard to ask Lord Hervey to bring Mr. Berrington to her apartments when the levee was over.

Mr. Berrington in after years always expressed a great admiration for Queen Caroline. She impressed his simple mind as a beautiful figure of royalty. She wore her powdered hair dressed low with ringlets hanging down her shapely shoulders. Knots of pearls laced her wide sleeves. There was regal fullness in the heavy yellow figured silk skirt which stood well away from the hips as fashion demanded. Her fresh complexion, dainty curved lips, keen, watchful eyes and smiling greeting to Master Nic won his loyalty at once. He would never concede the stout homeliness of the German house-wife, which even the cleverest court painter could not wholly eliminate. "A great queen," Mr. Berrington would insist, "a wise, tactful managing woman of sense and courage." Here he was right.

Lord Hervey took Mr. Berrington to his own rooms and asked him to remain there until Her Highness was ready to give him a private audience. He then returned to the Princess's apartments, where he found her seated at her knotting in the centre of her little band of courtiers. The young princesses, Emily and Caroline, girls of thirteen and fourteen, were working at their tambour frames under Mrs. Purcell's directions. Mrs. Clayton, Mrs. Howard, Lord Lifford and other ladies and gentlemen regaled the Princess with the news and gossip of the day.

"Well, Hervey," said Her Highness as my lord came in, "have they decided yet to hang the rogue that attacked me?"

"Madam," replied my lord, in tones of apology and despair, "the Lord Chancellor tells me it cannot be done."

The Princess frowned.

"But I spoke to him myself," she cried petulantly.

"It seems there are Acts of Parliament——" began Lord Hervey.

"Parliament, Mon Dieu! and lawyers! Your English institutions are *ennuyants*," replied the Princess with a sneer.

"They will not let such a wretch live, mamma, will they?" asked Princess Emily, with a troubled look on her child face.

"He will not go unpunished," said Lord Hervey reassuringly. "He will be whipped at the cart's tail from Somerset House to Charing Cross, and there will be a fine loyal crowd to see the sight."

"I wish they would bring him past our windows," said little Emily, pouting disappointment.

Her mother and the court ladies laughed pleasantly at her eager spirit.

At that moment the Prince entered, and they all rose. The dapper little man in his glory of gold brocade went from one of the pretty ladies to the other uttering some vapid criticism of the embroidery, or making some foolish remark upon the world's affairs, with a solemn stare of his empty cod-fish eyes, which his courtiers outwardly regarded as lamps of wisdom. How could all those pretty girls hide their contempt for the creature? But schooling and ambition will work wonders. Smiling Mary Bellenden beamed gratitude, beautiful Molly Lepell shone admiration, roguish Sophia Howe extinguished a wink beneath her pretty eyelashes, and the solemn prude, Miss Meadows, abased herself before his god-like wisdom. They fooled him to the top of his bent. When we laugh at the absurdity of kings, we should in charity remember their temptations.

Lord Bassett reminded the Princess that Miss Chilcote, the glove-seller of Westminster Hall, was in attendance.

"Bring her in then," said Her Highness; "they say she has English gloves equal to any that come from Flanders and Spain. It was the Prince commanded that we should wear everything that was English."

The Prince may not have remembered this, but he nodded approval. In this wise did Caroline lead her stupid bear to dance to her will.

"It is thoughts like these that touch the heart of the people," said Lord Hervey, as if thinking aloud.

A murmur of approval filled the apartment.

The Prince smiled thoughtfully.

Old Nan was introduced with Hetty, who carried boxes of her wares. The girl unpacked them, and Mrs. Chilcote explained their strength and beauty. The Princess prompted her husband to practical words of critical wisdom and chose some gloves for herself, asking his advice about each.

Hetty was dazzled with the glory of the costumes of the men and women who moved about the gilded apartment, and cast glances of satisfaction at themselves in the long mirrors which panelled the walls. She sought to pick out specimens of gloves to please the young ladies, who were full of pleasure at turning over the treasures that lay on the table. But old Nan knew her business.

"Find the fringed gloves for my lord," she ordered sharply, and Hetty had to help my Lord Hervey, whose cherub face covered with paint, mumbling smiles and pretty compliments, sickened her with disgust. The Prince gazed at her with passing admiration, but she had not the mature charms of his fair Howard. Still, he would have liked to romp with her at a masquerade, and if Lord Bassett brought her with him, as he had promised to do, he made a resolution that he would satisfy his whim. The Princess frowned slightly. She did not approve of the men of her own circle buzzing round the girl in her presence.

"What are these gloves for?" she asked, picking up some rough cut pairs of a very tender skin.

"They are chicken skin, your Highness," replied Hetty, glad to move away from my Lord Hervey.

"Ladies wear them to sleep in," added old Nan. "They keep the skin tender and white."

"Indeed!" said the Princess. "I must try them."

"Can they make perfection more perfect?" asked Lord Hervey with his obsequious smile.

The Princess laughed at his folly.

"And about the young man Berrington?" continued Lord Hervey.

Hetty started.

"Shall I send him about his business?"

"No, by no means," replied the Princess eagerly. "I had forgotten my Don Quixote. Send for him at once."

Lord Hervey motioned to Lord Bassett, who left the room and returned in a few moments in company with Mr. Berrington.

The stout Princess ambled across the room to greet him.

It was as though a young god had entered a grove of pigmies, fauns and attendant nymphs, who looked up from their frolics and were silent in admiration of their master. Dressed in the height of fashion, his full flung wig, the ringlets reaching the shoulders, hiding his own natural curls, the ample grey satin coat reaching below the knee, covering his lithe, graceful figure, the square-toed, high-heeled shoes hindering the free movement of the body— even these ungainly burdens could not obscure the beauty of the youth.

The good Princess gave her hand to the young hero who had rescued her, and her eyes gave him a grateful welcome, for he was good to look upon. Her young daughters feasted their eyes on his joyous presence almost greedily, and the ladies of the Court were at once his friends and his slaves. Even the Prince and Lord Hervey and the other gentlemen were more admiring than jealous. He was so young, so unassuming, so natural. It was my Lord Hervey who said to the Princess: "He comes among us as a sun child on a visit to the earth."

P

Hetty, whose eyes were fixed on him from the far end of the room, observed with dismay that even these great ones had no terrors for her lover, who accepted their homage as a matter of daily routine. Would that he, too, had caught a sight of his beloved as he entered the room.

But to the bright insight of Master Nic, who had the genius to walk by instinct into the centre of the stage and accept the devotion of the minor players, these men and women, though cast for high-sounding parts, were of no account when he himself, the real star, appeared on the horizon of their world. It was his royal whim to accept the Princess as a fairy godmother, but he could not make believe about the puppet Prince, or these dumpy, gawky girls who eyed him so greedily, or Lord Hervey, painted and perfumed for his part of Sporus, or Mrs. Clayton, whose big earrings grew bigger with every place she sold. These were all as common clay as any in Bohemia.

Her Highness gave him the cue. She had heard that he was making claim to extensive estates in Oxfordshire, and he must tell them all about it. Gloves were forgotten. Nan Chilcote withdrew humble but scowling. Hetty in her corner trembled tearfully. Mr. Berrington told his story in a few words with becoming modesty. The Princess, seated on a sofa gazing with matronly pleasure at the young figure in front of her, listened attentively to The Child's pleasant romance pictures of ancient halls and parks and lawns and farms and broad acres.

" There is only one thing wanting, Mr. Berrington," said the Princess laughing, "and that must be our care to find for you."

"Madam, you honour me. I cannot guess your meaning."

"When you come into your kingdom, sir, we will find you a mistress worthy of it."

"Ah, madam, how can one so unworthy hope for such happiness?" replied Mr. Berrington with feigned humility.

"Faint heart ne'er won fair lady," mocked Lord Hervey.

"Perhaps not faint but already disposed of," suggested Mrs. Howard.

"My good Howard has a true instinct for a faithful heart. Has my young knight already a lady-love?"

"Is it fair to ask him to make his confession here before us all?" asked saucy Mistress Howe, laughing.

"Then will you place your happiness in our hands?" asked the Princess gaily. "We will be like the Parliament gentlemen and form a committee of selection to find you a bride."

Mr. Berrington was in no way outfaced by the women's folly, and entered into the jest with pleasure. With a gracious swing of the arm he made a low bow, reaching to the knees of the Princess.

"Your humble petitioner will ever pray that you will do him so much honour as to nominate some fair lady who will deign to accept so unworthy an esquire——"

"You are indeed an obedient courtier, Mr. Berrington, and I can see that you are still heart-whole."

"Madam," replied the foolish youth, with his hand upon his heart, "my affections are as free as air."

Hetty was no longer trembling. Anger and bitter indignation had given her strength. She had no knowledge or experience of the chaff and badinage of courts. The false coinage of words used in her world to express golden truths and here thrown from tongue to tongue, meaning less than nothing, utterly deceived her. In her world yea was yea, and nay was nay. There could be no middle values in spoken words, which must express the light of truth or the darkness of lies. She had heard with her own ears, and they could not play her false.

It was the sin of Peter without a divinity to forgive. Hetty was but yet a woman. That her lover should openly deny her before these worldlings was too gross an insult. She stood rooted to the spot, drinking in the foolish talk as if it were a poison syrup. In vain did Nan Chilcote gather her samples together and seek to distract her attention and draw her away. She would lose no moment of her agony.

The careless Child, for he was nothing better, poised his supple body in an exquisite bow to his fairy godmother, drawling out a second time the fool phrase, "affections free as air."

Hetty moved forward a pace or two as if to denounce him in her anger, and stopped shamefaced. Nic looked up and saw for a moment the scorn on her face. There was only one real outstanding figure in the room for him—the woman he loved, and he could not speak to her. The rest seemed to vanish like dream persons. This was his last memory of her. He could never wipe that form off his tablets—Hetty and her brown eyes flashing fire and revenge, sweeping with dignity out of his path as she threw a last glance of contemptuous farewell to her lover, and her lips curled scornfully as they seemed to form an echo of his own words: "Free. Yes. Free as air."

CHAPTER XX

THERE was a certain irony in Mr. Berrington's fastening on Thrift Street, Soho, as the site of his new lodgings. The place was in the centre of fashion, and the rooms were to be had at a reasonable price, as the late tenant, a young country squire who had lost his bearings in the uncharted seas of London's libertinism, had been redeemed from the Marshalsea by an irate father and carried back to an impoverished estate on the wolds of Lincolnshire.

Brick walls tell no tragedies, and Master Nic entered upon his new domain with a light and easy heart. He admired his marble mantelpieces and their white Corinthian columns, and accepted the heavy crimson curtains and blue silk bed hangings of his predecessor, until such time as he could adorn the place to his own taste. Already his table was littered with cards and invitations, appeals for subscriptions, announcements of routs and fetes and humble offers of service from all the fashionable traders of the West End.

A week had passed since his visit to Leicester House. He had opened his heart to Counsellor Annesley and told him in confidence much of the real truth of his story; and the old man thoroughly convinced of the justice of his claim, had undertaken the direction of matters with the lawyer, Oldcastle. Meanwhile that worthy had arranged to advance the youth on certain documents signed, sealed and delivered, five hundred guineas for present needs. This sudden and unbounded wealth and his new position in the world of fashion had rendered a change of lodging necessary. During all this time he had not seen Hetty. He could not bring himself to face the brown eyes of scorn nor could his fertile brain plan out the exact dramatic excuse to be uttered at their meeting. Many rehearsals passed in his mind of how the scene of his forgiveness should be opened, but none seemed to him to meet the needs of the case. Words which came so readily to him failed his imagination as he entered her presence. He could not even shape her attitude. Sometimes she was soft and yielding, and again he saw her angry and revengeful, and though he felt serenely certain that he would be received into favour again, there were moments when he was enough of a traitor to wonder whether he wished to be taken back into her heart and be forgiven. He had picked up a pen to write to her, but the words laughed at him from the paper, and he tore it angrily. He had started to walk to Westminster, he had made a determined onset for Fetter Lane, but on each occasion a coffee house and a chance acquaintance and a bottle had seemed a deliverance from a task beyond his strength.

That afternoon he was to dine with the Counsellor at his house in Great Queen Street. Mr. Annesley was a widower and had an only daughter, Belinda, a charming girl of eighteen, much admired by the younger Templars, who were honoured by The Vulture's hospitality.

Mr. Berrington found himself once again exploring a new world. He had never before entered the house of a professional man, and experienced the charm of educated domesticity offered to him as a welcome friend with generous hospitality and good taste.

The Vulture, in a handsome brown and orange suit, sat at the head of his new mahogany table, his grave, kindly face alert to watch every movement of his dear Belinda, who did the honours of the table with a grace and certainty that vastly contented Mr. Berrington. The fool compared her in his heart to Hetty in the same situation.

There was but one other guest, young Robert Melvil. "He rides the Northern Circuit, Mr. Berrington. He will be their leader some day—aye, and go further than that."

"Counsellor, you make me blush."

"Papa doesn't praise everyone, Mr. Melvil, as I know to my cost," said Belinda pleasantly.

"Papa waits until there is something worthy of praise, Mistress Pert," replied the Counsellor, laughing.

Looking at Melvil across the table, Nic admired his round humorous face and the merry way he told amusing stories of the courts, clever and entertaining, but thoughtfully within the measure of modesty. Then the talk changed to books and music and painting and an article in *The Crafts-man* was touched upon, and some law cases had almost broken the happy thread of the converse, but Belinda sternly forbade "trade talk," and The Vulture nodded assent and approval. Then Belinda, to set the talk in pleasant paths, described a pantomime she had seen at the theatre at Lincoln's Inn Fields.

"It was perfectly wonderful, papa. There was an egg which grew larger and larger, until at length it cracked open and out came a little harlequin, and he grew and grew until he became a full-sized man, and then, when the serpent came on covered with gold and green scales and red spots making a hissing noise, one of the grenadiers on guard—for the King was there that night—was so frightened that he dropped his musket and drew his sword to defend himself from the monster. We were all terrified."

"It must have been a real pleasure, my dear," said her father drily.

"Ah, but when you came to the scene where the trees grew up and blossomed flowers, and the whole stage became a dense forest,—that was wonderful and beautiful. I wonder how it is all done."

This gave Mr. Berrington a chance to speak, for he had been at the making of some of these properties and seen them rehearsed. He could tell them secrets from that abode of mystery "behind the scenes," which all playgoers of all ages have rejoiced to hear about, and he could tell them that this pantomime had cost Mr. Rich over £4,000, and could explain to them all about the costly ingenuity of the serpent and the machinery of the forest.

The Vulture admired the cleverness of his daughter in finding a theme of talk in which his young friend could take a part. He became eloquent against Italian opera and foreign music, and loud in praise of the English stage and angry at the apathy and neglect with which it was treated.

Melvil and his daughter praised Cuzzoni and Mr. Berrington upheld the argument of his host.

"You play yourself, sir?" asked Belinda.

"I can strum a little on the spinet. At school we were all taught to play some instrument."

"I remember," said the Counsellor, nodding. "Mr. De La Place boasted of his boys' orchestra."

"So you were there, too," said Belinda, remembering her brother and smiling almost affectionately at Master Nic.

"We will have music after tea," said her father, "but it shall be English music, mind you."

The cloth was now removed, the King's health drunk in the first glass, and Belinda rose to go. Mr. Berrington, as he held open the door for her, admired her tall, lithe figure and confident carriage and the parting word of command she flung over her shoulder that they should not sit over-long with the wine. This well-bred courtesy of woman was a new and dainty pleasure to him.

At the end of the first bottle Mr. Melvil asked leave to go. He had work to attend to at the Temple. The Counsellor did not seek to stay him, and as he and his guest sat down to a second bottle, he spoke the praises of the young man and plainly intimated that he and Belinda were more than mere friends, and that some day his daughter might well be a judge's lady.

"She deserves the first in the land, sir," said Berrington with enthusiasm, and raising his glass, drank her health in a bumper. He felt an unreasoning dislike of young Melvil.

"Oldcastle was at my chambers this morning," continued the Counsellor. "This fellow Crowley makes delays and difficulties, but Oldcastle thinks he will not fight. It would be a great thing to take possession without a lawsuit. I have told Oldcastle to put our cards on the table—that is to say, all our good cards."

"It is often a sure bite," laughed Mr. Berrington knowingly.

"I was speaking to him about your friend Verrall, who seems to have been very forward in offers of money and assistance. You do not mind an older man offering you advice about these matters?"

He pushed the bottle towards Nic, who helped himself and expressed his gratitude.

"Mr. Verrall," continued the Counsellor, "is an excellent

citizen, no doubt, and a man of substance, but he belongs
to a pestilent set of country schismatics which an honest
English government should put down with a strong hand."

"I have no liking for his religious opinions," said Mr.
Berrington very honestly.

It relieved him to hear so clear an opinion of their
demerits from so learned a source.

"I tread on delicate ground, I know, but I speak as a
father would or, let us say, a father's friend, who can often
speak to a son with more discretion and less chance of
offence."

Nic's heart beat more quickly. He would have liked to
stop him, but he sipped his glass and bowed his thanks.

"Mr. Verrall seems to have told Oldcastle there was
something in the nature of an engagement between you and
his daughter. You mentioned the girl to me, I know. I must
have seen her often in Westminster Hall, for I buy my
gloves off Mother Chilcote. But we old men are blinder
than Cupid himself."

Mr. Berrington's good angel was calling upon him to
jump up and stop this discourse by declaring that Hetty was
the only woman he could ever love, and claim her before
all the world as his for better or worse, but he sat still, sipping his wine and nodding his head and telling his conscience that it was his duty to listen to the advice of his
elders. He would never desert Hetty, of course, but he must
know what he was doing. He must be cautious and consider
matters.

"I will not ask you how far things have gone between you
and the girl. You met in the country?"

Master Nic caught a glimpse of the chalk-pit in the
crystal of his glass and was going to burst out, but the
Counsellor pushed the bottle his way and the moment
darted past him.

"I know what you would say. We have all been young,
and the country in June was made for lovers. Why, I remember in eighty-five—or was it eighty-six?—at my uncle
Egerton's in Dorsetshire, there was a farmer's daughter; she
lived at the mill——" The old man broke off and emptied
his glass with half a sigh. "You have yourself to consider.

With the prospects and duties before you, and after your acceptance by the Prince and Princess, you must see that you cannot marry a girl of this class. For her sake, then, as well as your own, make a clean end of the whole affair."

Nic's good angel had fled in shame and disgust. A little hastily, perhaps, since this novice in the world's affairs had not himself capitulated to the superior arguments of his preceptor. Fair to the youth to remember that he had not been mean enough to concur in speech with the stale platitudes of social wisdom that the old Vulture had scattered lavishly in the hope that they would seed in his heart.

"Believe me, sir," concluded The Vulture, wagging his head kindly at the lad, "some day you will be thankful to me."

"I assure you I am grateful," stammered Nic, "but you don't know——" He paused and sighed. "It is all very difficult."

"Life is difficult, my dear boy. But my daughter waits."

As the Counsellor moved to the door, he placed his hand on Nic's shoulder. "Put an end to it, my boy, and remember the line: 'If it were done when 'tis done, then 'twere well it were done quickly.' "

"There was murder in that thought," said Berrington, shuddering. Then he laughed over loudly as if he had spoken in joke.

It was the Counsellor's pleasure to have a few friends to tea and music on occasion, and about a dozen guests were assembled in the big drawing-room when he and Mr. Berrington entered. Mr. Annesley introduced his young friend to the company. Mr. Justice Raymond, and his two lovely daughters, Linda's bosom friends, and fellow-pupils of Mr. Mercer, the music master, young Willie Murray, a law student and a great friend of Robert Melvil, Alderman Humphreys and his wife—he and the Counsellor were fellow-members of the Georgia Board—Mr. Tripland, one of the Chancery clerks, and his son, a lad of fifteen who played with great skill upon the fiddle, and several other young ladies and gentlemen.

Belinda presided at the tea-table and, when these duties

were accomplished, opened the spinet and herself played a simple piece by way of invitation and encouragement of her friends. But there was no false bashfulness about any of them. Within their powers all were ready to sing or play on their instruments, and the Counsellor and his friends sat round to listen and applaud.

To poor Nic the social peace and courtesy of these kind folk was as strange a dream as the blossoming stage forest had been to Belinda. He watched her long, graceful arms stretched over the keyboard, her bright, intelligent face intent upon the bow of young Tripland's fiddle, that she might take the time from him and play in harmony with his tune.

The murmur of thanks died away, and Mr. Justice Raymond was heard asking Belinda for a favourite song.

"I would sing it willingly, but the accompaniment, alas, I do not know it."

"We can never hear Linda's best songs unless Mr. Mercer joins us," said her father impatiently.

Mr. Berrington had walked across to the spinet and looked at the music. It was within his spirit of adventure.

"May I try it for you?" he asked.

Belinda was delighted. She loved to sing her best songs, standing to her full height, with her throat free and not bending over the instrument. Nic played a verse of it, Belinda nodding and smiling at his proficiency and humming the air to secure the time and the pauses. It was a triumphant success, and the young ladies were all ready to sing their best songs now that they were free of the dangers of accompaniments and had so skilful and handsome a companion in their efforts. When they had all achieved their success with his assistance, they demanded that he himself should sing.

"And let us have an old ballad, Mr. Berrington," called out the Counsellor. "'Drink to me only' or 'Who is Sylvia?' or——"

"Oh, papa!" groaned Belinda.

Even in those days the younger generation thought the old songs were out of date.

"There was a pretty song Mrs. Clive sang in a farce the

other day, if I can remember it," said Nic, trying a few notes
on the spinet.

"Kitty! That dainty rogue. I heard her sing it. It goes
like this——" The Counsellor hummed the air.

"That's it, sir. I have it," said Nic, and he played a few
bars. Then, with a spritely imitation of the incomparable
Kitty, and sufficient exaggeration of languishing conceit,
which made his young companions giggle with pleasure, he
started a popular love-song of the stage.

> "What need I trust your words precise,
>   Your soft desires denying,
> When O! I read within your eyes
>   Your tender heart's complying!
>   Your tongue may cheat
>   And with deceit
>   Your softer wishes cover,
>   But O! your eyes
>   Know no disguise,
>   Nor ever cheat your lover."

His eyes met Belinda's and they laughed assent to the
nonsense. There were more verses for the same refrain. The
song ended in joy and laughter.

"Capital! Capital!" cried the learned judge, clapping his
hands.

"I could see Kitty when I shut my eyes—the beautiful
wretch," said the Counsellor.

"Very merry, very merry!" laughed the alderman, "and
a lot of truth in it, too."

"My dear!" murmured his wife, frowning at him.

The young girls laughed and thanked Mr. Berrington
and assured him it was the purest nonsense they had ever
listened to.

When the party broke up Mr. Berrington walked towards
his lodgings with a heavy heart. The Counsellor's good advice weighed down his spirits. He turned into Button's to
see if there was anyone he knew who would make a night
of it with him. There were but few guests at Button's, and
no one that Master Nic knew. He sat himself down in a box

in the corner of the room, and calling for a bottle and a pipe, pretended to read *The Craftsman*, but he only followed the words on the page with his eyes.

All his mind was on Hetty. He rehearsed his every movement since their return from Sussex, and remembered his last evening with Turquet. He, too, was an older and wiser man, and perhaps had seen more of the real world than even The Vulture. He set their advice in parallel columns before his soul and hankered for the best of both schedules.

He laughed grimly and emptied another glass. He was a fool. Turquet was wiser than The Vulture. Riches without Hetty were dust and ashes. He would go back. He would recover the jewel. And then he saw Belinda sitting at the head of the table and the old man calm, sensible and full of kindly wisdom laying down the eternal law of class. The Vulture became old Verrall mouthing a grace before meat at Fetter Lane, with the stepmother turning the whites of her eyes to the ceiling and sleek Ziba clasping his humble hands, and pretty Hetty drooping her eyes to the table. She was of their class; she belonged to them. That was true enough. But not for ever. He was her brave knight riding to her rescue. He would snatch her away from them, carry her in triumph to his palace, build one more worthy of her, compel those who sneered at "a girl of that class" to accept her as his wife, the only woman in the world, his Hetty, his beloved! He drained a last glass to Hetty and seized his hat and cane and looked at his watch. It was only half-past nine. He had made up his mind.

He was in the Strand by now and pushing through Temple Bar and along Fleet Street, with the words on his lips, "I have sinned and am no more worthy," but with the sure thought in his heart that he was sealed for pardon and that ready arms would be thrown open to fold him in forgiveness.

He knocked at Mr. Verrall's door. Peace came over his heart as he heard the echo of the knock in the empty street. He had made the right choice at last. Nothing could turn him from his course now. He would not defend himself. He would cast himself at her feet and wait to be raised to the throne. He knocked a second time in his impatience and then a third.

At last the bolts were grudgingly drawn. The chain was removed. His heart beat rapidly. Was it Hetty herself! The door was opened a few inches, and Ziba's pale face looked out at him. He was holding a candle.

"Mr. Berrington!" he cried in surprise.

"I want to see Mr. Verrall at once. I must see him," said Master Nic, putting his foot forward as if to hinder the door being closed.

"Mr. Verrall is away."

"Then I will see Mrs. Verrall," cried Berrington.

"You have not heard, then?"

"Heard what?" asked Berrington, frightened at the subdued tones of Ziba's voice.

"Mrs. Verrall died of smallpox last week, and was buried on Saturday. Mr. Verrall and his daughter have gone. Poor man, he takes it badly. He thinks it was a judgment on his family for their pride and ambition. Verily it may be so, for 'pride goeth before destruction and an haughty spirit before a fall.' "

Berrington saw the door close slowly in his face. He had no fight in his heart. God would not forgive him, nor let Hetty forgive him. He was alone in the street, alone in the world. He turned his face to the west and walked away in sullen despair.

CHAPTER XXI

BELINDA

To chronicle in detail the days and nights of Berrington's descent into the hell of London's wealth and fashion would be a waste of vain words. But I spare myself the weariness of it, since anyone who thirsts for these things may find them for himself in the farces and comedies of the time. You may cast Nic Berrington if you will, for the parts of Gaywit, Sotmore, Bellamour, Wilding and the rest, but he wore their livery with a difference.

For he played his scenes of evil-doing with an air of grace and lighthearted insincerity in vice that robbed them of much of their grossness. An affair with the pretty wife of an alderman who had made eyes at him at the opera was more a gambling venture, to win a hundred guineas from Lord Bassett by producing at White's a ringlet of the frail one as a token of success, than a serious assignation. The fact, too, that his success had been marred by an enforced concealment in the lady's wardrobe, and an early morning escape with the loss of his coat and sword, made merry laughter for a generation of foolish youths whose limits of humour found in such exploits a tinsel glory of achievement.

Hetty had vanished from his horizon, and he plunged into the pleasures that fortune seemed to throw at his feet with the joy of a child. His parlour in Thrift Street soon became a morning centre for fashionable idlers. Not to know Nic Berrington was to be behind the hour. Certainly he played the part of host and patron with dazzling brilliancy. He was the gadfly of a summer afternoon, flashing gaily above the dung-hill of the town. Tailors, milliners, jockeys, prize-fighters, actors, musicians, gamblers and the lords and gentlemen of the day, who best loved such society accepted his sway and crowded his daily levee. Lord Bassett, whom his familiars called "Bunny," was his bosom friend and companion. A certain Colonel Sabine, a game-

ster of surprising skill and good fortune, had already drawn
him into some small parties at whist and ombre, at which
Nic had been reasonably successful, and it was noted
that he was a cool and knowing person at any game of
cards.

There was a young fellow about his own age, Roger
Mytton, from the West Riding of Yorkshire, reported to be
spending a large fortune, that had recently tumbled into his
lap, who resented the fuss that was made about Nic Berrington, since he seemed to be drawing away from his own circle
many who had danced attendance upon him for what
crumbs they could gather.

Young Mytton, though a spendthrift and a gambler, had
not those generous instincts of lavish waste which rejoice
the hearts of the idle and dissolute who live on the follies
and vices of their masters. There was a trait of meanness in
his character, and a grasping desire to win that made the
youngster a bad loser, an unloved character in the world of
sport in which he tried to shine. Mr. Berrington was always
the perfect loser, when loss came his way, paying his forfeit
with genial ease in the grand manner. It was a virtue that
the wasters of his company set great store by, and the
practice of it brought him many admirers.

It was Lord Bassett who brought Mytton to Thrift
Street to take his morning chocolate with Mr. Berrington,
who at the moment was enjoying a fencing lesson from the
famous M. Dubois. The foils were put aside, and coffee and
chocolate produced, but Berrington shouted to Billinge for
a mug of ale. He could never acquire the fashionable taste
for the slops that even in that day were ousting English
drink. Several other young fellows dropped in, and the talk
ran on racing, prize-fights, plays and the opera.

"What do we do this afternoon?" asked Nic, yawning.

"Whitehall cockpit," said one of his companions.

"A grand sport!" cried Nic, who, like that great schoolmaster, Roger Ascham, regarded cock-fighting as a pastime
very fit for a gentleman.

"Have you any birds?" asked Mytton.

"A few in the country," replied Nic airily; and for aught
he knew, it was the truth.

"Will you make a match with me?" asked Mytton eagerly.

"You will want a brave bird to beat Roger's best," said Lord Bassett warningly.

"My dear Bunny," said Mr. Berrington reprovingly, "surely you can trust me to find a bird to put up a good fight. Give me a week."

"Thursday week, then," said Mytton. "Fifty guineas. Is it a match?"

"Willingly," said Berrington, reaching for his book from the table to make a note of it. Several bets were made, but Nic had to take them all, and finding this, he demanded odds which were forthcoming at three to two, to which he nodded "Done" and pencilled the bets in the book.

When Billinge heard of it, he threw up his hands in despair. He knew all about Mytton's farms and the reputation of his pedigree birds at the cockpit. "It is a fair bite," he said angrily. "They have caught you this time."

"Maybe," said his master pleasantly, "but never say die, Toby. There is a blacksmith named Hilder at Alfriston who could train fighting-cocks with any man in the kingdom. He trained for Gage in the old days. We have more than a week to find our bird, and you shall ride down there at once. If he fails us, then you must go and pick up something over the river, and we will trust to luck."

But Hilder did not fail. He was proud of the chance to bring his birds to London and put up a fight for Sussex at Whitehall with the best that Yorkshire could produce.

The pit was crowded, for there had been much talk over the match. Most of the spectators were sorry for Berrington, since it was not to be supposed that a novice at the game could produce a cock to fight an owner of Mytton's reputation. They pressed near the small arena in which the birds fought. Mytton's cock-fighter placed his bird on the stand, and it walked round proudly for a few seconds. Some of the learned ones thought its legs too long and its feathers too plentiful, but the power of its neck and the strength of its limbs as it strutted on the board were favourably commented upon.

The bird was caught up, and Hilder produced his Sussex

Q

champion. An ugly fellow enough, not 'quite so big as the Mytton bird, but strong and sturdy on its short legs, with no crest to speak of.

"Not the blood of the other," as Colonel Sabine said; "a good farmyard fighter, no doubt, but not of the class for Whitehall."

Their silver spurs were put on and adjusted. The fighters held their birds at either end of the stage, and at the word given the champions rushed at each other with fury. The fight had commenced. Odds were yelled on Mytton. The Sussex bird was almost overpowered by the first onset of his opponent, but encouraged by Hilder, he pulled himself together, and a dogged fight ensued. Contrary to expectations, the fight turned out to be a great affair. The Mytton bird grew more careful. Both were torn and bleeding. The noise and yelling increased, the odds lessened to evens, and half an hour of wild, intense excitement and terrifying din saw two weary birds gradually weakening in their attack and a hundred haggard men hoarse and exhausted, but still yelling with the enthusiasm of greed, the sharp thrills of fear or the wild joy of contest.

Then in a moment the Sussex bird made a feint, followed by a furious rush which might have ended the fight, but he seemed to slip, and the Mytton bird was on to him at the moment and dropped him for dead on the boards. Yells went up: 5—1, 7—1, 10—1 guineas to shillings, but no call of "done." There was a sob of pity from Billinge. Berrington's face went white. Roger Mytton shouted aloud with joy, his greedy little eyes flashed triumph. The Mytton bird in the glory of his victory jumped on the dead body of his opponent and crowed in shrill derision and contempt. It had been well for him had he taken his winning more modestly. The great heart of the Sussex bird was still beating. The trumpet of triumph roused it to action. With a sudden effort he revived and almost leaped into the air and, falling on his astonished adversary, struck him dead to the ground with a blow.

"The case is altered," murmured Hilder thankfully. A yell of wild triumph was started by Billinge. Odds of a hundred to one were shouted in a wild mockery of enthusiasm by Berrington's friends. Good Master Hilder gathered up his bird into his arms and a few tears of joy fell on the bleeding crest of the noble creature that had brought him the happiest and proudest moment of his life.

And so it was with all his ventures. The gambler's luck continued with Berrington. His encounter with Colonel Sabine when he was rumoured to have pocketed the Colonel's faked cards was highly applauded ; and when it became known that the Colonel did not ask for satisfaction, and M. Dubois was reported to have said that he showed a wise discretion, Berrington was more than ever the hero of the hour.

But his great coup was in the hazard room at White's, where he won £5,000 at a sitting. From this moment the eyes of all London were upon him. "Lucky Berrington" was a nine days' wonder; his chariot was looked for in the Ring; his presence was sought after at Vauxhall. No party to a masquerade was complete without him. The fairest and best of women sat in his box at the opera. He frequented the Green Room and, to Belinda's surprise and delight, his word was taken (coupled with a guarantee of the costs of production) that Mr. Melvil's tragedy was indeed worthy of the stage. It was at this period of his story that Mr. Hogarth painted his portrait and, as many have noticed, used his figure, as well he might, for the hero of his Rake's Progress.

It was one of the duties of a man of fashion to frequent auctions. At these shows city madams met their west-end gallants, amateurs collected bric-a-brac and pictures, as they do to-day, and idle folk were there to see and be seen and waste the hours between chocolate and dinner.

Mr. Berrington had taken Belinda at her earnest request to one of these auctions at Mr. Dalton's print warehouse in Pall Mall. The room was crowded with dealers and buyers and onlookers. It was an auction of pictures. Mr. Berrington had come to the conclusion that his rooms in Thrift Street required a few old masters such as hung in Lord Hervey's drawing-room, and he was here to collect them.

The auctioneer, however, had little to display this morning but modern pictures and portraits. The bidding was by no means brisk and much in the hands of the dealers who had made a ring to cut prices. It was this that tempted Mr. Berrington to throw his voice into the medley to purchase a big Dutch landscape of windmills and frozen canals. Then the dealers, angry that some one from the outside should spoil their market, ran the picture up to fifty guineas, when Nic, who understood those cunning cheats as well as they did, smilingly left them with their bargain and refused to be drawn further into the contest.

A little later a portrait of a lady was held up, and the auctioneer announced that it was a masterpiece of Sir James Thornhill.

"What a beautiful face," murmured Belinda, touching her companion's arm to call attention to it.

Berrington turned round and looked at it. In his excitement he grasped her arm. "It is my mother," he whispered to her. "My mother."

"Twenty guineas," called a dealer.

"And ten," from another.

"Thirty," called the auctioneer, registering a bid from an old man who stood beneath the rostrum and nodded his wishes silently.

"Fifty," called out Mr. Berrington in a clear voice.

The old man nodded another ten.

"Sixty," cried the auctioneer.

The dealers stood aside. The picture had passed out of commercial figures as far as they were concerned.

"Seventy!" called out Mr. Berrington.

"And five," said the old man.

"Seventy-five," repeated the auctioneer, looking in pleasant expectation at Mr. Berrington.

"Make it a hundred, sir," he said.

"A hundred guineas, going at a hundred guineas!" cries the auctioneer, leaning towards the old man and poising his hammer in the air.

"At a hundred guineas! A hundred! Going!—going!—at a hundred!"

The old man made no movement. He was gazing across the room at his opponent, taking in every feature of his face. He seemed to have forgotten the picture and the bidding for it, in his interest in the human face of the buyer. There was a pause and a silence, and the hammer fell to a buzz of talk and the calling of another lot.

"I want your father to see that picture," said Berrington.

"What on earth do you want with one of Thornhill's domestic beauties?" asked Roger Mytton sneeringly as he joined them. "Is it to hang side by side with Bacchus and Venus and the rest of them at Thrift Street?"

"I did not buy it for myself," said Mr. Berrington quietly. "Miss Annesley expressed a liking for it."

Belinda coloured and was about to explain, but her companion added quickly, "The Counsellor is a great admirer of Sir James's work, and we are going to make him a birthday present."

Belinda laughed pleasantly. His readiness and impudence were not to be denied.

Mr. Berrington paid for the picture and went out to find his chariot. "We will carry it home at once," he said, and it was put into his carriage and they drove away.

It was in this way that the picture remained with the Counsellor, and was afterwards sent across the seas to Georgia.

The old man who had failed at the bidding came to the door of the auction room and watched Mr. Berrington hand Belinda into the chariot and jump in after her and drive away.

Mr. Mytton was standing on the steps of the house waving his hat to them. As he was turning back into the auction room, the old man stopped him.

"Could you tell me the name of the young gentleman who bought that picture?"

Mytton looked at the old man contemptuously.

"Is there anyone in London who does not know Nic Berrington? Wealthy Nic. Lucky Nic. Heir to boundless estates in Oxfordshire. 'The Golden Claimant,' Dick Steele calls him. With his luck at dice and cards, why he should have estates as well, God only knows."

"So he calls himself Nic Berrington," said the old man musingly.

"Calls himself Nic Berrington. What do you mean? They

say his claim is clear enough, though no one knows his story."

"I know his story," said the old man surlily, "and I know the story of the picture he bought and why he bought it."

Mytton was full of curiosity. "Well, what of it?" he asked.

"The picture was stolen from my house and became the property of the late Mr. Jonathan Wild."

"The thief-taker."

"Ask anyone who has been in his house at Newgate Street. It hung there for years."

"But what has that got to do with Berrington?"

"Your Mr. Berrington was a pickpocket in the London streets a year ago—born and bred to it. He lived with Wild and his gang. Wild called him Berrington, and it was his plot to bring him up as a claimant for these estates in Oxfordshire, but that young man has no more right to the name of Berrington than you have. He is a bastard son of Jonathan Wild."

Roger Mytton whistled and stared at the old man. "How do you come to know all this?" he asked.

"My name is Crowley, Luke Crowley of Witney. I am in London on this very business."

"Come across to 'The Eagle,' Mr. Crowley, and have a bottle of wine with me. I should like to know more about this. I like Nic Berrington well enough, and so do the rest of us. He's free and pleasant, and I've always found him straight, I must say that. But a pickpocket, you know! Damn it, a pickpocket! That's more than a joke."

It was at "The Eagle" that they met Jonas Craven, the poet, whose dedication Mr. Berrington had refused that morning, with the promise that when he wanted an epitaph he would give the poet the refusal of the job. It is never wise to fall out with the fretful tribe of Grub Street, and Craven smacked his lips over Crowley's story. It would make a telling scandal for *The Syllabub*, a society sheet in which the daily life and misdoings of the great ones of the earth were retailed in the guise of naughty histories from imaginary countries.

Now while these things were plotting against his peace,

Mr. Berrington was with Belinda telling her something of the story of the picture they had brought to the Counsellor's house. Of late he had spent many pleasant hours in her company. She allowed him to play her accompaniments, to fetch her books and music from the libraries, to figure in her entertainments as a devoted admirer, until Nic, always supreme in impudence, began to compare himself to the sturdy, clever, downright Melvil and to wonder whether he ought not to rescue this porcelain gem from such unimpassioned custody.

In these days Belinda swam into all his dreams, and in his facile, careless way he used to remember his own words to her father, "She is worthy of the best," and laughingly wonder whether the superlative belonged to Melvil or himself. Moreover, he allowed these silly notions such hospitality in his thoughts that at times it seemed almost his duty to offer Belinda eternal happiness by throwing himself at her feet.

They had set up Sir James Thornhill's masterpiece in the drawing-room by the side of the window to catch the light, and seated themselves on a couch opposite to look at it critically.

"How do you know it is your mother's portrait?" asked Belinda.

"I have known the picture for years," replied Nic.

"There is a likeness in the eyes and the brow—above this," she said, placing her hand across the lower part of his face.

He caught her hand and kissed it, and she snatched it away, shaking her head at him, with a mock frown.

"Tell me the story of the picture."

"It is my earliest memory," he said. "I can remember her. Sometimes in dreams I see her gliding gracefully in large rooms, and I am a little child pattering along the floor after her. Or she stands on the terrace as she does there. The trees and the mansion behind are always part of the dream. I have stood upon the stone parapet there by her side watching and waiting for someone. My father, perhaps. But I have no memory of him. Still, when I see the house again, I shall know that spot and the big room, where the crowds were, all dressed in black, carrying torches. That was the end of it. I know now. The Counsellor told me. They died of the plague, and both were buried the same day. I must have been about five years old then."

"And have you never seen the picture again until to-day?" asked Belinda.

"That is the strange thing," replied Mr. Berrington thoughtfully. "Years afterwards it was hanging in the house of——" he hesitated a moment. "Yes, a friend."

"How came it there?"

"I never knew. He would never speak of it."

She knew from the tone in which he spoke that the friend was dead.

"It is a kind face, but there is sorrow in it."

"I do not see that," said Nic. "She must have had everything a woman could want."

"You cannot say that. You never know. You were only her child. A child knows nothing."

She nearly patted his hand as she spoke, as if he were one child and she another, but something impelled her to rise and move to her spinet. She was minded to end his dreams.

"Listen to this," she cried. "It is a song of Herrick that papa is very fond of."

She began to sing:

> "He that will not love must be
> My scholar and learn this of me."

Mr. Berrington had moved to the window and stood by the curtain looking across at the charming figure of the girl, her clear face upraised, bright with the joy of music. The song was an invitation to him to speak. He saw in her, not perhaps the woman he loved, but the ideal mistress of the house that was to be his, the companion of his stately future, a great possession, the ownership of which would be envied by others, a token of his triumph, the seal of his success. As she finished her song, he had stolen across to the spinet and knelt by her side, seizing her hands and kissing them devoutly.

"Will you be mistress of mine, and all that is mine, and

stand on the terrace, as she did, to welcome me to our home?"

The girl drew her hands away and looked down upon him sorrowfully.

"Oh, Nic, Nic!" she cried, "you have spoiled everything. Why cannot we be friends?"

She rose and stood at a distance from him with her hands behind her, and he slowly drew to his feet, but remained at the spinet.

"Why cannot we be more than friends, Belinda?"

"Because we do not love each other," she replied calmly. "If you were not such a child, I should hate you for it. You are thinking of your great house and your wealth, and you picture me an elegant hostess, part of the furniture of it all. Oh, fie, Nic! It was not kind of you."

She laughed at him to put him at his ease, but the clear insight of her words stung him and he winced. He did not dare deny the truth of what she said, and had the wit to raise no subtle defence.

"Am I forgiven?" he asked, with a faint effort at his most winning smile.

She put out her hand, and he raised it reverently to his lips.

"So this is farewell, Belinda."

"This is farewell, Mr. Berrington."

He walked to the door and turned to bow to her and acknowledge her graceful and most formal curtsey. She was at the window at the back of the curtain watching him as he jumped into his chariot, and her eyes followed him as he clattered down the street. At the corner he nearly ran over a fellow who stood staring at him and his splendid chariot. As he swerved to avoid him, he saw it was Ziba. He laughed to himself. His heart was lighter. He, too, had had a narrow escape. He thought of Hetty, and then he was angry with himself, touched the horse with his whip, and raced through the streets as though the devil were after him.

It was many years before Mr. Robert Melvil heard anything of this incident, and Mrs. Melvil was almost piqued that the lucky fellow could not believe how near he had been to losing the best woman who ever lived, so complacent are husbands when their suit is over and the *chose* in action is reduced into possession.

The next number of *The Syllabub* had an unusual sale, and it was buzzed around the coffee-houses that the thing was not to be missed. The story of Eugenio went from mouth to mouth, and everyone in the little world between Bow Street and St. James's accepted the truth of the scandal and had met someone, who knew somebody, who could vouch for every detail of the story.

The narrative of Luke Crowley which Jonas Craven wittily displayed as an old-time romance in the imaginary city of Atlantis, was so told that no one in the world of fashion could miss the interpretation of it. Eugenio was a little herd boy on the Arcadian plains, and a certain robber chief named Ferox, thief taker as well as thief teacher, thought by many to be the lad's father, having discovered that certain fruitful estates were awaiting a missing heir, determined to adopt little Eugenio, and whilst teaching him the trade of a pickpocket, also educate him up to the playing of the part of the missing heir. How Ferox was caught and executed, leaving Eugenio destitute, how the youth supported himself by crime, and ultimately imposed himself upon society as the missing heir—these things were set out with so much of the truth that it surprised even Berrington himself when at long last the paper fell into his hands.

Robert Melvil picked up a copy of it at Nando's and walked across to The Vulture's chambers in Middle Temple Lane. Counsellor Annesley skimmed it through.

"An enemy hath done this," he said, "and the pity of it is that it is so accurate in detail."

"Was young Berrington among Wild's gang then?" said Melvil in surprise.

"Mr. Berrington is my client," replied the Counsellor, "and his confidences are sacred, but you may take it from me that he is Nic Berrington, son of the late Nicholas Berrington, of Steeple Berrington, and that can be proved."

Melvil accepted the verdict in silence. He was not bound to endorse it until he had heard the evidence. Meanwhile, in the clubs and coffee-houses, young Mytton and Colonel Sabine and many others shrugged their shoulders and spread the scandal merrily, but Lord Bassett declared with an oath that Nic Berrington was a straight fellow and a gentleman, and that for his part he still believed he would prove his claim, and that the story in *The Syllabub* was a pack of lies.

The great scene in the drama was staged at the Thatched House Tavern. Mr. Berrington had strolled in to dinner, and would have sat down at a table opposite to young Mytton.

"The place is reserved," said Mytton curtly. "I am expecting a friend."

"By all means," replied Berrington, turning away. "Are you at White's for piquet to-night?"

Mytton made no reply and ostentatiously continued eating.

Nic tingled with angry excitement. He repeated his question calmly but in a louder voice: "I asked, are you for piquet to-night?"

He stood at the corner of the table waiting an answer.

"I do not play to-night," muttered the other.

"I have a right to my revenge," said Mr. Berrington angrily.

"You have no right to be here at all, Mr. Eugenio, and you know it," said Mytton bravely, and one or two at a table near by murmured approval.

"Eugenio!" repeated Nic in amazement, "Eugenio! What is the jest?"

"Brazen it out how you will," continued Mytton, "the Thatched House and White's are not for apprentices of Jonathan Wild."

At the name of the Master, Berrington turned pale. He would not let his tongue deny him, and to confess him meant ruin. In a flash of rage he picked up Mytton's glass and was about to fling the contents in his face when he felt a strong hand upon his shoulder, and the glass was taken from his hand.

"Jonathan Wild was a great man. I drink to his blessed memory," said the newcomer, and he emptied Roger Mytton's glass and threw it on the floor.

Nic uttered a cry of astonishment. Mytton and several

others sprang to their feet and would have flung themselves on the stranger. The landlord and one or two of the waiters hurried to the table to prevent a fracas. Lord Bassett and Colonel Sabine came across from the other side of the room.

"What has happened, Roger? Tell me, Nic!" called out his lordship.

The tall stranger interposed.

"It is my quarrel," he said. "My friend, Squire Berrington, has been libelled and insulted in a low Grub Street news-sheet. This gentleman"—he looked towards Mytton —"makes himself Grub Street's champion. Be it so. I, Count Turquet de Grillac, King's Messenger, know the story to be a pack of lies. If this offends, I am ready to give satisfaction. Next week Mr. Berrington moves into his house at Steeple Berrington, and has honoured me with an invitation."

"My dear de Grillac," cries Nic, picking up the cue with a laugh, "you have spoiled the surprise I had prepared for my friends. I want you all to ride down with me. We must have a rare house-warming. The old place will want it after all these years."

"For my part," said Lord Bassett kindly, "I look forward to the visit."

"Gad!" said Colonel Sabine, "a week or two in the country would do us all good."

Roger Mytton looked uneasily at Turquet. He was in no humour to take up the challenge. Besides, if Mr. Berrington was really going to Oxfordshire next week, the story of Eugenio must be a foul libel, and he had made a fool of himself.

"When we get down to Oxfordshire," said Turquet pleasantly, "if anyone is still dissatisfied with my conduct to-night, we can arrange matters very pleasantly among ourselves."

He bowed low to Mytton and the rest with grave ceremony, and drawing his arm within Mr. Berrington's, they strolled leisurely out of the tavern.

CHAPTER XXII

THE COMEDY OF MASTER CROWLEY

TURQUET and Nic took coach to Thrift Street, where Toby welcomed them with wine and tobacco. Master Nic cast off his coat and sword, wrapped himself in a handsome blue silk gown and lolled on the sofa a perfect picture of indolent ease and conceit, whilst he told Turquet his recent adventures.

Hetty had thrown him over and gone away, and he was too brave a man of the world to break his heart over a girl, and "Damme, sir, I am well pleased to be rid of her psalm-singing relations."

Turquet had walked down to the edge of the pit himself. He had watched many a golden lad tripping down the steep sides of its foot-hills. It was to him the natural resting-place of youth and folly, but in spite of his haggard outlook on the affairs of the world, there was pain at his heart as he listened to the glib chatter of Nic's apologia.

"That was a fine jest of yours, Turquet, about taking possession of Steeple Berrington," cries Nic, changing the subject, "and what on earth was all that cackle about *The Syllabub*? What is *The Syllabub*?"

"You are as ignorant as one of the innocent old judges in Westminster Hall. What is *The Syllabub*? It is the *dernier cri* of the newsmonger, and Jonas Craven, the editor, is a Triton among the minnows of Grub Street, and he has shouted to the world your life history."

"That accounts for smug Mr. Oldcastle deserting the ship," said Nic, nodding wisely at Turquet.

"We have no lawyers, then? A nice mess we have made of things. What else have we done in my absence?"

Master Nic in a modest narrative related his variance with the Annesley household, laying stress on the fortunate escape he had made from the arms of the fair Belinda, who might have caged him for ever within the gilded bars of gentility. He touched lightly on his triumph at the cockpit, and then burst into an indignant tirade against the fickle men and women who deserted their friend at the first whisper of a libellous rumour.

Turquet was sitting at the window looking out across the gardens of the neighbouring houses and watching the autumn leaves fall into the wind and eddy towards the lawns.

"What did you win at White's, Nic?" he asked, as the youth's eloquence came to a period.

"Some five or six thousand pounds," said Nic nonchalantly enough, though a tremor in his voice betrayed his pleasure and excitement. "So you see, Turquet, I have not made such a muddle of things. I can run on my own. I have money in the bank, an estate to take possession of, and there are plenty of women in the world——"

"Most of them priced to a sequin and ready and willing for sale and delivery," cried Turquet, finishing his sentence. Nic laughed assent and filled Turquet's glass. "Welcome back, dear friend, to this world of fraud and chicane, and set your wits working. For me, I have accepted your challenge at White's. This week I take possession of my estates, at least so you told my friends at the Thatched House. How is it to be done?"

"I am thinking," said Turquet, "that Crowley must have been the author of the libel and therefore Crowley has been in London."

"Crowley is in London," said Billinge, "I have seen him."

"You might have told me that before," said Turquet shortly.

"You might have asked me," said Billinge.

Nic laughed merrily at both of them. Turquet rose and paced the room in thought.

"Ha, ha, Toby," cries Nic, winking at Billinge, and looking impudently at Turquet. "This kind of thing comes of chumming with statesmen and ambassadors. Here you see our English Machiavelli in the act of hatching a new-laid plot for the destruction of poor Crowley. Shall we lure him into a lonely house by the river and drop him into the

Thames ? Even then I suppose we should have his executors to deal with."

" A lonely house by the river," repeated Turquet, musing. " Toby, who has the ' Fox and Grapes ' at Lambeth now ?"

" Old Knapp and his wife," replied Billinge.

" We must deal with this affair as the Master would have dealt with it," said Turquet. " We will take Crowley with us to Steeple Berrington and get him to open the doors for us."

" It sounds simple," said Berrington critically, " but The Vulture told me Oldcastle had offered all sorts of favourable terms but he could not buy peace. The old fox is in posses- sion of the earth and you will not lure him with gold."

Turquet was not listening to him.

" To dictate terms of peace," he said with grim deter- mination, " you must have the army of the enemy at your mercy."

" The rats have got to the upper-storey and are nibbling at our friend's brains," cried impudent Nic, touching his forehead as a sign to Toby that he considered Turquet was losing his wits.

But Turquet was too intent on his scheme to heed Nic's folly.

" You must find out Crowley's lodging in London to- night, Toby. Some of Oldcastle's people will know."

Billinge nodded.

" And where can we find Jenny ? " asked Turquet. " Jenny is essential."

" I'll bet you a guinea Jenny is at Drury Lane Theatre," called out Nic looking at his watch.

" Done with you," cried Turquet, " and let us get a coach and go find her. If Jenny will come in we can't fail."

" And what part is Jenny to play in this mysterious drama ? "

" Did you ever hear of a leading lady in your visits behind the scenes ? That is to be Jenny's part."

The Count laughed knowingly at his little jest.

Toby made off to enquire about Crowley's whereabouts, leaving Turquet and Nic who drove to Drury Lane Theatre where they arrived about an hour before the close of the play. They climbed up to the top of the gallery, which was but half full, and looked down on the men and women in it from above.

Mr. Berrington pointed to the second row and Turquet smiled content as he handed him his guinea.

It was Jenny, staid, demure Jenny, dressed in the garb of a city madam, and by her side a young spark from the country pressing attentions on her, which, coldly received at first, were now as the play drew to an end, being met by greater kindness and a shrinking coy surrender to an invitation to supper.

Nic stepped lightly across the back benches until he sat behind them and touched the girl gently on the shoulder. She turned round with a start of surprise. Her companion looked angered and half ashamed.

" My dear brother Nic! Who would have thought to see you here ? "

She paused on the word of relationship and carefully accented it. Master Nic picked up the hint.

" My dear sister, your uncle Turquet is here. You must return home with us at once."

She seemed overcome with vexation and cast eyes at the young fellow next her. Master Nic moved away and gave her time to whisper to the youth.

" I must go back to the City with them. Another evening."She pressed his hand at leaving him, pouting vexation. The youngster gazed in awe at the charming girl and her handsome brother and was filled with the rapture of conceit at the thought that he was the hero of a real intrigue with a beautiful unknown.

" What the hell is all this about, Turquet ? " cries laughing Jenny, slapping him on the shoulder. " You have lost me a supper and a lover with money to burn."

" You shall have the best supper that they can give us at ' The Rose,' " said Nic, " and two lovers with money to burn."

At supper the Count outlined his plan of campaign. Jenny,who had a healthy appetite, listened with her mouth full and nodded approval. At the end of it her practical mind turned to ways and means and the assessment of the value of her services.

" You shall be mistress of Steeple Berrington for as long as you will and share it all," cried Nic, lifting his glass towards her with wide, admiring eyes.

" Is that an offer of marriage, young Nic ? " she asked mischievously, leaning across the table to him.

He seized her arm and drew her towards him and kissed her.

" If you will," he said hoarsely. " I have always loved you, Jenny."

" You have grown a saucy Child, Nykin," and she boxed his ears gently and threw his arm away from her. " I shall want fifty guineas for expenses and a hundred guineas if we succeed."

The Child gave her twenty pounds in notes to start with.

" Saucy or not, Jenny, I shall carry you to Steeple Berrington with me if I will."

" We shall see, Mr. Nicolas," she replied, pushing the notes into her bosom and nodding at him defiantly.

" Mr. Nicolas," said Turquet. " It is a good name. Start your adventure under the name of Mrs. Nicolas."

" As you please, Count," said the girl.

Crowley was lodging in Little Rider Street. His landlady a buxom widow, Mrs. Pierce, had some sort of cousinship with Mrs. Metyard of Wych Street where Turquet still kept his London foothold. The introduction of Mrs. Nicolas into the household presented no difficulties. Crowley, like many another elderly respectable citizen from outside, regarded London as a place where, when business was over, much relaxation, which in the domestic domicile would have been irregular and dissolute, was part of a man's rights, seeing that his person and identity were unknown to the world and there were no witnesses to record his erring footsteps. He was pleased with the results of his employ-ment of Jonas Craven who had fairly earned his wage as a hack writer of libel, and Craven had added to his rewards by carrying Mr. Crowley to plays and masquerades and suppers at which Crowley was the honoured paymaster, and Craven supplied willing guests. But these adventures were too

R

extravagant for the old man who found himself a mere looker-on at the entertainment until the curtain fell on the payment of bills when he was always alone in the centre of the stage.

The visits of young Mrs. Nicolas to her friend Mrs. Pierce were very opportune.

" Poor soul," says Mrs. Pierce to her lodger. " Poor little Jenny : and she a young wife and her husband a leather merchant leaving her for Sturbridge Fair within three months of marriage. A hard world I call it, and I'm glad the young woman should come here a-visiting. For she's a lively puss and men have no conscience nowadays, I declare."

The first time Crowley drank tea with them in Mrs. Pierce's parlour he and Mrs. Nicolas had changed eyes across the teacups. The old man imagined the twinkle of her eye had been specially directed towards him and youthful fire kindled a fitful blaze which crackled in his dry heart; so that when Mrs. Pierce left them together for a few moments, he had called her Jenny and taken her hand, and she had sighed and withdrawn it, almost reluctantly he thought, as Mrs. Pierce stumbled against the door before she entered.

So away to the theatre with them both and Crowley sitting between them holding Jenny's hand in his the most of the time, and caring little for the love affairs of the actors so eager was he in the progress of his own. Then to a tavern for supper and after much wine and food and amorous talk Crowley was for carrying Jenny home in a coach, but good Mrs. Pierce would have none of it. Only it was arranged that Jenny should be at Little Rider Street early on the morrow and they would all have a day's pleasuring together. On which terms, and another bottle to bind the bargain, they parted.

It was a glorious summer day in autumn. Had Crowley been a poet he would have likened this elderly sun dispersing the early morning mist to his own triumphant display with the simple Jenny. He was now enraptured. He talked over the good Pierce to his evil schemes. They would take oars to Lambeth. Crowley suggested a snug

little dinner at the " Fox and Grapes." Mrs. Pierce shook
her head. It had an evil reputation nowadays she thought.
Crowley chuckled but declared it to be an honest house.
But suppose Mrs. Pierce were called away after dinner and
left him and the fair Jenny alone. Mrs. Pierce was shocked.
Money was spoken of. Again, she shook her head. Guineas
were produced. She weakened and remembered she was a
poor woman. Guineas were passed across the table. Mrs.
Pierce became businesslike and practical. If Mr. Nicolas
left his wife in her own keeping, who was she to stand
between the poor child and a day's pleasuring ? So the sun
shone high in the heavens and Crowley beamed triumphant.
The mists vanished in a golden shower.

When Jenny arrived, blushing and roseate beneath a
straw hat and cherry ribbons, in a dainty summer gown to
fit St. Martin's weather, Crowley began to wish he had
found this delight of his eyes before the wretched leather
merchant had won her. However, she was his for to-day.
The outing to Lambeth was mentioned. Jenny sparkled
with pleasure and then clouded over. What would Mr.
Nicolas say to it ?

" Why should he ever hear of it ? " asked Crowley.

" Besides if Mrs. Pierce is with us, and you come as her
friend," he continued.

" Well I do say it's a lovely day for an outing," said Mrs.
Pierce, looking at the sunshine in the street and then
hurrying out of the room.

Mrs. Nicolas dissembled hesitation. Crowley advanced to
the sofa and sat near her. He produced a little gold watch.

" I can never show this to my husband," she cried with
delight—as her hand closed upon it.

" You shall have an uncle in Oxfordshire," said Crowley
passing his arm round her waist. " He shall send you many
presents and come and visit you if you are a good girl."

She laughed merrily at the thought of it.

" And to-day Uncle shall take you to dine at Lambeth,
eh ? " he asked.

" Of course he shall. The dear ! Uncle ! "

She sprang up clapping her hands and then threw her
arms round the old fellow's neck and kissed him.

He held her in his arms for a moment. What a day of sunshine it was. Mrs. Pierce entered.

" So that's settled I see," she cried, and laughed heartily.

The women had a few words of talk in the kitchen. Mrs. Pierce had to change her clothes and make herself " fit to be seen " in her own phrase and Jenny must run home for a cloak and would meet them at Temple Stairs where they would take oars for Lambeth.

Billinge brought word of these movements of the enemy to Turquet and Nic who were carefully perusing a legal document which Turquet had brought with him from an attorney. There were certain affidavits and other papers accompanying it which were duly signed and initialled.

" Is it all legal and binding ? " asked Mr. Berrington.

" It will stand so, the attorney says, unless the Courts set it aside for duress and fraud."

" What are duress and fraud ? " asked Nic pleasantly.

" The powers that rule the world, keep the strong in high places, and the weak at their feet," answered Turquet bitterly.

" Statesmanship," said Mr. Berrington joyfully. " It is as good a career as the road."

Turquet gathered the papers together and gave his orders. " Five o'clock is the hour. You, Toby, bring the portmanteau from Mrs. Pierce's. Not a shred of him to be left at his lodgings, and word to any caller he has ridden to Witney. You, Nic, bring the notary. We will have the papers signed and witnessed in form."

Nic knocked the neck off a bottle of champagne and filled three tumblers.

"Gentlemen, I give you Jenny. Dear, delightful Jenny."

They clinked glasses and drank to the heroine of their stratagem.

Luke Crowley's party was a success. The garden of the inn reached to the river and there were arbours at which in summer time refreshments were served. When dinner was ordered and whilst it was cooking Mrs. Pierce suggested they should sit in the sun in the alcove and watch the crowded thoroughfare of the river, a rare treat to the City woman. Mr. Knapp, the landlord, hinted at a barrel o

oysters. Jenny clapped her hands. The oysters were brought
and consumed at leisure with mugs of stout and the shells
thrown on to the river beach below.

Dinner was served in a snug private parlour of the inn
with a bow window through the square panes of which the
vessels drifting up the tide distorted themselves into strange
shapes. Jenny sat near Crowley who patted her hand and
beamed at her with an air of possession, to which Jenny
replied with pouts and ripples of laughter. Mrs. Pierce filled
her mouth and emptied her glass with steady purpose
declaring that oysters always gave her an appetite.

Dinner over, cheese and cakes and fruit and more wine
prolonged the feast into the afternoon until Mrs. Pierce,
who had hitherto made no response to Crowley's winks and
coughs prompting her exit, rose and declared it was time
they must be going.

Jenny protested that there were hours of daylight before
them and Crowley filled her glass and piled grapes and
apples on her plate and bade Mrs. Pierce rest content.
Mrs. Pierce was obdurate. Go she must. She had duties at
home. Jenny laughed at her and she grew angry and picked
up her cloak and flung herself out of the room. This sobered
Jenny and she was for following her, but Crowley caught
her and pulled her back to the table promising her Mrs.
Pierce would return anon. They would finish the bottle and
then they would take oars and be back by daylight. And
while they were discussing and debating and wrangling the
matter Crowley chuckled and pointed to the window and
there was a boat shooting into the current carrying Mrs.
Pierce homeward and they were alone.

Jenny rose indignant and would have cried out but
Crowley caught her in his arms and soothed her with
endearing words until she laughed at him and patted him
on the cheek and whispered " Uncle " so demurely that he
laughed too and struggled for kisses, pulling her on to the
sofa by his side so roughly that her hair came down her
shoulders and she cried out to him to have done. She
looked more bewitching and attractive than ever and he
seized her hands and poured out his love, promising
constancy and affection and rich presents if she would stay

with him in the inn. Her husband was away. No one would ever know, and here was a purse of gold to prove his honesty. He threw it into her lap. She put it aside and rose from the sofa. He followed her with it and pressed it on her. There should be more to-morrow and more and more to follow. She thrust the purse into her dress and and he seized her in his arms. They were near the window and she uttered a wild cry, gazing out in horror at the landing stage.

" Mr. Nicolas ! My husband ! "

Mr. Crowley dropped his arms and stood sobered. Jenny sank back upon the sofa crying out she was undone. A tall man was striding up the path from the river to the house whilst two companions followed him more leisurely. Crowley was like the man in the comedy he had laughed at the night before. But this was no play scene, there was no closet to hide in and no screen to cover a retreat. Moreover, there was no comic terror in his heart and a real enraged husband was rushing up the stairs of the house with murder in his heart.

Turquet flung into the room with his sword drawn.

" Mercy ! Murder ! Help ! " cried Jenny, throwing herself on his sword arm.

Turquet pushed her roughly aside. Crowley crouched behind a chair whimpering for mercy.

Mr. Knapp and his wife came tumbling into the room and begged Turquet for the sake of the reputation of the house to be pacified. Turquet pointed to the condition of Jenny and called on them to witness what he had found. The landlady carried away Jenny who was sobbing hysterically. The landlord soothed Mr. Nicolas with prospects of damages.

" The gentleman is surely rich and will pay for the wrong done."

" He shall pay to the last farthing," said the injured husband and flung his sword on the table.

" Let us have no violence," said the landlord. " There is a notary below. Let him come up and let right be done."

Turquet shrugged assent. He sat at the head of the table, and pointed to a seat at the bottom of it which Crowley took in fear and trembling. The notary came in and he and the landlord having at Turquet's order placed more wine on the board, stood aside to see fair play.

"This fellow has seduced my wife," said Turquet.

The notary nodded. Crowley would have spoken but Turquet had his hand on his sword and had not yet addressed him.

"He will pay me damages and I for my part agree to bring no action against him."

The notary nodded.

"The damages are a thousand pounds."

The notary nodded again and Mr. Knapp the landlord looked relieved at the honourable and pacific turn the affair had taken and nodded his congratulations to Crowley.

"Draw us an agreement to that effect to be signed and witnessed."

"And the gentleman's name?" asked the notary.

Crowley's tongue clove to the roof of his mouth. He tried to think of any name other than his own.

"Your name, sir," shouted Turquet angrily.

"Luke Crowley," was all he could remember and he murmured the syllables of it.

"Attorney of Witney, Oxfordshire," added Mr. Nicolas.

Crowley gasped.

Mr. Nicolas waved the notary away to draw his agreement and pouring out a bumper for himself and another for Mr. Knapp and a third for his prisoner, sat drinking in silence whilst he tapped the table impatiently with the hilt of the sword. The bumpers were repeated until the third was swallowed and the sun was sinking across the river when the notary brought in the paper and an ink horn and set it before the unhappy Crowley.

Fuddled and terror-stricken as he was, he fumbled for his spectacles and demanded like an honest attorney that he might read the document first.

Turquet rose in anger and hit the table with the flat of his sword.

The attorney seized the pen and muttering to himself, "I sign under duress, you witness all of you I sign under duress."

"Sign and be damned," shouted Turquet.

The notary and Mr. Knapp duly witnessed this strange document.

Luke Crowley rose shattered and staggering.

" Get me a boat," he beseeched the landlord. " A boat. I must get back."

" By no means," called out Turquet. " We will have supper first. Lights and the curtains, and a bowl of punch and we make a night of it. Landlord, about your business smartly." Then turning with a laugh to his victim he said, " Mr. Knapp tells me you have engaged a room here, Mr. Crowley, and you shall make use of it. Alone," he added and burst into a loud guffaw, shaking with the fun of the notion.

He slapped Crowley heartily on the back, vowed he was forgiven and should feast with him, and the landlord and his servants bustled about to re-set the table, well pleased at the end of the trouble. They brought candles and drew curtains. Jenny returned repentant and forgiven, and there followed the merriment of a wild comedy of reconciliation which pleased the actors mightily. Healths were drunk and toasts were honoured, to all of which Crowley was compelled, until at last he sat dazed and drunken at the bottom of the table, his head in his hands, trying to remember where he was and what had happened.

He dreamed uneasily of a merry party ; of young Mr. Berrington seizing him by the hand and promising to make him factor of his estates as long as he was true to him ; of pretty Mrs. Nicolas sitting next him at supper plying him with wine and of a certain Count de Grillac, who got mingled in his dream with Mr. Nicolas, laughing with tears in his eyes as he toasted his darling wife ; of Toby Billinge and Mr. Knapp propping him up and putting his spectacles on his nose whilst he read his promise and full acknowledgment that Mr. Berrington here present was rightful heir of the estates of Steeple Berrington. Here he broke down and wept on young Nic's shoulder.

How it ended he never knew. But on the morning he awoke in the cabin of a hay-barge, sailing up the Thames. Seated on his portmanteau, holding custody of his body and his worldly effects was Toby Billinge, offering him a mug of small beer as an unfailing remedy for the morning symptoms of a glorious overnight.

CHAPTER XXIII

THE barge *Lady-bird* was a large vessel which had brought about fifty or sixty tons of meal and malt from Reading and was returning with a miscellaneous cargo of salt and grocery wares, at the bottom of which were stowed away a few parcels in which Captain Roger Johnson had a trader's interest. The skippers of these Thames barges like the waggoners on the roads had friendly relations with the Free Traders, whose services to the commerce of the country were held in high esteem by the average citizen. That the drunken man in the cabin was probably contraband also, did not worry the skipper or his mate. Turquet had promised them that their prisoner should be taken ashore at Datchet and no opportunity given to him to identify them or their vessel.

Turquet and Berrington sat on the deck of the barge, smoking peacefully in the morning sun and watching the pleasant houses and gardens on the shore as a favouring breeze and tide carried them rapidly up the river.

" We have done well up to now," said Turquet thoughtfully, " but we must consolidate our victory and make it firm for the future."

" I like this barge business vastly," said Mr. Berrington stretching himself. " I could drift along like this for years dreaming, well, dreaming of Jenny. But at Hampton Court I leave you and go back to the girl."

" Business is what we must come to, Nic, and it must be settled within an hour if you are to leave us at Hampton Court."

" It has to be, dear fellow," replied Mr. Berrington with a look of importance. " I have urgent affairs in London. I must find a new lawyer."

" Your lawyer for the next few years, my clever child, is in the cabin downstairs."

" Crowley ! I wouldn't trust the brute."

" No sane man trusts his lawyer, he uses him, and Crowley is the most useful lawyer you could have. It is only a question of terms. You will have to pay him and pay him handsomely."

" I hate the sight of the beast. He has betrayed me for years."

" Forgive us our trespasses," said Turquet with a smile, " as we forgive those who have the cudgel in their hand and will get the best of the fight if we try and throw them off our ground. We must go and parley with the fellow. The best terms we can get are these : Crowley to fully acknowledge that you are Nicholas Berrington and the Squire of Steeple Berrington. You to appoint him steward for seven years certain."

Mr. Berrington whistled his dissent, but Turquet proceeded with his judgment and took no notice of this contempt of court.

" For seven years certain. I think he will accept that. The fellow is sixty at least. You to enter your kingdom at once. He to pass his accounts to the satisfaction of Count Turquet de Grillac. These terms to be signed on board the *Lady-bird* and ratified by myself and Crowley at Datchet before my friend Mr. Anthony Fowden, the Windsor Attorney."

"Fowden ! Do you know him ? He acts for Bassett and many about the Court."

" I did him a service once. He had a son——"

" I mind the young fool well."

" Fathers love the fools they bring into the world. It is nothing to the purpose of our business. If you are to leave us at Hampton Court we have not more than an hour to finish our task. Let us get to work."

Berrington sighed. It went against the grain. But he was convinced that Turquet was right. It was clearly the nearest way to his kingdom and his princess. Like a wise monarch he would adopt the wisdom of his minister as his own.

" Turquet," he said affectionately, " you are a good friend. What must be must be. We will sign the treaty at our Palace of Hampton Court."

" In the cabin of your gracious Majesty's sloop the *Lady-bird*, " added Turquet, rising to his feet.

" Let us go and draw the old badger at once," said Mr. Berrington, jumping to his feet.

They walked to the hatchway and let themselves down into the cabin.

Crowley was in a state of hopeless despondency. The happenings of the night before, the respectable comments of his conscience on his own actions, and his craven fear of what his captors intended to do with him, had reduced him to an abject condition of melancholy. He supped his small beer with inattention to its qualities and shaking his head moodily repeated the lines of a play he had seen in London :

" ' The dawn is overcast, the morning lowers
And heavily in clouds brings on the day.' "

" Crowley, thou reasonest well," said Mr. Berrington laughing, as he and Turquet entered the stuffy little cabin.

" You must not listen to the folly of youth, Mr. Crowley," said Turquet gravely. " We come here to make amends for the freedom with which we interfered with your pleasures last night and remember the maxim, ' all is fair in war.' So far from the dawn being overcast I am coming to show you that your own particular sun is about to rise above the horizon."

Berrington listened with admiration to the politic argument of the Count. He seemed to prove to demonstration that every step that had been taken was taken in the sole interest of Luke Crowley himself. The old man also listened intently, with approval of his opponent's skill, but with critical appreciation of the real points of the discourse.

Turquet readily admitted that the document they had obtained would not stand the racket of a law-suit, but it could be used to put Crowley in a very evil light, for their case would be that for years Crowley had known of the rightful heir, had kept the estate from him and robbed him of the profits of it and that he had executed the deed voluntarily and in a fit of remorse. That would be the

story of the witnesses to it and it would be left to Crowley
to tell the story of his squalid intrigue with Mrs. Nicolas
and call her as a witness if he chose to do so.

Crowley blinked at them in a puzzled way and nodded to
the Count to continue, saying politely :

" Proceed, Mr. Nicolas ; proceed."

" Let us forget Mr. Nicolas," replied the Count graciously. " You speak to Count Turquet de Grillac who to help
his young friend and the cause of right has condescended to
play a part in his foolish farce."

The Count then told him shortly the terms he had stated
to Master Nic. An amnesty as to the past, Crowley to be
agent for seven years certain, subject to the supervision of
accounts by the Count.

Crowley began to see that these were better terms than
would be obtained after a law-suit as to the rightful
ownership of the estates. After all, a young spendthrift
like Nic Berrington was no bad passenger for an astute
coachman with the reins of government in his hands. He
condescended to details.

" How were these matters to be secured ? " he asked the
Count.

" A most sensible question, for we must admit as wise
ambassadors that knowing what we do of each other's
characters neither would be justified in trusting the word
of the other. Are you ready to agree to these terms, Mr.
Crowley ? "

The attorney was not a man of " Yes " and " No."
Billinge had to bring an ink horn and paper. Notes were
made. Turquet and Crowley wrangled over phrases.
Master Nic, weary of their quibbles, went on deck and
watched the skipper handling the sails of the heavy barge
to bring his vessel round the bends of the river. Presently
Billinge called him below.

" Mr. Crowley has been most reasonable," said Turquet
affably. " He has signed a paper of his own free will
admitting you to be the rightful Nicholas Berrington. You
will sign a paper expressing satisfaction with his past
stewardship and appointing him your steward for the next
seven years."

Mr. Berrington made a wry face but sat down and signed as he was told to do.

"It has further been agreed that Mr. Crowley and I proceed by water to Windsor, where we have all necessary papers drawn up by Mr. Anthony Fowden."

"A gentleman I shall be proud to meet in any business," said Crowley, who by now had recovered his self-respect.

"So now I can leave you at Hampton Court as I planned?" asked Nic eagerly as he rose from the table.

"When you have thanked Mr. Crowley for the care he has taken of your interests and the pleasure you feel that you are not to lose his services in the future," replied Turquet with great seriousness.

Mr. Berrington had sufficient wit to obey Turquet's order and approaching Crowley with inward disgust and outward smiling courtesy he took his hand, saying: "Within a few weeks I shall be taking possession of my house. I hope when I bring friends down you will do me the honour to be my guest for a week or two."

"For certain Mr. Crowley will be there to welcome you, for he and I will move into the house without delay that we may keep the workmen to their work. There will be much to do."

Billinge put his head into the cabin and called out that they were off Hampton Court. A wherry was signalled to and approached the barge. Nic bade farewell to Turquet saying:

"You had best beware of the old fox."

"I shall never leave him until you are in possession of your own," said Turquet emphatically.

Nic leaped lightly into the wherry and the brown sail of the barge was allowed to fill so that by the time he had reached the shore and scrambled on to the bank and stood to wave farewell to Turquet she was already rounding the bend of the river.

Turquet and Crowley spent the hours of the voyage to Windsor in long and interesting discussion of the future and the attorney was much impressed by the Count's knowledge of men and affairs.

Mr. Anthony Fowden, the Windsor attorney, was a man of letters and an antiquary and in high favour with the

Court and the best families in the County. If there had been any lingering thought in Crowley's mind that he might appeal to him for assistance it vanished when he saw the interest and concern that Mr. Fowden took in anything that the Count desired. Two days were spent at Mr. Fowden's house at Windsor. Papers were drawn up under his directions and signed, sealed and delivered and left in his custody. Turquet wrote a full account of the matter to Master Nic and handing his despatches to Billinge for conveyance to London he carried off Mr. Crowley to Steeple Berrington.

On Mr. Berrington's return to London he at once began to give large orders to London tradesmen, upholsterers, decorators, caterers and especially vintners, to be ready to advance upon Steeple Berrington at word of command. The stationers had already submitted to him samples of gilt-edged note-paper decorated with the family crest of the Berringtons. He looked forward with a child's glee to writing invitations to Bassett, Mytton and his friends of the cockpit and the gaming table, who were all to join in the revelries on the occasion of his ascent to the throne of the Berringtons.

He had already despatched several heavy waggons of hangings and furniture to Oxfordshire and was meditating the advisability of interviewing Mr. Jonas Craven with a horsewhip and demanding an apology when the genial editor of *The Syllabub* called at Thrift Street with a proof of an article signed by Mr. Crowley and a note of his compliments and regret that anything should have appeared in his newspaper calculated to give pain to so honourable and excellent a gentleman as Mr. Nicholas Berrington.

The fiction that had appeared to the detraction of Mr. Berrington was out-fictioned by the stories that were now published singing his praises and congratulating him on his well-deserved fortune. Anecdotes were remembered of his services to good Princess Caroline, his friendship with the estimable Mr. Quin, his success at the cockpit, and when memories of true incidents failed, more glorious ones were readily invented in Grub Street or borrowed from the common stock of these trappings of fame.

So that when Mr. Berrington showed himself in the Mall again, all his former companions gathered round him. Every man of fashion sought for an invitation to the forthcoming festival at Steeple Berrington and once again our hero was a real hero moving in the circle of his choice and feasted and flattered by those who looked to batten on his prosperity.

Mr. Berrington accepted this outward homage with a cool grace tinged with cynical amusement and inward contempt. He was now the wise youth of experience, who had weighed out the worthlessness of the world, and sampled the dead sea apples and was forever immune from delusions about his fellow-men and women, being firmly convinced that there was no honest fruit worthy of the human palate. Yet in his heart he made exceptions to his rules of pessimism, remembering that he had luck, health and riches, and that with these attributes, much pleasure could still be had in a world wisely used.

In the business and pleasure that had engaged him since his return to London he had not forgotten Jenny. He had expected that after their successful adventure together she would have come to him at Thrift Street but she made no appearance there. He sought her at the Play house and in the Park and at Spring Gardens and Vauxhall, but without success. When Billinge returned he was set upon her track but failed to pick up the scent. Mr. Berrington now became eager in pursuit of her. He had pledged his word to carry her as his princess to Steeple Berrington and he had already fixed his accession for the last week in October. Never before had the human companionship of woman in the shape of Jenny been so desirable and necessary to his happiness.

Mr. Berrington was kept very busy buying furniture in the latest style for his palace of Steeple Berrington and business led him to Mr. Coates, the draper of Ludgate Hill. As he strolled up to the door a yellow coach passed him and drew up in front of him. The footman opened the door and the handsome gentleman usher who stood outside the shop assisted a young woman to alight and then handed down an elderly woman who, taking her charge by the arm, carried her into the shop. There was something about her that reminded him of Jenny.

When he entered the shop the two ladies were seated at the counter. They were already deep in converse with a brisk foppish apprentice who was calling for silks, throwing them out on the counter and gazing at the material on his arm murmuring in an affected voice, " There, madam ; a diverting silk ; it suits madam wondrously. The weavers must have had madam in their eyes when they thought of it." He dexterously made a wide sleeve of it and placed it on the young woman's arm. She turned her head. It was Jenny. Her eyes twinkled merrily. Mr. Berrington approached with a gracious bow.

" I trust my lady has not forgotten our last meeting."

" Really, Sir—" began the old lady somewhat angrily.

" My dear Aunt," said the girl, looking at Nic with amusement, " Monsieur is of course mistaken. Indeed, Sir," she added modestly dropping her eyes, " I have been so little in the world that it is not possible we have met."

Mr. Berrington bowed low, apologising for his error with gracious compliments to both the ladies, and crossed the shop to discourse with the manager. Still there was no doubt it was Jenny. The manager knew nothing of the ladies. They were making purchases for cash and carrying them away. When Mr. Berrington left the shop, the yellow coach was no longer at the door. He strolled down Ludgate Hill. As he passed the Belle Sauvage, he saw the coach standing in the yard. The coachman and footman were not with it, having gone into the inn. He noticed the coat of arms upon it. He decided that any effort to interview the coachman might be injurious to Jenny's scheme so he called a hackney coach and drove to " The Bedford " coffee-house. Here as he expected he found his old friend Mr. Quin, who expressed great delight at meeting him again and congratulated him on his good fortune.

Nic knew that Mr. Quin was learned on matters of genealogy and heraldry and sought information about the coat of arms on the yellow coach.

" The crest you can tell me ? " asked Quin.

" A hand holding a pair of tongs."

" Yes, and the arms ? "

" There was a pig and three stars as I remember."

" Really, Mr. Berrington," said Quin somewhat shocked, " you mean three mullets and a sanglier passant of the second."

" Very likely, Sir, and on one side was a vulture moulting and on the other a knight in armour with a wooden sword."

" I know them well. The supporters are dexter, an eagle with wings inverted proper and sinister a chevalier in a coat of mail."

"But to whom do they belong?" insisted Mr. Berrington.

" To Lord Posso of Dunkeld, a wealthy Scots Lord," replied Quin. " He is staying in London, I have heard. At one time he was a patron of the theatre and I regret to say carried off some of our prettiest and most hopeful actresses."

Mr. Quin deprecating a second bottle at that hour, Mr. Berrington left him and went in search of Billinge. The next morning Toby brought him word that Lord Posso was lodging in fashionable apartments on the first floor of No. 20 Bond Street with a beautiful young lady who was kept in strict custody by an elderly German woman.

" The nymph is Jenny," said Nic laughing.

" The devil she is," replied Billinge. " She might have let us know."

" She is playing a game of her own but I intend to cut in," said Master Nic with decision.

One good thing Nic Berrington had learned from the strange education fate had decreed him and that was rapidity of action following decision. He had eaten the sour grapes and his teeth were on edge. But if he had to go down into the pit he would make a brave show of it. Fate had made Jenny the companion of his youth. He would show the world, from Prince to peasant, his contempt for all of them, and Master Nic would carry Jenny as his Princess with pomp and glory to his inheritance and his triumph should be the talk of the town.

At this time in Hyde Park near by the little river or stream which flowed through the park and formed an ornamental pond was the Ring. Mr. Berrington's great

resolve was to drive Jenny in the Ring at the fashionable
hour of five or six o'clock on a Sunday afternoon to show
the world of fashion that he had chosen her as his Princess
before they started off to Oxfordshire.

That Jenny would accompany him he made no doubt.
Her patrons were many of them generous and hospitable.
They would carry her to Islington or Vauxhall and live
in sin with her, but they would not sin against the decrees
of fashion and the world by driving her in the Ring, which
was sacred to the Court and the gentry and those ladies
with whom they were joined in holy matrimony.

Even now the Ring was nearing the end of its fashionable
history and indeed soon after this time when Queen
Caroline made the Serpentine it was abolished or fell into
decay. It stood to the north of the water and was merely a
circle of some three hundred paces' diameter with a sorry
kind of balustrade made of poles placed upon stakes three
feet from the ground. For some hundred years the rank and
fashion of England had driven round and round this Ring
every afternoon during the season. When they tired of
going round one way they faced about and drove round
the other. Whether they took any joy in this dull and dusty
pursuit, who knows ? But they created envy and hatred and
malice in the hearts of hundreds of men and thousands of
women who knew that they could never enter this sphere
of fashion. As an old writer says in describing these
perambulations with tolerant disdain, " So rowls the
world," and for the life of me it seems to continue to
" rowl " to-day in a very similar circle.

When Master Nic announced his intention to Jenny,
she fluttered with excitement, but absolutely refused to
give any promise to leave the brazen tower in which Lord
Posso held her captive, for the more alluring adventure
with young Nic and his showers of gold. But Berrington
merely laughed and appointed the Sunday and the afternoon
hour at which the event should happen.

It was not Berrington's way to waste time in argument
that should be used in actions, and he had much to do
to make ready for his triumph. For nearly every day Mr.
Berrington spent several hours at Mr. Hatchet's, the coach

builder in Long Acre, superintending the building and
decoration of his new coach. He would have naught to do
with the new fashion of grey and silver but insisted on the
glorious yellow with gilt framing which he used to say was
the only colour for a gentleman's coach. The body of his
coach was of small French design and was slung on wide
leather braces. The interior was hung with plate-glass
mirrors. The hammer cloth cushion in front where Toby
was to preside as coachman rested on a carved footboard
supported by Tritons blowing horns, a piece of French
carving that greatly pleased Master Nic's simple taste.
Four black horses had been carefully chosen and matched
by Mr. Berrington with Billinge's expert assistance, and the
turn-out had already been tried in the early mornings on the
north road and pronounced fit for its first appearance in the
Ring.

The day fixed for the great adventure opened au-
spiciously. It was a glorious autumn morning when Mr.
Berrington woke about noon and called for his valet and
his chocolate. He spent some hours on his toilet. It was a
matter of concern with him to choose the most befrilled,
belaced, and embroidered shirt in his collection to grace
the occasion. His periwig he was satisfied had been skilfully
curled, powdered and scented. With deliberate care he
donned his orange silken hose and coloured shoes. The
velvet breeches, embroidered waistcoat and silken coat
were making their first appearance in public and he smiled
contentedly as he thought of seeing them at strange angles
in the mirrors of the coach. He dined in his rooms and at
four o'clock his coach was announced. He looked out of the
window and saw with pride that a considerable crowd had
gathered round. His footmen kept them away from the
coach and they stood about in awed silence gazing at the
glory of his equipage.

Nic was childishly pleased at this homage to his taste.
He smiled at himself in the glass as he arranged his cravat
and placed a patch cunningly on the right spot. He sprink-
led scent on his handkerchief and admired the Valenciennes
lace by which it was surrounded; then he carelessly attached
his dangling sword and accurately adjusted his hat at the

proper angle. This done he picked up his snuff-box from the dressing-table, surveyed the whole effect with the pride of an accomplish eartist an d set forth on his quest of Jenny.

When the equipage drew up in Bond Street at the door of Lord Posso's lodging, Jenny and her German duenna were called to the window of the drawing-room by a cry of delight from Jenny's maid Peggy, who was wild with excitement at the sight of so much splendour on their threshold.

Mr. Berrington's footmen flung themselves from the tail-board and rushed to the door. The runners stood at the horses' heads. Billinge sat like a dignified idol on his grey hammer cloth. The door of the coach was thrown open and Mr. Berrington stepped lightly on to the cobble-stones.

"Was there ever anyone like Nykin," cries Jenny, clapping her hands in a whirl of delight.

His lordship's footman was deeply impressed by the costly grandeur of Mr. Berrington's entourage and expressed humble regret at his master's absence.

"I will pay my respects to the ladies, then," said Nic and throwing the flunkey a guinea he proceeded upstairs as though he were my lord's dearest friend.

Opening the door of the sitting-room he found Jenny in a loose morning gown with cherry ribbons, her favourite colour, looking her most mischievous. She had run back from the window and was resting on the sofa and welcomed him with a pleasant smile.

The German woman uttered an exclamation of fear and surprise.

"It is my cousin Nic, Aunt. Nic, salute your Aunt, my dear boy, and talk German to her if you can, she speaks worse English than His Majesty."

"Alas, I cannot wait," said Mr. Berrington. "I have come to take you for a drive in the Ring, my dear."

Jenny chuckled. The German lady looked shocked, for she knew that the Ring was only for people of family and fashion, and that Jenny had not the *entree*.

"Do you hear that, Aunt? Mr. Berrington is going to drive me in the Ring."

" Ach ! What shall I do ? " cried the old lady in despair.
" My Lord will hear of it. He will kill both of us."

" Everyone will hear of it, of course. It will be the talk
of London. My dear Nykin, don't be absurd."

" I mean what I say. Your friend Posso will not drive
you in the Ring. But I will, Jenny, and in a few days will
drive you down with me to Steeple Berrington."

" Do you hear that, Aunt ? That is a proposal if it is
anything."

" I mean it so, Jenny."

" Really, Nykin, will you never grow up ? You must
know, Aunt, that I care nothing for Mr. Berrington and he
cares nothing for me. But to drive in the Ring with the
heir to Steeple Berrington ! It will be the talk of the town."

If my Lord Posso had appeared at the moment and
offered her the title of " my lady " coupled with appropriate settlements it would have been naught. To ride
in the Ring side by side with this young sun-god clothed in
fine raiment and sitting in a gilded coach was a pleasure
Jenny would not have bartered even for an honest and
ancient name.

" Peggy ! Peggy ! " she cried to her maid. " I am going
to drive in the Park with Mr. Berrington. My big hat ! My
scarlet gloves ! And the muff. Tell me, should I have a
muff, Nykin ? "

" Ach, what shall I do ? " groaned the poor duenna.

" By all means a muff, Jenny," said Mr. Berrington
authoritatively. " The Princess carries one."

" Yes, yes, my dear," cries the old woman. " Of course
a muff. Ach ! What must I do ? "

She gave a practical answer to her own question by
helping to adorn the pretty girl for her mad excursion. No
woman can refrain from the joy of decorating a sacrifice
for the altar. Peggy and the German woman vied with
each other in their efforts to fit the girl to sit beside the
glorious youth who called her forth to so much joy and
happiness.

At last the finishing touch was given. Jenny kissed her
friends and gave her arm to Master Nic and they passed
down the stairs. Peggy and the old lady stood at the window

watching Mr. Berrington hand his prize into the golden coach. He raised his hat to them as he followed her. The footmen jumped on to the tail-board. The runners gave the leaders their heads and Billinge cracked his whip over the shoulders of the mob. The women watched the noble coach swinging down Bond Street until it was out of sight.

" Ach ! What have I done ? " cried the older woman, wringing her hands. " I am ruined. The girl will never come back."

" Come back ! " cries Miss Peggy scornfully. " Come back ! I should think not indeed ! "

CHAPTER XXIV

THE ENTHUSIASTS

EVEN before the death of his second wife Simon Verrall had shewn signs of a desire to return to the mission that was always tugging at his heart-strings. His early life had been spent in Somerset, which was the home of religious enthusiasts. These outbreaks have geographical situations and move like storms and diseases in their appointed paths. A revival in Wales, for instance, always spreads from South to North. Even in our own day Somerset has had its Agapemone and other strange communities.

A new sect of some of Verrall's early companions had formed a band of missionary preachers. The orthodox called them in derision " The Enthusiasts " and they had accepted the title as one of challenge to the dead-heads of orthodoxy. For a considerable time Verrall's friends had reminded him of his early heroism, flattered his powers of preaching, dinned into his ears their grief at his backsliding. But for his wife, he would have listened to their folly, for she had held him in the leash of business, and now she was taken, he believed that this was the hand of God releasing him for His own service.

After the death of his wife Verrall carried his daughter away to Somerset, where he was received by " The Enthusiasts " with real love and affection. He shut himself into a room and for many days wrestled in prayer for guidance. His friends were unceasing in their petitions that he should throw in his lot with the faithful. Even Hetty added her simple prayers to that effect since she felt that only in that way could he gain happiness.

His prayers were at last answered by a vivid dream or vision which he willingly accepted as a command from heaven and took pride in narrating it with dramatic detail and not without some vainglory, to his excited brethren. His experience had indeed been a strange one. He had knelt in prayer at his pillow and had perhaps sunk upon his bed in sleep when he heard a voice calling to him by the name of Jonah the son of Amittai. From that moment, though he never lost his own identity, he passed through all the adventures of Jonah, from Tarshish to the time of his sacrifice in the ship, and he knew the moment when the sailors caught his unresisting body and swung it gently into the waves, and how he dropped silently and gradually through the waters until black night and horrible darkness closed upon him and he was in the belly of the whale. Then he seemed endowed with a giant's strength and fought and cried out and threw his body about uneasily among the sheets, which seemed to close round and hold him down, until at length he sprang on to the floor of his room and heard the voice of the Lord calling upon him through the dim morning light : " Arise, go forth and preach."

Although he at once told his companions he would obey this command, he approached his daughter on the subject with some hesitation. He proposed, he said, that Ziba should have a power of attorney to carry on the business at Fetter Lane, and as for Hetty herself he was sure that Mrs. Chilcote would give her a home unless she had any thought that Ziba——

But here Hetty interrupted him saying : " Where you go, father, I go too."

The old man looked pleased at her decision.

" Your will is the Lord's will, my dear," he said with calm satisfaction, kissing her on the forehead to signify his own and divine approbation.

Thus it came to pass that Verrall and his daughter once again started off on the war-path of Methodism to preach the doctrines of " The Enthusiasts." There was no doubt that Verrall had the gift of tongues and knew all the technique of the revivalists. Like many of the humbler forerunners of greater prophets, he was able to prepare the way, and was ready to sacrifice even his life, in a cause which at that date had no worldly or financial rewards to offer, and his sermons, like those of his successors, found favour among the melancholy, the hypochondriacal, the hysterical and the epileptic. It is a common experience of such preaching that it is followed by manifestations of demoniacal possession and fits of religious mania. These portents followed the ministration of Verrall's crusade. They convinced him with greater certainty that he was indeed doing the Lord's work. Every day his language became more violent. Vicars and curates were twining serpents; bishops, deans and prebendaries vipers damned by the fire. His actions, too, became every day more eccentric and unbalanced, so that at times Hetty began to fear that his brain was affected.

Everywhere they went, crowds came to hear him preach. He became more voluble and terrifying in his demeanour, but with Hetty herself, he was always kind and affectionate. Often she sought to persuade him to return home and rest himself, but he turned a deaf ear to her entreaties, and they continued their Crusade. At Shrewsbury, they received urgent letters from the faithful at Lancaster, that they would join the faithful brethen in a mission to convert that heathen church-ridden town, and Verrall, Hetty and their friends turned their footsteps northwards.

The Enthusiasts of Lancaster were a strong and militant body. The Rector was also a man of energy and determination who resented the abuse levelled by the vagabond ministers at himself and his brother clergy. During the summer on Sunday evenings the brethren had met in the Town Square to listen to one of their preachers and sing hymns, and this outburst of irreligion had gravely troubled the orthodox. The Rector had called upon the Constable to stop these meetings. The Constable had wisely consulted Mr. Ambrose and other magistrates who held that as long as the meetings were orderly they were best let alone.

The people of Lancaster and the neighbourhood were in a very excited state about the arrival of Verrall. Many strange stories of the miracles he had worked, the sudden conversion of sinners that had followed his preaching, and his eloquent denunciation of the orthodox, had aroused a strong desire in the minds of enemies as well as friends to hear the message of the prophet of " The Enthusiasts."

There had been several gatherings of the faithful during the week, but the great meeting of all was publicly announ-

ced to be held at the Town Square on Sunday evening
after the hours of evening service. To this meeting the
orthodox flocked with their friends in a resentful frame of
mind. Like all good Tories, they were angry with the
authorities for allowing these madmen so much liberty.
When Mr. Ambrose, of The Clough, who as a county
magistrate thought it wise to ride into the town that
evening for fear there might be trouble, arrived at Lancaster
he found the streets crowded with men, women and
children of all ages hustling and pushing their way to the
great Square in the centre of the town.

He made his way to the " Royal Oak " and sat at the
window of the parlour looking down on the crowd below.
The Constable and a few of his men stood on the edge of the
the crowd. Verrall and the elders of his party sat on a stage
which their friends had built of some planks and market-
stalls. Mr. Ambrose noted with displeasure a group of
youths armed with sticks and cudgels, some of whom he
knew to be friends of the Rector. These young fellows kept
edging their way towards the platform when opportunity
occurred.

The service opened with prayer and hymns. Hetty sang
well and many of the women on the platform and in the
congregation joined heartily in the singing. Mr. Ambrose
could not but enjoy and respect the honest fervour of these
simple folk, and was vexed at the conduct of the Rector,
who came into the room and having ordered a bottle of
port of the drawer, stood at the window and began sneering
at the prayers and the singing.

" I see no harm in it myself," said Mr. Ambrose. " It
were better they used the prayers of the Church, but how
does it injure anyone ? There are worse ways of spending a
Sunday evening than in prayer and praise."

" Are you turning Enthusiast, Mr. Ambrose ? " asked
the Rector laughing. " But bide a while. You will hear
worse than this before they are done."

Several addresses were given before Verrall's turn came.
He had been in consultation with the leaders of the Lancaster brethren and had heard many stories, true and
otherwise, of the indolence of the local clergy. It is a

subject that has always appealed to Methodists and their audiences for, like politics, popular religion is generally a religion of hate and scores its best points in the detraction of its opponents.

That Verrall intended to start a tumult in the town seems improbable. It is quite unlikely that he knew of the friction that already existed between the Church and the mob, or that the stalwarts who gathered round the platform carried sticks and cudgels beneath their coats. He opened the Bible at random as he rose to address the people and his eye fell on the text: "What is that to thee? Follow thou me."

" Blasphemer ! " muttered the Rector.

"Hush!" said Mr. Ambrose. "Let us listen to the man."

For a while his discourse was sane and persuasive, but as he felt the audience sway to his voice he was lured into the eloquence of hate against the unchristian principles and practices of the generality of the clergy. " They do not preach or live up to the truth. They do not follow Jesus. Woe unto such blind leaders of the blind. How can these wolves in sheep's clothing escape the damnation of hell ? The scarlet whore of Babylon is not more corrupt than the Church of England."

A groan of sympathy and approval ran through the congregation. Even the supporters of the Church seemed stunned by the vigour of his denunciation.

Suddenly the Rector stood at the window of the inn and, throwing out his arms, bellowed out : " Liar ! Blasphemer ! Away with him ! "

The friends of the Church scarcely needed a call to battle. The young men waved their sticks and shouted oaths and foul names at the preacher as they rushed towards the platform, intent on destroying both the prophet and his pulpit. But a bodyguard of the faithful, who had taken precaution to carry staves with them and stood below the preacher, met the onset of the church party with a counter-attack and a fierce fight ensued.

Women screamed and fainted. Hetty instinctively jumped from the platform to pick up a fallen child whose mother had hurried up a side street in fear of the mob. As she struggled to carry the child out of the Square to a place of safety she looked back and could see her father, who stood in the centre of the fighting mob, still waving his arms as if he were continuing his prophecy.

Suddenly the platform gave way with a crash and Verrall seemed literally to dive into the human sea beneath him. To save his fall he had clutched at the throat of a burly churchwarden who was leading the church militant and they fell to the ground together locked in each other's arms.

By this time Mr. Ambrose and another magistrate had run to the stables and, mounting their horses, ridden into the Square and held up their hands for peace. Mr. Ambrose was greatly liked by the people, many of whom listened to his advice and scattered apart or ceased to fight. The constables advanced with their truncheons and proceeded to arrest the ring-leaders. Whether by chance or selection, or that the constables thought them the easier prey, their prisoners consisted of Verrall and three of " The Enthusiasts " who had come with him from Blackburn, and a young Irish papist who was not clear on what side he had entered the quarrel but was exceedingly fierce and troublesome with the constable for interfering with his pleasure.

Mr. Ambrose rode up and down dispersing the mob. Each side carried off its wounded, the police took their prisoners to the Castle, followed by despondent women and children and some friends of the Irishman, who supported him with their wails and cheers. Long before nightfall the Town Square was deserted and at peace.

The Quarter Sessions for the County of Lancaster were held early in October. The case that raised the greatest interest was the indictment against Simon Verrall, Charles Milson, Thomas Veer, John Brightman and Michael O'Leary, who were charged with divers other persons unknown, for tumultuous congregation and breach of the peace to the great terror and disturbance of the King's liege people and subjects to the ill-example of all others in the like case offenders and against the peace of the said lord the King, his crown and dignity.

The Clerk of the Peace was very proud of the indictment and read it out to the prisoners at the bar with the just pride of a successful author. Mr. John Rigby of Ellel

Grange, who as senior magistrate was in the chair, listened to the reading with critical approval. He had been a Templar in his youth and was accredited with much judicial learning.

A long list of thieves and vagabonds had first to be duly sentenced to be hanged or whipped or transported, and it was not until the afternoon of the second day that the trial of Verrall and his friends was reached. Several witnesses were called who stated generally that there were hundreds of people in the Town Square and that Verrall was abusive to the clergy. As to who struck the first blow there was no very clear agreement, but several spoke to Verrall's language and saw him fall on top of the churchwarden. No one gave evidence of the Rector's intemperate interruption. Verrall told the jury that he left himself in the hands of God. The other prisoners said a few halting words in their own defence, and then Mr. Rigby made a short summing-up to the jury and the court adjourned for half-an-hour whilst the members of the jury were locked up to consider their verdict.

On returning into court the prisoners were brought to the Bar and the jury returned.

" Are you agreed on your verdict ? " asks the Clerk.

The foreman stood up with a paper in his hand.

" What say you ? " asks the Clerk. " Is Simon Verrall guilty in manner and form as he stands indicted, or not guilty ? "

" We find him guilty of speaking in the Town Square."

Mr. Rigby threw down his pen in anger. " You had as good say nothing as that."

" Was it not an unlawful assembly ? " asked the Clerk of the Peace. " You mean that he was speaking to a tumult of people."

But the foreman said he had no commission to say more than what was written down and Verrall wanted to argue with the Bench that this was an acquittal. So Mr. Rigby bade them be seated again and told the jury in very round words that their verdict must be to the indictment "Guilty" or " Not guilty," and that no sane man could possibly find the prisoners " Not guilty," and further, that if the jury were perverse and would not find a just verdict they should be locked up without meat, drink, fire or tobacco.

" You must not think to abuse the court," he continued very angrily. " We will have a verdict by the help of God, or you shall starve for it."

Verrall began an harangue against this treatment of the jury, but Mr. Rigby shouted him down.

" Stop that prating fellow's mouth," he cried to the jailors, " or take him to the cells. Consider your verdict, gentlemen, and consider it well. If there are factious fellows among you I will find them out."

The jury retired again and the Bench withdrew to discuss the affair over wine and tobacco.

Within an hour or less word came that the jury were agreed, and on returning into court after the usual formalities had been gone through, the craven jury through their foreman murmured the word " Guilty " as the name of each prisoner was put to them. A girl's cry rang through the court ; Mr. Ambrose looked up and saw Hetty Verrall being led out in a fainting condition. He felt deeply sorry for the girl and by no means pleased at the verdict of the jury or satisfied with the justice administered by the court. He was not learned in the law and natural instincts rebelled against all forms of cruelty and injustice.

The jury having been sent away, the magistrates retired to discuss the fate of the prisoners. Mr. Rigby considered they should all be whipped and then transported, but Mr. Ambrose stood out strongly against such a sentence. Mr. Bradshaw of Garstang desired O'Leary the Irishman should be released as he was a good worker and was coming to him to work on a new road he was making.

This seemed very reasonable and Mr. Rigby agreed that O'Leary should be whipped round the Castle yard and then be liberated without paying his fees. The three " Enthusiasts" as minor offenders were to be kept in gaol for a year and Verrall, as ringleader, to be transported for seven years.

These sentences having been awarded, not without some interruption from Verrall and loud lamentations from poor O'Leary, Mr. Ambrose rode home, not too well satisfied with the day's work. He had made enquiries as to where

Hetty was lodging, and when he got home he told the whole story of the business to his wife, and she, with great charity and concern, promised to drive into Lancaster the next morning and see if anything could be done for the poor girl. Mr. Ambrose explained to his wife that it might be many months before Verrall could be transported and, meanwhile, if the Verralls had friends, they might petition for his reprieve.

The next day Mrs. Ambrose was as good as her word, and was so pleased with poor Hetty that she carried her home with her, for the girl was distraught with grief and fear, and the poor woman who was caring for her had no means to give her the rest and attention that was necessary.

Mrs. Ambrose soon learned her history, and her husband was interested to find that Hetty was the girl who used to serve at old Nan Chilcote's stall in Westminster Hall. He wrote a long letter to Ziba Grime and urged him to come to Lancaster to see his master. He also visited the Castle and had an interview with Verrall, who was very grateful to him for his wife's kindness to Hetty. The preacher himself seemed perfectly resigned to his fate, and expressed the belief that it was a divine method of calling him to a new sphere of usefulness. Mr. Ambrose closely examined him as to any friends he had in London who would speak for him, but he would name no one.

It was Mrs. Ambrose, who had conceived a great friendship for poor Hetty, who discovered her story, and when she heard that young Nic Berrington was a friend of the Princess, now good Queen Caroline, Mrs. Ambrose at once went to her husband and asked him to write to his young friend and see if he would use his influence at court to obtain a pardon for poor Verrall.

Mr. Ambrose had heard some months back from his friend, Captain Oglethorpe, strange stories of Mr. Berrington's entry into his kingdom and of the extravagant revels that succeeded his accession. Nevertheless, he felt that the young man, whatever may have been his folly and dissipations, had a good heart and would probably make an effort to save his former friend, so he wrote to him a full account of the matter, which he handed to the London carrier for despatch.

CHAPTER XXV

COURSING AT BLEWBERRY BOTTOM

THERE is no speed limit for the descent into hell, and no earthly policeman can check the driver of a chariot bent upon a Gadarene joy-ride. Only God's pity or a woman's could have saved Berrington at this stage of his career. Jenny had no pity, only selfish ambitions and greed. She was a skilled companion for youth bent on destruction, and knew the moment to step off the coach before it rushed over the last brink of the precipice. Poor Nic, who believed himself so masterful with the wench, was like all the strong, silent males of fiction and history, since the days of Samson, merely a woman's toy.

The two young people had their moment of triumph, and Nic Berrington's drive in the Ring with the flamboyant Jenny was twenty-four hours' town talk. The impudence of the fellow in escorting the girl into the sacred circle had delighted the mob, staggered the high priests of fashion and roused the industry of the wits to sharpen their pens towards epigram.

Things might have gone better for them had not Mr. Berrington's good Princess—now Queen Caroline—been making the Tour with her daughters that very afternoon. Nic made a graceful salutation. He was certain Her Majesty had recognised him. Jenny was equally certain that Her Majesty had duly appraised her status. The Queen gazed coldly into space and made no acknowledgment of the youth she had formerly befriended. Her Majesty had official knowledge of *les maitresses*, and did not suffer them gladly. Counsellor Annesley and Belinda were also making the Tour, but Nic saw a stern look in the old man's face and sat back in the coach out of his sight.

But for the welcome of the orange women, who openly expressed their coarse delight in the glorious equipage and

274

the golden girl in the coach, the adventurers were clearly told that they were strangers within the gates. After a few turns round the dreary, dusty circle Nic turned to Jenny and acknowledged defeat.

"This is but poor sport," he cried. "Let us drive out to 'The Pigeons' at Brentford."

And Jenny, who looked very glum and unhappy, answered snappishly: "If this is your world of fashion, for God's sake take me out of the dust and dirt of it before my clothes are ruined."

They turned out of the Park at the under-keeper's lodge at Hyde Park Corner, and took the road past Knightsbridge and Kensington towards Hammersmith. Once more in their own world of the open country road both were happy again, and had quite recovered their content as they encountered the adoration of the knowing eyes of the villagers of Turnham Green, and shortly afterwards rattled into the courtyard of "The Pigeons" at Brentford. Here they found Billinge on the steps of the inn and the landlord and landlady eager to welcome their splendid guests. For Berrington in his masterful way had never doubted his success and arranged that this should be the resting-place at the end of the first stage of the journey to his kingdom.

After an excellent supper served in the best parlour of the inn, Jenny looked across at Master Nic with smiling defiance, saying, "Tell me, Nic, how did you know I should come with you on this mad jaunt?"

"My dear girl, surely you must have observed that I make it my business in life to order things my own way." He elegantly dusted his sleeves with his kerchief and continued in the same complacent tone: "To-morrow we revisit London and then continue our journey to Steeple Berrington."

"Why do we go back on our road?" asked the girl eagerly, for she scented danger.

"We visit the Fleet, and there, my dear, a certain chaplain——"

Jenny stopped him with contemptuous laughter.

"Nykin!" she cried, "you talk and act like the fool child you are. Why should I ruin your life and mine by mar-

T

riage? In less than a year you will have run through your money and I shall be living on my wits again."

Master Nic looked at her despondently.

"Surely, Jenny, you knew I would do the honest thing by you."

"A curse on your honesty, Mr. Berrington, for truly I see little honesty in it. And why should I give up my liberty and hand you over my savings, which, let me tell you, Nic, amount to a very comfortable sum, for the sake of marrying a man who is certain to end his life in a debtors' prison?"

"Do you absolutely refuse my offer, Jenny?" he asked at last, looking very melancholy.

"You may thank your stars I have the good sense to do so. You are a good lad, Nykin. You do not forget old friends, and I like you for it. You have brought us all together again. You and I and old Turquet and Billinge. Perhaps for the last time. What would the Master have said about it?"

Mr. Berrington winced at the recollection of the Master.

"Well, what would Wild have said about it?" he asked impatiently.

" 'There is honour among thieves.' So I will come into the venture with the others as a comrade on equal terms, but not as a slave and humble servant."

And having delivered judgment, she threw her arms round her prisoner and kissed him masterfully—or should we write mistressfully?

Three days afterwards Mr. Nicholas Berrington and his lady arrived in triumph at the gates of the great house at Steeple Berrington. The church bells rang at the price agreed upon between Turquet and the vicar. The villagers turned out and gazed open-mouthed at the equipage and cheered the young couple as an instalment of gratitude in advance for beef and beer awaiting them in the white tents on the lawns. The sun shone in the heavens and the hearts of men and women were glad, but some of the shrewder matrons in the village pursed their lips and half closed their eyes at the beauty of smiling Jenny. Mrs. Vicar, too, and her husband differed in opinion about the girl, and the latter said some wise things to his wife about obedience and charity, strengthening his discourse with authoritative texts of Scripture, to which his wife replied: "Nevertheless, Henry, sin is sin, and I will never set foot in the Hall as long as that woman remains there."

The Reverend Henry Playseed made no reply. He had been a sea chaplain and had not lost all his sea manners. He remembered the wisdom of an old messmate, who used to say that "though he might make short trips for pastime, he would never embark with woman on the voyage of life, because he was afraid of foundering in the first foul weather." The vicar had more charity than his wife, and his cassock was often seen running before the wind across the village green that separated the vicarage from the park; and at early morn he might be heard rehearsing the choruses he had sung at Mr. Berrington's table as he returned to his duties.

Not that these duties were neglected, though his spiritual gifts would not have met with the approval of the Methodists. But he knew his Bible and could cap their texts aptly, and he had the Prayer Book services by heart. These he honoured as though they were the King's Regulations, and declaimed them clearly in the church, in the voice of a boatswain, nor did he forget to visit the sick, or catechise the young, or give alms to the poor.

And that his visits to Berrington Hall did something to leaven the atmosphere of waste and dissipation seems not unlikely, for Nic had a real respect for the man and used to make it his duty to please him by appearing in the family pew at Sunday service.

There was no longer any doubt expressed that Mr. Berrington was the rightful heir. Crowley had fully acknowledged that the young man was the real Nicholas Berrington. Berrington Hall was once again open house, and the squires and gentlemen of the neighbourhood gathered to drink the health of their new neighbour, and he and his friends were welcome guests at the great houses round.

To chronicle the days of waste and riot and sport and conviviality would be a dull task. Whilst Turquet was

Prime Minister he had tried to interest Mr. Berrington in
the management of the estate, but the young prince preferred riding over his fields after the hounds rather than
wasting his substance in repairing the farm fences.

One improvement he made at Berrington Hall, and that
was in the lighting of it, the like of which had never been
seen in the countryside before. For he had the stables and
out-buildings and passages in the house illuminated with
beautiful oil lamps composed of one entire glass of a globular shape which he bought from the shop opposite the Hay-
market. These wonderful lamps were then the wonder of
the age. His rooms also were always lit with a multitude of
wax candles echoing from shining mirrors. But of late he
had experimented with these new lamps and found them
savoury enough to use in the kitchens and minor rooms.
Berrington always revelled in light. It was part of his nature.

Though most of his guests were of the old set from
White's and the Thatched House Tavern, there were others.
Old Quin drove down for a few days and Captain Oglethorpe with him, who tried to interest Nic in his new
scheme for a plantation in America to be called Georgia in
honour of the King. Mr. Berrington listened with respect
to the Captain's project, and expressed polite regret that his
duties as an English landlord made it impossible for him to
accompany the Captain on his venture, but he pressed upon
him a handsome draft as a donation to the scheme which
the Captain received very gratefully.

Months passed in luxury and pleasure and schemes of
extravagance, and at length Crowley began to protest that
money could not be advanced at the present rate and that
creditors were beginning to clamour for payments. Unfortunately at this juncture Turquet was away on a mission to
the Continent for Sir Robert Walpole. Before he had gone
Turquet, like a good minister, had frankly warned his
prince that he was draining the exchequer beyond its power
of replevin, to which his young master had royally referred
him to the master of all evil and gone his way of prodigality
rejoicing.

The latest extravagance was coursing, and sad it is that
so noble a pursuit should have been the last step in our

young friend's road to ruin. But it is ever the best gifts of life that tempt the unwary to destruction. And though each form of hunting and sport has its element of cruelty, yet the wisdom of the world has rightly decided in favour of coursing. And for my part in this matter, I am of the school of Solomon and Flavius Arrianus, and I would have added Mr. Wordsworth, but that local tradition declares he preferred cock-fighting, in which taste he followed the academic example of Roger Ascham.

The great course at Blewberry Bottom between Berrington Blackguard and Harcourt Heriot is classic coursing history. Uncle John or many another Altcar expert could tell you, what his great-grandfather had told him he had learned at first hand of the business. I have been at pains to investigate the true history of the matter, and make no apology for the meticulous detail of the narrative, since this was one of the decisive battles of the world, not only to the brave greyhounds who fought it out at Blewberry, but to God and the devil in their contest for the soul of The Child. For though Mr. Berrington was no longer a legal infant, one cannot say that he put away childish things until after the day of the battle.

Soon after Turquet left for France, Berrington had started a kennel, and bought for a considerable price all the greyhounds of the late Mr. Dews, of Newbold Pacey. At this time Oxfordshire and Berkshire were great coursing rivals, and Berrington's neighbours were delighted to hear that he had seriously set himself to vindicate their county's superiority in this noble sport.

These county battles continued into our own day, as admirers of that sweet lady, Mary Mitford, will remember. For who has not read of the triumph on Ilsley Downs of her pet, Lufra, a little Northumbrian bitch, bred by a collier, which romped away from one of Lord Rivers' famous dogs and lost the Oxfordshire squires a pot of money.

It was considered a great honour in coursing to challenge for your county, and for many years Simon, the young Viscount Harcourt, had done this as of right, as his kennels at Stanton Harcourt contained the best greyhounds in the district. Mr. Berrington, however, had tried several of his greyhounds against the Harcourt dogs, and on occasion had been successful, and the two young men were regarded as aspirants for the honour of challenging for their county at the close of the season. Before Berrington could do this a serious match must be arranged, and the community had to be satisfied that Berrington had the best greyhound.

Mr. Berrington had made up his mind to claim the honour, and an opportunity occurred at a meeting at Ashdown Park. A clever bitch called Harcourt Heriot had won several courses for the Viscount. There was a legal jest in the name, for everyone knew the dog had been seized as a heriot on the death of its owner, one of the Harcourt tenants, and public opinion condemned the action and the nomenclature. Still, the bitch was clever and won her matches, and after dinner young Harcourt started to cry odds on Heriot against all comers, with such aggressive insolence, that Nic could stand it no longer and, though modestly admitting that he was a new hand at the sport, told the Viscount he would find a match for the brindle in his own kennel. The Oxfordshire squires were delighted. The challenge was accepted. Large sums of money were laid against Mr. Berrington's nomination, and he rode home having pledged his kennel to the amount of several thousand pounds.

When he arrived at Steeple Berrington he found Turquet had returned from foreign parts looking very weary and tired. When he heard of this new folly, he groaned in spirit, for he had stopped at Witney and had a talk with Crowley, and was greatly worried about his friend's financial affairs. These matters, however, Nic refused to so much as discuss. A new fortune was to be made out of this coursing match, always supposing they nominated the right dog. Over this there was an unfortunate difference of opinion between Nic and Jenny.

Jenny, too, was as eager as Mary Mitford herself about coursing, and had a greyhound of whom she made a great pet, and she insisted that Nic should nominate Berrington Blackguard. He was a black dog of great size and strength, with one white spot on the middle of his neck and white shoe linings under his feet. This glossy giant had attached himself to Jenny from the first, and followed her wherever she went. Nic had christened him Blackguard because he declared that on occasion he only wrenched and rushed his hares, not turning them as a good greyhound should. He had intended to nominate his own pet, a little blue and white bitch, called Berrington Beauty.

There were endless discussions on this weighty subject. Trials were run and the Blackguard being on his best behaviour, even Nic himself had to agree that he was the right nomination. A meeting took place between the Viscount and Mr. Berrington. It was arranged between them that instead of each appointing an umpire who should choose an arbitrator as referee, which was much the custom in those days, they should leave the affair to the judgment of old Mr. Fairford of Wantage, who was a very honest gentleman and a sound judge of coursing. Indeed, he had all the qualifications of a great judge, since he had an eye like a hawk, was as deaf as a post, and rode like the devil. Deafness is a great attribute in a judge (of coursing), as it prevents him hearing any outside discussion that might influence his judgment. It was further arranged that the match should be decided in the best out of three courses, two to be decided the first day and the deciding course if necessary on the next day.

A large company assembled at Blewberry Bottom on the day of the match. Nearly all the men and most of the women were on horseback, but a few preferred to follow on foot. Those who have only seen the enclosed coursing of modern times must remember that from the days of Solomon and Arrianus coursing the hare with greyhounds was enjoyed on the great open wolds and uplands of the world which the greedy have long ago taken from us. But in Berrington's England there were plenty of real open coursing grounds with merry brown hares waiting to try their speed against the greyhounds. Blewberry Bottom was one of the most famous of them.

The way of it was thus. The hare-finder, who was a very important official in those days, went forth to start the hare. No horseman or footman was allowed to go before or on either side of the finder, but had to keep directly behind the finder and not to come nearer to him than forty yards. The slipper with the greyhounds followed the finder, and behind them the judge whose duty was to keep up with the course at all hazards, but always to be behind the dogs.

It was a brilliant morning early in March. A light southeast wind blew across the downs, and the larks were singing gaily, as the eager procession followed the hare-finder across the Bottom. At the foot of a small nob or mound, where there was some gorse, the finder stopped. The dogs strained at the leash. The slipper controlled them cleverly, and three times, as by law commanded, the finder called out "Sol ho!" before he put the hare from her form.

Jenny's heart was in her mouth; even Nic was excited, but neither he nor Viscount Harcourt displayed their feelings. Mr. Fairford held up his hand, to keep back the riders behind him. Suddenly a great hare leaped out of the bush and made for over the hill above some gravel pits. The two greyhounds struggled and barked, but not until the hare had her full twelve score yards' law did Mr. Fairford drop his hand and shout the word "Go!" There was a splendid slip, and nose to nose brindle and black raced up the hill after the disappearing hare.

Mr. Fairford took the risk of an ascent up a narrow slip of grass between the two pits, and Berrington followed him. The rest of the company spread right and left and did not see anything of the run up, which went to Blackguard, who outpaced Heriot several lengths. Then, to Nic's delight, the great black flung himself at the hare and fell, but it was a fair turn, and later he gathered himself again and took another fall, turning his hare, and the brindle fell over him. They were now near a covert, and the remaining points were evenly distributed before the gallant hare found a drain and left the combatants panting at the mouth of it.

Lord Harcourt rode up to Mr. Fairford, shouting out: "Did you see my dog fall? Did you see my dog fall?"

"I don't know which is your dog, damn you!" said the honest judge, "but the black fell and the brindle fell over him, and the black made a turn just over the hill."

"Then you give it to the black?" said the young Viscount ungraciously.

Mr. Fairford turned away and shouted in a mighty voice that all the company might hear: "Black! Black!" Then he rode to the finder to discuss with him where they should find for the next course, for several other matches were to be run that day.

In the afternoon Blackguard seemed to resent being called on for a second effort. He waited on the brindle, letting her do all the work and score all the points, though he came in at the finish cleverly enough to kill the hare. There are many men as well as greyhounds who ruin their careers by like selfishness. Even Jenny could take no exception to Mr. Fairford's judgment in favour of the brindle.

Mr. Berrington and his friends rode across the hills to the river at Wantage fairly satisfied with the day's work, leaving Blackguard at a neighbouring farm-house in the care of Billinge. At supper Jenny and Nic and their friends had a noisy discussion over the merits of Berrington Black-guard and Berrington Beauty, and the chances of the former against Harcourt Heriot, whilst Turquet, who was in a sullen humour, sat and smoked at the parlour fire.

The next morning it was drizzling and rather misty, but by nine o'clock, when they met at Blewberry, the sun was shining and the mist had cleared sufficiently for sport. They went to the other end of the Bottom and found a strong hare in the valley. When the slip was made Heriot, at the moment they were loosed, paused as though she were un-sighted for a moment, and the black got forty yards' start, or perhaps more.

Jenny was in a heaven of delight, Master Nic chuckled complacently and even Turquet smiled. Lord Harcourt volubly cursed the bitch, and the judge, and the slipper and the noble sport of coursing. Blackguard made two or maybe three turns, and then Miss Heriot joined him, and the hare being a gallant fellow, she put in a turn or so, though it was not much more than turn for turn, for Blackguard kept up his pace. But then his speed began to decrease, and now Heriot made all the turns, keeping the hare away from covert, and as Berrington judged it, Blackguard did not serve a single turn out of the eight or ten which the brindle gave successively before the hare got to covert.

Jenny, and indeed many of the spectators, thought the black dog was the winner. Nic, who had reined in his horse near to his friend Turquet, looked across at him with enquiring eyes, and Turquet, to put him out of his misery, nodded, saying: "Brindle gained nearly double the number of points that Black did, and in half the time. If Mr. Fairford knows his business——"

At this moment the judge cantered up to the waiting group and shouted, "Brindle! Brindle!" The Viscount threw up his hat with a joyous oath.

"The judge does know his business," said Mr. Berrington pleasantly, and he rode across to thank Mr. Fairford for his services and congratulate his opponent.

Jenny had cantered to where Billinge had captured her defeated greyhound. She shot from her horse, threw her arms round the lazy black giant, and wept bitterly. Even had he won, she could not have honoured him more. But that is the way of women; and those who know say it is also a characteristic of angels.

CHAPTER XXVI

THE DEATH OF TURQUET

At the end of the day's coursing Berrington's friends had all with one consent begun to make excuse about returning with him to Steeple Berrington, and had ridden off to their homes. The retreat of the Blackguard and his followers was a dismal affair. Jenny was broken-hearted at her favourite's defeat. Turquet was silent and morose, and when Nic rallied him on his depression, confessed to headache. Billinge reviled their champion until Jenny cursed him to silence. Even Nic's sunny nature seemed clouded by this untoward misfortune.

Supper and abundant claret put life into the little party, and after Jenny had retired for the night. Turquet and Nic drew their chairs to the fire for a council of war.

"Why do you take this set-back so sadly, Turquet?" asked Berrington pleasantly.

"You are a ruined man, Nic," replied Turquet gloomily.

"Crowley must find props for the ruin then," said Nic, laughing.

Turquet poured himself out half a tumbler of brandy and shook his head. Nic had never seen his friend in so mournful a humour.

"To-morrow I shall ride into Witney," continued Nic cheerily, "and see the fox in his den, and find out what he can do for us."

"To-morrow! To-morrow!" muttered Turquet hazily, and then with an effort he continued: "Keep house, Nic. There are writs out for you already. Crowley is no friend. Had we won——"

His voice broke in tears. Nic saw he was over-tired or ill, and chattered away merrily to distract his thoughts.

"My dear Turquet, you forget your own proverb, 'Let the past bury the past.' We can stand our losses readily

285

enough. The whole affair is my error. We should have run Berrington Beauty, but Jenny would have me nominate the Blackguard, and lovely woman must have her own way."

Turquet's chin had fallen on his breast. Nic was frightened at the grey pallor of his face.

"Turquet! Turquet!" he cried, raising his voice and leaning across the table to look into his eyes. "Turquet, are you ill? Let me help you to bed, Turquet."

His friend's eyes opened and gazed stupidly at Nic. Suddenly he rose to his feet and tried to put his glass on the table, but it fell on the floor with a crash. Turquet stumbled to his feet and then, to save himself, fell back in his chair, smiling feebly.

"I should have left the brandy alone. Away to bed, Nic. I shall sleep by the fire."

"You are ill, Turquet," cried Nic frightened.

"Yes, yes. I should have kept my bed to-day. I was a fool."

He tried to rise again, pulling at the table, but was too weak and dizzy to stand, and fell back again. Nic was now in grave distress for his friend, and ran to the kitchen for Toby, shouting for him to come to his aid. He hurried him back to the parlour, followed by Berrington Beauty tripping daintily along the passage after her master.

At the door they stopped and gazed at Turquet in terror. He had risen to his feet, and was clinging to the mantelpiece, on which stood one of Nic's large lamps. He had torn his waistcoat open and bared his chest to the mirror, and was gazing with grim intent at several foul red spots on his skin. His eyes turned and he saw his friends.

"For Christ's sake, get away!" he whispered hoarsely. "Away! I know it. It is plague. I have seen it before. Plague!"

He staggered into his chair a huddled mass of human unconsciousness.

Billinge would have faced any mortal enemy or the Evil One in person to save a friend, but this was the return of the curse on the house following the defeat at Blewberry, and the horror of it overset the little wits he had. He uttered a wild cry and rushed from the room to the kitchen, where some of the servants were dozing by the fire.

"Save yourselves! Save yourselves!" he cried.

"What the hell is all this?" said a fellow half awake.

"The plague! The Count has the plague. He is dying in the hall."

The men awoke as though they had heard the last trump and with one accord rushed into the open and fled from the stricken house.

Nic heard them go. His heart sank. He was alone. He did not see the anxious look on the face of the faithful greyhound at his side. He was alone with a man dying of plague within two yards of him, his limp body lying on a chair. He could hear Turquet breathing heavily, and he could hear his own heart thumping against his ribs. He knew that he was as white as a sheet, and his soul shouted at him that he was a coward. He stepped on tiptoe towards his friend and, taking down a candle from the mantelpiece in his trembling hand, pulled aside the man's vest and saw the red pustules on his skin. He took up his wrist and felt the pulse was moving. When he had done so much, he knew that he was in the same jeopardy of death as his friend, and that gave him courage. Master Nic was himself again. He whistled "Lilli-Bullero" softly but defiantly to cheer his spirits and promote sane thought. Billinge, poor fool, was a deserter. He thought of the vicar, but no, it was not fair to drag another into the business; he must save Jenny and then look after his friend on his own.

He himself slept on the first floor in a room next Jenny's He took a candle and went to the girl's room, opening the door but a crack. He called her twice by name. There must still have been an accent of terror in his voice, for she jumped up and called out to him to ask what was amiss. He ordered her back roughly in a whisper of command. At the word "plague" the girl whimpered miserably.

"You are safe enough, Jenny," he said, "if you act at once. Dress as soon as you can: make for the back door. Do not enter the hall. Toby must be somewhere in the stables. There is the chaise and horses enough, and a clear moon. Off with you."

"But you, Nykin," the girl called out tearfully, "what will you do?"

His answer was to shut her door with a snap and go to his own room. As there was no possibility of carrying the Count to his apartments, he had determined to haul his own mattress and blankets down the staircase into the hall. This he did, making two journeys with all the things he thought necessary for the moment.

Then he made up a bed in a corner near the fire, close to the Count's chair, and placed a screen at the head of it to prevent the draughts from the doorway. All this took some time, and ever and anon he paused in his task to listen for sounds of Jenny. At last he heard the creaking of the stairs and the opening and shutting of the back door. Jenny was safe.

Then he began to work on the Count, who was lying in a stupor in his chair. He managed to pull his boots off, and in doing so roused Turquet, who asked in a dazed voice what was happening.

"Nothing new, old friend," said Berrington, "but a drunken man should never sleep in his boots. Help me with your coat, can't you?"

Turquet rose and steadied himself by the chair, muttering, "Drunk? Never. What has happened?"

"Even the strongest of us are overcome by the fumes of brandy. It has happened to me, my dear Turquet, even to me," said Nic saucily.

Turquet swore several oaths in a puzzled delirium to show that he was intensely exasperated with his young friend, but he seemed eager to get his clothes off, and when he was sufficiently undressed, he caught hold of Nic's arms and slid on to the mattress with a groan of gratitude like a tired child.

"That is the way of it. Yarely! Yarely! Let go the top mast," called out Nic, as he released his arm from his friend's grasp. "Now you can sleep in comfort."

He piled the blankets on him, for his friend's hands felt deathly cold, and then straightened him out in bed and tucked him safely in. Turquet lay still, breathing heavily. Berrington put some logs on the fire and went into the kitchen for more candles. Then he returned, put out the lamp and placed the candles where the light could not fall on the

sick man's face. Satisfying himself that Turquet was resting
and perhaps sleeping, he went upstairs to make sure that
Jenny had fled.

He was soon back again and, finding that his patient was
really asleep, he opened a bottle of claret, pulled a chair to
the fire and, wrapping his cloak round him, sat listening
to the crackling logs. The clock struck one. Turquet was
now breathing regularly. Berrington filled a pipe and
lighted it from a brand which he pulled deftly out of the fire.
He and his dying friend were alone in the house. The fire
and the clock, he thought, were his only live companions.

He was almost dozing off when he felt a cold hand placed
on his own. Berrington Beauty, his pretty favourite, had
followed him about patiently waiting for a word of kindness, but that her master should make for sleep without a
word of good-night to her was unthinkable, and was more
than her ladyship could permit. So she thrust her cold nose
into his hand as a protest against this lack of the courtesies
of life.

Berrington started awake, overjoyed to find he had one
comrade left.

"Beauty, my dear!" he cried, taking her head in his hands.
"You would have beaten Harcourt's dog, wouldn't you?
I shall open another bottle and drink your health. It is something to have one bitch faithful unto death. Here's to you,
little lady. It has not been one of our lucky days, has it? But
sufficient for the day. You just keep your nose there, little
lady, and see I do not go to sleep. I've got to watch! Do
you understand, watch!"

The morning sun shining through the upper windows of
the hall fell on the face of the sleeping watcher. Nature had
conquered his "resolution," and it was well for him it was
so. The waking youth turned his face from the sun's rays.
The movement woke him. Berrington Beauty barked a
rousing welcome. Nic sprang up from his chair. Where was
he? His eyes fell on the figure lying like a log asleep or unconscious on the mattress. He felt ashamed and angry with
himself. However, no harm was done. He walked across to
the windows and pulled open the curtains. It was a fine
spring morning.

Having made certain that Turquet lived and slept, Berrington went forth to explore the house. Not a living soul remained. All the servants had fled. In the stables only his own horse was standing in his box. His master saw to his feed. He found some corn for the hens and scattered it among them. Then he washed at the pump and returned to the house and breakfasted in the kitchen on the remains of a meat pie and a tankard of ale. So far all was well. But for his anxiety about Turquet, there was a Robinson Crusoe touch about the general outlook that was not without its charm. If he ever met his truant servant again, he thought what fun he would have roasting him mercilessly with the sauce of odorous comparison between Toby and Man Friday.

For the present, however, his puzzle was how to help his poor friend, and after prolonged thought he came to the conclusion that his best course was to ride into Witney in search of a doctor. With this intent he returned to the stables to groom and saddle his horse.

Ill news travels apace in all centres, but more quickly perhaps across scattered country than through crowded cities. For countryside travellers stop to greet each other and pass the news. It was known the same night in three counties that Harcourt Heriot had beaten Berrington Blackguard and that Mr. Berrington had lost ten thousand pounds. Early next morning more terrible news ran like wildfire across the fields. It was whispered that everyone had fled from the great house at Steeple Berrington and that Count de Grillac, the King's Messenger, was dead of the plague.

The waggoner from London began to hear this story in varied forms some miles the other side of Witney. He carried a letter for Mr. Berrington that he had collected from a waggon from Lancaster, and on arrival at Steeple Berrington the villagers told him that it was but too true and that every living being had fled in the night. Old people who remembered the death of the late squire and his wife shook their heads gloomily and declared that they always knew the house was under a curse.

The waggoner had a parcel of books for the Rev. Henry Playseed, and having no wish to deliver Mr. Berrington's letter to a plague-stricken house, he asked his advice about the matter.

The Vicar, who had been writing a sermon in his study and had heard nothing of the disaster at the Hall, promised the waggoner that he would deliver the letter himself without delay. There was never any hesitation about this old sailor in the hour of danger. He threw on his cassock and, taking his hat and stick, started off, letter in hand. As he clicked the garden gate in opening it, he heard a shrill voice from the bedroom window.

"Where are you going, Henry?" called his wife excitedly.

"I have heard terrible news, my dear," said her husband, holding the open gate in his hand. "I must go up to the Hall at once."

"I know all about it, Henry," replied Mrs. Playseed, in a superior tone of voice, as she came to the window and looked out. "The milkmaid told Alice this morning. That wicked Frenchman has the plague. You must not go near them."

"But, my dear, it may not be true."

"Of course it is true. It is a judgment on them for their sins."

"And they may want help and succour."

"Let their friends succour them. If you go to that house, Henry, I shall lock the door against you. You shall not bring the plague home here."

The good lady slammed the window angrily.

"Well, I can sleep in the barn then," said the Vicar to himself, and he hurried on his way, muttering as if to keep up his courage. "'I was sick and ye visited me.' Yes, of course, and I always visited them when they were well. Maria is quite wrong about it. After all, it may not be the plague."

He went up to the front door of the Hall and rang the bell. He could hear it sounding within the house, but no one came. He peered through the lower windows and could dimly see the figure of a man lying on a mattress in the corner of the room. Perhaps this was the dead count. He shuddered slightly and turned away, making for the back of the house. As he approached the stables, Berrington

U

Beauty bounded out, barking violently. The Vicar called to her, and she went up to greet him, for she knew her master's friends. At this moment Berrington came out of the stable and stood holding his hand out to stop the Vicar coming near him.

"I have a letter for you, Mr. Berrington."

"Drop it where you stand. I will fetch it later. There is illness in the house."

"That is why I came," said Mr. Playseed.

"The plague," whispered Nic.

"Who says so?" asked the Vicar.

"The Count himself."

"What does he know of these things? Let me see him."

"Leave him to me, sir," cried Nic eagerly. "Why should you risk your life? I am riding into Witney at once for a doctor."

"If you tell a Witney doctor it is plague he won't travel this side of Witney," said Mr. Playseed, laughing. "I know them. Let me have a look at the man first. 'I was sick and ye visited me.' Those are the sailing orders!"

With these words the Vicar took command of the ship, as it were, and strode into the kitchen and across into the hall, followed by Mr. Berrington and the faithful Beauty.

Turquet was lying half unconscious, shifting uneasily from time to time and muttering incoherent words. The Vicar knelt by the side of his bed and felt his pulse. Then he gently opened his vest and carefully examined the spots on his chest. Then he turned the man's face round to the light and peered into his eyes and touched his skin gently. Poor Nic admired his courage; it put new heart into him.

When he had finished his examination he turned to Nic with a smile, saying: "There's no plague about the man at all. He's only got small-pox, that's all."

"Are you sure, sir?" gasped Nic excitedly.

"Nothing more. Small-pox. Have you had them yourself?"

"At school."

"That's pure fortune, anyhow. Well, you can ride into Witney for a doctor if you wish. But I can find you an old woman in the village to nurse him, who knows more about small-pox than all the doctors in Oxfordshire."

"I should like to get a doctor to him."

"As you think best, Mr. Berrington. By the bye, here's your letter. The waggoner left it with me. I'll be back with the nurse in less than no time."

Mr. Berrington followed the Vicar out of the house, profuse in his thanks, which the good man waved aside. The reaction seemed too much for him. "Only small-pox!" He sat on a seat on the terrace and laughed aloud. How he would smoke Billinge for his cowardice, and as soon as Turquet got well again, what a theme for witty reproof when the old man became didactic. When he got well again —but would he recover? "Only small-pox," he thought hopefully, yet he seemed to remember that in older people the disease was often fatal.

The Vicar returned with Mrs. Goadby, a stout, motherly body, who took possession of the Hall, the sick man, and Mr. Berrington, and all the appurtenances thereof without fuss or demur. The three carried the patient in his blankets up to his own room. The hall was tidied down, the kitchen fire lighted, hot bricks wrapped in flannel placed in the patient's bed, and Mrs. Goadby announced that he had fallen asleep.

"Then we can do no more for him," said Nic cheerfully, "and after we have had a bowl of punch, Vicar, I will be off to Witney."

"The ride will do you good, and the punch will do us both good, but before the punch let us not forget prayer. By the regulations prayer should be said in the sick man's room, but as sleep is better for him at the moment than prayer, we will kneel here."

So saying, the good man knelt at the hall table, Berrington following his example, and in a clear, businesslike voice, Mr. Playseed made his appeal to the Maker of mankind in the statutory language of the Prayer Book. This duty fulfilled, the punch was brewed and discussed, and the Vicar declining a second bowl, Nic mounted his horse and rode to Witney.

Various stories were afloat in the town, and the arrival of

Mr. Berrington at the inn with the news that his friend was only ill of small-pox was received with great relief. The doctor gave Mr. Berrington a bottle of physic and readily agreed to ride out next day and see the patient, and this matter settled, Mr. Berrington called at Crowley's office. Mr. Crowley, however, was from home, but the head clerk, who was very fond of Mr. Berrington, warned him as he went away that he had reason to believe that bailiffs were already out with warrants of arrest against him, and though Mr. Crowley had told him not to trouble Mr. Berrington about the matter, yet he thought he ought to know, and strongly advised him to keep house for a while. Mr. Berrington thanked him for his information and returned home.

The next day Billinge returned to duty. He had driven Jenny to Oxford, and seen her into the stage coach and left the chaise and one of the horses with a livery man. He was very contrite at his cowardice, and Nic was too worried about Turquet and his own affairs to rally him as he would have done under happier circumstances. Not wanting his services, he sent him back to Oxford to sell the chaise and horse and return with the money, commanding him to keep an open eye for bailiffs and to report on their movements.

This done, Berrington locked his doors against strangers and devoted himself, with the aid of Mrs. Goadby and the Reverend Henry Playseed, who called daily and read regulation prayers to the unconscious Count, to the care of his sick friend.

It was not until Billinge returned that Nic remembered something of a letter that Mr. Playseed had brought him on the morning after Turquet was taken ill. He recollected now that he had placed it in his desk when he rode to Witney. He went in search of it. It was from Mr. Ambrose, and as he read it he felt so helpless and troubled in spirit that he almost wished that the plague had in truth descended once more on the house and carried him off as it had carried away his parents; for then he could have lain still and been quiet and slept, and been with them and found rest. But now he was called upon to do things that were beyond his power, and there was no one near him to help.

Mr. Ambrose's letter told the story of Mr. Verrall's trial

and how Hetty was being cared for by his wife. He begged
Mr. Berrington would inform him whether he would use
his influence with the Queen and the Court to obtain a
pardon for Verrall. If this could not be done, then Hetty
had made up her mind to follow her father to the plantations. Mr. Ambrose continued to explain that he and his
friend, Captain Oglethorpe, the Member for Haslemere,
were both on the board of the Georgia trustees, and he had
some hope that it might be arranged that Verrall and his
daughter should sail with some of the new settlers, many of
whom were of the same way of thinking in religious matters
as Mr. Verrall and his daughter. He concluded by telling
Mr. Berrington that he was on his way to London and
would be found at the Belle Sauvage.

As he read Mr. Ambrose's kindly and courteous phrases,
Nic was stricken with remorse. Face to face with the help-
lessness of his position and his inability to rush to the aid of
his dear Hetty, whose image he had tried with no great
success to push out of his mind, the wickedness and folly of
his life fell like a great burden on his soul, and he found
himself encompassed by the net of his own sin and
realised the bitter fate of bearing the yoke of his own
wrongdoing. Darkness and despair shut in his thoughts on
all sides. He could not ride to the rescue of his beloved. He
could not bring succour to her since he was a ruined man.
He could not even hope for her forgiveness, and even if he
tried to make his way to London and Mr. Ambrose, the
hunters of the law would be on to him and he would be
kennelled in the Fleet and left there to rot and die without
hope of release.

All these things his conscience kept repeating to him
with pedantic iteration, rudely reminding him that he had
been duly warned from time to time of the fate in store for
him. Indeed, this conscience of his seemed to him a useless,
gloomy companion of his sleepless nights, offering him no
consolation, but seeming to take malicious pleasure in
bringing his thoughts back to the cheering truth that his
misery and dismay were of his own making.

As he sat with his head in his hands, vainly wishing that
Turquet was fit to be consulted about his affairs, he heard

the weighty figure of Mrs. Goadby descending from he sick room. She opened the door and beckoned to him.

"He is calling for you," she said gravely.

"Is he better, then?"

The woman shook her head.

"He is passing. You had best hurry."

Nic ran up the stairs. Turquet, who had been comatose for many hours, had roused himself and lay propped against two pillows. He smiled at Nic and pointed with a thin finger to the chair near the bed.

"The game is over," he whispered.

Nic took his hand and rested his face upon it, sobbing.

"Shall I fetch Mr. Playseed?" he whispered.

"We have no time to waste. Man can neither teach us to live nor to die. It is our own business. When you come to the door of death you will find it opens easily enough."

Nic tried to speak and to urge him not to exert himself, but Turquet gripped his shoulder and raised himself to point to his portmanteau. Berrington gathered he was to bring it to him, and he opened it at his bedside.

"There are some papers there endorsed in French."

Nic found them and held them out to him.

"If you carry them to Geneva you can turn them into money. There is a purse there, too. Enough for present needs. Take them now. You are ruined, Nic, and if you go back to the old game without Turquet to guard you, you will be hanged on the gallows. You have run past your luck, you must go back and pick up the trail."

He stopped for want of breath and seemed to choke. Nic moved as though he would go for assistance, but the dying man's thin hand fastened on to his own and he sat beside him, neither of them moving for several minutes. It seemed to Nic that his friend's eyes were glazing over, and he feared that death had already claimed him.

But on a sudden life blazed into his eyes again with a last vigour, and he raised himself.

"God knows why I love you, Child," he whispered. "There has been no other love in my life but what you brought. And, remember—" He paused, his voice sank; then he continued; "Find the girl, Hetty :—a good girl

Hetty : . . . Geneva . . . Hetty ! . . . Kiss me, Nic . . .
Your last chance . . . Hetty ! "

Turquet fell back exhausted and Nic leaned over and
kissed him on the brow. He seemed to hear the Count
breathing as he sat holding his hand. Mrs. Goadby entered
the room silently. She came to the bedside and took
Turquet's hand away from Nic and held it for a moment
and then laid it softly on the counterpane. Tenderly she
drew down the Count's eyelids to hide the staring eyes,
murmuring as she did so ; " The Lord gave and the Lord
hath taken away ; blessed be the name of the Lord."

CHAPTER XXVII

BACK TO HETTY

THE day after the funeral the Vicar came to see his young friend and asked him what his plans might be and in what way he could assist him. Nic showed his gratitude, as youth does to the elder brother who is ready to listen, by pouring out all the complicated story of his sins and wickedness and the difficulties to which they had given birth.

Mr. Playseed pointed out that under his sailing orders he was not entitled to judge or condemn, but that his business was to assist human wrecks to a safe harbour, and asked Berrington to tell him plainly how his affairs stood. Nic was very grateful and at once showed him the papers the Count had handed to him from which it appeared that substantial sums of money were lodged with one M. Lefroi, a goldsmith at Geneva, to be handed to Mr. Nicholas Berrington on the death of the Count. Mr. Berrington also told his friend something of Mr. Ambrose's letter and his own financial position and his fear that unless some arrangement could be made with his creditors he might be imprisoned for debt.

Mr. Playseed advised that it would be well to ride to London and consult with Mr. Ambrose and Captain Oglethorpe, and both he and Nic agreed that the New World of Georgia in which these gentlemen were interested offered a tempting future to a youth of his abilities, and that if he could evade arrest and make across to Geneva and secure the money the Count had left to him, he might purchase an estate in the new colony. He said nothing to the Vicar about Hetty at first, but as they discussed the question of emigration, Mr. Playseed himself thought right to read his young friend a lecture on the duty of matrimony which, he explained over their second bowl of punch, was held by the Church to be an honourable and holy state, though in actual daily experience he had found that there were drawbacks attendant upon it owing to the inability of some women to remember and act upon the scriptural duty of obedience. Nevertheless, he assured his young friend that in going to a new colony, it was a very essential thing to carry out with him a wife, not only as the Church pointed out for the procreation of children, but to do the work of the house whilst he was hunting and adventuring.

The next day Billinge came in with news that he had met two evil-looking fellows outside the park gate, and knew one to be a London tipstaff. Mr. Berrington determined to ride that night for London alone, and ordered Billinge to join him at the " Duke's Head " in Redcross Street, Southwark, at the end of the week. Mr. Playseed agreed to come up from the Vicarage to see him safely off, and it was settled the three of them should have a farewell supper, and that the Vicar and Billinge should keep the lights going after Mr. Berrington had ridden away so that if the bailiffs were watching the house it would appear that the Squire and his friends were making merry as usual.

That night Nic Berrington sat in the great hall of the house of his fathers feasting his friends for the last time. Two of the great globular lamps had been brought in and stood on the dinner wagon, the wax candles in the great candelabra were all lighted, and though the lower windows were curtained, through the upper windows the light shone forth to the world so that, as Nic said with a grin of satisfaction, " the fellows outside will know that ' the king doth wake to-night and takes his rouse.' "

It was after midnight when Berrington rose and taking Mr. Playseed by the hand, thanked him with tears of gratitude for all his kindness and especially for having taken under his guardianship Berrington Beauty. The Vicar made light of his services and assured him that he hoped to run the greyhound at Cotswold and make money out of her.

Mr. Berrington now left them, and went out to the stables, Billinge going with him to fasten the back door behind him, and had he done so without delay all had been well. But after his master had crept out and vanished into the darkness Toby must needs keep the door ajar to look after him. The bailiffs must have been hanging about, and noticed the door ajar. They were not entitled to break and enter for fear of the law, yet if they could get an entrance by strategy the law was on their side. They evidently thought that one of the servants had gone out into the yard for some necessary service and stealthily approached the doorway and suddenly threw all their weight on it, knocking Toby backwards. By this ruse their small army entered the citadel and rushed into the hall, their leader shouting out that he had a warrant for Mr. Berrington.

The Vicar was mixing a last bowl of punch when the ruffians rushed at him, blinded by the light, and taking him for the moment to be their prisoner. With great presence of mind he flung the contents of the bowl in the leader's face and Billinge, now recovered from the surprise, came in with a stout cudgel and attacked the party in the rear. There was a fierce struggle in the midst of which one of the fellows was knocked against the dinner wagon which fell with its two noble lamps and their great glass globes crash upon the floor.

The whole party stood amazed at the disaster, for the oil was running across the boards and one of the curtains and some papers and packing-cases which Mr. Berrington had been filling were already alight and blazing.

" Rouse Mr. Berrington," shouted the Vicar, not without diplomacy " He is asleep in his room ! "

" Let him be and help put the fire out," grumbled Billinge.

" Is that the way of it ? " cries the bailiff and he and his men rushed to the staircase to hunt for their prey.

As soon as they were gone Mr. Playseed ordered Billinge out of the house telling him to ride after his Master with all haste he could, and whilst he was shouting his command at him he kept crying "Fire !" and heaped rugs and flung carpets on the flames which had now gained a hold upon the room.

Billinge knew full well that when the bailiffs had finished their search they would certainly arrest him so he made his way to the stables and rode off as fast as his horse could carry him.

The fire was now more than a match for one man or many men and had a good hold of the lower rooms of the building. The Vicar concluded that the best hope was to rouse the village and form a fighting line of pails between the house and the pond and he raced down the hill calling for help.

The bailiffs who had ransacked every room upstairs in search of their prisoner now found the staircase in flames and their retreat cut off, and had to drop from the first floor windows on to the beds below. For miles round the great blaze of Steeple Berrington Hall lighted the sky. Farmers and neighbours ran to the place but no efforts could save the building and by early morning only the charred walls, the smoking rafters and the shameless debris of wasteful destruction remained to be seen. So ended the short reign of Nicholas Berrington in the house of his fathers.

But as the owner of the Hall rode across the wolds and looked back for a moment at the flames and smoke destroying his property there was little sorrow in his heart. For what had his inheritance brought him ? Now that he could no longer reign there himself it was something to know that neither could his enemies dwell there in triumph. The smoke and the flame were typical of the pit from which he was escaping. Already his buoyant young spirit was full of glorious dreams of a New World and he was looking forward to more splendid palaces built by his own strong hand for Hetty and their children and grandchildren to inhabit. For not even the greatest disasters could for long depress Nic's gay, sunny spirit and at the darkest hour of night God had given him the blessed gift of looking forward to the rosy-fingered dawn giving colour to new horizons.

He pushed across the South Wolds and made towards Lambourn where he put up for a few hours and breakfasted and rested his horse. As he rode forward towards Farnborough he began to hold inquest in a more business-like spirit on his future prospects. He must get in touch

with Mr. Ambrose. He must show him the papers Turquet
had given him and advise with him about a visit to Geneva.
He must learn from him about the possibilities of reaching
this new land in which he and Captain Oglethorpe were
interested and then he must throw himself at the feet of
Hetty and ask for forgiveness.

It was in this frame of mind that he rode across Kingston
Bridge into Surrey, thinking it safer to ride through the
pleasant villages of Richmond, Wimbledon, Tooting and
Clapham and so through Camberwell and Peckham into
Southwark, than to enter London and risk visiting Mr.
Ambrose at La Belle Sauvage before he had some infor-
mation of the movements of his enemies.

Arrived at Red Cross Street, Southwark, Mr. Berrington
put up at the " Duke's Head " and found that Billinge,
who had taken the straight road from Oxford, had been
enquiring for him and would probably be looking in about
dinner-time. Mr. Berrington took possession of the inn
parlour and ordered a roast fowl to be made ready for his
dinner, and whilst this was doing he took the Count's
papers from his saddle bag and made a careful study of
them. There seemed no doubt that if he could reach
Geneva, and satisfy M. Lefroi of his identity, he would be
the master of several hundred pounds and could start a
new life in Georgia on an equality with other settlers who
were making the venture. As Hetty was desirous to follow
her father into exile all this seemed most satisfactory and he
already saw himself installed as a magistrate and burgher
of Georgia, when his dreams were interrupted by the
arrival of Billinge.

Toby was overjoyed to see his master in safety but he had
no very cheerful news for him. He had seen Mr. Luke
Crowley in Paternoster Row, but he had wisely kept out of
his way. Indeed he had moved warily enough and had only
dared to show his face to one or two trusty friends among
the runners. From these he learned that there were many
writs out against Mr. Berrington and that if he put his nose
into London he would very surely follow it to the Fleet.

" That is as may be," cried Nic merrily, " but to-
morrow I must visit Mr. Ambrose and after dinner you

shall carry a letter to make an appointment where I am to meet him."

As Toby could by no means dissuade him from this rash adventure, he went off with Mr. Berrington's letter to La Belle Sauvage where he learned that Mr. and Mrs. Ambrose and a young lady with them had left the inn and gone to some fashionable lodgings in Bow Street. A more unfortunate neighbourhood could not have been chosen, but Billinge made his way there and delivered the letter with his own hands. He had been commanded by his master to say nothing of the happenings in Oxfordshire and merely to repeat the message of the letter that Mr. Berrington desired to wait upon Mr. Ambrose at any hour he should name.

As Mr. Ambrose could make nothing out of the impenetrable stupidity of the messenger, for Billinge was an adept at the portrayal of natural vacancy of mind, and could not even get Mr. Berrington's address which Toby seemed to think was " somewhere over the river," he sat down and wrote him a cordial invitation to dinner the next day at two. He had heard enough gossip about Mr. Berrington's affairs to know that it might be unwise for him to show himself in Bow Street. He therefore added a postscript that if Mr. Berrington preferred that he should visit him at his present lodgings and would send word of his address he would be very pleased to call upon him.

Nic was delighted at this invitation and sent Billinge again across the river with a note of grateful acceptance and then he himself set off to visit a certain Jew clothes dealer of his acquaintance who had a warehouse at the back of St. Mary's Church. Mr. Levy was the honest trader who in Nic's early professional rambles about town had supplied him with many excellent costumes from his store, so that at one time he would be a young student of the Temple, at another an ensign of a marching regiment, or a naval lieutenant home from a foreign voyage. Mr. Levy shipped a large quantity of gentlemen's second-hand clothing to Holland and Germany and in Wild's day had been a receiver and worked with Captain Roger Johnson and other Free Traders.

He was overjoyed to see his young friend, Mr. Berrington again and very ready to supply his needs. After careful
consultation and much inspection and choice, Nic got all
that he wanted and returned to the "Duke's Head"
followed by a boy with a large bundle and a long cane.

That night Mr. Berrington was in great spirits. He and
Billinge sat over a bowl of punch, the latter begging him
not to risk his liberty by appearing in Bow Street, the
former trying to fire his friend's sluggish imagination with
pictures of the glories of the new world of which in real
fact he knew very little himself. The thought that he was to
see Hetty coloured the future for him with a rosy hue. A
second bowl of punch was called for and they sat late into
the night, Billinge dozing over his pipe and Nic pouring
forth to him rhapsodies of happiness to come.

The next morning Mr. Berrington rose late. He ordered
Billinge to be ready to attend him to the river steps. There
he was to leave him and make his way to the "Magpie and
Stump" to enquire for Captain Roger Johnson and to
remain there until he joined him.

Mr. Berrington, having broken his fast with a tankard of
small beer and some bread and cheese, opened his bundle
and proceeded to adorn himself for his visit to Bow Street. He
first made use of a preparation to heighten the pallor of his
face and put some dark shadows under the hollows beneath his eyes. Then he put on a handsome suit of black
and some plain knee bands, silk stockings and square-toed
shoes with plain buckles. He now adjusted a huge three-
tailed periwig and grinned happily at his appearance in the
cracked mirror over the mantelpiece. To this disguise he
added a pair of horn spectacles and pulled down the
corners of his mouth to give his merry face a sour aspect.
Pleased with this, he arranged his black hat at a sober angle
and placing his left hand in a small muff, a recent fashion
among the men of medicine, took up a gold-headed cane
with a pomander on top, shaped like a parish beadle
staff, and called for Billinge to applaud his creation.

As the full splendour of him dawned on Toby he
chuckled admiration. "You should have been a play
actor, Sir. Mr. Quin himself wouldn't recognise you."

Mr. Berrington now sauntered boldly into the street followed by his humble servitor. He crossed the fields towards Cuper's Gardens where he dismissed his servant and took oars across the river to Somerset Stairs, this being, as he considered, the most direct and strategic method of reaching his destination in safety. Across the river he hailed a coach and drove to Bow Street, and but for his fatal habit of playing The Child all had been well.

When the doctor arrived at Mr. Ambrose's lodgings and was mounting the steps the servant was showing out a gentleman whose figure was familiar to Mr. Berrington. The doctor removed his hat, placed it under his arm and bowing, gravely, stood aside to let the man pass. It was Ziba Grime. He stared at the doctor without recognising him and acknowledging his courtesy stepped into the street. Poor foolish Nic, however, chuckling with infantile joy at the success of his disguise, screwed up his face and put out his tongue at the retreating figure. Unfortunately at this moment Ziba had turned round and witnessed this unprofessional conduct of the learned man. Mr. Berrington turned and hurried into the house. Ziba walked towards Temple Bar wondering where he had seen the doctor before and puzzling over his strange behaviour.

When Dr. Bowlus was announced in the drawing-room, Mr. Ambrose, who was alone and writing at his desk, rose and looked at him in surprise.

" To what cause, Sir, am I indebted for this honour ? "

" My unhappy patient, Mr. Berrington," began the doctor in a grave voice.

Mr. Ambrose came towards him with a look of anxious enquiry. At this moment the servant closed the door behind him and the doctor, bursting into a merry laugh, seized his host by both hands crying, " Toby was right ; I should have been a play actor. But really, Mr. Ambrose, I dare not let a soul in London know I am about, else these bailiffs will have me by the heels and then farewell to happiness and a new world."

Mr. Ambrose could not help laughing at the perfection of the deceit and the two sat down to discuss the position of affairs. Soon afterwards Captain Oglethorpe joined them and was at once let into the secret of Mr. Berrington's disguise and the three had a long conversation on the subject of Georgia.

The Captain, it appeared, was the moving spirit on the board of trustees and himself intended to take the first ship of settlers to the new colony in about two months' time. The members of the board, Lord Derby, Mr. Page and Captain Coram, in particular, were eager that young married people should be chosen to accompany him as they were more likely than single men to make the new land their permanent home.

Mr. Berrington listened with deep interest to all these matters and showed Mr. Ambrose Turquet's papers, saying that if he could get to Geneva and bring back his money he should like to place it with Captain Oglethorpe to purchase land in his new colony. The idea of taking with him a young fellow so full of spirit and adventure appealed greatly to the Captain who promised him his support. Mr. Ambrose was already doing his best to get Verrall pardoned on condition he sailed with the Georgia expedition and all this seemed so eminently fair and reasonable to the three men that they had concluded it was as good as settled when Mr. Berrington with natural hesitation and shame asked if Mr. Ambrose had done anything to pave the way for his reconciliation to Hetty.

The mention of the girl's name was a caveat to their conclusions. Captain Oglethorpe pished and poohed that so sensible a scheme should wait on the whims of a young woman who was offered such a prize as a husband and an estate in his new Garden of Eden. Mr. Ambrose looked grave and said his wife's ward, for so they now regarded her, was greatly troubled by the addresses of Mr. Grime, her father's late manager. She was eager to go with her father abroad, but had refused to discuss even with Mrs. Ambrose the possibility of forgiving her lover whose cruel desertion of her had convinced her of his faithlessness.

Nic accepted her outlook as very natural and expressed his sorrow and penitence for all his misdeeds, but trusted that Mr. Ambrose would use his influence with her to grant him the favour of an interview and allow him to plead his cause in person. But even as to this Mr. Ambrose expressed grave doubts, as the young lady, on being informed that Mr. Berrington had expressed his intention of joining them at dinner, had asked Mrs. Ambrose's leave to keep her room.

" She cannot object to meeting Dr. Bowlus," said Captain Oglethorpe, " who may be able to gain her sympathy for our misguided young friend by describing the painful ravages to a sound constitution brought about by a broken heart."

At this rough allusion to sacred subjects the gallant Captain laughed loudly, but the other two looked grave.

" I should dearly love to see her again, even in this absurd disguise," said Berrington simply.

" I see no harm in that, Mr. Berrington. I will go and speak to my wife about it," and Mr. Ambrose left the room.

Mr. Ambrose explained to his wife that Mr. Berrington was unable to join them but that his doctor had kindly called to acquaint him of his indisposition and he had asked him to stay to dinner.

" Then, my dear," said Mrs. Ambrose kindly to Hetty who was sitting near her, " your fears of meeting poor Mr. Berrington were unnecessary. How often have I chided you about the evil of useless dejection ? "

" Is he seriously ill ? " asked Hetty eagerly.

" The doctor makes light of it," said Mr. Ambrose.

The ladies rose and followed him to the drawing-room.

Dr. Bowlus stood with his back to the window as they entered and made an elegant bow as he was introduced. Hetty was more beautiful than ever, but her brown eyes were graver than he had seen them and her face paler and there was no smile in her greeting. She made him a formal curtsey but scarce looked at him. He could have thrown himself at her feet but Mrs. Ambrose was asking after his patient and he found himself replying :

" The young man has had a serious breakdown, Madam; You know something of his troubles. Lightly as I esteem him, foolish as he has been in many ways, I cannot desert the fellow. I have known him from his youth."

W

" Like my husband, Dr. Bowlus, you too think well of him."

" I have always thought well of him," replied the doctor earnestly.

" There must be something in a youth that inspires friendship in older minds," mused Mrs. Ambrose, " some day I shall hope to judge for myself."

" I trust, Madam, that my young friend will gain your verdict too."

" He will have a friendly jury, for when I was a girl I knew the young man's mother."

" My — His — Mr. Berrington's mother ! " stammered the doctor, stepping forward excitedly.

Hetty looked up at him for the first time and watched him eagerly.

The servant announced dinner.

The doctor gallantly gave his hand to Mrs. Ambrose. They passed in to the dining-room.

CHAPTER XXVIII

WHEN Dr. Bowlus took his seat at the dinner-table next to Mrs. Ambrose he had quite recovered his professional tone and manner. Hetty kept her eyes on the table but listened eagerly to his talk. Mr. Ambrose and the Captain were discoursing of a motion that the latter had recently carried in the House of Commons to enquire into the misconduct of the Warden of the Fleet Prison. Dr. Bowlus expressed his strong disapprobation of imprisonment for debt. Captain Oglethorpe quoted Solon and other learned authors in favour of its abolition and Mrs. Ambrose remembered an apt story from the Scriptures about Elisha and the widow of Samaria.

" A miracle of that kind might free your young friend Mr. Berrington from the shackles of debt, eh doctor ? " said Mr. Ambrose laughing.

The doctor in his elderly dull voice replied with great solemnity : " As I understand Mr. Berrington, he has quite made up his mind to lead a new life as soon as I can allow him out of my hands. He is all for a new life in a new country."

" Hear ! Hear ! " cried Captain Oglethorpe.

" And I have great hopes he will keep his word, great hopes. He is full of good intentions, I can assure you."

" We know where those lead to, doctor," said Mrs. Ambrose slily.

" Georgia, my dear, in his case ; Georgia, I believe, Doctor ? " said Mr. Ambrose.

The doctor nodded gravely and then they all laughed hilariously.

Hetty peeped curiously at the doctor from under her lashes. When Mrs. Ambrose had mentioned Mr. Berrington's mother the note of his real voice had touched the strings of her heart. But so cunning was his disguise and so finished his play acting, that as dinner went on she had nearly convinced herself that she had but dreamed dreams. This made her angry with herself and the doctor, and as he sprang up and opened the door when the ladies rose from the table she passed him without so much as a look and her chin was high in the air.

Doctor Bowlus sat down again with a deep sigh.

" You must let me see the dear girl before I go, Mr. Ambrose. I must know my fate. What is the use of troubling about Geneva and escaping from my creditors if she will not forgive me ? You see that, Captain."

" I see nothing of the kind, Sir," replied Captain Oglethorpe, who by no means wished to lose so excellent a recruit for his scheme. " Miss Verrall is a charming girl, I allow, but——"

" We will drink her health," interrupted Mr. Ambrose.

" Willingly ! " said the others and bumpers were emptied in Hetty's honour.

" But I maintain," continued Captain Oglethorpe doggedly, " that if her heart is hardened against you, there are others."

The doctor denied this proposition and whilst he and the Captain were debating it their host slipped away.

When he returned in about twenty minutes he found the two poring over a map of Georgia, and the Captain was indicating to his eager comrade the position of the country owned by the Spaniards and the hinterlands over which the various tribes of Indians still held sway.

Mr. Ambrose interrupted their discourse.

" If you care to leave us for a cup of tea, doctor, Miss Hetty is waiting for you in the drawing-room."

" Alone ? " cried Nic eagerly.

Mr. Ambrose nodded.

" And have you told her ? "

" I meddle with no lover's secrets," said Mr. Ambrose pleasantly. " Go and make your own peace."

The doctor was outside the door in a second.

" I would not miss taking that young fellow with me for a ship-load of convicts," said Captain Oglethorpe as he poured himself out a bumper of claret.

" With a wife like Miss Verrall, and a Governor like
you, James, and in a new country away from temptation
he may do well," said Mr. Ambrose rather sententiously.

" He shall do well," replied Oglethorpe. " He is a lad
after my own heart. I love that young fellow."

" And for the matter of that, so do I," said Mr. Ambrose
heartily. " They are a fine young couple. I give you their
health and prosperity."

The gentlemen raised their glasses and drank. Meanwhile, the doctor was standing at the door of the drawing-
room with as uncertain a courage as the poor cat i' the
adage. But it was never Nic's way to falter at the fences of
life and in a second he had recovered his nerve, thrown
open the door and stalked professionally into the room.

A charming sight met his eyes. His beloved was alone,
sitting at the tea-table in her modest quaker-like dress, for
she had an instinctive distaste for the rufflings and pinkings
and patchings of modern London. Miss Hetty gave him a
smiling welcome and seemed to be laughing at him with her
merry eyes. And had it been any other woman Nic would
have accepted her sweet invitation to an armistice with
equal candour. But he was always at his worst with Hetty,
since he felt that nothing but his best was worthy of her,
and the wiles with which he came and conquered in the
world of women, he could not practise in the presence of
his beloved. He misread the twinkle in her eyes. That she
had discovered his disguise had not entered his mind. That
he had thought he could disguise himself from Hetty
seemed to her presumptuous.

" Madam," said our doctor, with a profound bow,
" good Mr. Ambrose tells me that you are interested in my
young patient."

The smile faded from her face that he should waste
precious moments in continuing such foolery.

" Do you take sugar, doctor ? Two lumps ? "

She handed him his cup and folded her hands on her lap.

" Mr. Ambrose assured me you were interested in the
young man," continued the doctor pompously.

" ' *Was* interested ' he must have meant," said Hetty
drily.

" Is it all over then ? " asked the doctor dismally.

" I do not care to discuss the matter with strangers, Sir. Besides, it is nothing to either of us."

" Is the poor fellow to give up all hope ? " said the absurd doctor, dropping into his natural voice.

His chagrin and the hopeless look he gave his beloved were worth all the art of the theatre for they set Hetty a-laughing and she cried out : " Why really doctor—sure you can say best. Do all your patients give up hope when you are called in ? "

He was on his knees at her side.

" Miss Verrall, Hetty. This disguise. It is not mere folly. It was my only chance to catch a glimpse of you again."

" Did you think you could deceive me ? I knew you from the first."

There was a touch of scorn in the girl's tone, but it was the scorn of love undervalued. Berrington was himself again and quick on the cue.

" You knew me," he whispered, taking her hand. " You knew me, Hetty. So now I know you still love me."

" Enough to wish you good-bye. I am going for a long voyage. I have made up my mind. I will follow my father into exile."

" But not alone, Hetty."

" The New World is not a world for fine gentlemen."

" You judge me harshly."

" More harshly than you judge yourself I daresay ? "

" That were impossible, Hetty," he called out in tones of despair. " I know there is no reason why you should have faith. But I have not come to ask for reason or justice or even pity. You must give me love, Hetty, or send me back to my old ways."

The girl instinctively put her hand on his arm as if to keep him near her, but she did not speak.

" I have nothing to give you. I am ruined. I do not want you to fear my danger, but at any moment I may be thrown into prison for my debts."

The girl had placed her other hand upon his arm. Now that he was ruined and in danger he was too precious to lose.

"If I can escape to France," he continued rapidly, "I can reach sufficient money to sail with Captain Oglethorpe to his new world. Hetty, it must be settled to-day. Can you forget the past and let me take you with me?"

She drew back her hands slowly.

"Nic! Nic dearest, you are making this sacrifice for my sake that I may go with my father."

Nic laughed triumphantly at her folly.

"Ask Mr. Ambrose, Hetty! Ask the Captain! What have I to sacrifice? Poor Turquet was right there. That is always the woman's part, he used to say. It is you who have to make the sacrifice, you who have to pick out of the gutter a man who has done all the things he should not and help him to make good. Only love can make such sacrifice. You must tell me the truth, Hetty.—Is there such love?"

Hetty's answer knew no words. And beautiful as were the thoughts in their minds and noble and eternal as were the aspirations of their souls, all that could be seen in the actual mirror of life was a sweet girl throwing her arms round the neck of an elderly physician and weeping tears of joy on his shoulder, whilst he clasped her in his arms as if he feared some evil spirit should tear her from his grasp.

When this torrent of emotion had somewhat subsided the two sat near to each other upon the sofa gradually recovering from this tremendous and unimaginable event, and there they were soon afterwards discovered by Mrs. Ambrose, who had never had the least doubt in the world that this would come to pass.

The good lady laughed her congratulations and clapped her hands with joy when she entered the room and her eyes were greeted by the pleasant sight of her young guest resting her head on the shoulder of the elderly doctor whose periwig was much out of the perpendicular.

The young people jumped up from the sofa. Mrs. Ambrose kissed the blushing Hetty and called in her husband and Captain Oglethorpe to join her in congratulating the happy couple. Mr. Ambrose bustled about to get a bottle of wine and glasses to drink the health of Mr. Berrington and his betrothed, and when this ritual was happily performed he turned to his wife and bade her carry off the young lady and discourse with her on wedding garments and leave the men to discuss ways and means.

Captain Oglethorpe's plan of campaign was that the young couple should go across to France, travel to Geneva and by no means return to London but make for Falmouth where his vessel would stay a while and join them there. Mr. Ambrose admitted to Berrington that in his youth he had had experience of catchpoles and bailiffs and assured him that once his presence in London was known he would be in a spunging house in forty-eight hours.

It was now time for the lovers to say farewell and while this was doing the elders continued to discuss kindly plans for their welfare. At length Mr. Ambrose thought it time to send for a coach, and Mrs. Ambrose had to intervene in the young people's farewell procedure, the methods of which threatened to be continuous and recurrent.

The ladies stood at the window and the two gentlemen went down to see the doctor into his coach. They shook him heartily by the hand and the ladies waved their kerchiefs. As the coach drove away the old gentleman gallantly put his head out of the window and kissed his hand to the ladies on the front floor.

On the steps of a tavern, opposite Mr. Ambrose's lodgings, a man stood watching these things with eager curiosity. His long vigil was rewarded. The suspicious-looking doctor was the man he had suspected. Mr. Ziba Grime was highly pleased with his insight and patience. He slipped into the road and followed the coach as it rumbled along the Strand towards Temple Bar.

At the " Magpie and Stump " the news was that Captain Johnson was across the Channel. This, however, was no great matter for the moment as Nic's hours were spent in plans for evading the bailiffs and meeting Hetty as often as it could be managed. Redcross Street was safe from their raids and when Berrington went abroad his disguises were so cleverly devised that hitherto he had escaped detection. Hetty had walked in the Park with a young country squire in boots and a jockey cap, also with a pleasant naval officer with but one arm, and she had sat in a box at the play with her old friend the doctor, though what the play was about neither she nor he could ever remember. Mr. Berrington kept away from Bow Street but Ziba constantly made excuses to visit Mr. Ambrose or Miss Verrall who both received him very civilly.

The plans for the wedding went secretly and speedily forward. A licence was obtained from the Archbishop of Canterbury. The Vicar of St. Paul's, Covent Garden, was notified of the day and the hour. A light chaise was ordered to carry the happy pair as far as " The Crown " at East Grinstead and on the following day they were to continue their journey to Cherry Croft.

We may picture to ourselves the delight of Granny Johnson when she received her boy's letter and heard that he was coming home to her again, bringing his bride with him, though the good news was tempered with the sad thought of a speedy parting with her dear one, a parting that the old woman's good sense told her must surely be a last parting on earth. However, she set her heart to think of the joy of possessing the young people as her own to love for these last few days, and she set her hands to baking and cooking and the adornment of her best bedroom with curtains and sweet linen, and she thanked God and was happy in her own sane fashion.

And if weddings and battles and statecraft proceeded according to their secret plans all this might have happened as arranged, but in practice one finds that the secrets of these great events are too often shared by women and the best-laid plans are addled in the hatching. And when it is a wedding that has to be kept secret, disaster is almost bound to happen, since no woman worthy of her name and dignity would refrain from telling her sister woman, always in the strictest confidence, the hour and date of a secret marriage. And such pleasant confidences being continually repeated the secret overflows the circle of the faithful and spreads itself abroad.

It was unfortunate perhaps that Betty, Mrs. Ambrose's maid, had to be trusted, but her aid was absolutely necessary to the making of many garments. Betty had never before been known to sew with such enthusiasm and energy. She even refused to take her evening out to work for so high a cause. This I fear prompted her to share her secret with the landlord's son with whom she walked out on these occasions. It was afterwards thought that this man was in the pay of Ziba and that it was he who learned the secret and sold it Judas-like to Crowley and the tipstaffs.

When the wedding party entered the door of Inigo Jones' handsome old barn of a church, there were very few folk about, but as soon as it was known that a wedding was forward a crowd of women and children and a few market loafers gathered at the gates to see the bride and bridegroom come out. Billinge stayed with the chaise but after waiting some ten minutes or so he put his head into the church and finding the parson was still at the splicing, took the driver across to the " Shakespeare " for a pint of ale, leaving a boy in charge of the horses.

It was at this moment that a couple of old hackney coaches drove up out of one of which jumped that well-known bailiff, Mr. Robert Ferret, followed by several rough-looking catchpoles who scattered themselves among the crowd round the church gates.

The bells of St. Paul's rang out a merry peal. Nic Berrington, his troubles over, his happy bride on his arm, followed by his friends, was making his way through the little crowd at the gate when Bob Ferret, with a slip of paper in his hand, stepped up from behind and touched him lightly on the shoulder. Mr. Berrington thinking there was another verger to fee, turned round, putting his hand in his pocket as he did so. He was instantly surrounded and seized by Mr. Ferret's ruffians and picked up and carried bodily into one of the coaches. Poor Hetty screamed and clung to Mr. Ambrose. Even if Mr. Ambrose and Captain Oglethorpe had dared to resist the powers of the law, Ferret had laid his plans too cleverly and had left no opportunity for resistance or rescue. His coaches were already half across the market place and Mr. Berrington's disconsolate friends were left to carry the unhappy bride back to Mr. Ambrose's lodgings.

Now the present Warden of the Fleet was a scoundrel called Thomas Bambridge, and Captain Oglethorpe was moving Parliament to strip him of his place and power to commit frauds and cruelties on his prisoners. When Bambridge heard that Berrington was a friend and protégé of his enemy, Captain Oglethorpe, he himself took part in planning his capture and he looked forward to taking his revenge on the Captain out of the purse and person of his prisoner.

By his command Berrington was carried to the spunging house of his servant, Richard Corbett, at Ludgate Hill. By the time they reached their destination Berrington who was at first stunned by his misfortune had to some extent recovered his self-possession. He had visited Corbett some years ago with Wild, when Turquet had been there. He knew something of the rights and wrongs of jailors and their prisoners, and he at once determined that he would not stay with Corbett to be fleeced and ruined, but that he would insist on his right to be carried to the Fleet.

Corbett received his prisoner in a crowded room and in a bullying tone demanded four shillings coach hire. Berrington threw him a couple of shillings, garnished with curses and told him to be careful how he tried his dirty tricks on a gentleman.

" But to satisfy you, Sir," continued Nic condescendingly, " that I do not desire to stint you in any lawful way, show me some private room I can hire from you whilst I stay here."

Corbett, who was a heavy lump of greed and stupidity and readily obedient to anyone who assumed the tone of a master, did as he was ordered.

The private room was a cold naked hovel with iron bars to the windows, but it had a table and chair. Berrington ordered some dinner and a bottle of wine and pen, ink and paper. Then he wrote a fervent letter to his beloved, bidding her be of good cheer, and desired Mr. Ambrose to visit him as soon as might be. He then sent for a messenger to despatch his letters and told Mr. Corbett he would be pleased to crack a bottle with him after dinner.

Mr. Corbett accepted the invitation with alacrity and when he came up to his rooms after dinner, handed him a bill of charges and fees amounting to over £45.

Mr. Berrington looked at it contemptuously and threw it on the table.

" Much as I enjoy your hospitable welcome, Mr. Corbett," he said, " I have made up my mind that I prefer the situation of the Fleet to this very extravagant palace of yours."

"Whether Mr. Bambridge will see it that way, Sir," said Corbett, sipping his wine, " I can't say."

" I must have a talk with my landlord then," said Nic, passing the bottle to his guest.

" He will be here this afternoon."

" Then I can tell Bambridge what I intend," replied Nic firmly.

Corbett regarded him with awe. He was not used to hear the name of Bambridge treated so lightly.

Soon after dinner Mr. Ambrose arrived. He seemed terribly cast down and dejected. It was the prisoner who cheered his guest. For Mr. Berrington had not as yet lost heart and he put some of his own buoyant courage into his friend's heart to carry back to his dear wife.

" Here," he said, " I do not intend to stay. These places are rightly called spunging houses. In a month they would squeeze me of the last penny I have. This is what I propose. My dear wife——" his voice faltered on the word but he continued quickly, " You will help me here, dear friend ? "

Mr. Ambrose could not speak but nodded assent.

"My dear wife must go down to Cherry Croft and wait me there."

" She already asks to come and visit you, poor thing."

" It must not be," replied Berrington firmly. " I go to the Fleet. Tell her I am full of hope and have plans in my mind for joining her. You must find me a good lawyer. At present I do not see any wisdom in giving security and seeking the freedom of the Rules. But tell Hetty—I almost feel I can promise her, that I will be at Cherry Croft within a month. But if I do not keep my word then she shall return and I must live within the rules. Unless my star has set for ever, I shall be in Sussex, never fear, and then we sail for the New World."

This joyful tirade of nonsense seemed to infect Mr.

Ambrose with some of its honest enthusiasm which was
what Nic desired, since he would carry the atmosphere of it
back to his beloved.

Mr. Ambrose promised Nic that he would himself drive
his wife and Mrs. Berrington down to Lewes and Nic
handed his friend letters for Captain Johnson and Billinge
who were to visit him in the Fleet.

That afternoon the great Thomas Bambridge, Warden of
the Fleet, was making his weekly tour of his spunging
houses to squeeze blackmail out of his victims and see that
his servants did not cheat him of his dues. He arrived at
Corbett's house about four o'clock. Corbett fetched Mr.
Berrington downstairs and carried him to the parlour
where Mr. Bambridge was interviewing a miserable
architect named Castell who seemed in an agony of
terror.

The Warden, an undersized, mean little man, with a
yellow wizened face and a shock head of hair, stood with
his arms folded and his back to the fire. The poor gentleman, who seemed half frantic, was stretching out his trembling hands to his judge as if crying for mercy.

"For the love of God, Master Bambridge," cried the
poor wretch, "let me go to the Fleet if I cannot be enlarged
or send for my securities."

"What is wrong with the man?" asked Bambridge
impatiently.

"It's the smallpox, Sir. He's devilish afraid of catching
them," said Corbett deferentially.

"Have we smallpox in the house?" asked Bambridge
carelessly.

"I told you last week, Sir. The man White is down with
them."

Mr. Castell had thrown his head on the table and was
moaning, "I've never had them! I know I shall die of
them!"

The tipstaff who had brought him in said in some
compassion; "He's been like that ever since he heard of
them, sir."

"Don't leave me here," cried the poor wretch who was
eally distraught with terror.

" Take him away," said Mr. Bambridge peremptorily.
Mr. Castell seemed mad with terror.

Corbett and the tipstaff carried him away shrieking in his
delirium, " It will kill me. It is murder ! murder ! "

The Warden took a pinch of snuff and muttered : " If the
smallpox carry him off we shall not lose much. We have had
all he has and most of what his friends are good for."

He looked up and saw Berrington standing at the door.
" And what may you want, young gentleman ? " he asked
with a patronising sneer.

" I too have made up my mind that this is not a healthy
spot," said Nic, taking a pace forward. " I too prefer the
Fleet. I have heard you make it as pleasant as Bath or the
Wells, Mr. Bambridge."

The Warden peered at him through his weasel eyes in
astonishment. He was not accustomed to raillery.

" Who the hell are you ? " he inquired scowling at
him.

" Nicholas Berrington of Steeple Berrington and,
expletives omitted, your very humble servant."

Mr. Bambridge whistled and looked at his guest.

" So you want to go across to the Fleet," he said
sneeringly. " When the fees are paid we will see about it
next week."

" The fees not being legal will not be paid. My lawyer
will settle that business with you."

As Berrington spoke he took the bill that Corbett had
given him and tore it slowly into small pieces and threw
them at the Warden's feet.

" Who taught you what fees were legal ? " he shouted
angrily.

" My friend, Captain Oglethorpe, Member for Haslemere," replied Berrington pleasantly. " He takes a mighty
interest in these things."

" A damned conceited meddling——"

" I said ' my friend,' Mr. Bambridge," interrupted Nic.
" I hear no ill words of my friends. And why, Sir, should
you and I quarrel over trifles ? You and I have had mutual
friends, and if I prefer the Fleet to this expensive pest-house
of yours, why should you disoblige me ? "

" We will see about it later on," grumbled Bambridge who was puzzled at the youth's impudence.

" Pardon me, Mr. Bambridge, we will settle it now, unless you prefer I should stand on my rights."

" Rights ! " shouted the Warden with a hoarse laugh.

" My lawyers can apply to the judges."

" I am the judge's servant, Mr. Berrington ; you forget that. You need not think the judges care to hear complaints of their servant."

This very sensible remark made Berrington more cautious. The judges he had played so triumphantly as aces might be merely knaves. The Warden knew the pack better than he did.

" I want no scandal, Mr. Bambridge," replied Berrington pleasantly. " But even judges I suppose are human, and will not take it amiss if I tell them some memories of the old days and your past services to our mutual friend Jonathan Wild. A great man, Sir, and it is a feather in your cap to have served under him."

Bambridge flushed at the name and looked angrily at his smiling prisoner.

" Wild's dead, thank God ! " he muttered.

" He is gone, poor man, and as you were thinking very truly, dead men tell no tales. But there are many who know your past, Mr. Bambridge. Captain Johnson, —Captain Roger. Curse my liver and bones ! you remember the old Captain ? I saw him only a few weeks back at the ' Magpie and Stump.' You remember the Magpie' ? "

The Warden was shrewd enough to see that it would be better for all parties that this youth of strange memories should be under his immediate supervision in the Fleet. He would find out from Roger Johnson all about him.

" You seem," he replied, looking curiously at the young man, " to have kept some very strange company, Mr. Berrington."

" And still do, Mr. Bambridge," said Nic with a sweet smile, " so that if I wish to come and live with you in the Fleet where we can gossip of old friends and old days, I take it you will not withhold your invitation."

The Warden turned and spat wrathfully into the fire.

"What the hell do I care where you go?" he cried angrily. "To the Fleet, if you will."

"Your very humble servant," replied Mr. Berrington, making his most graceful and ceremonious leg, to the intense disgust of the Warden.

Even with the scum of the earth he had the power to prevail pleasantly.

CHAPTER XXIX

THE DIPLOMACY OF CAPTAIN JOHNSON

WE who live in the modern glass houses of bureaucracy would do well to refrain from stoning our forefathers of the eighteenth century. The cruelties to prisoners of that date shock our sense of justice, but in our own mild way we commit social sins against the oppressed which will make our great-grandchildren wag their wise heads and give tongue.

Captain Oglethorpe's crusade against the iniquities of Bambridge and his crew of miscreants makes very modern reading. When the gallant member for Haslemere cited the foul deeds done in the name of the law all generous souls were horrified that such things should be. But the wise big-wigs, the elder statesmen of the day, shook their heads at this outburst of sentiment, and deprecated any hasty interference with the perfection of our legal system.

Moreover, said business men, let us remember here are questions of property at stake. Public offices in those days were bought and sold openly and more or less honestly. Old John Huggins had bought the wardenship of the Fleet for £5,000 and now, old in years and fat in fortune, had sold his patent to his deputy and fellow-rascal, Thomas Bambridge. These good citizens had to write off their capital and make a provision for their future, and the raw material of their business was debtors.

Berrington had taken up his abode on the Master's side of the prison and had at once become a popular figure at the skittle-alley and the racket-court. He had been visited by Captain Johnson who gave him to understand that he was deeply engaged in business schemes with Bambridge, and that on his return from Bordeaux, in a few weeks' time, he thought they might arrange an escape, as he knew all the secrets of old John Huggins and the present Warden and they dared not quarrel with him.

323

X

This put Mr. Berrington in good heart and he wrote his beloved a long letter full of the certainty he felt that his release was not far distant.

The particular conspiracy which Captain Johnson and Bambridge were working at the moment was a variant of what we call a long-firm fraud. A certain French prisoner, Monsieur Dumay, was supposed to be ill in bed in his room in the Fleet. He had often been ill in this way. In fact, during these supposed illnesses Dumay made trips to Bordeaux. There he bought wine and drew bills on Mr. Bishop, one of Huggins' late tipstaffs. These bills on presentation were properly met. Credit with the sellers in France was now firmly established and the merchants became careless and ready to deliver wine before the bills were presented.

Dumay was away on the final trip. He was to purchase for paper as much wine as *The Lively Kate* would hold and then return to the Fleet. Bishop would refuse to accept the bills and the rascals would sell the wine they had stolen in this way and divide the price, leaving the foreign sellers to whistle for their money with Dumay as their debtor.

Now that Captain Oglethorpe was stirring up the muddy waters of the Fleet, Bambridge was particularly eager to get Dumay back into his own custody again, for he had really as much trouble on his hands as any government official could well handle, and right on top of all his anxieties the poor fool Castell goes and dies of smallpox at Corbett's spunging-house. As ill-luck would have it the family of the unfortunate architect was well known to Captain Oglethorpe, who at once set to work to investigate the matter and brought the facts to the attention of his Committee. Great indignation was felt by all of them at the way the poor wretch had been treated. The affair was made public and his death was openly spoken of as a murder. The Committee fixed a day to visit the Fleet and hold an inquiry into this and other scandals. Notice was served upon Bambridge that he would be called upon for a strict account of his dealings with the late Mr. Castell and that he must have ready for their inspection all the papers, documents and witnesses relating to his case.

When Bambridge received this notice he sent an invitation to Mr. Berrington to crack a bottle with him at the Master's apartments, which his prisoner accepted with some curiosity, as since his arrival his jailer had taken little or no notice of his existence.

After a few compliments Mr. Bambridge came to the business in hand and asked Mr. Berrington if he remembered seeing at Corbett's house a poor devil called Castell.

" Very well indeed," replied Nic. " Has he caught the smallpox as he feared ? "

" Not only that, but he has died of them."

" I am sorry for it. I am very sorry for it," repeated Berrington gravely.

" And so am I, for this precious Committee want to know why he was kept there."

" The devil they do ? " said his prisoner smiling pleasantly. " And why was he kept there, Mr. Bambridge ? Now you see how thoughtful I was in your interests to move over here."

" This is not a jesting business, Mr. Berrington. I sent for you to tell you that I do not want you mixed up in this business."

" There, Sir, we are of one mind."

" Good," continued the jailer, more pleased with his prisoner. " It is a great pity you remember anything about the affair. You had best say you know nothing of it."

Berrington shook his head : " I shall never forget the poor wretch squealing with his face in his hands. I dream of him."

" Pah ! We must all die."

" We need not all be murdered," said Nic simply.

Bambridge looked at him angrily. " At all events," he said, striking the table with his fist, " there is no need to talk about the business."

" I do not intend to do so."

" Or of giving evidence before this damned Committee."

" I shall not volunteer my evidence."

" They may have heard you were present and send for you and then——"

" I must speak the truth," said Nic emptying his glass and rising as if to go.

"Why the hell should you speak the truth?" cries Bambridge spluttering with rage. "It will be the worse for you if you do. You are here in my power. It will be the worse for you."

"You must take it from me, Mr. Bambridge, that I don't care that for your threats," cried Nic, and he snapped his fingers in the Warden's face. "I have always made it a habit in matters in which I have no personal interest to speak the truth. I shall not alter my ways at your bidding."

"You had best keep out of this, Mr. Berrington," shouted Bambridge, standing up and leaning over the table and thrusting out his yellow face at his prisoner. "Keep out of it, you young fool. By God, if you let me down before the Committee I will have my revenge of you. They cannot throw me out of my office to-morrow."

"Then you are a damned lucky fellow," cried Nic laughing at his antics. "You need not worry yourself about me. I shall stay in my room all to-morrow. You may say I am indisposed if you wish. I am glad you think that they cannot throw you out of your post to-morrow, for frankly when Captain Johnson returns I want you to do me a favour and if they send you to Newgate at once it would to some extent disturb my plans."

"Your plans! My God——"

The imperturbable badinage of Mr. Berrington left this coarse fellow inarticulate as to any form of printable expletives, and Nic, seeing he could get no sense out of his host, rose and bowed to him with great ceremony and left the room. Mr. Bambridge with a quivering hand took a clay pipe from the mantelpiece and having loaded and lighted it with difficulty proceeded to the cupboard for a bottle of brandy and poured himself out a stiff glass. Then he threw himself into his chair and kept muttering and repeating until he felt somewhat calmer: "I shall kill that youth! I shall kill him!"

The next day the members of the Parliamentary Commission met at the prison. They had many horrible tragedies to enquire into and the details of the bestial cruelty of the jailers can be read by the curious in the official reports of the Commissioners, and the futile trials of Huggins, Bambridge and the minor scoundrels who acted under their orders.

The Commissioners were a worthy collection of English citizens. Sir James Thornhill was one of the number and he got permission for his son-in-law, Mr. Hogarth, to paint a picture of one of the sessions held in the Fleet Prison. There in our National Portrait gallery to-day you may see for yourself Captain Oglethorpe presiding with dignity over the proceedings, a wretched prisoner with a heavy wooden collar round his neck kneeling at the feet of his fellow-citizens praying for redress, and the yellow livid scoundrel Bambridge cowering before his judges in fear and hatred.

It was late in the afternoon before the Commissioners started their inquiry into the death of Mr. Castell. The only witnesses called by Bambridge were Mr. and Mrs. Corbett. Needless to say, these two worthies were loud in praise of the care and attention they had lavished on the unfortunate gentleman. Captain Oglethorpe asked Mrs. Corbett, who was, like many of her sex, an expansive talker, whether Mr. Berrington had met Mr. Castell in the spunging-house. Bambridge, who was standing behind the Chairman, winked and nodded an answer in the negative, but the good lady chattered away in full enjoyment of her importance.

"Well, now you remind me, Captain, that was so. I had been just speaking by chance about smallpox and saying a gentleman in the house had them and Mr. Castell seemed in a fair fright about it and then in comes Mr. Berrington,"— she caught her master's frantic signals and stammered— "no, was it Mr. Berrington? No, gentlemen, of course not. Now I remember it was Mr. Bambridge that came in. Yes, that was it, and after that I took Mr. Castell to his room and Mr. Berrington came in afterwards."

"The woman was stopped by the Warden making signs to her, Mr. Chairman," said My Lord Percival angrily.

"Let us have the witnesses in apart from Mr. Bambridge," proposed Sir James Thornhill.

"No, no," ruled Captain Oglethorpe, "Mr. Bambridge

is, as it were, the accused person, and it is fair he should be
present and hear all that is said."

Several of the older members murmured their approval,
but the younger ones seemed to think human vermin
and brutes of this type might be destroyed with less
formality.

" But Mr. Berrington," continued their Chairman, " is,
I grieve to say, a prisoner in this building, and if the
Committee think it advisable, they can hear his evidence."

There was a general " Hear ! Hear ! " at this suggestion.
Mr. Bambridge urged the gentleman's indisposition and the
lateness of the hour and asked for an adjourment, but two
members were sent with a tipstaff to Mr. Berrington's
room and finding him in excellent health returned with him
to the tribunal.

The evidence that he gave was a true account of what
had happened in Corbett's parlour, and though it was rudely
interrupted by some foul expressions of Bambridge's,
which Captain Oglethorpe sternly rebuked, it greatly
impressed the members of the Committee, who thanked
Mr. Berrington very heartily for the frank way in which he
had given evidence. The Committee then adjourned for
three weeks.

Captain Oglethorpe had a few words in private with Mr.
Berrington before he left and was surprised to find that he
spoke very confidently of leaving the Fleet before long and
joining his wife in Sussex to carry her across to Geneva. He
would not, however, disclose any details of his plans and
the Captain came away with the idea that the young man's
head was turned by his terrible misfortunes and that his
mind was filled with some mad dream which he took for a
feasible plan of escape.

When the last of the Committeemen had driven off, Mr.
Bambridge in a foul distemper of rage and hatred went to
his room and sat there pouring brandy down his throat and
cursing Mr. Berrington, the Commissioners, good Mrs.
Corbett and, more deservedly, Thomas Bambridge
himself.

It was his beastly habit to steep himself in drink when
he meditated some cruelty or fraud against an unhappy

prisoner. Drink was not the cause of his crimes, but a good weapon that he misused to commit crime, and when he started on one of these bouts his servants knew what to expect.

There was a brute named James Barnes, the head of his bodyguard, a discredited prize-fighter, who enjoyed assisting his Master to bully the defenceless. He and Corbett had been drinking with the other turnkeys and as it was now time for Corbett to return to Ludgate Hill, they went up together to the Master's room.

Barnes reported that there was a good deal of excitement among the prisoners about the visit of the Commission and suggested that it would be wise to turn the keys on them without delay even at the loss of some profit, through clearing the drinking bars.

The Warden rose unsteadily and began shouting his orders : " Turn out the guard. I'm still Warden here. I'll show them who is Master. Where's that fellow Berrington ? Curse him, he's at the bottom of this."

Mr. Corbett begged him to leave the young fellow alone.

But Bambridge was beyond reason.

" I'll have his blood. I'll have his blood. Turn out the guard," he cried, and seizing a thick cane that he carried on his rounds he staggered after Barnes down to the guard-room.

The guard consisted of seven or eight of the lusty scum of mankind armed with rifles with long bayonets, and when the wretched prisoners saw the Warden starting on a tour of his kingdom with this ragged retinue they scuttered quickly to cover. It was already dusk and some of the guard carried lanthorns with them.

Bambridge then called on his second-in-command, William Pindar, to get some irons and carry them down to the Strong Room and led his posse to the first floor where Mr. Berrington was lodging.

The Strong Room was a shrine erected by Mr. Huggins in which he had tortured to death and despair many a poor wretch who refused to submit to his exactions. It was built over the common sewer near a laystall where the filthy matter was lodged. There was no fire, nor fireplace, no

light, but through a hole over the door, and a little hole by
the side big enough to put a quart pot in at, and the place
was so moist that drops of wet ran down the wall and the
dampness and stench were indescribable. .

Bambridge knocked with his cane at Mr. Berrington's
door and before he could reply kicked it open. His prisoner
was seated at his table writing a letter to his beloved by the
light of a guttering candle. He rose at their entrance.
Bambridge ran his lanthorn into his prisoner's face, seized
him by the collar and told him with many curses to come
along with him.

Mr. Berrington struggled to throw him off when Barnes
and another man flung themselves upon him and threw a
rope in a noose round his arms and drew it tight so that he
was powerless to defend himself. Bambridge, cursing him
with his foul tongue, hit him several times on the head and
shoulders with his cane until even Barnes was disgusted
with his drunken cruelty and catching his wrist made him
drop his weapon. The men then ran their victim along the
corridor, carried him down the staircase to the door of the
Strong Room, where Pindar was waiting with heavy irons
which the wretches now fastened on his arms and legs.

Mr. Berrington saw it was of no avail to plead for mercy
to these brutes or to the drunken Warden who stood by to
see his orders carried out, cursing and threatening his
prisoner. One of the men, less cruel than the rest, had
carried down the prisoner's bed which he flung into the
noisome den. Barnes having fastened his irons to his own
satisfaction pushed him to the door.

"You will be hanged for this if I die," said Mr.
Berrington sternly.

"Die and be damned to you," shouted Bambridge.

Barnes laughed heartily at his Master's reply and threw
his manacled prisoner into the Strong Room and slammed
the iron door. Bambridge turned the key and taking it out
of the lock put it safely in his pocket.

Poor Nic crawled as best he could in the foul darkness
of his dungeon to find his bed. For once his spirit was
broken and when he thought of Hetty and remembered the
stories the prisoners had told him of poor men done to

death in this noisome den his soul could not uphold him and he wept in despair.

Whilst these events were happening *The Lively Kate* was lying in the Pool and her wine casks were being lightered through the bridge and stored in a warehouse on Vintner's Quay. This business being finished before midday the next morning Captain Johnson and Monsieur Dumay made their way to the " Magpie and Stump " where they enjoyed a hearty meal. Whilst this was forward Billinge found them and narrated what he had heard about Nic's evidence before the Committee and expressed his fears that Bambridge would do him an injury.

" For," said he, " the Warden is the blackest-hearted scoundrel in the wide world."

" If he touches a hair of the lad's head," cries the Captain rising from the table, " damn my liver and bones if I don't shoot him like a dog. Fetch me a coach, Toby."

Monsieur Dumay was left at the Inn and Toby and the Captain drove to the Fleet.

When Mr. Barnes opened the gate to the two visitors and heard their enquiries for Mr. Berrington he muttered something about trouble in the prison and a row overnight and suggested to the Captain he had better ask permission of the Warden himself.

On hearing this, Captain Johnson, having damned the anatomy of Barnes in much detail, and threatened him with worldly and eternal punishment, strode upstairs to the Warden's lodging followed by Billinge.

Bambridge was sitting at his table gazing at an untasted mug of small ale with a toast in it. The drink and the rage of anger were out of him. He cowered and looked up in fright at Captain Johnson. His yellow blotchy face and bloodshot eyes gave him the look of a loathly beast of prey rather than a man after God's image.

" Where's Dumay, Captain ? " he hiccupped as the Captain approached him.

" What have you done with my friend, Mr. Berrington?" shouted the Captain in reply.

" He's got his deserts. Where's Dumay ? "

'If you've injured my boy, Thomas Bambridge, I've sworn I'll shoot you dead, and I'll keep my word."

The Captain pulled a pistol out of his pocket and sat down at the table opposite the Warden.

" Now friend Thomas," he continued more calmly, " let us have a quiet chat and conference, damn your eyes, and first and foremost, where is Nic Berrington ? "

" Under lock and key, curse him."

" Where, I say ? " shouted the Captain angrily.

" In the Strong Room."

Captain Johnson jumped up and caught Bambridge by the throat and shook him.

" You've put my boy in the den where you killed Solas, the Portugal and poor Captain Macpheadris. Fetch him out. Fetch him out I say."

" Steady, Captain ! " called out Toby. " You said a quiet chat you know. Reason with him. Reason with him."

"Aye, aye, Toby, I'll reason with him," said the Captain, and he shook his victim violently and threw him back into his chair. "Now, friend Thomas," he said, tapping the table with his pistol, "don't you go to provoke a peaceable man again. Where's the key of the den? Come now."

Bambridge scowled and shook his head sullenly.

"Now see here, my friend," says the Captain persuasively, "if you injure the lad, you've Tyburn before you as sure as carts is carts and hemp's hemp. But if you act reasonable it will be all for your good. Now listen to reason, Thomas Bambridge. Just remember I've got Dumay back. The wine is in warehouse, and your share is ready. A tidy sum, Thomas, my friend. You shall have Dumay back to-night. He comes in at the private door at midnight as usual, and you hand me over young Berrington in exchange."

"If I let that young devil out he'd kill me."

"If you keep him in I'll kill you. But leave the youngster to me. I'll make him write a confession that he rushed the gates. That was the story you put up when we released Boyce the smuggler. He shall write a fine letter cracking you up to Captain Oglethorpe. The Captain's a rare friend of his."

Billinge looked a bit doubtful. He did not see Nic writing such a letter. But Bambridge seemed to scent a way out of his troubles. If it could be put to the committee that Nic Berrington had bolted, his evidence would be discounted.

"If he would write a letter like that, Captain, and would clear out of the country," said Bambridge hesitatingly.

"Damn my tongue and slit it out if the lad don't write what I tell him. Haven't I been a father to him? Ain't I taking him back to his wife and carrying him across to France next week——?"

"You promise to take him abroad then?" said Bambridge eagerly.

"This day week he will be in France, and then he sails for the plantations and never sets foot in this country again. Come, friend Thomas, throw the key of that damned den on the table and I'll pocket my pistol."

Bambridge thought a moment and, putting his hand in his pocket, pulled out the key and told Billinge to go in search of Barnes. When he returned the warden gave orders that Mr. Berrington was to be taken out of the Strong Room and taken to his own room and kept there under guard, but that Billinge might attend to him.

When Toby found his poor master half unconscious and calling out vengeance on his persecutors in the horrible dungeon where he was interned, he could have flung himself at Barnes and destroyed him. But his good sense prevailed, and he made Barnes and Pindar help him to carry Nic upstairs and find him clean bedding, and then he sent for a woman nurse from the poor side to help wash him and make him comfortable. After some toast and a strong sherry posset, Mr. Berrington, who recognised that he was under the care of Toby, fell into a sound sleep whilst his servant watched at his side.

When he awoke he was feeling greatly refreshed and exceedingly vindictive against Bambridge and his servants. So that when Billinge told him Captain Johnson was closeted with the warden and making some sort of treaty with him for his release, Nic was exceedingly vexed about it. He insisted on getting up and dressing himself, and sent Toby to command a joint and potatoes from the kitchen and some bottles of wine and inform Captain Johnson that he expected him to dinner at four o'clock.

The Captain's business with Mr. Bambridge took some time, but at last the wine accounts were settled, the exchange of prisoners agreed, and nothing remained but for the Captain to obtain the letter he had promised Mr. Berrington would write. That done, Billinge was to be sent for Monsieur Dumay, and the Captain was to remain in charge of his young friend.

The Captain was delighted to see Nic again, and being a man of sense and discretion, he ate a good meal and drank his wine to a running accompaniment of Nic's account of his woes and the beastly conduct of the warden and his servants, and his plan of writing a true history of the matter and presenting it to Captain Oglethorpe.

Billinge looked up and winked at Captain Johnson as much as to say "I told you so," though, in fact, he had said nothing about it, and the Captain winked back as much as to say "Wait and see," and poor Nic went on blethering about his wrongs.

After dinner, when the punch was made and pipes and tobacco were produced, Captain Johnson claimed a right to be heard, and Berrington graciously giving permission, the Captain informed Nic of the arrangement he had made. But when he described the letter to be written, Berrington threw his pipe fiercely on the table and refused to have any truck with such cowardly nonsense.

"Justice, Captain," he cried, "justice and nothing less!"

Billinge winked again. The Captain smoked peacefully.

"Think of Hetty, my boy," he said soothingly. "Think of Hetty."

"I can't do it, Captain."

"Think of Granny, my boy."

"I can't write a lot of lies to save that brute's skin."

"Think of your own skin first."

"That's sense, master," said Billinge.

"I won't save my skin by writing a lot of lies. Dammel I won't."

"Curse my fingers and thumbs and stow swearing at me, my boy. If I'd learned to hold a pen I'd write myself, but

I've given my word you shall write, Nic, and you will, my boy. You won't break my word for me, will you? You've had a fine education. What's writing to you, and what's the good of education if you can't write lies to look like truth. Toby! The standish!"

Toby brought paper, pens and ink and put them on the table. Nic took up a quill and threw it down in disgust.

"I can't do it."

"Hetty's waiting for you, my lad," said the Captain, puffing his pipe. "Hetty's waiting. Get to it. It's got to be done."

Nic took up his pen again and scribbled, and struck words out and tore the paper in shreds. Then a smile of pleasure lighted up his face. He had caught the trick of it, and the vanity of the author had conquered the stupid honesty of the man.

The Captain smiled in peace and nodded his head to Toby. The battle was won.

"Read it up, Nic, and remember to date it this day week. By then I'll have the boat round to Freston and you and your wife across to Dunkirk.

Nic, with a chuckle of pride over his composition, read out his letter:

"SIR,—I desyre to say how greaved I am to leave you in this hayste, but I wold have you knowe my affayres were urgent, and your turnkeys not to blame that I rushed the gaites."

"True enough," said the Captain.

"I cold have wished to tell Capt. Oglethorpe and his committy of all the care and hospitalitty you use to your prisoners. Wold I cold write you any fayrer complement of the wellcome you gave to me than I have told you with myne own tong.

"Your dutifull servant,
"NIC BERRINGTON."

"There's a letter for you, Toby! Not a word of truth in it and no lies neither," cried the triumphant Captain. "I knew he could do it!"

A further bowl of punch was ordered to drink success to

their plans, and then Toby was sent off to find Dumay, whilst the Captain carried the letter to show Bambridge and Nic betook himself to bed and rest before his journey.

That night, after midnight, Bambridge, preceded by Barnes with a lanthorn, led Captain Johnson and Mr. Berrington across the Fleet yard, through the racket court, down to the little yard where the dogs were kept, behind which Huggins had built a private door in the prison wall that he might let prisoners in and out of the prison unknown to the inmates. Outside the door Billinge and Monsieur Dumay were waiting. There were no farewells to make. The three friends did not linger in the streets, but made their way down to the river, where a boat awaited them. The tide was on the flow, and the rowers took them up to Lambeth, where they found Mr. Knapp, of the "Fox and Grapes," had an excellent supper prepared for them and good horses ready for to-morrow's journey.

The start was made at dawn. Captain Johnson saw Toby and Nic ride away, his last warning to Nic being that he must be ready to sail that day week. But Nic scarce heard him. His eyes and ears were all for the road, and his mind was at Cherry Croft. He waved a farewell to the Captain, and shouted for joy as they cantered down the lane to join the high road. Even his good horse seemed to step proudly at the thought that he was carrying so splendid a groom to the arms of so sweet a bride, and Toby clucked over the joy of his bantling like an old hen.

They breakfasted at Croydon and dined at East Grinstead, where fresh horses were in readiness, and they were at the "White Hart" at Lewes before it was dark. Toby was for ordering supper here, but Nic was too impatient to be away, and it was settled that he should ride forward at once and Toby should come along as soon as he had finished a few mugs of ale and a pasty.

It was about half-past nine when Nic Berrington rode past Freston Church, and by the rookery of old elm-trees, and saw an orange light in the best bedroom above the parlour of Cherry Croft. And Hetty heard the clatter of hoofs on the flints and rushed to the window to hear the voice of her beloved calling her name in the garden below.

POSTSCRIPT.

THERE are no further adventures to chronicle, at all events
for the present, and the future story of Mr. and Mrs.
Berrington is to be found in the early history of Georgia,
where Nic was a brave lieutenant to his gallant friend
Captain Oglethorpe, and played a worthy part in those
heroic and perilous days. The journey to Geneva passed off
with no untoward event, the legacy of poor Turquet was
found to be greater than was expected, and the young pair
joined Captain Oglethorpe's vessel at Falmouth and sailed
for the plantations. Hetty had already heard that the Captain, through the kind offices of good Queen Caroline, had
released her father on Captain Oglethorpe's undertaking
that he should sail with his expedition.

Billinge continued as a runner for some years, and on the
death of Mr. Knapp, took over his widow and the freehold
of the "Fox and Grapes." Jenny also retired from her
activities and married an elderly Irish peer, the Baron
Kilbrachan, who traced his descent to Connogh, King of
Thomond, but unfortunately died without issue. Lady
Kilbrachan lived at Bath in her later years, where she was a
regular attendant at the Countess of Huntingdon's chapel.

Granny and Captain Johnson remained at Cherry Croft,
and were both living when Mr. Berrington and his good
lady and their eldest son and daughter visited the old
country with General Oglethorpe in 1743. But after this
date I have not found any trace of Nic Berrington or his
family and his friends.

THE END

www.ingramcontent.com/pod-product-compliance
Lightning Source LLC
Chambersburg PA
CBHW022205010726
47493CB00002B/421